ROBERT SILVERBERG

SAILING TO BYZANTIUM

ROBERT SILVERBERG's many novels include *The Alien Years*; the most recent volume in the Majipoor Cycle, *Lord Prestimion*; the bestselling Lord Valentine trilogy; and the classics *Dying Inside* and *A Time of Changes*. He has been nominated for the Nebula and Hugo awards more times than any other writer; he is a five-time winner of the Nebula and a four-time winner of the Hugo.

"Robert Silverberg is the binary master of science fiction; better than anyone else in the field, he can write of epic events, perceived at a human scale . . ."

—K. W. Jeter, author of *Noir* and *Dr. Adder*

AVAILABLE NOW

The Deceivers
by Alfred Bester

The Computer Connection
by Alfred Bester

Arthur C. Clarke's Venus Prime: Volumes 1, 2, and 3
by Paul Preuss

Isaac Asimov's Robot City: Volume 1
by Michael P. Kube-McDowell and Mike McQuay

Isaac Asimov's Robot City: Volume 2
by William F. Wu and Arthur Byron Cover

Isaac Asimov's Robot City: Volume 3
by Rob Chilson and William F. Wu

West of Eden
by Harry Harrison

Mirage
An Isaac Asimov Robot Mystery
by Mark W. Tiedemann

Heavy Metal: F.A.K.K.²: The Novelization
by Kevin B. Eastman and Stan Timmons

Moebius' Arzach
by Jean-Marc Lofficier

The Sentinel
by Arthur C. Clarke

COMING SOON

The Touch
Created by Steven-Elliot Altman

re: demolished
by Alfred Bester

SAILING TO BYZANTIUM

ROBERT SILVERBERG

ibooks
new york
www.ibooksinc.com

DISTRIBUTED BY SIMON & SCHUSTER, INC

An Original Publication of ibooks, inc.

Pocket Books, a division of Simon & Schuster, Inc.
1230 Avenue of the Americas, New York, NY 10020

An ibooks, inc. Book

ibooks, inc.
24 West 25th Street
New York, NY 10010

The ibooks World Wide Web Site Address is:
http://www.ibooksinc.com

ISBN 0-7434-0718-0
First Pocket Books printing September 2000
10 9 8 7 6 5 4 3 2 1
POCKET and colophon are registered trademarks of
Simon & Schuster, Inc.

Cover art:
"Expectations," 1885 by Sir Lawrence Alma-Tadema (1836-1912)
Private Collection/Bridgeman Art Library

Cover design by Debbie Silva
Interior design by Michael Mendelsohn at MM Design 2000, Inc.

Printed in the U.S.A.

CONTENTS

INTRODUCTION

The short novel—or "novella," as it is often called—is one of the richest and most rewarding of literary forms. Spanning twenty to thirty thousand words, usually, it allows for more extended development of theme and character than does the short story, without making the elaborate structural demands of the full-length book. Thus it provides an intense, detailed exploration of its subject, providing to some degree both the concentrated focus of the short story and the broad scope of the novel.

Some of the greatest works of modern literature fall into the novella class. Consider Mann's "Death in Venice," Joyce's "The Dead," Melville's "Billy Budd," and Conrad's "Heart of Darkness"—or Faulkner's "The Bear," Tolstoy's "The Death of Ivan Ilych," Carson McCuller's "Ballad of the Sad Cafe."

In science fiction, too, the novella has been particularly fruitful, from the time of H. G. Wells's "The Time Machine" onward. The roster of classic science-fiction novellas includes such masterpieces as Robert A. Heinlein's "By His Bootstraps," Wyman Guin's "Beyond Bedlam," Isaac Asimov's "The Dead Past," Roger Zelazny's "A Rose for Ecclesiastes," James Blish's "A Case of Conscience," and James Tiptree, Jr.'s "Houston, Houston, Do You Read?"

I have long found the novella a valuable form myself. One of the prime tasks of the science-fiction writer is to create carefully detailed worlds of the imagination, and therefore room for invention is a necessity. The short story can give only a single vivid glimpse of the invented world; the full-length novel frequently becomes so enmeshed in the obligations of plot and counterplot that the background recedes to a secondary position. But the short novel, leisurely without being discursive, is ideal for the sort of world-creation that is science fiction's specialty. And so, from "Hawksbill Station" of 1966 and "Nightwings" of 1968, I have returned again and again to the novella length with special pleasure and rewarding results: I have won more Hugo and Nebula awards for novellas than for stories of any other lengths.

Here, in one volume, are five of my best novella-length stories. They were exciting stories to write and I'm delighted to have the opportunity to bring them together in collected form.

Robert Silverberg
March 2000

SAILING TO BYZANTIUM

SAILING TO BYZANTIUM
AN INTRODUCTION

It was the spring of 1984. I had just completed my historical/fantasy novel *Gilgamesh the King* set in ancient Sumer, and antiquity was very much on my mind when Shawna McCarthy, who had just begun her brief and brilliant career as editor of *Isaac Asimov's Science Fiction Magazine*, came to the San Francisco area, where I live, on holiday. I ran into her at a party and she asked me if I'd write a story for her. "I'd like to, yes." And, since the novella is my favorite form, I added, "a long one."

"How long?"

"Long," I told her. "A novella."

"Good," she said. We did a little haggling over the price, and that was that. She went back to New York and I got going on "Sailing to Byzantium" and by late summer it was done.

It wasn't originally going to be called "Sailing to Byzantium." The used manila envelope on which I had jotted the kernel of the idea out of which "Sailing to Byzantium" grew—I always jot down my story ideas on the backs of old envelopes—bears the title, "The Hundred-Gated City." That's a reference to ancient Thebes, in Egypt, and this was my original note:

"Ancient Egypt has been re-created at the end of time, along with various other highlights of history—a sort of Disneyland. A twentieth-century man, through error, has been regenerated in Thebes, though he belongs in the replica of Los Angeles. The misplaced Egyptian has been sent to Troy, or maybe Knossos, and a Cretan has been displaced into a Brasilia-equivalent of the twenty-ninth century. They move about, attempting to return to their proper places."

It's a nice idea, but it's not quite the story I ultimately wrote, perhaps because I decided it might turn out to be nothing more than an updating of Murray Leinster's classic novella "Sidewise in Time," a story that was first published before I was born but which is still well remembered in certain quarters. I *did* use the "Hundred-Gated" tag in an entirely different story many years later—"Thebes of the Hundred Gates." (I'm thrifty with titles as well as old envelopes.) But what emerged in the summer of 1984 is the story you are about to read, which quickly acquired the title it now bears as I came to understand the direction my original idea had begun to take.

From the earliest pages I knew I was on to something special, and it remains one of my favorite stories, out of all the millions and millions of words of science fiction I've published in the past five decades. Shawna had one or two small editorial suggestions for clarifying the ending, which I accepted gladly, and my friend Shay Barsabe, who read the story in manuscript, pointed out one subtle logical blunder in the plot that I hastily corrected; but otherwise the story came forth virtually in its final form as I wrote it.

It was published first as an elegant limited-edition book, now very hard to find, by the house of Underwood-Miller, and soon afterward it appeared in *Asimov's* for February, 1985. It met with immediate acclaim, and that year it was chosen with wonderful editorial unanimity for all three of the best-science-fiction-of-the-year anthologies, those edited by Donald A. Wollheim, Terry Carr, and Gardner Dozois. "A possible classic," is what Wollheim called it, praise that gave me great delight, because the crusty, sardonic Wollheim had been reading science fiction almost since the stuff was invented, and he was not one to throw such words around lightly. "Sailing to Byzantium" won me a Nebula award in 1986, and was nominated for a Hugo, but finished in second place, losing by four votes out of 800. Since then the story has been reprinted many times and translated into a dozen languages or more. It's a piece of which I'm extremely proud, and a virtually automatic choice to lead off this collection of my novellas.

SAILING TO BYZANTIUM

At dawn he arose and stepped out onto the patio for his first look at Alexandria, the one city he had not yet seen. That year the five cities were Changan, Asgard, New Chicago, Timbuctoo, Alexandria: the usual mix of eras, cultures, realities. He and Gioia, making the long flight from Asgard in the distant north the night before, had arrived late, well after sundown, and had gone straight to bed. Now, by the gentle apricot-hued morning light, the fierce spires and battlements of Asgard seemed merely something he had dreamed.

The rumor was that Asgard's moment was finished anyway. In a little while, he had heard, they were going to tear it down and replace it, elsewhere, with Mohenjo-daro. Though there were never more than five cities, they changed constantly. He could remember a time when they had had Rome of the Caesars instead of Chang-an, and Rio de Janeiro rather than Alexandria. These people saw no point in keeping anything very long.

It was not easy for him to adjust to the sultry intensity

of Alexandria after the frozen splendors of Asgard. The wind, coming off the water, was brisk and torrid both at once. Soft turquoise wavelets lapped at the jetties. Strong presences assailed his senses: the hot heavy sky, the stinging scent of the red lowland sand borne on the breeze, the sullen swampy aroma of the nearby sea. Everything trembled and glimmered in the early light. Their hotel was beautifully situated, high on the northern slope of the huge artificial mound known as the Paneium that was sacred to the goat-footed god. From here they had a total view of the city: the wide noble boulevards, the soaring obelisks and monuments, the palace of Hadrian just below the hill, the stately and awesome Library, the temple of Poseidon, the teeming marketplace, the royal lodge that Marc Antony had built after his defeat at Actium. And of course the Lighthouse, the wondrous many-windowed Lighthouse, the seventh wonder of the world, that immense pile of marble and limestone and reddish-purple Aswan granite rising in majesty at the end of its mile-long causeway. Black smoke from the beacon fire at its summit curled lazily into the sky. The city was awakening. Some temporaries in short white kilts appeared and began to trim the dense dark hedges that bordered the great public buildings. A few citizens wearing loose robes of vaguely Grecian style were strolling in the streets.

There were ghosts and chimeras and phantasies everywhere about. Two slim elegant centaurs, a male and a female, grazed on the hillside. A burly thick-thighed swordsman appeared on the porch of the temple of Poseidon holding a Gorgon's severed head and waved it in a wide arc, grinning broadly. In the street below the hotel gate three small pink sphinxes, no bigger than housecats, stretched and yawned and began to prowl the curbside. A larger one, lion-sized, watched warily from an alleyway: their mother, surely. Even at this distance he could hear her loud purring.

Shading his eyes, he peered far out past the Lighthouse and across the water. He hoped to see the dim shores of Crete or Cyprus to the north, or perhaps the great dark curve of Anatolia. *Carry me toward that great Byzantium*, he thought. *Where all is ancient, singing at the oars.* But he beheld only he endless empty sea, sun-bright and blinding though the morning was just beginning. Nothing was ever where he expected it to be. The continents did not seem to be in their proper places any longer. Gioia, taking him aloft long ago in her little flitterflitter, had shown him that. The tip of South America was canted far out into the Pacific, Africa was weirdly foreshortened; a broad tongue of ocean separated Europe and Asia. Australia did not appear to exist at all. Perhaps they had dug it up and used it for other things. There was no trace of the world he once had known. This was the fiftieth century. "The fiftieth century after *what*?" he had asked several times, but no one seemed to know, or else they did not care to say.

"Is Alexandria very beautiful?" Gioia called from within.

"Come out and see."

Naked and sleepy-looking, she padded out onto the white-tiled patio and nestled up beside him. She fit neatly under his arm. "Oh, yes, yes!" she said softly. "So very beautiful, isn't it? Look, there, the palaces, the Library, the Lighthouse! Where will we go first? The Lighthouse, I think. Yes? And then the marketplace—I want to see the Egyptian magicians—and the stadium, the races—will they be having races today, do you think? Oh, Charles, I want to see everything!"

"Everything? All on the first day?"

"All on the first day, yes," she said. "Everything."

"But we have plenty of time, Gioia."

"Do we?"

He smiled and drew her tight against his side.

"Time enough," he said gently.

He loved her for her impatience, for her bright bubbling eagerness. Gioia was not much like the rest in that regard, though she seemed identical in all other ways. She was short, supple, slender, dark-eyed, olive-skinned, narrow-hipped, with wide shoulders and flat muscles. They were all like that, each one indistinguishable from the rest, like a horde of millions of brothers and sisters—a world of small lithe childlike Mediterraneans, built for juggling, for bull-dancing, for sweet white wine at midday and rough red wine at night. They had the same slim bodies, the same broad mouths, the same great glossy eyes. He had never seen anyone who appeared to be younger than twelve or older than twenty. Gioia was somehow a little different, although he did not quite know how; but he knew that it was for that imperceptible but significant difference that he loved her. And probably that was why she loved him also.

He let his gaze drift from west to east, from the Gate of the Moon down broad Canopus Street and out to the harbor, and off to the tomb of Cleopatra at the tip of long slender Cape Lochias. Everything was here and all of it perfect, the obelisks, the statues and marble colonnades, the courtyards and shrines and groves, great Alexander himself in his coffin of crystal and gold: a splendid gleaming pagan city. But there were oddities—an unmistakable mosque near the public gardens, and what seemed to be a Christian church not far from the Library. And those ships in the harbor, with all those red sails and bristling masts—surely they were medieval, and late medieval at that. He had seen such anachronisms in other places before. Doubtless these people found them amusing. Life was a game for them. They played at it unceasingly. Rome, Alexandria, Timbuctoo—why not? Create an Asgard of translucent bridges and shimmering ice-girt palaces, then grow weary of it and take it away? Replace it with Mohenjo-daro? Why not? It seemed to him a great pity to destroy those lofty Nordic feasting halls for the sake of building a squat brutal sun-baked city of brown brick; but these people did not look at things the way he did. Their cities were only temporary. Someone in Asgard had said that Timbuctoo would be the next to go, with Byzantium rising in its place. Well, why not? Why not? They could have anything they liked. This was the fiftieth century, after all. The only rule was that there could be no more than five cities at once. "Limits," Gioia had informed him solemnly when they first began to travel together, "are very important." But she did not know why, or did not care to say.

He stared out once more toward the sea.

He imagined a newborn city congealing suddenly out of mists, far across the water: shining towers, great domed palaces, golden mosaics. That would be no great effort for them. They could just summon it forth whole out of time, the Emperor on his throne and the Emperor's drunken soldiery roistering in the streets, the brazen clangor of the cathedral gong rolling through the Grand Bazaar, dolphins leaping beyond the shoreside pavilions. Why not? They had Timbuctoo. They had Alexandria. Do you crave Constantinople? Then behold Constantinople! Or Avalon, or Lyonesse, or Atlantis. They could have anything they liked. It is pure Schopenhauer here: the world as will and imagination. Yes! These slender dark-eyed people journeying tirelessly from miracle to miracle. Why not Byzantium next? Yes! Why not? *That is no country for old men*, he thought. *The young in one another's arms, the birds in the trees*—yes! Yes! Anything they liked. They even had him. Suddenly he felt frightened. Questions he had not asked for a long time burst through into his consciousness. *Who am I? Why am I here? Who is this woman beside me?*

"You're so quiet all of a sudden, Charles," said Gioia, who could not abide silence for very long. "Will you talk to me? I want you to talk to me. Tell me what you're looking for out there."

He shrugged. "Nothing."

"Nothing?"

"Nothing in particular."

"I could see you seeing something."

"Byzantium," he said. "I was imagining that I could look straight across the water to Byzantium. I was trying to get a glimpse of the walls of Constantinople."

"Oh, but you wouldn't be able to see as far as that from here. Not really."

"I know."

"And anyway Byzantium doesn't exist."

"Not yet. But it will. Its time comes later on."

"Does it?" she said. "Do you know that for a fact?"

"On good authority. I heard it in Asgard," he told her. "But even if I hadn't, Byzantium would be inevitable, don't you think? Its time would have to come. How could we not do Byzantium, Gioia? We certainly will do Byzantium, sooner or later. I know we will. It's only a matter of time. And we have all the time in the world."

A shadow crossed her face. "Do we? Do we?"

He knew very little about himself, but he knew that he was not one of them. That he knew. He knew that his name was Charles Phillips and that before he had come to live among these people he had lived in the year 1984, when there had been such things as computers and television sets and base-ball and jet planes, and the world was full of cities, not

merely five but thousands of them, New York and London
and Johannesburg and Paris and Liverpool and Bangkok
and San Francisco and Buenos Aires and a multitude of
others, all at the same time. There had been four and a half
billion people in the world then; now he doubted that there
were as many as four and a half million. Nearly everything
had changed beyond comprehension. The moon still seemed
the same, and the sun; but at night he searched in vain for
familiar constellations. He had no idea how they had
brought him from then to now, or why. It did no good to
ask. No one had any answers for him; no one so much as
appeared to understand what it was that he was trying to
learn. After a time he had stopped asking; after a time he
had almost entirely ceased wanting to know.

He and Gioia were climbing the Lighthouse. She scam-
pered ahead, in a hurry as always, and he came along behind her in his more stolid fashion. Scores of other tourists,
mostly in groups of two or three, were making their way up
the wide flagstone ramps, laughing, calling to one another.
Some of them, seeing him, stopped a moment, stared,
pointed. He was used to that. He was so much taller than
any of them; he was plainly not one of them. When they
pointed at him he smiled. Sometimes he nodded a little ac-
knowledgment.

He could not find much of interest in the lowest level,
a massive square structure two hundred feet high built of
huge marble blocks: within its cool musty arcades were
hundreds of small dark rooms, the offices of the Lighthouse's keepers and mechanics, the barracks of the garrison,
the stables for the three hundred donkeys that carried the
fuel to the lantern far above. None of that appeared inviting
to him. He forged onward without halting until he emerged
on the balcony that led to the next level. Here the Lighthouse grew narrower and became octagonal: its face, gran-

ite now and handsomely fluted, rose in a stunning sweep above him.

Gioia was waiting for him there. "This is for you," she said, holding out a nugget of meat on a wooden skewer. "Roast lamb. Absolutely delicious. I had one while I was waiting for you." She gave him a cup of some cool green sherbet also, and darted off to buy a pomegranate. Dozens of temporaries were roaming the balcony, selling refreshments of all kinds.

He nibbled at the meat. It was charred outside, nicely pink and moist within. While he ate, one of the temporaries came up to him and peered blandly into his face. It was a stocky swarthy male wearing nothing but a strip of red and yellow cloth about its waist. "I sell meat," it said. "Very fine roast lamb, only five drachmas."

Phillips indicated the piece he was eating. "I already have some," he said.

"It is excellent meat, very tender. It has been soaked for three days in the juices of—"

"Please," Phillips said. "I don't want to buy any meat. Do you mind moving along?"

The temporaries had confused and baffled him at first, and there was still much about them that was unclear to him. They were not machines—they looked like creatures of flesh and blood—but they did not seem to be human beings, either, and no one treated them as if they were. He supposed they were artificial constructs, products of a technology so consummate that it was invisible. Some appeared to be more intelligent than others, but all of them behaved as if they had no more autonomy than characters in a play, which was essentially what they were. There were untold numbers of them in each of the five cities, playing all manner of roles: shepherds and swineherds, street-sweepers, merchants, boatmen, vendors of grilled meats and cool drinks, hagglers in the marketplace, schoolchildren, charioteers, policemen, grooms, gladiators, monks, artisans, whores and cutpurses, sailors—whatever was needed to sustain the illusion of a thriving, populous urban center. The darkeyed people, Gioia's people, never performed work. There were not enough of them to keep a city's functions going, and in any case they were strictly tourists, wandering with the wind, moving from city to city as the whim took them, Chang-an to New Chicago, New Chicago to Timbuctoo, Timbuctoo to Asgard, Asgard to Alexandria, onward, ever onward.

The temporary would not leave him alone. Phillips walked away and it followed him, cornering him against the balcony wall. When Gioia returned a few minutes later, lips prettily stained with pomegranate juice, the temporary was still hovering about him, trying with lunatic persistence to sell him a skewer of lamb. It stood much too close to him, almost nose to nose, great sad cowlike eyes peering intently into his as it extolled with mournful mooing urgency the quality of its wares. It seemed to him that he had had trouble like this with temporaries on one or two earlier occasions. Gioia touched the creature's elbow lightly and said, in a short sharp tone Phillips had never heard her use before, "He isn't interested. Get away from him." It went at once. To Phillips she said, "You have to be firm with them."

"I was trying. It wouldn't listen to me."

"You ordered it to go away, and it refused?"

"I asked it to go away. Politely. Too politely, maybe."

"Even so," she said. "It should have obeyed a human, regardless."

"Maybe it didn't think I was human," Phillips suggested. "Because of the way I look. My height, the color of my eyes. It might have thought I was some kind of temporary myself."

"No," Gioia said, frowning. "A temporary won't solicit another temporary. But it won't ever disobey a citizen, either. There's a very clear boundary. There isn't ever any confusion. I can't understand why it went on bothering you." He was surprised at how troubled she seemed: far more so, he thought, than the incident warranted. A stupid device, perhaps miscalibrated in some way, over-enthusiastically pushing its wares—what of it? What of it? Gioia, after a moment, appeared to come to the same conclusion. Shrugging, she said, "It's defective, I suppose. Probably such things are more common than we suspect, don't you think?" There was something forced about her tone that bothered him. She smiled and handed him her pomegranate. "Here. Have a bite, Charles. It's wonderfully sweet. They used to be extinct, you know. Shall we go on upward?"

The octagonal midsection of the Lighthouse must have been several hundred feet in height, a grim claustrophobic tube almost entirely filled by the two broad spiraling ramps that wound around the huge building's central well. The ascent was slow: a donkey team was a little way ahead of them on the ramp, plodding along laden with bundles of kindling for the lantern. But at last, just as Phillips was growing winded and dizzy, he and Gioia came out onto the second balcony, the one marking the transition between the octagonal section and the Lighthouse's uppermost story, which was cylindrical and very slender.

She leaned far out over the balustrade. "Oh, Charles, look at the view! Look at it!"

It was amazing. From one side they could see the entire city, and swampy Lake Mareotis and the dusty Egyptian plain beyond it, and from the other they peered far out into the gray and choppy Mediterranean. He gestured toward the innumerable reefs and shallows that infested the waters leading to the harbor entrance. "No wonder they needed a lighthouse here," he said. "Without some kind of gigantic landmark they'd never have found their way in from the open sea."

A blast of sound, a ferocious snort, erupted just above him. He looked up, startled. Immense statues of trumpet-wielding Tritons jutted from the corners of the Lighthouse at this level; that great blurting sound had come from the nearest of them. A signal, he thought. A warning to the ships negotiating that troubled passage. The sound was produced by some kind of steam-powered mechanism, he realized, operated by teams of sweating temporaries clustered about bonfires at the base of each Triton.

Once again he found himself swept by admiration for the clever way these people carried out their reproductions of antiquity. Or *were* they reproductions, he wondered? He still did not understand how they brought their cities into being. For all he knew, this place was the authentic Alexandria itself, pulled forward out of its proper time just as he himself had been. Perhaps this was the true and original Lighthouse, and not a copy. He had no idea which was the case, nor which would be the greater miracle.

"How do we get to the top?" Gioia asked.

"Over there, I think. That doorway."

The spiraling donkey-ramps ended here. The loads of lantern fuel went higher via a dumbwaiter in the central shaft. Visitors continued by way of a cramped staircase, so narrow at its upper end that it was impossible to turn around while climbing. Gioia, tireless, sprinted ahead. He clung to the rail and labored up and up, keeping count of the tiny window slits to ease the boredom of the ascent. The count was nearing a hundred when finally he stumbled into the vestibule of the beacon chamber. A dozen or so visitors were crowded into it. Gioia was at the far side, by the wall that was open to the sea.

It seemed to him he could feel the building swaying in the winds up here. How high were they? Five hundred feet, six hundred, seven? The beacon chamber was tall and narrow, divided by a catwalk into upper and lower sections. Down below, relays of temporaries carried wood from the dumbwaiter and tossed it on the blazing fire. He felt its intense heat from where he stood, at the rim of the platform on which the giant mirror of polished metal was hung. Tongues of flame leaped upward and danced before the mirror, which hurled its dazzling beam far out to sea. Smoke rose through a vent. At the very top was a colossal statue of Poseidon, austere, ferocious, looming above the lantern.

Gioia sidled along the catwalk until she was at his side. "The guide was talking before you came," she said, pointing. "Do you see that place over there, under the mirror? Someone standing there and looking into the mirror gets a view of ships at sea that can't be seen from here by the naked eye. The mirror magnifies things."

"Do you believe that?"

She nodded toward the guide. "It said so. And it also told us that if you look in a certain way, you can see right across the water into the city of Constantinople."

She is like a child, he thought. They all are. He said, "You told me yourself this very morning that it isn't possible to see that far. Besides, Constantinople doesn't exist right now."

"It will," she replied. "You said that to me, this very morning. And when it does, it'll be reflected in the Lighthouse mirror. That's the truth. I'm absolutely certain of it." She swung about abruptly toward the entrance of the beacon chamber. "Oh, look, Charles! Here come Nissandra and Aramayne! And there's Hawk! There's Stengard!" Gioia laughed and waved and called out names. "Oh, everyone's here! *Everyone!*"

They came jostling into the room, so many newcomers that some of those who had been there were forced to scramble down the steps on the far side. Gioia moved among them, hugging, kissing. Phillips could scarcely tell one from another—it was hard for him even to tell which were the men and which the women, dressed as they all were in the same sort of loose robes—but he recognized some of the names. These were her special friends, her set, with whom she had journeyed from city to city on an endless round of gaiety in the old days before he had come into her life. He had met a few of them before, in Asgard, in Rio, in Rome. The beacon-chamber guide, a squat wide-shouldered old temporary wearing a laurel wreath on its bald head, reappeared and began its potted speech, but no one listened to it; they were all too busy greeting one another, embracing, giggling. Some of them edged their way over to Phillips and reached up, standing on tiptoes, to touch their fingertips to his cheek in that odd hello of theirs. "Charles," they said gravely, making two syllables out of the name, as these people often did. "So good to see you again. Such a pleasure. You and Gioia—such a handsome couple. So well suited to each other."

Was that so? He supposed it was.

The chamber hummed with chatter. The guide could not be heard at all. Stengard and Nissandra had visited New Chicago for the water-dancing—Aramayne bore tales of a feast in Chang-an that had gone on for *days*—Hawk and Hekna had been to Timbuctoo to see the arrival of the salt caravan, and were going back there soon—a final party soon to celebrate the end of Asgard that absolutely should not be missed—the plans for the new city, Mohenjodaro—we have reservations for the opening, we wouldn't pass it up for anything—and, yes, they were definitely going to do Constantinople after that, the planners were already deep into their Byzantium research—so good to see you, you look so beautiful all the time—have you been to the Library yet? The zoo? To the temple of Serapis?—

To Phillips they said, "What do you think of our Alexandria, Charles? Of course, you must have known it well in your day. Does it look the way you remember it?" They were always asking things like that. They did not seem to comprehend that the Alexandria of the Lighthouse and the Library was long lost and legendary by the time his twentieth century had been. To them, he suspected, all the places they had brought back into existence were more or less contemporary. Rome of the Caesars, Alexandria of the Ptolemies, Venice of the Doges, Chang-an of the T'angs, Asgard of the Aesir, none any less real than the next nor any less unreal, each one simply a facet of the distant past, the fantastic immemorial past, a plum plucked from that dark backward abysm of time. They had no contexts for separating one era from another. To them all the past was one borderless timeless realm. Why, then, should he not have seen the Lighthouse before, he who had leaped into this era from the New York of 1984? He had never been able to explain it to them. Julius Caesar and Hannibal, Helen of Troy and Charlemagne, Rome of the gladiators and New York of the Yankees and Mets, Gilgamesh and Tristan and Othello and Robin Hood and George Washington and Queen Victoria—to them, all equally real and unreal, none of them any more than bright figures moving about on a painted canvas. The past, the past, the elusive and fluid past—to them it was a single place of infinite accessibility and infinite connectivity. Of course, they would think he had seen the Lighthouse before. He knew better than to try again to explain things. "No," he said simply. "This is my first time in Alexandria."

*   *   *

They stayed there all winter long, and possibly some of the spring. Alexandria was not a place where one was sharply aware of the change of seasons, nor did the passage of time itself make itself very evident when one was living one's entire life as a tourist.

During the day there was always something new to see. The zoological garden, for instance: a wondrous park, miraculously green and lush in this hot dry climate, where astounding animals roamed in enclosures so generous that they did not seem like enclosures at all. Here were camels, rhinoceroses, gazelles, ostriches, lions, wild asses; and here, too, casually adjacent to those familiar African beasts, were hippogriffs, unicorns, basilisks, and fire-snorting dragons with rainbow scales. Had the original zoo of Alexandria had dragons and unicorns? Phillips doubted it. But this one did; evidently it was no harder for the backstage craftsmen to manufacture mythic beasts than it was for them to turn out camels and gazelles. To Gioia and her friends all of them were equally mythical, anyway. They were just as awed by the rhinoceros as by the hippogriff. One was no more strange—or any less—than the other. So far as Phillips had been able to discover, none of the mammals or birds of his era had survived into this one except for a few cats and dogs, though many had been reconstructed.

And then the Library! All those lost treasures, reclaimed from the jaws of time! Stupendous columned marble walls, airy high-vaulted reading rooms, dark coiling stacks stretching away to infinity. The ivory handles of seven hundred thousand papyrus scrolls bristling on the shelves. Scholars and librarians gliding quietly about, smiling faint scholarly smiles but plainly preoccupied with serious matters of the mind. They were all temporaries, Phillips realized. Mere props, part of the illusion. But were the scrolls illu-

sions, too? "Here we have the complete dramas of Sopho-
cles," said the guide with a blithe wave of its hand,
indicating shelf upon shelf of texts. Only seven of his hundred twenty-three plays had survived the successive burnings of the library in ancient times by Romans, Christians,
Arabs: were the lost ones here, the *Triptolemus*, the *Nausi-
caa*, the *Jason*, and all the rest? And would he find here,
too, miraculously restored to being, the other vanished
treasures of ancient literature—the memoirs of Odysseus,
Cato's history of Rome, Thucidydes' life of Pericles, the
missing volumes of Livy? But when he asked if he might
explore the stacks, the guide smiled apologetically and said
that all the librarians were busy just now. Another time,
perhaps? Perhaps, said the guide. It made no difference,
Phillips decided. Even if these people somehow had brought
back those lost masterpieces of antiquity, how would he
read them? He knew no Greek.

The life of the city buzzed and throbbed about him. It
was a dazzlingly beautiful place: the vast bay thick with
sails, the great avenues running rigidly east-west, north-
south, the sunlight rebounding almost audibly from the
bright walls of the palaces of kings and gods. They have
done this very well, Phillips thought: very well indeed. In
the marketplace hard-eyed traders squabbled in half a dozen
mysterious languages over the price of ebony, Arabian incense, jade, panther skins. Gioia bought a dram of pale
musky Egyptian perfume in a delicate tapering glass flask.
Magicians and jugglers and scribes called out stridently to
passerby, begging for a few moments of attention and a
handful of coins for their labor. Strapping slaves, black and
tawny and some that might have been Chinese, were put up
for auction, made to flex their muscles, to bare their teeth,
to bare their breasts and thighs to prospective buyers. In the
gymnasium naked athletes hurled javelins and discuses, and

wrestled with terrifying zeal. Gioia's friend Stengard came rushing up with a gift for her, a golden necklace that would not have embarrassed Cleopatra. An hour later she had lost it, or perhaps had given it away while Phillips was looking elsewhere. She bought another, even finer, the next day. Anyone could have all the money he wanted, simply by asking: it was as easy to come by as air for these people.

Being here was much like going to the movies, Phillips told himself. A different show every day: not much plot, but the special effects were magnificent and the detail work could hardly have been surpassed. A megamovie, a vast entertainment that went on all the time and was being played out by the whole population of Earth. And it was all so effortless, so spontaneous: just as when he had gone to a movie he had never troubled to think about the myriad technicians behind the scenes, the cameramen and the costume designers and the set builders and the electricians and the model makers and the boom operators, so, too, here he chose not to question the means by which Alexandria had been set before him. It felt real. It *was* real. When he drank the strong red wine it gave him a pleasant buzz. If he leaped from the beacon chamber of the Lighthouse he suspected he would die, though perhaps he would not stay dead for long: doubtless they had some way of restoring him as often as was necessary. Death did not seem to be a factor in these people's lives.

By day they saw sights. By night he and Gioia went to parties, in their hotel, in seaside villas, in the palaces of the high nobility. The usual people were there all the time, Hawk and Hekna, Aramayne, Stengard and Shelimir, Nissandra, Asoka, Afonso, Protay. At the parties there were five or ten temporaries for every citizen, some as mere servants, others as entertainers or even surrogate guests, mingling freely and a little daringly. But everyone knew, all the time, who was a citizen and who just a temporary. Phillips began to think his own status lay somewhere between. Certainly they treated him with a courtesy that no one ever would give a temporary, and yet there was a condescension to their manner that told him not simply that he was not one of them but that he was someone or something of an altogether different order of existence. That he was Gioia's lover gave him some standing in their eyes, but not a great deal: obviously he was always going to be an outsider, a primitive, ancient and quaint. For that matter he noticed that Gioia herself, though unquestionably a member of the set, seemed to be regarded as something of an outsider, like a tradesman's great-granddaughter in a gathering of Plantagenets. She did not always find out about the best parties in time to attend; her friends did not always reciprocate her effusive greetings with the same degree of warmth; sometimes he noticed her straining to hear some bit of gossip that was not quite being shared with her. Was it because she had taken him for her lover? Or was it the other way around: that she had chosen to be his lover precisely because she was *not* a full member of their caste?

Being a primitive gave him, at least, something to talk about at their parties. "Tell us about war," they said. "Tell us about elections. About money. About disease." They wanted to know everything, though they did not seem to pay close attention: their eyes were quick to glaze. Still, they asked. He described traffic jams to them, and politics, and deodorants, and vitamin pills. He told them about cigarettes, newspapers, subways, telephone directories, credit cards, and basketball. "Which was your city?" they asked. New York, he told them. "And when was it? The seventh century, did you say?" The twentieth, he told them. They exchanged glances and nodded. "We will have to do it," they said. "The World Trade Center, the Empire State Building, the Citicorp

23

Center, the Cathedral of St. John the Divine: how fascinating! Yankee Stadium. The Verrazano Bridge. We will do it all. But first must come Mohenjo-daro. And then, I think, Constantinople. Did your city have many people?" Seven million, he said. Just in the five boroughs alone. They nodded, smiling amiably, unfazed by the number. Seven million, seventy million—it was all the same to them, he sensed. They would just bring forth the temporaries in whatever quantity was required. He wondered how well they would carry the job off. He was no real judge of Alexandrias and Asgards, after all. Here they could have unicorns and hippogriffs in the zoo, and live sphinxes prowling in the gutters, and it did not trouble him. Their fanciful Alexandria was as good as history's, or better. But how sad, how disillusioning it would be, if the New York that they conjured up had Greenwich Village uptown and Times Square in the Bronx, and the New Yorkers, gentle and polite, spoke with the honeyed accents of Savannah or New Orleans. Well, that was nothing he needed to brood about just now. Very likely they were only being courteous when they spoke of doing his New York. They had all the vastness of the past to choose from: Nineveh, Memphis of the Pharaohs, the London of Victoria or Shakespeare or Richard the Third, Florence of the Medici, the Paris of Abelard and Heloise or the Paris of Louis XIV, Moctezuma's Tenochtitlan and Atahuallpa's Cuzco; Damascus, St. Petersburg, Babylon, Troy. And then there were all the cities like New Chicago, out of time that was time yet unborn to him but ancient history to them. In such richness, such an infinity of choices, even mighty New York might have to wait a long while for its turn. Would he still be among them by the time they got around to it? By then, perhaps, they might have become bored with him and returned him to his own proper era. Or possibly he would simply have grown old and died. Even here, he supposed, he would eventually die, though no one else ever seemed to. He did not know. He realized that in fact he did not know anything.

The north wind blew all day long. Vast flocks of ibises appeared over the city, fleeing the heat of the interior, and screeched across the sky with their black necks and scrawny legs extended. The sacred birds, descending by the thousands, scuttered about in every crossroad, pouncing on spiders and beetles, on mice, on the debris of the meat shops and the bakeries. They were beautiful but annoyingly ubiquitous, and they splashed their dung over the marble buildings; each morning squadrons of temporaries carefully washed it off. Gioia said little to him now. She seemed cool, withdrawn, depressed; and there was something almost intangible about her, as though she were gradually becoming transparent. He felt it would be an intrusion upon her privacy to ask her what was wrong. Perhaps it was only restlessness. She became religious, and presented costly offerings at the temples of Serapis, Isis, Poseidon, Pan. She went to the necropolis west of the city to lay wreaths on the tombs in the catacombs. In a single day she climbed the Lighthouse three times without any sign of fatigue. One afternoon he returned from a visit to the Library and found her naked on the patio; she had anointed herself all over with some aromatic green salve. Abruptly she said, "I think it's time to leave Alexandria, don't you?"

She wanted to go to Mohenjo-daro, but Mohenjo-daro was not yet ready for visitors. Instead they flew eastward to Chang-an, which they had not seen in years. It was Phillips's suggestion: he hoped that the cosmopolitan gaudiness of the old T'ang capital would lift her mood.

They were to be guests of the Emperor this time: an

unusual privilege, which ordinarily had to be applied for far in advance, but Phillips had told some of Gioia's highly placed friends that she was unhappy, and they had quickly arranged everything. Three endlessly bowing functionaries in flowing yellow robes and purple sashes met them at the Gate of Brilliant Virtue in the city's south wall and conducted them to their pavilion, close by the imperial palace and the Forbidden Garden. It was a light, airy place, thin walls of plastered brick braced by graceful columns of some dark, aromatic wood. Fountains played on the roof of green and yellow tiles, creating an unending cool rainfall of recirculating water. The balustrades were of carved marble, the door fittings were of gold.

There was a suite of private rooms for him, and another for her, though they would share the handsome damask-draped bedroom at the heart of the pavilion. As soon as they arrived, Gioia announced that she must go to her rooms to bathe and dress. "There will be a formal reception for us at the palace tonight," she said. "They say the imperial receptions are splendid beyond anything you could imagine. I want to be at my best." The Emperor and all his ministers, she told him, would receive them in the Hall of the Supreme Ultimate; there would be a banquet for a thousand people; Persian dancers would perform, and the celebrated jugglers of Chung-nan. Afterward everyone would be conducted into the fantastic landscape of the Forbidden Garden to view the dragon races and the fireworks.

He went to his own rooms. Two delicate little maidservants undressed him and bathed him with fragrant sponges. The pavilion came equipped with eleven temporaries who were to be their servants: soft-voiced unobtrusive catlike Chinese, done with perfect verisimilitude, straight black hair, glowing skin, epicanthic folds. Phillips often wondered what happened to a city's temporaries when the

city's time was over. Were the towering Norse heroes of Asgard being recycled at this moment into wiry dark-skinned
Dravidians for Mohenjo-daro? When Timbuctoo's day was
done, would its brightly robed black warriors be converted
into supple Byzantines to stock the arcades of Constantinople? Or did they simply discard the old temporaries like so
many excess props, stash them in warehouses somewhere,
and turn out the appropriate quantities of the new model? He
did not know; and once when he had asked Gioia about it she
had grown uncomfortable and vague. She did not like him to
probe for information, and he suspected it was because she
had very little to give. These people did not seem to question
the workings of their own world; his curiosities were very
twentieth-century of him, he was frequently told, in that gently patronizing way of theirs. As his two little maids patted
him with their sponges he thought of asking them where they
had served before Chang-an. Rio? Rome? Haroun al-
Raschid's Baghdad? But these fragile girls, he knew, would
only giggle and retreat if he tried to question them. Interrogating temporaries was not only improper but pointless: it
was like interrogating one's luggage.

When he was bathed and robed in rich red silks he wandered the pavilion for a little while, admiring the tinkling
pendants of green jade dangling on the portico, the lustrous
auburn pillars, the rainbow hues of the intricately inter-
woven girders and brackets that supported the roof. Then,
wearying of his solitude, he approached the bamboo curtain
at the entrance to Gioia's suite. A porter and one of the
maids stood just within. They indicated that he should not
enter; but he scowled at them and they melted from him
like snowflakes. A trail of incense led him through the pavilion to Gioia's innermost dressing room. There he halted,
just outside the door.

Gioia sat naked with her back to him at an ornate dressing table of some rare flame-colored wood inlaid with bands of orange and green porcelain. She was studying herself intently in a mirror of polished bronze held by one of her maids: picking through her scalp with her fingernails, as a woman might do who was searching out her gray hairs.

But that seemed strange. Gray hair, on Gioia? On a citizen? A temporary might display some appearance of aging, perhaps, but surely not a citizen. Citizens remained forever young. Gioia looked like a girl. Her face was smooth and unlined, her flesh was firm, her hair was dark: that was true of all of them, every citizen he had ever seen. And yet there was no mistaking what Gioia was doing. She found a hair, frowned, drew it taut, nodded, plucked it. Another. Another. She pressed the tip of her finger to her cheek as if testing it for resilience. She tugged at the skin below her eyes, pulling it downward. Such familiar little gestures of vanity; but so odd here, he thought, in this world of the perpetually young. Gioia, worried about growing old? Had he simply failed to notice the signs of age on her? Or was it that she worked hard behind his back at concealing them? Perhaps that was it. Was he wrong about the citizens, then? Did they age even as the people of less blessed eras had always done, but simply have better ways of hiding it? How old was she, anyway? Thirty? Sixty? Three hundred?

Gioia appeared satisfied now. She waved the mirror away; she rose; she beckoned for her banquet robes. Phillips, still standing unnoticed by the door, studied her with admiration: the small round buttocks, almost but not quite boyish, the elegant line of her spine, the surprising breadth of her shoulders. No, he thought, she is not aging at all. Her body is still like a girl's. She looks as young as on the day they first had met, however long ago that was—he could not say; it was hard to keep track of time here; but he was sure some years had passed since they had come together. Those gray hairs, those wrinkles and sags for which she had searched just now with such desperate intensity, must all be imaginary, mere artifacts of vanity. Even in this remote future epoch, then, vanity was not extinct. He wondered why she was so concerned with the fear of aging. An affectation? Did all these timeless people take some perverse pleasure in fretting over the possibility that they might be growing old? Or was it some private fear of Gioia's, another symptom of the mysterious depression that had come over her in Alexandria?

Not wanting her to think that he had been spying on her, when all he had really intended was to pay her a visit, he slipped silently away to dress for the evening. She came to him an hour later, gorgeously robed, swaddled from chin to ankles in a brocade of brilliant colors shot through with threads of gold, face painted, hair drawn up tightly and fastened with ivory combs: very much the lady of the court. His servants had made him splendid also, a lustrous black surplice embroidered with golden dragons over a sweeping floor-length gown of shining white silk, a necklace and pendant of red coral, a five-cornered gray felt hat that rose in tower upon tower like a ziggurat. Gioia, grinning, touched her fingertips to his cheek. "You look marvelous!" she told him. "Like a grand mandarin!"

"And you like an empress," he said. "Of some distant land: Persia, India. Here to pay a ceremonial visit on the Son of Heaven." An excess of love suffused his spirit, and, catching her lightly by the wrist, he drew her toward him, as close as he could manage it considering how elaborate their costumes were. But as he bent forward and downward, meaning to brush his lips lightly and affectionately against the tip of her nose, he perceived an unexpected strangeness, an anomaly: the coating of white paint that was her makeup seemed oddly to magnify rather than mask the contours of her skin, highlighting and revealing details he had never observed before. He saw a pattern of fine lines radiating from the corners of her eyes, and the unmistakable beginning of a quirk mark in her cheek just to the left of her mouth, and perhaps the faint indentation of frown lines in her flawless forehead. A shiver traveled along the nape of his neck. So it was not affectation, then, that had had her studying her mirror so fiercely. Age was in truth beginning to stake its claim on her, despite all that he had come to believe about these people's agelessness. But a moment later he was not so sure. Gioia turned and slid gently half a step back from him—she must have found his stare disturbing— and the lines he had thought he had seen were gone. He searched for them and saw only girlish smoothness once again. A trick of the light? A figment of an overwrought imagination? He was baffled.

"Come," she said. "We mustn't keep the Emperor waiting."

Five mustachioed warriors in armor of white quilting and seven musicians playing cymbals and pipes escorted them to the Hall of the Supreme Ultimate. There they found the full court arrayed: princes and ministers, high officials, yellow-robed monks, a swarm of imperial concubines. In a place of honor to the right of the royal thrones, which rose like gilded scaffolds high above all else, was a little group of stern-faced men in foreign costumes, the ambassadors of Rome and Byzantium, of Arabia and Syria, of Korea, Japan, Tibet, Turkestan. Incense smoldered in enameled braziers. A poet sang a delicate twanging melody, accompanying himself on a small harp. Then the Emperor and Empress entered: two tiny aged people, like waxen images, moving with infinite slowness, taking steps no greater than a child's. There was the sound of trumpets as they ascended their thrones. When the little Emperor was seated—he looked like a doll up there, ancient, faded, shrunken, yet still somehow a figure of extraordinary power—he stretched forth both his hands, and enormous gongs began to sound. It was a scene of astonishing splendor, grand and overpowering.

These are all temporaries, Phillips realized suddenly. He saw only a handful of citizens—eight, ten, possibly as many as a dozen—scattered here and there about the vast room. He knew them by their eyes, dark, liquid, knowing. They were watching not only the imperial spectacle but also Gioia and him; and Gioia, smiling secretly, nodding almost imperceptibly to them, was acknowledging their presence and their interest. But those few were the only ones in here who were autonomous living beings. All the rest—the entire splendid court, the great mandarins and paladins, the officials, the giggling concubines, the haughty and resplendent ambassadors, the aged Emperor and Empress themselves, were simply part of the scenery. Had the world ever seen entertainment on so grand a scale before? All this pomp, all this pageantry, conjured up each night for the amusement of a dozen or so viewers?

At the banquet the little group of citizens sat together at a table apart, a round onyx slab draped with translucent green silk. There turned out to be seventeen of them in all, including Gioia; Gioia appeared to know all of them, though none, so far as he could tell, was a member of her set that he had met before. She did not attempt introductions. Nor was conversation at all possible during the meal: there was a constant astounding roaring din in the room. Three orchestras played at once and there were troupes of strolling musicians also, and a steady stream of monks and their attendants marched back and forth between the tables loudly chanting sutras and waving censers to the deafening accompaniment of drums and gongs. The Emperor did not descend from his throne to join the banquet; he seemed to be asleep, though now and then he waved his hand in time to the music. Gigantic half-naked brown slaves with broad cheekbones and mouths like gaping pockets brought forth the food, peacock tongues and breast of phoenix heaped on mounds of glowing saffron-colored rice, served on frail alabaster plates. For chopsticks they were given slender rods of dark jade. The wine, served in glistening crystal beakers, was thick and sweet, with an aftertaste of raisins, and no beaker was allowed to remain empty for more than a moment. Phillips felt himself growing dizzy: when the Persian dancers emerged he could not tell whether there were five of them or fifty, and as they performed their intricate whirling routines it seemed to him that their slender muslin-veiled forms were blurring and merging one into another. He felt frightened by their proficiency, and wanted to look away, but he could not. The Chung-nan jugglers that followed them were equally skillful, equally alarming, filling the air with scythes, flaming torches, live animals, rare porcelain vases, pink jade hatchets, silver bells, gilded cups, wagon wheels, bronze vessels, and never missing a catch. The citizens applauded politely but did not seem impressed. After the jugglers, the dancers returned, performing this time on stilts; the waiters brought platters of steaming meat of a pale lavender color, unfamiliar in taste and texture: filet of camel, perhaps, or haunch of hippopotamus, or possibly some choice chop from a young dragon. There was more wine. Feebly Phillips tried to wave it away, but the servitors were implacable. This was a drier sort, greenish-gold, austere, sharp on the tongue. With it came a silver dish, chilled to a polar coldness, that held shaved ice flavored with some potent smoky-flavored brandy. The jugglers were doing a second turn, he noticed. He thought he was going to be ill. He looked helplessly toward Gioia, who seemed sober but fiercely animated, almost manic, her eyes blazing like rubies. She touched his cheek fondly. A cool draft blew through the hall: they had opened one entire wall, revealing the garden, the night, the stars. Just outside was a colossal wheel of oiled paper stretched on wooden struts. They must have erected it in the past hour: it stood a hundred fifty feet high or even more, and on it hung lanterns by the thousands, glimmering like giant fireflies. The guests began to leave the hall. Phillips let himself be swept along into the garden, where under a yellow moon strange crook-armed trees with dense black needles loomed ominously. Gioia slipped her arm through his. They went down to a lake of bubbling crimson fluid and watched scarlet flamingolike birds ten feet tall fastidiously spearing angry-eyed turquoise eels. They stood in awe before a fat-bellied Buddha of gleaming blue tilework, seventy feet high. A horse with a golden mane came prancing by, striking showers of brilliant red sparks wherever its hooves touched the ground. In a grove of lemon trees that seemed to have the power to wave their slender limbs about, Phillips came upon the Emperor, standing by himself and rocking gently back and forth. The old man seized Phillips by the hand and pressed something into his palm, closing his fingers tight about it; when he opened his fist a few moments later he found his palm full of gray irregular pearls. Gioia took them from him and cast them into the air, and they burst like exploding firecrackers, giving off splashes of colored light. A little later, Phillips realized that he was no longer wearing his surplice or his white silken undergown. Gioia was naked, too, and she drew him gently down into a carpet of moist blue moss, where they made love until dawn, fiercely at first, then slowly, languidly, dreamily. At sunrise he looked at her tenderly and saw that something was wrong.

"Gioia?" he said doubtfully.

She smiled. "Ah, no. Gioia is with Fenimon tonight. I am Belilala."

"With—Fenimon?"

"They are old friends. She had not seen him in years."

"Ah. I see. And you are—?"

"Belilala," she said again, touching her fingertips to his cheek.

It was not unusual, Belilala said. It happened all the time; the only unusual thing was that it had not happened to him before now. Couples formed, traveled together for a while, drifted apart, eventually reunited. It did not mean that Gioia had left him forever. It meant only that just now she chose to be with Fenimon. Gioia would return. In the meanwhile he would not be alone. "You and I met in New Chicago," Belilala told him. "And then we saw each other again in Timbuctoo. Have you forgotten? Oh, yes, I see that you have forgotten!" She laughed prettily; she did not seem at all offended.

She looked enough like Gioia to be her sister. But, then, all the citizens looked more or less alike to him. And apart from their physical resemblance, so he quickly came to realize, Belilala and Gioia were not really very similar. There was a calmness, a deep reservoir of serenity, in Belilala, that Gioia, eager and volatile and ever impatient, did not seem to have. Strolling the swarming streets of Chang-an with Belilala, he did not perceive in her any of Gioia's restless feverish need always to know what lay beyond, and beyond, and beyond even that. When they toured the Hsing-ch'ing Palace, Belilala did not after five minutes begin—as Gioia surely would have done—to seek directions to the Fountain of Hsuan-tsung or the Wild Goose Pagoda. Curiosity did not consume Belilala as it did Gioia. Plainly she believed that there would always be enough time for her to see everything she cared to see. There were some days when Belilala chose not to go out at all, but was content merely to remain at their pavilion playing a solitary game with flat porcelain counters, or viewing the flowers of the garden.

He found, oddly, that he enjoyed the respite from Gioia's intense world-swallowing appetites; and yet he longed for her to return. Belilala—beautiful, gentle, tranquil, patient—was too perfect for him. She seemed unreal in her gleaming impeccability, much like one of those Sung celadon vases that appear too flawless to have been thrown and glazed by human hands. There was something a little soulless about her: an immaculate finish outside, emptiness within. Belilala might almost have been a temporary, he thought, though he knew she was not. He could explore the pavilions and palaces of Chang-an with her, he could make graceful conversation with her while they dined, he could certainly enjoy coupling with her; but he could not love her or even contemplate the possibility. It was hard to imagine Belilala worriedly studying herself in a mirror for wrinkles and gray hairs. Belilala would never be any older than she was at this moment; nor could Belilala ever have been any younger. Perfection does not move along an axis of time. But the perfection of Belilala's glossy surface made her inner being impenetrable to him. Gioia was more vulnerable, more obviously flawed—her restlessness, her moodiness, her vanity, her fears—and therefore she was more accessible to his own highly imperfect twentieth-century sensibility.

Occasionally he saw Gioia as he roamed the city, or thought he did. He had a glimpse of her among the miracle-vendors in the Persian Bazaar, and outside the Zoroastrian temple, and again by the goldfish pond in the Serpentine Park. But he was never quite sure that the woman he saw was really Gioia, and he never could get close enough to her to be certain: she had a way of vanishing as he approached, like some mysterious Lorelei luring him onward and onward in a hopeless chase. After a while he came to realize that he was not going to find her until she was ready to be found.

He lost track of time. Weeks, months, years? He had no idea. In this city of exotic luxury, mystery, and magic all was in constant flux and transition and the days had a fitful, unstable quality. Buildings and even whole streets were torn down of an afternoon and reerected, within days, far away. Grand new pagodas sprouted like toadstools in the night. Citizens came in from Asgard, Alexandria, Timbuctoo, New Chicago, stayed for a time, disappeared, returned. There was a constant round of court receptions, banquets, theatrical events, each one much like the one before. The festivals in honor of past emperors and empresses might have given some form to the year, but they seemed to occur in a random way, the ceremony marking the death of T'ai Tsung coming around twice the same year, so it seemed to him, once in a season of snow and again in high summer, and the one honoring the ascension of the Empress Wu being held twice in a single season. Perhaps he had misunderstood something. But he knew it was no use asking anyone.

One day Belilala said unexpectedly, "Shall we go to Mohenjo-daro?"

"I didn't know it was ready for visitors," he replied.

"Oh, yes. For quite some time now."

He hesitated. This had caught him unprepared. Cautiously he said, "Gioia and I were going to go there together, you know."

Belilala smiled amiably, as though the topic under discussion were nothing more than the choice of that evening's restaurant.

"Were you?" she asked.

"It was all arranged while we were still in Alexandria. To go with you instead—I don't know what to tell you, Belilala." Phillips sensed that he was growing terribly flustered. "You know that I'd like to go. With you. But on the other hand I can't help feeling that I shouldn't go there until I'm back with Gioia again. If I ever am." How foolish this sounds, he thought. How clumsy, how adolescent. He found that he was having trouble looking straight at her. Uneasily he said, with a kind of desperation in his voice, "I did promise her—there was a commitment, you understand—a firm agreement that we would go to Mohenjo-daro together—"

"Oh, but Gioia's already there!" said Belilala in the most casual way.

He gaped as though she had punched him.

"What?"

"She was one of the first to go, after it opened. Months and months ago. You didn't know?" she asked, sounding surprised, but not very. "You really didn't know?"

That astonished him. He felt bewildered, betrayed, furious. His cheeks grew hot, his mouth gaped. He shook his head again and again, trying to clear it of confusion. It was a moment before he could speak. "Already there?" he said at last. "Without waiting for me? After we had talked about going there together—after we had agreed—"

Belilala laughed. "But how could she resist seeing the newest city? You know how impatient Gioia is!"

"Yes. Yes."

He was stunned. He could barely think.

"Just like all short-timers," Belilala said. "She rushes here, she rushes there. She must have it all, now, now, right away, at once, instantly. You ought never expect her to wait for you for anything for very long: the fit seizes her, and off she goes. Surely you must know that about her by now."

"A short-timer?" He had not heard that term before.

"Yes. You knew that. You must have known that." Belilala flashed her sweetest smile. She showed no sign of comprehending his distress. With a brisk wave of her hand she said, "Well, then, shall we go, you and I? To Mohenjo-daro?"

"Of course," Phillips said bleakly.

"When would you like to leave?"

"Tonight," he said. He paused a moment. "What's a short-timer, Belilala?"

Color came to her cheeks. "Isn't it obvious?" she asked.

Had there ever been a more hideous place on the face of the earth than the city of Mohenjo-daro? Phillips found it difficult to imagine one. Nor could he understand why, out of all the cities that had ever been, these people had chosen to restore this one to existence. More than ever they seemed alien to him, unfathomable, incomprehensible.

From the terrace atop the many-towered citadel he peered down into grim claustrophobic Mohenjo-daro and shivered. The stark, bleak city looked like nothing so much as some prehistoric prison colony. In the manner of an uneasy tortoise it huddled, squat and compact, against the gray monotonous Indus River plain: miles of dark burnt-brick walls enclosing miles of terrifyingly orderly streets, laid out in an awesome, monstrous gridiron pattern of maniacal rigidity. The houses themselves were dismal and forbidding too, clusters of brick cells gathered about small airless courtyards. There were no windows, only small doors that opened not onto the main boulevards but onto the tiny mysterious lanes that ran between the buildings. Who had designed this horrifying metropolis? What harsh sour souls they must have had, these frightening and frightened folk, creating for themselves in the lush fertile plains of India such a Supreme Soviet of a city!

"How lovely it is," Belilala murmured. "How fascinating!"

He stared at her in amazement.

"Fascinating? Yes," he said. "I suppose so. The same way that the smile of a cobra is fascinating."

"What's a cobra?"

"Poisonous predatory serpent," Phillips told her. "Probably extinct. Or formerly extinct, more likely. It wouldn't surprise me if you people had recreated a few and turned them loose in Mohenjo to make things livelier."

"You sound angry, Charles."

"Do I? That's not how I feel."

"How do you feel, then?"

"I don't know," he said after a long moment's pause. He shrugged. "Lost, I suppose. Very far from home."

"Poor Charles."

"Standing here in this ghastly barracks of a city, listening to you tell me how beautiful it is, I've never felt more alone in my life."

"You miss Gioia very much, don't you?"

He gave her another startled look.

"Gioia has nothing to do with it. She's probably been having ecstasies over the loveliness of Mohenjo just like you. Just like all of you. I suppose I'm the only one who can't find the beauty, the charm. I'm the only one who looks out there and sees only horror, and then wonders why nobody else sees it, why in fact people would set up a place like this for *entertainment*, for *pleasure*—"

Her eyes were gleaming. "Oh, you are angry! You really are!"

"Does that fascinate you, too?" he snapped. "A demonstration of genuine primitive emotion? A typical quaint twentieth-century outburst?" He paced the rampart in short quick anguished steps. "Ah. Ah. I think I understand it now, Belilala. Of course: I'm part of your circus, the star of the sideshow. I'm the first experiment in setting up the next stage of it, in fact." Her eyes were wide. The sudden harshness and violence in his voice seemed to be alarming and exciting her at the same time. That angered him even more. Fiercely he went on, "Bringing whole cities back out of time was fun for a while, but it lacks a certain authenticity, eh? For some reason you couldn't bring the inhabitants, too; you couldn't just grab a few million prehistorics out of Egypt or Greece or India and dump them down in this era, I suppose because you might have too much trouble controlling them, or because you'd have the problem of disposing of them once you were bored with them. So you had to settle for creating temporaries to populate your ancient cities. But now you've got me. I'm something more real than a temporary, and that's a terrific novelty for you, and novelty is the thing you people crave more than anything else: maybe the *only* thing you crave. And here I am, complicated, unpredictable, edgy, capable of anger, fear, sadness, love, and all those other formerly extinct things. Why settle for picturesque architecture when you can observe picturesque emotion, too? What fun I must be for all of you! And if you decide that I was really interesting, maybe you'll ship me back where I came from and check out a few other ancient types—a Roman gladiator, maybe, or a Renaissance pope, or even a Neanderthal or two—"

"Charles," she said tenderly. "Oh, Charles, Charles, Charles, how lonely you must be, how lost, how troubled! Will you ever forgive me? Will you ever forgive us all?"

Once more he was astounded by her. She sounded entirely sincere, altogether sympathetic. Was she? Was she, really? He was not sure he had ever had a sign of genuine caring from any of them before, not even Gioia. Nor could he bring himself to trust Belilala now. He was afraid of her, afraid of all of them, of their brittleness, their slyness, their elegance. He wished he could go to her and have her take him in her arms; but he felt too much the shaggy prehistoric just now to be able to risk asking that comfort of her.

He turned away and began to walk around the rim of the citadel's massive wall.

"Charles?"

"Let me alone for a little while," he said.

He walked on. His forehead throbbed and there was a pounding in his chest. All stress systems going full blast, he thought: secret glands dumping gallons of inflammatory substances into his bloodstream. The heat, the inner confusion, the repellent look of this place—

Try to understand, he thought. Relax. Look about you. Try to enjoy your holiday in Mohenjo-daro.

He leaned warily outward, over the edge of the wall. He had never seen a wall like this; it must be forty feet thick at the base, he guessed, perhaps even more, and every brick perfectly shaped, meticulously set. Beyond the great rampart, marshes ran almost to the edge of the city, although close by the wall the swamps had been dammed and drained for agriculture. He saw lithe brown farmers down there, busy with their wheat and barley and peas. Cattle and buffaloes grazed a little farther out. The air was heavy, dank, humid. All was still. From somewhere close at hand came the sound of a droning, whining stringed instrument and a steady insistent chanting.

Gradually a sort of peace pervaded him. His anger subsided. He felt himself beginning to grow calm again. He looked back at the city, the rigid interlocking streets, the maze of inner lanes, the millions of courses of precise brickwork.

It is a miracle, he told himself, that this city is here in this place and at this time. And it is a miracle that I am here to see it.

Caught for a moment by the magic within the bleakness, he thought he began to understand Belilala's awe and delight, and he wished now that he had not spoken to her so sharply. The city was alive. Whether it was the actual Mohenjo-daro of thousands upon thousands of years ago, ripped from the past by some wondrous hook, or simply a cunning reproduction, did not matter at all. Real or not, this was the true Mohenjo-daro. It had been dead, and now, for the moment, it was alive again. These people, these *citizens*, might be trivial, but reconstructing Mohenjo-daro was no trivial achievement. And that the city that had been reconstructed was oppressive and sinister-looking was unimportant. No one was compelled to live in Mohenjo-daro any more. Its time had come and gone, long ago; those little dark-skinned peasants and craftsmen and merchants down there were mere temporaries, mere inanimate things, conjured up like zombies to enhance the illusion. They did not need his pity. Nor did he need to pity himself. He knew that he should be grateful for the chance to behold these things. Someday, when this dream had ended and his hosts had returned him to the world of subways and computers and income tax and television networks, he would think of Mohenjo-daro as he had once beheld it, lofty walls of tightly woven dark brick under a heavy sky, and he would remember only its beauty.

Glancing back, he searched for Belilala and could not for a moment find her. Then he caught sight of her carefully descending a narrow staircase that angled down the inner face of the citadel wall.

"Belilala!" he called.

She paused and looked his way, shading her eyes from the sun with her hand. "Are you all right?"

"Where are you going?"

"To the baths," she said. "Do you want to come?"

He nodded. "Yes. Wait for me, will you? I'll be right there." He began to run toward her along the top of the wall.

The baths were attached to the citadel: a great open tank the size of a large swimming pool, lined with bricks set on edge in gypsum mortar and waterproofed with asphalt, and eight smaller tanks just north of it in a kind of covered arcade. He supposed that in ancient times the whole complex had had some ritual purpose, the large tank used by common folk and the small chambers set aside for the private ablutions of priests or nobles. Now the baths were maintained, it seemed, entirely for the pleasure of visiting citizens. As Phillips came up the passageway that led to the main bath he saw fifteen or twenty of them lolling in the water or padding languidly about, while temporaries of the dark-skinned Mohenjo-daro type served them drinks and pungent little morsels of spiced meat as though this were some sort of luxury resort. Which was, he realized, exactly what it was. The temporaries wore white cotton loincloths; the citizens were naked. In his former life he had encountered that sort of casual public nudity a few times on visits to California and the south of France, and it had made him mildly uneasy. But he was growing accustomed to it here.

The changing rooms were tiny brick cubicles connected by rows of closely placed steps to the courtyard that surrounded the central tank. They entered one and Belilala swiftly slipped out of the loose cotton robe that she had worn since their arrival that morning. With arms folded she stood leaning against the wall, waiting for him. After a moment he dropped his own robe and followed her outside. He felt a little giddy, sauntering around naked in the open like this.

On the way to the main bathing area they passed the

private baths. None of them seemed to be occupied. They were elegantly constructed chambers, with finely jointed brick floors and carefully designed runnels to drain excess water into the passageway that led to the primary drain. Phillips was struck with admiration for the cleverness of the prehistoric engineers. He peered into this chamber and that to see how the conduits and ventilating ducts were arranged, and when he came to the last room in the sequence he was surprised and embarrassed to discover that it was in use. A brawny grinning man, big-muscled, deep-chested, with exuberantly flowing shoulder-length red hair and a flamboyant, sharply tapering beard was thrashing about merrily with two women in the small tank. Phillips had a quick glimpse of a lively tangle of arms, legs, breasts, buttocks.

"Sorry," he muttered. His cheeks reddened. Quickly he ducked out, blurting apologies as he went. "Didn't realize the room was occupied—no wish to intrude—"

Belilala had proceeded on down the passageway. Phillips hurried after her. From behind him came peals of cheerful raucous booming laughter and high-pitched giggling and the sound of splashing water. Probably they had not even noticed him.

He paused a moment, puzzled, playing back in his mind that one startling glimpse. Something was not right. Those women, he was fairly sure, were citizens: little slender elfin dark-haired girlish creatures, the standard model. But the man? That great curling sweep of red hair? Not a citizen. Citizens did not affect shoulder-length hair. And *red*? Nor had he ever seen a citizen so burly, so powerfully muscular. Or one with a beard. But he could hardly be a temporary, either. Phillips could conceive no reason why there would be so Anglo-Saxon-looking a temporary at Mohenjo-daro;

and it was unthinkable for a temporary to be frolicking like that with citizens, anyway.

"Charles?"

He looked up ahead. Belilala stood at the end of the passageway, outlined in a nimbus of brilliant sunlight. "Charles?" she said again. "Did you lose your way?"

"I'm right here behind you," he said. "I'm coming."

"Who did you meet in there?"

"A man with a beard."

"With a what?"

"A beard," he said. "Red hair growing on his face. I wonder who he is."

"Nobody I know," said Belilala. "The only one I know with hair on his face is you. And yours is black, and you shave it off every day." She laughed. "Come along, now! I see some friends by the pool!"

He caught up with her, and they went hand in hand out into the courtyard. Immediately a waiter glided up to them, an obsequious little temporary with a tray of drinks. Phillips waved it away and headed for the pool. He felt terribly exposed: he imagined that the citizens disporting themselves here were staring intently at him, studying his hairy primitive body as though he were some mythical creature, a Minotaur, a werewolf, summoned up for their amusement. Belilala drifted off to talk to someone and he slipped into the water, grateful for the concealment it offered. It was deep, warm, comforting. With swift powerful strokes he breast-stroked from one end to the other.

A citizen perched elegantly on the pool's rim smiled at him. "Ah, so you've come at last, Charles!" *Char-less.* Two syllables. Someone from Gioia's set: Stengard, Hawk, Aramayne? He could not remember which one. They were all so much alike.

Phillips returned the man's smile in a halfhearted, tentative way. He searched for something to say and finally asked, "Have you been here long?"

"Weeks. Perhaps months. What a splendid achievement this city is, eh, Charles? Such utter unity of mood—such a total statement of a uniquely single-minded esthetic—"

"Yes. Single-minded is the word," Phillips said dryly.

"Gioia's word, actually. Gioia's phrase. I was merely quoting."

Gioia. He felt as if he had been stabbed.

"You've spoken to Gioia lately?" he said.

"Actually, no. It was Hekna who saw her. You do remember Hekna, eh?" He nodded toward two naked women standing on the brick platform that bordered the pool, chatting, delicately nibbling morsels of meat. They could have been twins. "There is Hekna, with your Belilala." Hekna, yes. So this must be Hawk, Phillips thought, unless there has been some recent shift of couples. "How sweet she is, your Belilala," Hawk said. "Gioia chose very wisely when she picked her for you."

Another stab: a much deeper one. "Is that how it was?" he said. "Gioia *picked* Belilala for me?"

"Why, of course!" Hawk seemed surprised. It went without saying, evidently. "What did you think? That Gioia would merely go off and leave you to fend for yourself?"

"Hardly. Not Gioia."

"She's very tender, very gentle, isn't she?"

"You mean Belilala? Yes, very," said Phillips carefully. "A dear woman, a wonderful woman. But of course I hope to get together with Gioia again soon." He paused. "They say she's been in Mohenjo-daro almost since it opened."

"She was here, yes."

"Was?"

"Oh, you know Gioia," Hawk said lightly. "She's moved along by now, naturally."

Phillips leaned forward. "Naturally," he said. Tension thickened his voice. "Where has she gone this time?"

"Timbuctoo, I think. Or New Chicago. I forget which one it was. She was telling us that she hoped to be in Timbuctoo for the closing-down party. But then Fenimon had some pressing reason for going to New Chicago. I can't remember what they decided to do." Hawk gestured sadly. "Either way, a pity that she left Mohenjo before the new visitor came. She had such a rewarding time with you, after all: I'm sure she'd have found much to learn from him also."

The unfamiliar term twanged an alarm deep in Phillips's consciousness. *"Visitor?"* he said, angling his head sharply toward Hawk. "What visitor do you mean?"

"You haven't met him yet? Oh, of course, you've only just arrived."

Phillips moistened his lips. "I think I may have seen him. Long red hair? Beard like this?"

"That's the one! Willoughby, he's called. He's—what?— a Viking, a pirate, something like that. Tremendous vigor and force. Remarkable person. We should have many more visitors, I think. They're far superior to temporaries, everyone agrees. Talking with a temporary is a little like talking to one's self, wouldn't you say? They give you no significant illumination. But a visitor—someone like this Willoughby— or like you, Charles—a visitor can be truly enlightening, a visitor can transform one's view of reality—"

"Excuse me," Phillips said. A throbbing began behind his forehead. "Perhaps we can continue this conversation later, yes?" He put the flats of his hands against the hot brick of the platform and hoisted himself swiftly from the pool. "At dinner, maybe—or afterward—yes? All right?" He set off at a quick half-trot back toward the passageway that led to the private baths.

As he entered the roofed part of the structure his throat grew dry, his breath suddenly came short. He padded quickly up the hall and peered into the little bath chamber. The bearded man was still there, sitting up in the tank, breast-high above the water, with one arm around each of the women. His eyes gleamed with fiery intensity in the dimness. He was grinning in marvelous self-satisfaction; he seemed to brim with intensity, confidence, gusto.

Let him be what I think he is, Phillips prayed. I have been alone among these people long enough.

"May I come in?" he asked.

"Aye, fellow!" cried the man in the tub thunderously. "By my troth, come ye in, and bring your lass as well! God's teeth, I wot there's room aplenty for more folk in this tub than we!"

At that great uproarious outcry Phillips felt a powerful surge of joy. What a joyous rowdy voice! How rich, how lusty, how totally uncitizenlike!

And those oddly archaic words! *God's teeth? By my troth?* What sort of talk was that? What else but the good pure sonorous Elizabethan diction! Certainly it had something of the roll and fervor of Shakespeare about it. And spoken with—an Irish brogue, was it? No, not quite: it was English, but English spoken in no manner Phillips had ever heard.

Citizens did not speak that way. But a *visitor* might.

So it was true. Relief flooded Phillips's soul. Not alone, then! Another relic of a former age—another wanderer—a companion in chaos, a brother in adversity—a fellow voyager, tossed even farther than he had been by the tempests of time—

The bearded man grinned heartily and beckoned to Phillips with a toss of his head. "Well, join us, join us, man! 'Tis good to see an English face again, amidst all these Moors and rogue Portugals! But what have ye done with thy lass? One can never have enough wenches, d'ye not agree?"

The force and vigor of him were extraordinary: almost too much so. He roared, he bellowed, he boomed. He was so very much what he ought to be that he seemed more a character out of some old pirate movie than anything else, so blustering, so real, that he seemed unreal. A stage Elizabethan, larger than life, a boisterous young Falstaff without the belly.

Hoarsely Phillips said, "Who are you?"

"Why, Ned Willoughby's son Francis am I, of Plymouth. Late of the service of Her Most Protestant Majesty, but most foully abducted by the powers of darkness and cast away among these blackamoor Hindus, or whatever they be. And thyself?"

"Charles Phillips." After a moment's uncertainty he added, "I'm from New York."

"*New* York? What place is that? In faith, man, I know it not!"

"A city in America."

"A city in America, forsooth! What a fine fancy that is! In America, you say, and not on the Moon, or perchance underneath the sea?" To the women Willoughby said, "D'ye hear him? He comes from a city in America! With the face of an Englishman, though not the manner of one, and not quite the proper sort of speech. A city in America! A city. God's blood, what will I hear next?"

Phillips trembled. Awe was beginning to take hold of him. This man had walked the streets of Shakespeare's London, perhaps. He had clinked canisters with Marlowe or Essex or Walter Raleigh; he had watched the ships of the Armada wallowing in the Channel. It strained Phillips's spirit to think of it. This strange dream in which he found himself was compounding its strangeness now. He felt like a weary swimmer assailed by heavy surf, winded, dazed. The hot close atmosphere of the baths was driving him toward vertigo. There could be no doubt of it any longer. He was not the only primitive—the only *visitor*—who was wandering loose in this fiftieth century. They were conducting other experiments as well. He gripped the sides of the door to steady himself and said, "When you speak of Her Most Protestant Majesty, it's Elizabeth the First you mean, is that not so?"

"Elizabeth, aye! As to the First, that is true enough, but why trouble to name her thus? There is but one. First and Last, I do trow, and God save her, there is no other!"

Phillips studied the other man warily. He knew that he must proceed with care. A misstep at this point and he would forfeit any chance that Willoughby would take him seriously. How much metaphysical bewilderment, after all, could this man absorb? What did he know, what had anyone of his time known, of past and present and future and the notion that one might somehow move from one to the other as readily as one would go from Surrey to Kent? That was a twentieth-century idea, late nineteenth at best, a fantastical speculation that very likely no one had even considered before Wells had sent his time traveler off to stare at the reddened sun of the earth's last twilight. Willoughby's world was a world of Protestants and Catholics, of kings and queens, of tiny sailing vessels, of swords at the hip and ox-carts on the road: that world seemed to Phillips far more alien and distant than was this world of citizens and temporaries. The risk that Willoughby would not begin to understand him was great.

But this man and he were natural allies against a world they had never made. Phillips chose to take the risk.

"Elizabeth the First is the queen you serve," he said. "There will be another of her name in England, in due time. Has already been, in fact."

Willoughby shook his head like a puzzled lion. "Another Elizabeth, d'ye say?"

"A second one, and not much like the first. Long after your Virgin Queen, this one. She will reign in what you think of as the days to come. That I know without doubt."

The Englishman peered at him and frowned. "You see the future? Are you a soothsayer, then? A necromancer, mayhap? Or one of the very demons that brought me to this place?"

"Not at all," Phillips said gently. "Only a lost soul, like yourself." He stepped into the little room and crouched by the side of the tank. The two citizen-women were staring at him in bland fascination. He ignored them. To Willoughby he said, "Do you have any idea where you are?"

The Englishman had guessed, rightly enough, that he was in India: "I do believe these little brown Moorish folk are of the Hindu sort," he said. But that was as far as his comprehension of what had befallen him could go.

It had not occurred to him that he was no longer living in the sixteenth century. And of course he did not begin to suspect that this strange and somber brick city in which he found himself was a wanderer out of an era even more remote than his own. Was there any way, Phillips wondered, of explaining that to him?

He had been here only three days. He thought it was devils that had carried him off. "While I slept did they come for me," he said. "Mephistophilis Sathanas, his henchmen seized me—God alone can say why—and swept me in a moment out to this torrid realm from England, where I had reposed among friends and family. For I was between one voyage and the next, you must understand, awaiting Drake and his ship—you know Drake, the glorious Francis? God's blood, there's a mariner for ye! We were to go to the Main again, he and I, but instead here I be in this other place—" Willoughby leaned close and said, "I ask you, soothsayer, how can it be, that a man go to sleep in Plymouth and wake up in India? It is passing strange, is it not?"

"That it is," Phillips said.

"But he that is in the dance must needs dance on, though he do but hop, eh? So do I believe." He gestured toward the two citizen-women. "And therefore to console myself in this pagan land I have found me some sport among these little Portugal women—"

"Portugal?" said Phillips.

"Why, what else can they be, but Portugals? Is it not the Portugals who control all these coasts of India? See, the people are of two sorts here, the blackamoors and the others, the fair-skinned ones, the lords and masters who lie here in these baths. If they be not Hindus, and I think they are not, then Portugals is what they must be." He laughed and pulled the women against himself and rubbed his hands over their breasts as though they were fruits on a vine. "Is that not what you are, you little naked shameless Papist wenches? A pair of Portugals, eh?"

They giggled, but did not answer.

"No," Phillips said. "This is India, but not the India you think you know. And these women are not Portuguese."

"Not Portuguese?" Willoughby said, baffled.

"No more so than you. I'm quite certain of that."

Willoughby stroked his beard. "I do admit I found them very odd, for Portugals. I have heard not a syllable of their Portugee speech on their lips. And it is strange also that they run naked as Adam and Eve in these baths, and allow me free plunder of their women, which is not the way of Portugals at home, God wot. But I thought me, this is India, they choose to live in another fashion here—"

"No," Phillips said. "I tell you, these are not Portuguese, nor any other people of Europe who are known to you."

"Prithee, who are they, then?"

Do it delicately, now, Phillips warned himself. *Delicately.*

He said, "It is not far wrong to think of them as spirits of some kind—demons, even. Or sorcerers who have magicked us out of our proper places in the world." He paused, groping for some means to share with Willoughby, in a way that Willoughby might grasp, this mystery that had enfolded them. He drew a deep breath. "They've taken us not only across the sea," he said, "but across the years as well. We have both been hauled, you and I, far into the days that are to come."

Willoughby gave him a look of blank bewilderment.

"Days that are to come? Times yet unborn, d'ye mean? Why, I comprehend none of that!"

"Try to understand. We're both castaways in the same boat, man! But there's no way we can help each other if I can't make you see—"

Shaking his head, Willoughby muttered, "In faith, good friend, I find your words the merest folly. Today is today, and tomorrow is tomorrow, and how can a man step from one to t'other until tomorrow be turned into today?"

"I have no idea," said Phillips. Struggle was apparent on Willoughby's face; but plainly he could perceive no more than the haziest outline of what Phillips was driving at, if that much. "But this I know," he went on. "That your world and all that was in it is dead and gone. And so is mine, though I was born four hundred years after you, in the time of the second Elizabeth."

Willoughby snorted scornfully. "Four hundred—"

"You must believe me!"

"Nay! Nay!"

"It's the truth. Your time is only history to me. And mine and yours are history to *them*—ancient history. They call us visitors, but what we are is captives." Phillips felt himself quivering in the intensity of his effort. He was aware how insane this must sound to Willoughby. It was beginning to sound insane to him. "They've stolen us out of our proper times—seizing us like gypsies in the night—"

"Fie, man! You rave with lunacy!"

Phillips shook his head. He reached out and seized Willoughby tightly by the wrist. "I beg you, listen to me!" The citizen-women were watching closely, whispering to one another behind their hands, laughing. "Ask them!" Phillips cried. "Make them tell you what century this is! The sixteenth, do you think? Ask them!"

"What century could it be, but the sixteenth of our Lord?"

"They will tell you it is the fiftieth."

Willoughby looked at him pityingly. "Man, man, what a sorry thing thou art! The fiftieth, indeed!" He laughed. "Fellow, listen to me, now. There is but one Elizabeth, safe upon her throne in Westminster. This is India. The year is Anno 1591. Come, let us you and I steal a ship from these Portugals, and make our way back to England, and peradventure you may get from there to your America—"

"There is no England."

"Ah, can you say that and not be mad?"

"The cities and nations we knew are gone. These people live like magicians, Francis." There was no use holding anything back now, Phillips thought leadenly. He knew that he had lost. "They conjure up places of long ago, and build them here and there to suit their fancy, and when they are bored with them they destroy them, and start anew. There is no England. Europe is empty, featureless, void. Do you know what cities there are? There are only five in all the world. There is Alexandria of Egypt. There is Timbuctoo in Africa. There is New Chicago in America. There is a great city in China—in Cathay, I suppose you would say. And there is this place, which they call Mohenjo-daro, and which is far more ancient than Greece, than Rome, than Babylon."

Quietly Willoughby said, "Nay. This is mere absurdity. You say we are in some far tomorrow, and then you tell me we are dwelling in some city of long ago."

"A conjuration, only," Phillips said in desperation. "A likeness of that city. Which these folk have fashioned somehow for their own amusement. Just as we are here, you and I: to amuse them. Only to amuse them."

"You are completely mad."

"Come with me, then. Talk with the citizens by the great pool. Ask them what year this is; ask them about England; ask them how you come to be here." Once again Phillips grasped Willoughby's wrist. "We should be allies. If we work together, perhaps we can discover some way to get ourselves out of this place, and—"

"Let me be, fellow."

"Please—"

"Let me be!" roared Willoughby, and pulled his arm free. His eyes were stark with rage. Rising in the tank, he looked about furiously as though searching for a weapon. The citizen-women shrank back away from him, though at the same time they seemed captivated by the big man's fierce outburst. "Go to, get you to Bedlam! Let me be, madman! Let me be!"

*   *   *

Dismally Phillips roamed the dusty unpaved streets of Mohenjo-daro alone for hours. His failure with Willoughby had left him bleak-spirited and somber: he had hoped to stand back to back with the Elizabethan against the citizens, but he saw now that that was not to be. He had bungled things; or, more likely, it had been impossible ever to bring Willoughby to see the truth of their predicament.

In the stifling heat he went at random through the confusing congested lanes of flat-roofed windowless houses and blank featureless walls until he emerged into a broad marketplace. The life of the city swirled madly around him: the pseudo-life, rather, the intricate interactions of the thousands of temporaries who were nothing more than wind-up dolls set in motion to provide the illusion that pre-Vedic India was still a going concern. Here vendors sold beautiful little carved stone seals portraying tigers and monkeys and strange humped cattle, and women bargained vociferously with craftsmen for ornaments of ivory, gold, copper, and bronze. Weary-looking women squatted behind immense mounds of newly made pottery, pinkish red with black designs. No one paid any attention to him. He was the outsider here, neither citizen nor temporary. They belonged.

He went on, passing the huge granaries where workmen ceaselessly unloaded carts of wheat and others pounded grain on great circular brick platforms. He drifted into a public restaurant thronging with joyless silent people standing elbow to elbow at small brick counters, and was given a flat round piece of bread, a sort of tortilla or chapatti, in which was stuffed some spiced mincemeat that stung his lips like fire. Then he moved onward down a wide shallow timbered staircase into the lower part of the city, where the peasantry lived in cell-like rooms packed together as though in hives.

It was an oppressive city, but not a squalid one. The

intensity of the concern with sanitation amazed him: wells and fountains and public privies everywhere, and brick drains running from each building, leading to covered cess-pools. There was none of the open sewage and pestilent gutters that he knew still could be found in the India of his own time. He wondered whether ancient Mohenjo-daro had in truth been so fastidious. Perhaps the citizens had rede-signed the city to suit their own ideals of cleanliness. No: most likely what he saw was authentic, he decided, a func-tion of the same obsessive discipline that had given the city its rigidity of form. If Mohenjo-daro had been a verminous filthy hole, the citizens probably would have re-created it in just that way, and loved it for its fascinating reeking filth.

Not that he had ever noticed an excessive concern with authenticity on the part of the citizens; and Mohenjo-daro, like all the other restored cities he had visited, was full of the usual casual anachronisms. Phillips saw images of Shiva and Krishna here and there on the walls of buildings he took to be temples, and the benign face of the mother-goddess Kali loomed in the plazas. Surely those deities had arisen in India long after the collapse of the Mohenjo-daro civiliza-tion. Were the citizens indifferent to such matters of chro-nology? Or did they take a certain naughty pleasure in mixing the eras—a mosque and a church in Greek Alexan-dria, Hindu gods in prehistoric Mohenjo-daro? Perhaps their records of the past had become contaminated with errors over the thousands of years. He would not have been sur-prised to see banners bearing portraits of Gandhi and Nehru being carried in procession through the streets. And there were phantasms and chimeras at large here again, too, as if the citizens were untroubled by the boundary between his-tory and myth: little fat elephant-headed Ganeshas blithely plunging their trunks into water fountains, a six-armed three-headed woman sunning herself on a brick terrace.

Why not? Surely that was the motto of these people: *Why not, why not, why not?* They could do as they pleased, and they did. Yet Gioia had said to him, long ago, "Limits are very important." In what, Phillips wondered, did they limit themselves, other than the number of their cities? Was there a quota, perhaps, on the number of "visitors" they allowed themselves to kidnap from the past? Until today he had thought he was the only one; now he knew there was at least one other; possibly there were more elsewhere, a step or two ahead or behind him, making the circuit with the citizens who traveled endlessly from New Chicago to Chang-an to Alexandria. We should join forces, he thought, and compel them to send us back to our rightful eras. *Compel?* How? File a class-action suit, maybe? Demonstrate in the streets? Sadly he thought of his failure to make common cause with Willoughby. We are natural allies, he thought. Together perhaps we might have won some compassion from these people. But to Willoughby it must be literally unthinkable that Good Queen Bess and her subjects were sealed away on the far side of a barrier hundreds of centuries thick. He would prefer to believe that England was just a few months' voyage away around the Cape of Good Hope, and that all he need do was commandeer a ship and set sail for home. Poor Willoughby: probably he would never see his home again.

The thought came to Phillips suddenly:

Neither will you.

And then, after it:

If you could go home, would you really want to?

One of the first things he had realized here was that he knew almost nothing substantial about his former existence. His mind was well stocked with details on life in twentieth-century New York, to be sure; but of himself he could say not much more than that he was Charles Phillips and had come from 1984. Profession? Age? Parents' names? Did he have a wife? Children? A cat, a dog, hobbies? No data: none. Possibly the citizens had stripped such things from him when they brought him here, to spare him from the pain of separation. They might be capable of that kindness. Knowing so little of what he had lost, could he truly say that he yearned for it? Willoughby seemed to remember much more of his former life, somehow, and longed for it all the more intensely. He was spared that. Why not stay here, and go on and on from city to city, sightseeing all of time past as the citizens conjured it back into being? Why not? Why not? The chances were that he had no choice about it, anyway.

He made his way back up toward the citadel and to the baths once more. He felt a little like a ghost, haunting a city of ghosts.

Belilala seemed unaware that he had been gone for most of the day. She sat by herself on the terrace of the baths, placidly sipping some thick milky beverage that had been sprinkled with a dark spice. He shook his head when she offered him some.

"Do you remember I mentioned that I saw a man with red hair and a beard this morning?" Phillips said. "He's a visitor. Hawk told me that."

"Is he?" Belilala asked.

"From a time about four hundred years before mine. I talked with him. He thinks he was brought here by demons." Phillips gave her a searching look. "I'm a visitor, too, isn't that so?"

"Of course, love."

"And how was I brought here? By demons also?"

Belilala smiled indifferently. "You'd have to ask someone else. Hawk, perhaps. I haven't looked into these things very deeply."

"I see. Are there many visitors here, do you know?"

A languid shrug. "Not many, no, not really. I've only heard of three or four besides you. There may be others by now, I suppose." She rested her hand lightly on his. "Are you having a good time in Mohenjo, Charles?"

He let her question pass as though he had not heard it. "I asked Hawk about Gioia," he said.

"Oh?"

"He told me that she's no longer here, that she's gone on to Timbuctoo or New Chicago, he wasn't sure which."

"That's quite likely. As everybody knows, Gioia rarely stays in the same place very long."

Phillips nodded. "You said the other day that Gioia is a short-timer. That means she's going to grow old and die, doesn't it?"

"I thought you understood that, Charles."

"Whereas you will not age? Nor Hawk, nor Stengard, nor any of the rest of your set?"

"We will live as long as we wish," she said. "But we will not age, no."

"What makes a person a short-timer?"

"They're born that way, I think. Some missing gene, some extra gene—I don't actually know. It's extremely uncommon. Nothing can be done to help them. It's very slow, the aging. But it can't be halted."

Phillips nodded. "That must be very disagreeable," he said. "To find yourself one of the few people growing old in a world where everyone stays young. No wonder Gioia is so impatient. No wonder she runs around from place to place. No wonder she attached herself so quickly to the barbaric hairy visitor from the twentieth century, who comes from a time when *everybody* was short-timer. She and I have something in common, wouldn't you say?"

"In a manner of speaking, yes."

"We understand aging. We understand death. Tell me: is Gioia likely to die very soon, Belilala?"

"Soon? Soon?" She gave him a wide-eyed childlike stare. "What is soon? How can I say? What you think of as soon and what I think of as soon are not the same things, Charles." Then her manner changed: she seemed to be hearing what he was saying for the first time. Softly she said, "No, no, Charles. I don't think she will die very soon."

"When she left me in Chang-an, was it because she had become bored with me?"

Belilala shook her head. "She was simply restless. It had nothing to do with you. She was never bored with you."

"Then I'm going to go looking for her. Wherever she may be, Timbuctoo, New Chicago, I'll find her. Gioia and I belong together."

"Perhaps you do," said Belilala. "Yes. Yes, I think you really do." She sounded altogether unperturbed, unrejected, unbereft. "By all means, Charles. Go to her. Follow her. Find her. Wherever she may be."

They had already begun dismantling Timbuctoo when Phillips got there. While he was still high overhead, his flitterflitter hovering above the dusty tawny plain where the River Niger met the sands of the Sahara, a surge of keen excitement rose in him as he looked down at the square gray flat-roofed mud brick buildings of the great desert capital. But when he landed he found gleaming metal-skinned robots swarming everywhere, a horde of them scuttling about like giant shining insects, pulling the place apart.

He had not known about the robots before. So that was how all these miracles were carried out, Phillips realized: an army of obliging machines. He imagined them bustling up out of the earth whenever their services were needed, emerging from some sterile subterranean storehouse to put

together Venice or Thebes or Knossos or Houston or whatever place was required, down to the finest detail, and then
at some later time returning to undo everything that they
had fashioned. He watched them now, diligently pulling
down the adobe walls, demolishing the heavy metal-studded
gates, bulldozing the amazing labyrinth of alleyways and
thoroughfares, sweeping away the market. On his last visit
to Timbuctoo that market had been crowded with a horde
of veiled Tuaregs and swaggering Moors, black Sudanese,
shrewd-faced Syrian traders, all of them busily dickering for
camels, horses, donkeys, slabs of salt, huge green melons,
silver bracelets, splendid vellum Korans. They were all gone
now, that picturesque crowd of swarthy temporaries. Nor
were there any citizens to be seen. The dust of destruction
choked the air. One of the robots came up to Phillips and
said in a dry crackling insect-voice, "You ought not to be
here. This city is closed."

He stared at the flashing, buzzing band of scanners and
sensors across the creature's glittering tapered snout. "I'm
trying to find someone, a citizen who may have been here
recently. Her name is—"

"This city is closed," the robot repeated inexorably.

They would not let him stay as much as an hour. There
is no food here, the robot said, no water, no shelter. This is
not a place any longer. You may not stay. You may not
stay. You may not stay.

This is not a place any longer.

Perhaps he could find her in Chicago, then. He took to
the air again, soaring northward and westward over the vast
emptiness. The land below him curved away into the hazy
horizon, bare, sterile. What had they done with the vestiges
of the world that had gone before? Had they turned their
gleaming metal beetles loose to clean everything away?
Were there no ruins of genuine antiquity anywhere? No

scrap of Rome, no shard of Jerusalem, no stump of Fifth Avenue? It was all so barren down there: an empty stage, waiting for its next set to be built. He flew on a great arc across the jutting hump of Africa and on into what he supposed was southern Europe: the little vehicle did all the work, leaving him to doze or stare as he wished. Now and again he saw another flitterflitter pass by, far away, a dark distant winged teardrop outlined against the hard clarity of the sky. He wished there was some way of making radio contact with them, but he had no idea how to go about it. Not that he had anything he wanted to say; he wanted only to hear a human voice. He was utterly isolated. He might just as well have been the last living man on Earth. He closed his eyes and thought of Gioia.

"Like this?" Phillips asked. In an ivory-paneled oval room sixty stories above the softly glowing streets of New Chicago he touched a small cool plastic canister to his upper lip and pressed the stud at its base. He heard a foaming sound; and then blue vapor rose to his nostrils.

"Yes," Cantilena said. "That's right."

He detected a faint aroma of cinnamon, cloves, and something that might almost have been broiled lobster. Then a spasm of dizziness hit him and visions rushed through his head: Gothic cathedrals, the Pyramids, Central Park under fresh snow, the harsh brick warrens of Mohenjo-daro, and fifty thousand other places all at once, a wild roller-coaster ride through space and time. It seemed to go on for centuries. But finally his head cleared and he looked about, blinking, realizing that the whole thing had taken only a moment. Cantilena still stood at his elbow. The other citizens in the room—fifteen, twenty of them—had scarcely moved. The strange little man with the celadon skin over by the far wall continued to stare at him.

"Well?" Cantilena asked. "What did you think?"

"Incredible."

"And very authentic. It's an actual New Chicagoan drug. The exact formula. Would you like another?"

"Not just yet," Phillips said uneasily. He swayed and had to struggle for his balance. Sniffing that stuff might not have been such a wise idea, he thought.

He had been in New Chicago a week, or perhaps it was two, and he was still suffering from the peculiar disorientation that that city always aroused in him. This was the fourth time that he had come here, and it had been the same every time. New Chicago was the only one of the reconstructed cities of this world that in its original incarnation had existed *after* his own era. To him it was an outpost of the incomprehensible future; to the citizens it was a quaint simulacrum of the archaeological past. That paradox left him aswirl with impossible confusions and tensions.

What had happened to *old* Chicago was of course impossible for him to discover. Vanished without a trace, that was clear: no Water Tower, no Marina City, no Hancock Center, no Timbune building, not a fragment, not an atom. But it was hopeless to ask any of the million-plus inhabitants of New Chicago about their city's predecessor. They were only temporaries; they knew no more than they had to know, and all that they had to know was how to go through the motions of whatever it was that they did by way of creating the illusion that this was a real city. They had no need of knowing ancient history.

Nor was he likely to find out anything from a citizen, of course. Citizens did not seem to bother much about scholarly matters. Phillips had no reason to think that the world was anything other than an amusement park to them. Somewhere, certainly, there had to be those who specialized in the serious study of the lost civilizations of the past—for how, otherwise, would these uncanny reconstructed cities be brought into being? "The planners," he had once heard Nissandra or Aramayne say, "are already deep into their Byzantium research." But who were the planners? He had no idea. For all he knew, they were the robots. Perhaps the robots were the real masters of this whole era, who created the cities not primarily for the sake of amusing the citizens but in their own diligent attempt to comprehend the life of the world that had passed away. A wild speculation, yes; but not without some plausibility, he thought.

He felt oppressed by the party gaiety all about him. "I need some air," he said to Cantilena, and headed toward the window. It was the merest crescent, but a breeze came through. He looked out at the strange city below.

New Chicago had nothing in common with the old one but its name. They had built it, at least, along the western shore of a large inland lake that might even be Lake Michigan, although when he had flown over it had seemed broader and less elongated than the lake he remembered. The city itself was a lacy fantasy of slender pastel-hued buildings rising at odd angles and linked by a webwork of gently undulating aerial bridges. The streets were long parentheses that touched the lake at their northern and southern ends and arched gracefully westward in the middle. Between each of the great boulevards ran a track for public transportation—sleek aquamarine bubble-vehicles gliding on soundless wheels—and flanking each of the tracks were lush strips of park. It was beautiful, astonishingly so, but insubstantial. The whole thing seemed to have been contrived from sunbeams and silk.

A soft voice beside him said, "Are you becoming ill?"

Phillips glanced around. The celadon man stood beside him: a compact, precise person, vaguely Oriental in appearance. His skin was of a curious gray-green hue like no skin

Phillips had ever seen, and it was extraordinarily smooth in texture, as though he were made of fine porcelain.

He shook his head. "Just a little queasy," he said. "This city always scrambles me."

"I suppose it can be disconcerting," the little man replied. His tone was furry and veiled, the inflection strange. There was something feline about him. He seemed sinewy, unyielding, almost menacing. "Visitor, are you?"

Phillips studied him a moment. "Yes," he said.

"So am I, of course."

"Are you?"

"Indeed." The little man smiled. "What's your locus? Twentieth century? Twenty-first at the latest, I'd say."

"I'm from 1984. A.D. 1984."

Another smile, a self-satisfied one. "Not a bad guess, then." A brisk tilt of the head. "Y'ang-Yeovil."

"Pardon me?" Phillips said.

"Y'ang-Yeovil. It is my name. Formerly Colonel Y'ang-Yeovil of the Third Septentriad."

"Is that on some other planet?" asked Phillips, feeling a bit dazed.

"Oh, no, not at all," Y'ang-Yeovil said pleasantly. "This very world, I assure you. I am quite of human origin. Citizen of the Republic of Upper Han, native of the city of Port Ssu. And you—forgive me—your name—?"

"I'm sorry. Phillips. Charles Phillips. From New York City, once upon a time."

"Ah, New York!" Y'ang-Yeovil's face lit with a glimmer of recognition that quickly faded. "New York—New York—it was very famous, that I know—"

This is very strange, Phillips thought. He felt greater compassion for poor bewildered Francis Willoughby now. This man comes from a time so far beyond my own that he barely knows of New York—he must be a contemporary of the real New Chicago, in fact; I wonder whether he finds this version authentic—and yet to the citizens this Y'ang-Yeovil too is just a primitive, a curio out of antiquity—

"New York was the largest city of the United States of America," Phillips said.

"Of course. Yes. Very famous."

"But virtually forgotten by the time the Republic of Upper Han came into existence, I gather."

Y'ang-Yeovil said, looking uncomfortable, "There were disturbances between your time and mine. But by no means should you take from my words the impression that your city was—"

Sudden laughter resounded across the room. Five or six newcomers had arrived at the party. Phillips stared, gasped, gaped. Surely that was Stengard—and Aramayne beside him—and that other woman, half hidden behind them—

"If you'll pardon me a moment—" Phillips said, turning abruptly away from Y'ang-Yeovil. "Please excuse me. Someone just coming in—a person I've been trying to find ever since—"

He hurried toward her.

"Gioia?" he called. "Gioia, it's me! Wait! Wait!"

Stengard was in the way. Aramayne, turning to take a handful of the little vapor-sniffers from Cantilena, blocked him also. Phillips pushed through them as though they were not there. Gioia, halfway out the door, halted and looked toward him like a frightened deer.

"Don't go," he said. He took her hand in his.

He was startled by her appearance. How long had it been since their strange parting on that night of mysteries in Chang-an? A year? A year and a half? So he believed. Or had he lost all track of time? Were his perceptions of the passing the months in this world that unreliable? She seemed at least ten or fifteen years older. Maybe she really was; maybe the years had been passing for him here as in a dream, and he had never known it. She looked strained, faded, worn. Out of a thinner and strangely altered face her eyes blazed at him almost defiantly, as though saying, *See? See how ugly I have become?*

He said, "I've been hunting for you for—I don't know how long it's been, Gioia. In Mohenjo, in Timbuctoo, now here. I want to be with you again."

"It isn't possible."

"Belilala explained everything to me in Mohenjo. I know that you're a short-timer—I know what that means, Gioia. But what of it? So you're beginning to age a little. So what? So you'll only have three or four hundred years, instead of forever. Don't you think I know what it means to be a short-timer? I'm just a simple ancient man of the twentieth century, remember? Sixty, seventy, eighty years is all we would get. You and I suffer from the same malady, Gioia. That's what drew you to me in the first place. I'm certain of that. That's why we belong with each other now. However much time we have, we can spend the rest of it together, don't you see?"

"You're the one who doesn't see, Charles," she said softly.

"Maybe. Maybe I still don't understand a damned thing about this place. Except that you and I—that I love you— that I think you love me—"

"I love you, yes. But you don't understand. It's precisely because I love you that you and I—you and I can't—"

With a despairing sigh she slid her hand free of his grasp. He reached for her again, but she shook him off and backed up quickly into the corridor.

"Gioia?"

"Please," she said. "No. I would never have come here

if I knew you were here. Don't come after me. Please. Please."

She turned and fled.

He stood looking after her for a long moment. Cantilena and Aramayne appeared, and smiled at him as if nothing at all had happened. Cantilena offered him a vial of some sparkling amber fluid. He refused with a brusque gesture. Where do I go now, he wondered? What do I do? He wandered back into the party.

Y'ang-Yeovil glided to his side. "You are in great distress," the little man murmured.

Phillips glared. "Let me be."

"Perhaps I could be of some help."

"There's no help possible," said Phillips. He swung about and plucked one of the vials from a tray and gulped its contents. It made him feel as if there were two of him, standing on either side of Y'ang-Yeovil. He gulped another. Now there were four of him. "I'm in love with a citizen," he blurted. It seemed to him that he was speaking in chorus.

"Love. Ah. And does she love you?"

"So I thought. So I think. But she's a short-timer. Do you know what that means? She's not immortal like the others. She ages. She's beginning to look old. And so she's been running away from me. She doesn't want me to see her changing. She thinks it'll disgust me, I suppose. I tried to remind her just now that I'm not immortal either, that she and I could grow old together, but she—"

"Oh, no," Y'ang-Yeovil said quietly. "Why do you think you will age? Have you grown any older in all the time that you've been here?"

Phillips was nonplussed. "Of course I have. I—I—"

"Have you?" Y'ang-Yeovil smiled. "Here. Look at yourself." He did something intricate with his fingers and a shimmering zone of mirrorlike light appeared between them.

Phillips stared at his reflection. A youthful face stared back at him. It was true, then. He had simply not thought about it. How many years had he spent in this world? The time had simply slipped by: a great deal of time, though he could not calculate how much. They did not seem to keep close count of it here, nor had he. But it must have been many years, he thought. All that endless travel up and down the globe—so many cities had come and gone—Rio, Rome, Asgard, those were the first three that came to mind—and there were others; he could hardly remember every one. Years. His face had not changed at all. Time had worked its harshness on Gioia, yes, but not on him.

"I don't understand," he said. "Why am I not aging?"

"Because you are not real," said Y'ang-Yeovil. "Are you unaware of that?"

Phillips blinked. "Not—real?"

"Did you think you were lifted bodily out of your own time?" the little man asked. "Ah, no, no, there is no way for them to do such a thing. We are not actual time travelers: not you, not I, not any of the visitors. I thought you were aware of that. But perhaps your era is too early for a proper understanding of these things. We are very cleverly done, my friend. We are ingenious constructs, marvelously stuffed with the thoughts and attitudes and events of our own times. We are their finest achievement, you know: far more complex even than one of these cities. We are a step beyond the temporaries—more than a step, a great deal more. They do only what they are instructed to do, and their range is very narrow. They are nothing but machines, really. Whereas we are autonomous. We move about by our own will; we think, we talk, we even, so it seems, fall in love. But we will not age. How could we age? We are not real. We are mere artificial webworks of mental responses. We are mere illusions, done so well that we deceive even ourselves. You did not know that? Indeed, you did not know?"

He was airborne, touching destination buttons at random. Somehow he found himself heading back toward Timbuctoo. *This city is closed. This is not a place any longer.* It did not matter to him. Why should anything matter?

Fury and a choking sense of despair rose within him. I am software, Phillips thought. I am nothing but software.

Not real. Very cleverly done. An ingenious construct. A mere illusion.

No trace of Timbuctoo was visible from the air. He landed anyway. The gray sandy earth was smooth, un-turned, as though there had never been anything there. A few robots were still about, handling whatever final chores were required in the shutting-down of a city. Two of them scuttled up to him. Huge bland gleaming silver-skinned insects, not friendly.

"There is no city here," they said. "This is not a permissible place."

"Permissible by whom?"

"There is no reason for you to be here."

"There's no reason for me to be anywhere," Phillips said. The robots stirred, made uneasy humming sounds and ominous clicks, waved their antennae about. They seemed troubled, he thought. They seem to dislike my attitude. Perhaps I run some risk of being taken off to the home for unruly software for debugging. "I'm leaving now," he told them. "Thank you. Thank you very much." He backed away from them and climbed into his flitterflitter. He touched more destination buttons.

We move about by our own will. We think, we talk, we even fall in love.

He landed in Chang-an. This time there was no reception committee waiting for him at the Gate of Brilliant Virtue. The city seemed larger and more resplendent: new pagodas, new palaces. It felt like winter: a chilly cutting wind was blowing. The sky was cloudless and dazzlingly bright. At the steps of the Silver Terrace he encountered Francis Willoughby, a great hulking figure in magnificent brocaded robes, with two dainty little temporaries, pretty as jade statuettes, engulfed in his arms. "Miracles and wonders! The silly lunatic fellow is here, too!" Willoughby roared. "Look, look, we are come to far Cathay, you and I!"

We are nowhere, Phillips thought. *We are mere illusions, done so well that we deceive even ourselves.*

To Willoughby he said, "You look like an emperor in those robes, Francis."

"Aye, like Prester John!" Willoughby cried. "Like Tamburlaine himself! Aye, am I not majestic?" He slapped Phillips gaily on the shoulder, a rough playful poke that spun him halfway about, coughing and wheezing. "We flew in the air, as the eagles do, as the demons do, as the angels do! Soared like angels! Like angels!" He came close, looming over Phillips. "I would have gone to England, but the wench Belilala said there was an enchantment on me that would keep me from England just now; and so we voyaged to Cathay. Tell me this, fellow, will you go witness for me when we see England again? Swear that all that has befallen us did in truth befall? For I fear they will say I am as mad as Marco Polo, when I tell them of flying to Cathay."

"One madman backing another?" Phillips asked. "What can I tell you? You still think you'll reach England, do you?" Rage rose to the surface in him, bubbling hot. "Ah, Francis, Francis, do you know your Shakespeare? Did you go to the plays? We aren't real. *We aren't real.* We are such stuff as dreams are made on, the two of us. That's all we are. O brave new world! What England? Where? There's no

England. There's no Francis Willoughby. There's no Charles Phillips. What we are is—"

"Let him be, Charles," a cool voice cut in.

He turned. Belilala, in the robes of an empress, coming down the steps of the Silver Terrace.

"I know the truth," he said bitterly. "Y'ang-Yeovil told me. The visitor from the twenty-fifth century. I saw him in New Chicago."

"Did you see Gioia there, too?" Belilala asked.

"Briefly. She looks much older."

"Yes. I know. She was here recently."

"And has gone on, I suppose?"

"To Mohenjo again, yes. Go after her, Charles. Leave poor Francis alone. I told her to wait for you. I told her that she needs you, and you need her."

"Very kind of you. But what good is it, Belilala? I don't even exist. And she's going to die."

"You exist. How can you doubt that you exist? You feel, don't you? You suffer. You love. You love Gioia: is that not so? And you are loved by Gioia. Would Gioia love what is not real?"

"You think she loves me?"

"I know she does. Go to her, Charles. Go. I told her to wait for you in Mohenjo."

Phillips nodded numbly. What was there to lose?

"Go to her," said Belilala again. "Now."

"Yes," Phillips said. "I'll go now." He turned to Willoughby. "If ever we meet in London, friend, I'll testify for you. Fear nothing. All will be well, Francis."

He left them and set his course for Mohenjo-daro, half expecting to find the robots already tearing it down. Mohenjo-daro was still there, no lovelier than before. He went to the baths, thinking he might find Gioia there. She was not; but he came upon Nissandra, Stengard, Fenimon.

"She has gone to Alexandria," Fenimon told him. "She wants to see it one last time, before they close it."

"They're almost ready to open Constantinople," Stengard explained. "The capital of Byzantium, you know, the great city by the Golden Horn. They'll take Alexandria away, you understand, when Byzantium opens. They say it's going to be marvelous. We'll see you there for the opening, naturally?"

"Naturally," Phillips said.

He flew to Alexandria. He felt lost and weary. All this is hopeless folly, he told himself. I am nothing but a puppet jerking about on its strings. But somewhere above the shining breast of the Arabian Sea the deeper implications of something that Belilala had said to him started to sink in, and he felt his bitterness, his rage, his despair, all suddenly beginning to leave him. *You exist. How can you doubt that you exist? Would Gioia love what is not real?* Of course. Of course. Y'ang-Yeovil had been wrong: visitors were something more than mere illusions. Indeed, Y'ang-Yeovil had voiced the truth of their condition without understanding what he was really saying: *We think, we talk, we fall in love.* Yes. That was the heart of the situation. The visitors might be artificial, but they were not unreal. Belilala had been trying to tell him that just the other night. *You suffer. You love. You love Gioia. Would Gioia love what is not real?* Surely he was real, or at any rate real enough. What he was was something strange, something that would probably have been all but incomprehensible to the twentieth-century people whom he had been designed to simulate. But that did not mean that he was unreal. Did one have to be of woman born to be real? No. No. No. His kind of reality was a sufficient reality. He had no need to be ashamed of it. And, understanding that, he understood that Gioia did not need to grow old and die. There was a way by which she could be saved, if only she would embrace it. If only she would.

When he landed in Alexandria he went immediately to the hotel on the slopes of the Paneium where they had stayed on their first visit, so very long ago; and there she was, sitting quietly on a patio with a view of the harbor and the Lighthouse. There was something calm and resigned about the way she sat. She had given up. She did not even have the strength to flee from him any longer.

"Gioia," he said gently.

She looked older than she had in New Chicago. Her face was drawn and sallow and her eyes seemed sunken; and she was not even bothering these days to deal with the white strands that stood out in stark contrast against the darkness of her hair. He sat down beside her and put his hand over hers and looked out toward the obelisks, the palaces, the temples, the Lighthouse. At length he said, "I know what I really am now."

"Do you, Charles?" She sounded very far away.

"In my age we called it software. All I am is a set of commands, responses, cross-references, operating some sort of artificial body. It's infinitely better software then we could have imagined. But we were only just beginning to learn how, after all. They pumped me full of twentieth-century reflexes. The right moods, the right appetites, the right irrationalities, the right sort of combativeness. Somebody knows a lot about what it was like to be a twentieth-century man. They did a good job with Willoughby, too, all that Elizabethan rhetoric and swagger. And I suppose they got Y'ang-Yeovil right. *He* seems to think so: who better to judge? The twenty-fifth century, the Republic of Upper Han, people with gray-green skin, half Chinese and half Martian for all I know. *Somebody* knows. Somebody here is very good at programming, Gioia."

She was not looking at him.

"I feel frightened, Charles," she said in that same distant way.

"Of me? Of the things I'm saying?"

"No, not of you. Don't you see what has happened to me?"

"I see you. There are changes."

"I lived a long time wondering when the changes would begin. I thought maybe they wouldn't, not really. Who wants to believe they'll get old? But it started when we were in Alexandria that first time. In Chang-an it got much worse. And now—now—"

He said abruptly, "Stengard tells me they'll be opening Constantinople very soon."

"So?"

"Don't you want to be there when it opens?"

"I'm becoming old and ugly, Charles."

"We'll go to Constantinople together. We'll leave tomorrow, eh? What do you say? We'll charter a boat. It's a quick little hop, right across the Mediterranean. Sailing to Byzantium! There was a poem, you know, in my time. Not forgotten, I guess, because they've programmed it into me. All these thousands of years, and someone still remembers old Yeats. *The young in one another's arms, birds in the trees.* Come with me to Byzantium, Gioia."

She shrugged. "Looking like this? Getting more hideous every hour? While *they* stay young forever? While *you*—" She faltered; her voice cracked; she fell silent.

"Finish the sentence, Gioia."

"Please. Let me alone."

"You were going to say, 'While *you* stay young forever, too, Charles,' isn't that it? You knew all along that I was never going to change. I didn't know that, but you did."

"Yes. I knew. I pretended that it wasn't true—that as I aged, you'd age, too. It was very foolish of me. In Chang-an, when I first began to see the real signs of it—that was when I realized I couldn't stay with you any longer. Because I'd look at you, always young, always remaining the same age, and I'd look at myself, and—" She gestured, palms upward. "So I gave you to Belilala and ran away."

"All so unnecessary, Gioia."

"I didn't think it was."

"But you don't have to grow old. Not if you don't want to!"

"Don't be cruel, Charles," she said tonelessly. "There's no way of escaping what I have."

"But there is," he said.

"You know nothing about these things."

"Not very much, no," he said. "But I see how it can be done. Maybe it's a primitive simpleminded twentieth-century sort of solution, but I think it ought to work. I've been playing with the idea ever since I left Mohenjo. Tell me this, Gioia: Why can't you go to them, to the programmers, to the artificers, the planners, whoever they are, the ones who create the cities and the temporaries and the visitors. And have yourself made into something like me!"

She looked up, startled. "What are you saying?"

"They can cobble up a twentieth-century man out of nothing more than fragmentary records and make him plausible, can't they? Or an Elizabethan, or anyone else of any era at all, and he's authentic, he's convincing. So why couldn't they do an even better job with you? Produce a Gioia so real that even Gioia can't tell the difference? But a Gioia that will never age—a Gioia-construct, a Gioia-program, a visitor-Gioia! Why not? Tell me why not, Gioia."

She was trembling. "I've never heard of doing any such thing!"

"But don't you think it's possible?"

"How would I know?"

"Of course it's possible. If they can create visitors, they can take a citizen and duplicate her in such a way that—"

"It's never been done. I'm sure of it. I can't imagine any citizen agreeing to any such thing. To give up the body—to let yourself be turned into—into—"

She shook her head, but it seemed to be a gesture of astonishment as much as of negation.

He said, "Sure. To give up the body. Your natural body, your aging, shrinking, deteriorating short-timer body. What's so awful about that?"

She was very pale. "This is craziness, Charles. I don't want to talk about it any more."

"It doesn't sound crazy to me."

"You can't possibly understand."

"Can't I? I can certainly understand being afraid to die. I don't have a lot of trouble understanding what it's like to be one of the few aging people in a world where nobody grows old. What I can't understand is why you aren't even willing to consider the possibility that—"

"No," she said. "I tell you, it's crazy. They'd laugh at me."

"Who?"

"All of my friends. Hawk, Stengard, Aramayne—" Once again she would not look at him. "They can be very cruel, without even realizing it. They despise anything that seems ungraceful to them, anything sweaty and desperate and cowardly. Citizens don't do sweaty things, Charles. And that's how this will seem. Assuming it can be done at all. They'll be terribly patronizing. Oh, they'll be sweet to me, yes, dear Gioia, how wonderful for you, Gioia, but when I turn my back they'll laugh. They'll say the most wicked things about me. I couldn't bear that."

"They can afford to laugh," Phillips said. "It's easy to be brave and cool about dying when you know you're going to live forever. How very fine for them: but why should you be the only one to grow old and die? And they won't laugh, anyway. They're not as cruel as you think. Shallow, maybe, but not cruel. They'll be glad that you've found a way to save yourself. At the very least, they won't have to feel guilty about you any longer, and that's bound to please them. You can—"

"Stop it," she said.

She rose, walked to the railing of the patio, stared out toward the sea. He came up behind her. Red sails in the harbor, sunlight glittering along the sides of the Lighthouse, the palaces of the Ptolemies stark white against the sky. Lightly he rested his hand on her shoulder. She twitched as if to pull away from him, but remained where she was.

"Then I have another idea," he said quietly. "If you won't go to the planners, *I* will. Reprogram me, I'll say. Fix things so that I start to age at the same rate you do. It'll be more authentic, anyway, if I'm supposed to be playing the part of a twentieth-century man. Over the years I'll very gradually get some lines in my face, my hair will turn gray, I'll walk a little more slowly—we'll grow old together, Gioia. To hell with your lovely immortal friends. We'll have each other. We won't need them."

She swung around. Her eyes were wide with horror.

"Are you serious, Charles?"

"Of course."

"No," she murmured. "No. Everything you've said to me today is monstrous nonsense. Don't you realize that?"

He reached for her hand and enclosed her fingertips in his. "All I'm trying to do is find some way for you and me to—"

"Don't say any more," she said. "Please." Quickly, as though drawing back from a suddenly flaring flame, she tugged her fingers free of his and put her hand behind her. Though his face was just inches from hers he felt an immense chasm opening between them. They stared at one another for a moment; then she moved deftly to his left, darted around him, and ran from the patio.

Stunned, he watched her go, down the long marble corridor and out of sight. It was folly to give pursuit, he thought. She was lost to him: that was clear, that was beyond any question. She was terrified of him. Why cause her even more anguish? But somehow he found himself running through the halls of the hotel, along the winding garden path, into the cool green groves of the Paneium. He thought he saw her on the portico of Hadrian's palace, but when he got there the echoing stone halls were empty. To a temporary that was sweeping the steps he said, "Did you see a woman come this way?" A blank sullen stare was his only answer.

Phillips cursed and turned away.

"Gioia?" he called. "Wait! Come back!"

Was that her, going into the Library? He rushed past the startled mumbling librarians and sped through the stacks, peering beyond the mounds of double-handled scrolls into the shadowy corridors. "Gioia? *Gioia!*" It was a desecration, bellowing like that in this quiet place. He scarcely cared.

Emerging by a side door, he loped down to the harbor. The Lighthouse! Terror enfolded him. She might already be a hundred steps up that ramp, heading for the parapet from which she meant to fling herself into the sea. Scattering citizens and temporaries as if they were straws, he ran within. Up he went, never pausing for breath, though his synthetic lungs were screaming for respite, his ingeniously designed heart was desperately pounding. On the first balcony he imagined he caught a glimpse of her, but he circled it without finding her. Onward, upward. He went to the top, to the beacon chamber itself: no Gioia. Had she jumped? Had she gone down one ramp while he was ascending the other? He clung to the rim and looked out, down, searching the base of the Lighthouse, the rocks offshore, the causeway. No Gioia. I will find her somewhere, he thought. I will keep going until I find her. He went running down the ramp, calling her name. He reached ground level and sprinted back toward the center of town. Where next? The temple of Poseidon? The tomb of Cleopatra?

He paused in the middle of Canopus Street, groggy and dazed.

"Charles?" she said.

"Where are you?"

"Right here. Beside you." She seemed to materialize from the air. Her face was unflushed, her robe bore no trace of perspiration. Had he been chasing a phantom through the city? She came to him and took his hand, and said, softly, tenderly, "Were you really serious, about having them make you age?"

"If there's no other way, yes."

"The other way is so frightening, Charles."

"Is it?"

"You can't understand how much."

"More frightening than growing old? Than dying?"

"I don't know," she said. "I suppose not. The only thing I'm sure of is that I don't want you to get old, Charles."

"But I won't have to. Will I?"

He stared at her.

"No," she said. "You won't have to. Neither of us will."

Phillips smiled. "We should get away from here," he said after a while. "Let's go across to Byzantium, yes, Gioia? We'll show up in Constantinople for the opening. Your friends will be there. We'll tell them what you've decided to do. They'll know how to arrange it. Someone will."

"It sounds so strange," said Gioia. "To turn myself into—into a visitor? A visitor in my own world?"

"That's what you've always been, though."

"I suppose. In a way. But at least I've been *real* up to now."

"Whereas I'm not?"

"Are you, Charles?"

"Yes. Just as real as you. I was angry at first, when I found out the truth about myself. But I came to accept it. Somewhere between Mohenjo and here, I came to see that it was all right to be what I am: that I perceive things, I form ideas, I draw conclusions. I am very well designed, Gioia. I can't tell the difference between being what I am and being completely alive, and to me that's being real enough. I think, I feel, I experience joy and pain. I'm as real as I need to be. And you will be, too. You'll never stop being Gioia, you know. It's only your body that you'll cast away, the body that played such a terrible joke on you anyway." He brushed her cheek with his hand. "It was all said for us before, long ago:

> 'Once out of nature I shall never take
> My bodily form from any natural thing,
> But such a form as Grecian goldsmiths make
> Of hammered gold and gold enamelling
> To keep a drowsy Emperor awake—' "

"Is that the same poem?" she asked.

"The same poem, yes. The ancient poem that isn't quite forgotten yet."

"Finish it, Charles."

—"Or set upon a golden bough to sing
To lords and ladies of Byzantium
Of what is past, or passing, or to come."

"How beautiful. What does it mean?"

"That it isn't necessary to be mortal. That we can allow ourselves to be gathered into the artifice of eternity, that we can be transformed, that we can move on beyond the flesh. Yeats didn't mean it in quite the way I do—he wouldn't have begun to comprehend what we're talking about, not a word of it—and yet, and yet—the underlying truth is the same. Live, Gioia! With me!" He turned to her and saw color coming into her pallid cheeks. "It does make sense, what I'm suggesting, doesn't it? You'll attempt it, won't you? Whoever makes the visitors can be induced to remake you. Right? What do you think: can they, Gioia?"

She nodded in a barely perceptible way. "I think so," she said faintly. "It's very strange. But I think it ought to be possible. Why not, Charles? Why not?"

"Yes," he said. "Why not?"

In the morning they hired a vessel in the harbor, a low sleek pirogue with a blood-red sail, skippered by a rascally-looking temporary whose smile was irresistible. Phillips shaded his eyes and peered northward across the sea. He thought he could almost make out the shape of the great city sprawling on its seven hills, Constantine's New Rome beside the Golden Horn, the mighty dome of Hagia Sophia, the somber walls of the citadel, the palaces and churches, the Hippodrome, Christ in glory rising above all else in brilliant mosaic streaming with light.

"Byzantium," Phillips said. "Take us there the shortest and quickest way."

"It is my pleasure," said the boatman with unexpected grace.

Gioia smiled. He had not seen her looking so vibrantly alive since the night of the imperial feast in Chang-an. He reached for her hand—her slender fingers were quivering lightly—and helped her into the boat.

HOMEFARING

HOMEFARING

AN INTRODUCTION

I had always had a sneaking desire to write the definitive giant-lobster story. Earlier science-fiction writers had preempted most of the other appealing monstrosities—including giant aunts (sic!), dealt with by Isaac Asimov in his classic story "Dream World," which I have just ruined forever for you by giving away its punchline. But giant lobsters remained fair game. And when George Scithers, the new editor of the venerable science-fiction magazine *Amazing Stories*, asked me in the autumn of 1982 to do a lengthy story for him, I decided that it was time at last for me to give lobsters their due.

The obvious giant-lobster story, in which horrendous pincer-wielding monsters twenty feet long come ashore at Malibu and set about the conquest of Los Angeles by terrorizing the surfers, might work well enough in a cheap Hollywood sci-fi epic, but it wouldn't have stood much chance of delighting a sophisticated science-fiction reader like Scithers. Nor did it have a lot of appeal for me as a writer. Therefore, following the advice of the brilliant, cantankerous editor Horace Gold, one of my early mentors, I searched for my story idea by turning the obvious upside down. Lobsters are pretty nasty things, after all. They're tough, surly, dangerous, and ugly—surely the ugliest food objects ever to be prized by mankind. A creature so disagreeable in so many ways must have some redeeming feature. (Other than the flavor of its meat, that is.) And so, instead of depicting them as the savage and hideous-looking critters they really are, what about putting them through a few hundred million years of evolution and turning them into wise and thoughtful civilized beings—the dominant life-form, in fact, of a vastly altered Earth?

A challenging task, yes. And made even more challenging for me, back there in the otherwise sunny and pleasant November of 1982, by the fact that I had just made the great leap from typewriter to computer. "Homefaring" marked my initiation into the world of floppy disks and soft hyphens, of backup copies and automatic pagination. It's all second nature to me now, of course, but in 1982 I found myself timidly stumbling around in a brave and very strange new world. Each day's work was an adventure in terror. My words appeared in white letters on a black screen, frighteningly impermanent: one electronic sneeze, I thought, and a whole day's brilliant prose could vanish like a time traveler who has just defenestrated his own grandfather. The mere making of backups didn't lull my fears: how could I be sure that the act of backing up itself wouldn't erase what I had just written? Pushing the button marked "Save"—did that really save anything? Switching the computer off at the end of my working day was like a leap into the abyss. Would the story be there the next morning when I turned the machine on again? Warily, I printed out each day's work when it was done, before backing up, saving, or otherwise jiggling with it electronically. I wanted to see it safely onto paper first. Sometimes when I put a particularly difficult scene together—for example, the three-page scene at the midpoint of the story, beginning with the line, "The lobsters were singing as they marched"—I would stop right then and there and print it out before proceeding, aware that if the computer somehow were to destroy it I would never be able to reconstruct it at that level of accomplishment. (It's an axiom among writers that material written to replace inadvertently destroyed copy can't possibly equal the lost passage—which gets better and better in one's memory all the time.)

Somehow, in fear and trembling, I tiptoed my way through the entire 88-page manuscript of "Homefaring" without any major disasters. The computer made it marvelously easy to revise the story as I went along; instead of typing out an 88-page first draft, then covering it with handwritten alterations and grimly typing the whole thing out again to make it fit to show an editor, I brought every paragraph up to final-draft status with painless little maneuvers of the cursor. When I realized that I had chosen a confusing name for a minor character, I ordered the computer to correct my error, and sat back in wonder as "Eitel" became "Bleier" throughout the story without my having to do a thing. And then at the end came the wondrous moment when I pushed the button marked "Print" and page after page of immaculate typed copy began to come forth while I occupied myself with other and less dreary tasks.

The readers liked the story and it was a finalist in the 1983 Nebula Award voting—perhaps might even have won, if it had been published in a magazine less obscure than dear old *Amazing*, which had only a handful of readers. That same year the veteran connoisseur of science fiction, Donald A. Wollheim, chose it for his annual World's Best SF anthology, an honor that particularly pleased me. I had deliberately intended "Homefaring" as a sleek and modern version of the sort of imagination-stirring tale of wonder that Wollheim had cherished in the s-f magazines of the 1930s, and his choice of the story for his book confirmed my feeling of working within a great tradition.

HOMEFARING

McCulloch was beginning to molt. The sensation, inescapable and unarguable, horrified him—it felt exactly as though his body was going to split apart, which it was—and yet it was also completely familiar, expected, welcome. Wave after wave of keen and dizzying pain swept through him. Burrowing down deep in the sandy bed, he waved his great claws about, lashed his flat tail against the pure white sand, scratched frantically with quick worried gestures of his eight walking-legs.

He was frightened. He was calm. He had no idea what was about to happen to him. He had done this a hundred times before.

The molting prodrome had overwhelming power. It blotted from his mind all questions, and, after a moment, all fear. A white line of heat ran down his back—no, down the top of his carapace—from a point just back of his head to the first flaring segments of his tail-fan. He imagined that all the sun's force, concentrated through some giant glass lens, was being inscribed in a single track along his shell.

And his soft inner body was straining, squirming, expanding, filling the carapace to overflowing. But still that rigid shell contained him, refusing to yield to the pressure. To McCulloch it was much like being inside a wet-suit that was suddenly five times too small.

—What is the sun? What is glass? What is a lens? What is a wet-suit?

The questions swarmed suddenly upward in his mind like little busy many-legged creatures springing out of the sand. But he had no time for providing answers. The molting prodrome was developing with astounding swiftness, carrying him along. The strain was becoming intolerable. In another moment he would surely burst. He was writhing in short angular convulsions. Within his claws, his tissues now were shrinking, shriveling, drawing back within the ferocious shell-hulls, but the rest of him was continuing inexorably to grow larger.

He had to escape from this shell, or it would kill him. He had to expel himself somehow from this impossibly constricting container. Digging his front claws and most of his legs into the sand, he heaved, twisted, stretched, pushed. He thought of himself as being pregnant with himself, struggling fiercely to deliver himself of himself.

Ah. The carapace suddenly began to split.

The crack was only a small one, high up near his shoulders—shoulders?—but the imprisoned substance of him surged swiftly toward it, widening and lengthening it, and in another moment the hard horny covering was cracked from end to end. Ah. Ah. That felt so good, that release from constraint! Yet McCulloch still had to free himself. Delicately he drew himself backward, withdrawing leg after leg from its covering in a precise, almost fussy way, as though he were pulling his arms from the sleeves of some incredibly ancient and frail garment.

Until he had his huge main claws free, though, he knew he could not extricate himself from the sundered shell. And freeing the claws took extreme care. The front limbs still were shrinking, and the limy joints of the shell seemed to be dissolving and softening, but nevertheless he had to pull each claw through a passage much narrower than itself. It was easy to see how a hasty move might break a limb off altogether.

He centered his attention on the task. It was a little like telling his wrists to make themselves small, so he could slide them out of handcuffs.

—Wrists? Handcuffs? What are those?

McCulloch paid no attention to that baffling inner voice. Easy, easy, there—ah—yes, there, like that! One claw was free. Then the other, slowly, carefully. Done. Both of them retracted. The rest was simple: some shrugging and wiggling, exhausting but not really challenging, and he succeeded in extending the breach in the carapace until he could crawl backward out of it. Then he lay on the sand beside it, weary, drained, naked, soft, terribly vulnerable. He wanted only to return to the sleep out of which he had emerged into this nightmare of shell-splitting.

But some force within him would not let him slacken off. A moment to rest, only a moment. He looked to his left, toward the discarded shell. Vision was difficult—there were peculiar, incomprehensible refraction effects that broke every image into thousands of tiny fragments—but despite that, and despite the dimness of the light, he was able to see that the shell, golden-hued with broad arrow-shaped red markings, was something like a lobster's, yet even more intricate, even more bizarre. McCulloch did not understand why he had been inhabiting a lobster's shell. Obviously because he was a lobster; but he was not a lobster. That was so, was it not? Yet he was under water. He lay on fine white sand, at a depth so great he could not make out any hint of sunlight overhead. The water was warm, gentle, rich with tiny tasty creatures and with a swirling welter of sensory data that swept across his receptors in bewildering abundance.

He sought to learn more. But there was no further time for resting and thinking now. He was unprotected. Any passing enemy could destroy him while he was like this. Up, up, seek a hiding-place: that was the requirement of the moment.

First, though, he paused to devour his old shell. That too seemed to be the requirement of the moment; so he fell upon it with determination, seizing it with his clumsy-looking but curiously versatile front claws, drawing it toward his busy, efficient mandibles. When that was accomplished—no doubt to recycle the lime it contained, which he needed for the growth of his new shell—he forced himself up and began a slow scuttle, somehow knowing that the direction he had taken was the right one.

Soon came the vibrations of something large and solid against his sensors—a wall, a stone mass rising before him— and then, as he continued, he made out with his foggy vision the sloping flank of a dark broad cliff rising vertically from the ocean floor. Festoons of thick, swaying red and yellow water plants clung to it, and a dense stippling of rubbery-looking finger-shaped sponges, and a crawling, gaping, slithering host of crabs and mollusks and worms, which vastly stirred McCulloch's appetite. But this was not a time to pause to eat, lest he be eaten. Two enormous green anemones yawned nearby, ruffling their voluptuous membranes seductively, hopefully. A dark shape passed overhead, huge, tubular, tentacular, menacing. Ignoring the thronging populations of the rock, McCulloch picked his way over and around them until he came to the small cave, the McCulloch-sized cave, that was his goal.

Gingerly he backed through its narrow mouth, knowing there would be no room for turning around, once he was inside. He filled the opening nicely, with a little space left over. Taking up a position just within the entrance, he blocked the cave-mouth with his claws. No enemy could enter now. Naked though he was, he would be safe during his vulnerable period.

For the first time since his agonizing awakening, McCulloch had a chance to halt: rest, regroup, consider.

It seemed a wise idea to be monitoring the waters just outside the cave even while he was resting, though. He extended his antennae a short distance into the swarming waters, and felt at once the impact, again, of a myriad sensory inputs, all the astounding complexity of the reef-world. Most of the creatures that moved slowly about on the face of the reef were simple ones, but McCulloch could feel, also, the sharp pulsations of intelligence coming from several points not far away: the anemones, so it seemed, and that enormous squid-like thing hovering overhead. Not intelligence of a kind that he understood, but that did not trouble him: for the moment, understanding could wait, while he dealt with the task of recovery from the exhausting struggles of his molting. Keeping the antennae moving steadily in slow sweeping circles of surveillance, he began systematically to shut down the rest of his nervous system, until he had attained the rest state that he knew—how?—was optimum for the rebuilding of his shell. Already his soft new carapace was beginning to grow rigid as it absorbed water, swelled, filtered out and utilized the lime. But he would have to sit quietly a long while before he was fully armored once more.

He rested. He waited. He did not think at all.

*　*　*

After a time his repose was broken by that inner voice, the one that had been trying to question him during the wildest moments of his molting. It spoke without sound, from a point somewhere within the core of his torpid consciousness.

　—Are you awake?

　—I am now, McCulloch answered irritably.

　—I need definitions. You are a mystery to me. What is a McCulloch?

　—A man.

　—That does not help.

　—A male human being.

　—That also has no meaning.

　—Look, I'm tired. Can we discuss these things some other time?

　—This is a good time. While we rest, while we replenish ourself.

　—Ourselves, McCulloch corrected.

　—Ourself is more accurate.

　—But there are two of us.

　—Are there? Where is the other?

McCulloch faltered. He had no perspective on his situation, none that made any sense.

　—One inside the other, I think. Two of us in the same body. But definitely two of us. McCulloch and not-McCulloch.

　—I concede the point. There are two of us. You are within me. Who are you?

　—McCulloch.

　—So you have said. But what does that mean?

　—I don't know.

The voice left him alone again. He felt its presence nearby, as a kind of warm node somewhere along his spine, or whatever was the equivalent of his spine, since he did not think invertebrates had spines. And it was fairly clear to him that he was an invertebrate.

He had become, it seemed, a lobster, or, at any rate, something lobster-like. Implied in that was transition: he had become. He had once been something else. Blurred, tantalizing memories of the something else that he once had been danced in his consciousness. He remembered hair, fingers, fingernails, flesh. Clothing: a kind of removable exoskeleton. Eyelids, ears, lips: shadowy concepts all, names without substance, but there was a certain elusive reality to them, a volatile, tricky plausibility. Each time he tried to apply one of those concepts to himself—"fingers," "hair," "man," "McCulloch"—it slid away, it would not stick. Yet all the same those terms had some sort of relevance to him.

The harder he pushed to isolate that relevance, though, the harder it was to maintain his focus on any part of that soup of half-glimpsed notions in which his mind seemed to be swimming. The thing to do, McCulloch decided, was to go slow, try not to force understanding, wait for comprehension to seep back into his mind. Obviously he had had a bad shock, some major trauma, a total disorientation. It might be days before he achieved any sort of useful integration.

A gentle voice from outside his cave said, "I hope that your Growing has gone well."

Not a voice. He remembered voice: vibration of the air against the eardrums. No air here, maybe no eardrums. This was a stream of minute chemical messengers spurting through the mouth of the little cave and rebounding off the thousands of sensory filaments on his legs, tentacles, antennae, carapace, and tail. But the effect was one of words having been spoken. And it was distinctly different from that other voice, the internal one, that had been questioning him so assiduously a little while ago.

"It goes extremely well," McCulloch replied: or was it the other inhabitant of his body that had framed the answer? "I grow. I heal. I stiffen. Soon I will come forth."

"We feared for you." The presence outside the cave emanated concern, warmth, intelligence. Kinship. "In the first moments of your Growing, a strangeness came from you."

"Strangeness is within me. I am invaded."

"Invaded? By what?"

"A McCulloch. It is a man, which is a human being."

"Ah. A great strangeness indeed. Do you need help?"

McCulloch answered, "No. I will accommodate to it."

And he knew that it was the other within himself who was making these answers, though the boundary between their identities was so indistinct that he had a definite sense of being the one who shaped these words. But how could that be? He had no idea how one shaped words by sending squirts of body-fluid into the all-surrounding ocean-fluid. That was not his language. His language was—

—words—

—English words—

He trembled in sudden understanding. His antennae thrashed wildly, his many legs jerked and quivered. Images churned in his suddenly boiling mind: bright lights, elaborate equipment, faces, walls, ceilings. People moving about him, speaking in low tones, occasionally addressing words to him, English words—

—Is English what all McCullochs speak?

—Yes.

—So English is human-language?

—Yes. But not the only one, said McCulloch. I speak English, and also German and a little—French. But other humans speak other languages.

—Very interesting. Why do you have so many languages?

—Because—because—we are different from one another,
we live in different countries, we have different cultures—

—This is without meaning again. There are many creatures, but only one language, which all speak with
greater or lesser skill, according to their destinies.

McCulloch pondered that. After a time he replied:

—Lobster is what you are. Long body, claws and antennae in front, many legs, flat tail in back. Different
from, say, a clam. Clams have shell on top, shell on
bottom, soft flesh in between, hinge connecting. You
are not like that. You have lobster body. So you are
lobster.

Now there was silence from the other.

Then—after a long pause—

—Very well. I accept the term. I am lobster. You are
human. They are clams.

—What do you call yourselves in your own language?

Silence.

—What's your own name for yourself? Your individual
self, the way my individual name is McCulloch and
my species-name is human being?

Silence.

—Where am I, anyway?

Silence, still, so prolonged and utter that McCulloch
wondered if the other being had withdrawn itself from his
consciousness entirely. Perhaps days went by in this
unending silence, perhaps weeks: he had no way of measuring the passing of time. He realized that such units as
days or weeks were without meaning now. One moment
succeeded the next, but they did not aggregate into anything continuous.

At last came a reply.

—You are in the world, human McCulloch.

Silence came again, intense, clinging, a dark warm garment. McCulloch made no attempt to reach the other mind. He lay motionless, feeling his carapace thicken. From outside the cave came a flow of impressions of passing beings, now differentiating themselves very sharply: he felt the thick fleshy pulses of the two anemones, the sharp stabbing presence of the squid, the slow ponderous broadcast of something dark and winged, and, again and again, the bright, comforting, unmistakable output of other lobster-creatures. It was a busy, complex world out there. The McCulloch part of him longed to leave the cave and explore it. The lobster part of him rested, content within its tight shelter.

He formed hypotheses. He had journeyed from his own place to this place, damaging his mind in the process, though now his mind seemed to be reconstructing itself steadily, if erratically. What sort of voyage? To another world? No: that seemed wrong. He did not believe that conditions so much like the ocean-floor of Earth would be found on another—

Earth.

All right: significant datum. He was human, he came from Earth. And he was still on Earth. In the ocean. He was—what?—a land-dweller, an air-breather, a biped, a flesh-creature, a human. And now he was within the body of a lobster. Was that it? The entire human race, he thought, has migrated into the bodies of lobsters, and here we are on the ocean floor, scuttling about, waving our claws and feelers, going through difficult and dangerous moltings—

Or maybe I'm the only one. A scientific experiment, with me as the subject: man into lobster. That brightly lit room that he remembered, the intricate gleaming equipment all about him—that was the laboratory, that was where they had prepared him for his transmigration, and then they had thrown the switch and hurled him into the body of—

No. No. Makes no sense. Lobsters, McCulloch reflected, are low-phylum creatures with simple nervous systems, limited intelligence. Plainly the mind he had entered was a complex one. It asked thoughtful questions. It carried on civilized conversations with its friends, who came calling like ceremonious Japanese gentlemen, offering expressions of solicitude and good will.

New hypothesis: that lobsters and other low-phylum animals are actually quite intelligent, with minds roomy enough to accept the sudden insertion of a human being's entire neural structure, but we in our foolish anthropocentric way have up till now been too blind to perceive—

No. Too facile. You could postulate the secretly lofty intelligence of the world's humble creatures, all right: you could postulate anything you wanted. But that didn't make it so. Lobsters did not ask questions. Lobsters did not come calling like ceremonious Japanese gentlemen. At least, not the lobsters of the world he remembered.

Improved lobsters? Evolved lobsters? Super-lobsters of the future?

—When am I?

Into his dizzied broodings came the quiet disembodied internal voice of not-McCulloch, his companion:

—Is your displacement then one of time rather than space?

—I don't know. Probably both. I'm a land creature.

—That has no meaning.

—I don't live in the ocean. I breathe air.

From the other consciousness came an expression of deep astonishment tinged with skepticism.

—Truly? That is very hard to believe When you are in your own body you breathe no water at all?

—None. Not for long, or I would die.

—But there is so little land! And no creatures live upon it. Some make short visits there. But nothing can dwell there very long. So it has always been. And so will it be, until the time of the Molting of the World.

McCulloch considered that. Once again he found himself doubting that he was still on Earth. A world of water? Well, that could fit into his hypothesis of having journeyed forward in time, though it seemed to add a layer of implausibility upon implausibility. How many millions of years, he wondered, would it take for nearly all the Earth to have become covered with water? And he answered himself: In about as many as it would take to evolve a species of intelligent invertebrates.

Suddenly, terribly, it all fit together. Things crystallized and clarified in his mind, and he found access to another segment of his injured and redistributed memory; and he began to comprehend what had befallen him, or, rather, what he had willingly allowed himself to undergo. With that comprehension came a swift stinging sense of total displacement and utter loss, as though he were drowning and desperately tugging at strands of seaweed in a futile attempt to pull himself back to the surface. All that was real to him, all that he was part of, everything that made sense—gone, gone, perhaps irretrievably gone, buried under the weight of uncountable millennia, vanished, drowned, forgotten, reduced to mere geology—it was unthinkable, it was unacceptable, it was impossible, and as the truth of it bore in on him he found himself choking on the frightful vastness of time past.

But that bleak sensation lasted only a moment and was gone. In its place came excitement, delight, confusion, and a feverish throbbing curiosity about this place he had entered. He was here. That miraculous thing that they had strived so fiercely to achieve had been achieved—rather too well, perhaps, but it had been achieved, and he was launched on the greatest adventure he would ever have, that anyone would ever have. This was not the moment for submitting to grief and confusion. Out of that world lost and all but forgotten to him came a scrap of verse that gleamed and blazed in his soul: Only through time time is conquered.

McCulloch reached toward the mind that was so close to his within this strange body.

—When will it be safe for us to leave this cave? he asked.

—It is safe any time, now. Do you wish to go outside?

—Yes. Please.

The creature stirred, flexed its front claws, slapped its flat tail against the floor of the cave, and in a slow ungraceful way began to clamber through the narrow opening, pausing more than once to search the waters outside for lurking enemies. McCulloch felt a quick hot burst of terror, as though he were about to enter some important meeting and had discovered too late that he was naked. Was the shell truly ready? Was he safely armored against the unknown foes outside, or would they fall upon him and tear him apart like furious shrikes? But his host did not seem to share those fears. It went plodding on and out, and in a moment more it emerged on an algae-encrusted tongue of the reef wall, a short distance below the two anemones. From each of those twin masses of rippling flesh came the same sullen pouting hungry murmurs: "Ah, come closer, why don't you come closer?"

"Another time," said the lobster, sounding almost playful, and turned away from them.

McCulloch looked outward over the landscape. Earlier, in the turmoil of his bewildering arrival and the pain and chaos of the molting prodrome, he had not had time to assemble any clear and coherent view of it. But now—despite the handicap of seeing everything with the alien perspective of the lobster's many-faceted eyes—he was able to put together an image of the terrain.

His view was a shortened one, because the sky was like a dark lid, through which came only enough light to create a cone-shaped arena spreading just a little way. Behind him was the face of the huge cliff, occupied by plant and animal life over virtually every square inch, and stretching upward until its higher reaches were lost in the dimness far overhead. Just a short way down from the ledge where he rested was the ocean floor, a broad expanse of gentle, undulating white sand streaked here and there with long widening gores of some darker material. Here and there bottom-growing plants arose in elegant billowy clumps, and McCulloch spotted occasional creatures moving among them over the sand that were much like lobsters and crabs, though with some differences. He saw also some starfish and snails and sea urchins that did not look at all unfamiliar. At higher levels he could make out a few swimming creatures: a couple of the squid-like animals—they were hulking-looking ropy-armed things, and he disliked them instinctively—and what seemed to be large jellyfish. But something was missing, and after a moment McCulloch realized what it was: fishes. There was a rich population of invertebrate life wherever he looked, but no fishes as far as he could see.

Not that he could see very far. The darkness clamped down like a curtain perhaps two or three hundred yards away. But even so, it was odd that not one fish had entered his field of vision in all this time. He wished he knew more about marine biology. Were there zones on Earth where no sea animals more complex than lobsters and crabs existed? Perhaps, but he doubted it.

Two disturbing new hypotheses blossomed in his mind. One was that he had landed in some remote future era where nothing out of his own time survived except low-phylum sea-creatures. The other was that he had not traveled to the future at all, but had arrived by mischance in some primordial geological epoch in which vertebrate life had not yet evolved. That seemed unlikely to him, though. This place did not have a prehistoric feel to him. He saw no trilobites; surely there ought to be trilobites everywhere about, and not these oversized lobsters, which he did not remember at all from his childhood visits to the natural history museum's prehistory displays.

But if this was truly the future—and the future belonged to the lobsters and squids—

That was hard to accept. Only invertebrates? What could invertebrates accomplish, what kind of civilization could lobsters build, with their hard unsupple bodies and great clumsy claws? Concepts, half-remembered or less than that, rushed through his mind: the Taj Mahal, the Gutenberg Bible, the Sistine Chapel, the Madonna of the Rocks, the great window at Chartres. Could lobsters create those? Could squids? What a poor place this world must be, McCulloch thought sadly, how gray, how narrow, how tightly bounded by the ocean above and the endless sandy floor.

—Tell me, he said to his host. Are there any fishes in this sea?

The response was what he was coming to recognize as a sigh.

—Fishes? That is another word without meaning.

—A form of marine life, with an internal bony structure—

—With its shell inside?

—That's one way of putting it, said McCulloch.

—There are no such creatures. Such creatures have never

existed. There is no room for the shell within the soft parts of the body. I can barely comprehend such an arrangement: surely there is no need for it!

—It can be useful, I assure you. In the former world it was quite common.

—The world of human beings?

—Yes. My world, McCulloch said.

—Anything might have been possible in a former world, human McCulloch. Perhaps indeed before the world's last Molting shells were worn inside. And perhaps after the next one they will be worn there again. But in the world I know, human McCulloch, it is not the practice.

—Ah, McCulloch said. Then I am even farther from home than I thought.

—Yes, said his host. I think you are very far from home indeed. Does that cause you sorrow?

—Among other things.

—If it causes you sorrow, I grieve for your grief, because we are companions now.

—You are very kind, said McCulloch to his host.

The lobster asked McCulloch if he was ready to begin their journey; and when McCulloch indicated that he was, his host serenely kicked itself free of the ledge with a single powerful stroke of its tail. For an instant it hung suspended; then it glided toward the sandy bottom as gracefully as though it were floating through air. When it landed, it was with all its many legs poised delicately en pointe, and it stood that way, motionless, a long moment.

Then it suddenly set out with great haste over the ocean floor, running so lightfootedly that it scarcely raised a puff of sand wherever it touched down. More than once it ran right across some bottom-grubbing creature, some slug or scallop, without appearing to disturb it at all. McCulloch thought the lobster was capering in sheer exuberance, after its long internment in the cave; but some growing sense of awareness of his companion's mind told him after a time that this was no casual frolic, that the lobster was not in fact dancing but fleeing.

—Is there an enemy? McCulloch asked.

—Yes. Above.

The lobster's antennae stabbed upward at a sharp angle, and McCulloch, seeing through the other's eyes, perceived now a large looming cylindrical shape swimming in slow circles near the upper border of their range of vision. It might have been a shark, or even a whale. McCulloch felt deceived and betrayed; for the lobster had told him this was an invertebrate world, and surely that creature above him—

—No, said the lobster, without slowing its manic sprint. That animal has no shell of the sort you described within its body. It is only a bag of flesh. But it is very dangerous.

—How will we escape it?

—We will not escape it.

The lobster sounded calm, but whether it was the calm of fatalism or mere expressionlessness, McCulloch could not say: the lobster had been calm even in the first moments of McCulloch's arrival in its mind, which must surely have been alarming and even terrifying to it.

It had begun to move now in ever-widening circles. This seemed not so much an evasive tactic as a ritualistic one, now, a dance indeed. A farewell to life? The swimming creature had descended until it was only a few lobster-lengths above them, and McCulloch had a clear view of it. No, not a fish or a shark or any type of vertebrate at all, he realized, but an animal of a kind wholly unfamiliar to him, a kind of enormous worm-like thing whose meaty yellow body was reinforced externally by some sort of chitinous struts running its entire length. Fleshy vane-like fins rippled along its sides, but their purpose seemed to be more one of guidance than propulsion, for it appeared to move by guzzling in great quantities of water and expelling them through an anal siphon. Its mouth was vast, with a row of dim little green eyes ringing the scarlet lips. When the creature yawned, it revealed itself to be toothless, but capable of swallowing the lobster easily at a gulp.

Looking upward into that yawning mouth, McCulloch had a sudden image of himself elsewhere, spreadeagled under an inverted pyramid of shining machinery as the countdown reached its final moments, as the technicians made ready to—

—to hurl him—

—to hurl him forward in time—

Yes. An experiment. Definitely an experiment. He could remember it now. Bleier, Caldwell, Rodrigues, Mortenson. And all the others. Gathered around him, faces tight, forced smiles. The lights. The colors. The bizarre coils of equipment. And the volunteer. The volunteer. First human subject to be sent forward in time. The various rabbits and mice of the previous experiments, though they had apparently survived the round trip unharmed, had not been capable of delivering much of a report on their adventures. "I'm smarter than any rabbit," McCulloch had said. "Send me. I'll tell you what it's like up there." The volunteer. All that was coming back to him in great swatches now, as he crouched here within the mind of something much like a lobster, waiting for a vast yawning predator to pounce. The project, the controversies, his co-workers, the debate over risking a human mind under the machine, the drawing of lots. McCulloch had not been the only volunteer. He was just the lucky one. "Here you go, Jim-boy. A hundred years down the time-line."

Or fifty, or eighty, or a hundred and twenty. They didn't

have really precise trajectory control. They thought he might go as much as a hundred twenty years. But beyond much doubt they had overshot by a few hundred million. Was that within the permissible parameters of error?

He wondered what would happen to him if his host here were to perish. Would he die also? Would he find himself instantly transferred to some other being of this epoch? Or would he simply be hurled back instead to his own time? He was not ready to go back. He had just begun to observe, to understand, to explore—

McCulloch's host had halted its running, now, and stood quite still in what was obviously a defensive mode, body cocked and upreared, claws extended, with the huge crusher claw erect and the long narrow cutting claw opening and closing in a steady rhythm. It was a threatening pose, but the swimming thing did not appear to be greatly troubled by it. Did the lobster mean to let itself be swallowed, and then to carve an exit for itself with those awesome weapons, before the alimentary juices could go to work on its armor?

"You choose your prey foolishly," said McCulloch's host to its enemy.

The swimming creature made a reply that was unintelligible to McCulloch: vague blurry words, the clotted outspew of a feeble intelligence. It continued its unhurried downward spiral.

"You are warned," said the lobster. "You are not selecting your victim wisely."

Again came a muddled response, sluggish and incoherent, the speech of an entity for whom verbal communication was a heavy, all but impossible effort.

Its enormous mouth gaped. Its fins rippled fiercely as it siphoned itself downward the last few yards to engulf the lobster. McCulloch prepared himself for transition to some new and even more unimaginable state when his host met its death. But suddenly the ocean floor was swarming with lobsters. They must have been arriving from all sides—summoned by his host's frantic dance, McCulloch wondered?—while McCulloch, intent on the descent of the swimmer, had not noticed. Ten, twenty, possibly fifty of them arrayed themselves now beside McCulloch's host, and as the swimmer, tail on high, mouth wide, lowered itself like some gigantic suction-hose toward them, the lobsters coolly and implacably seized its lips in their claws. Caught and helpless, it began at once to thrash, and from the pores through which it spoke came bleating incoherent cries of dismay and torment.

There was no mercy for it. It had been warned. It dangled tail upward while the pack of lobsters methodically devoured it from below, pausing occasionally to strip away and discard the rigid rods of chitin that formed its superstructure. Swiftly they reduced it to a faintly visible cloud of shreds oscillating in the water, and then small scavenging creatures came to fall upon those, and there was nothing at all left but the scattered rods of chitin on the sand.

The entire episode had taken only a few moments: the coming of the predator, the dance of McCulloch's host, the arrival of the other lobsters, the destruction of the enemy. Now the lobsters were gathered in a sort of convocation about McCulloch's host, wordlessly manifesting a commonality of spirit, a warmth of fellowship after feasting, that seemed quite comprehensible to McCulloch. For a short while they had been uninhibited savage carnivores consuming convenient meat; now once again they were courteous, refined, cultured—Japanese gentlemen, Oxford dons, gentle Benedictine monks.

McCulloch studied them closely. They were definitely more like lobsters than like any other creature he had ever seen, very much like lobsters, and yet there were differences. They were larger. How much larger, he could not tell, for he had no real way of judging distance and size in this undersea world; but he supposed they must be at least three feet long, and he doubted that lobsters of his time, even the biggest, were anything like that in length. Their bodies were wider than those of lobsters, and their heads were larger. The two largest claws looked like those of the lobsters he remembered, but the ones just behind them seemed more elaborate, as if adapted for more delicate procedures than mere rending of food and stuffing it into the mouth. There was an odd little hump, almost a dome, midway down the lobster's back—the center of the expanded nervous system, perhaps.

The lobsters clustered solemnly about McCulloch's host and each lightly tapped its claws against those of the adjoining lobster in a sort of handshake, a process that seemed to take quite some time. McCulloch became aware also that a conversation was under way. What they were talking about, he realized, was him.

"It is not painful to have a McCulloch within one," his host was explaining. "It came upon me at molting time, and that gave me a moment of difficulty, molting being what it is. But it was only a moment. After that my only concern was for the McCulloch's comfort."

"And it is comfortable now?"

"It is becoming more comfortable."

"When will you show it to us?"

"Ah, that cannot be done. It has no real existence, and therefore I cannot bring it forth."

"What is it, then? A wanderer? A revenant?"

"A revenant, yes. So I think. And a wanderer. It says it is a human being."

"And what is that? Is a human being a kind of Mc-Culloch?

"I think a McCulloch is a kind of human being."

"Which is a revenant."

"Yes, I think so."

"This is an Omen!"

"Where is its world?"

"Its world is lost to it."

"Yes, definitely an Omen."

"It lived on dry land."

"It breathed air."

"It wore its shell within its body."

"What a strange revenant!"

"What a strange world its world must have been."

"It is the former world, would you not say?"

"So I surely believe. And therefore this is an Omen."

"Ah, we shall Molt. We shall Molt."

McCulloch was altogether lost. He was not even sure when his own host was the speaker.

"Is it the Time?"

"We have an Omen, do we not?"

"The McCulloch surely was sent as a herald."

"There is no precedent."

"Each Molting, though, is without precedent. We cannot conceive what came before. We cannot imagine what comes after. We learn by learning. The McCulloch is the herald. The McCulloch is the Omen."

"I think not. I think it is unreal and unimportant."

"Unreal, yes. But not unimportant."

"The Time is not at hand. The Molting of the World is not yet due. The human is a wanderer and a revenant, but not a herald and certainly not an Omen."

"It comes from the former world."

"It says it does. Can we believe that?"

"It breathed air. In the former world, perhaps there were creatures that breathed air."

"It says it breathed air. I think it is neither herald nor Omen, neither wanderer nor revenant. I think it is a myth and a fugue. I think it betokens nothing. It is an accident. It is an interruption."

"That is an uncivil attitude. We have much to learn from the McCulloch. And if it is an Omen, we have immediate responsibilities that must be fulfilled."

"But how can we be certain of what it is?"

—May I speak? said McCulloch to his host.

—Of course.

—How can I make myself heard?

—Speak through me.

"The McCulloch wishes to be heard!"

"Hear it! Hear it!"

"Let it speak!"

McCulloch said, and the host spoke the words aloud for him, "I am a stranger here, and your guest, and so I ask you to forgive me if I give offense, for I have little understanding of your ways. Nor do I know if I am a herald or an Omen. But I tell you in all truth that I am a wanderer, and that I am sent from the former world, where there are many creatures of my kind, who breathe air and live upon the land and carry their—shells—inside their body."

"An Omen, certainly," said several of the lobsters at once. "A herald, beyond doubt."

McCulloch continued, "It was our hope to discover something of the worlds that are to come after ours. And therefore I was sent forward—"

"A herald—certainly a herald!"

"—to come to you, to go among you, to learn to know you, and then to return to my own people, the air-people, the human people, and bring the word of what is to come.

But I think that I am not the herald you expect. I carry no message for you. We could not have known that you were here. Out of the former world I bring you the blessing of those that have gone before, however, and when I go back to that world I will bear tidings of your life, of your thought, of your ways—"

"Then our kind is unknown to your world?"

McCulloch hesitated. "Creatures somewhat like you do exist in the seas of the former world. But they are smaller and simpler than you, and I think their civilization, if they have one, is not a great one."

"You have no discourse with them, then?" one of the lobsters asked.

"Very little," he said. A miserable evasion, cowardly, vile.

McCulloch shivered. He imagined himself crying out, "We eat them!" and the water turning black with their shocked outbursts—and saw them instantly falling upon him, swiftly and efficiently slicing him to scraps with their claws. Through his mind ran monstrous images of lobsters in tanks, lobsters boiling alive, lobsters smothered in rich sauces, lobsters shelled, lobsters minced, lobsters rendered into bisques—he could not halt the torrent of dreadful visions. Such was our discourse with your ancestors. Such was our mode of interspecies communication. He felt himself drowning in guilt and shame and fear.

The spasm passed. The lobsters had not stirred. They continued to regard him with patience: impassive, unmoving, remote. McCulloch wondered if all that had passed through his mind just then had been transmitted to his host. Very likely; the host earlier had seemed to have access to all of his thoughts, though McCulloch did not have the same entree to the host's. And if the host knew, did all the others? What then, what then?

Perhaps they did not even care. Lobsters, he recalled, were said to be callous cannibals, who might attack one another in the very tanks where they were awaiting their turns in the chef's pot. It was hard to view these detached and aloof beings, these dons, these monks, as having that sort of ferocity: but yet he had seen them go to work on that swimming mouth-creature without any show of embarrassment, and perhaps some atavistic echo of their ancestors' appetites lingered in them, so that they would think it only natural that McCullochs and other humans had fed on such things as lobsters. Why should they be shocked? Perhaps they thought that humans fed on humans, too. It was all in the former world, was it not? And in any event it was foolish to fear that they would exact some revenge on him for Lobster Thermidor, no matter how appalled they might be. He wasn't here. He was nothing more than a figment, a revenant, a wanderer, a set of intrusive neural networks within their companion's brain. The worst they could do to him, he supposed, was to exorcise him, and send him back to the former world.

Even so, he could not entirely shake the guilt and the shame. Or the fear.

Bleier said, "Of course, you aren't the only one who's going to be in jeopardy when we throw the switch. There's your host to consider. One entire human ego slamming into his mind out of nowhere like a brick falling off a building—what's it going to do to him?"

"Flip him out, is my guess," said Jake Ybarra. "You'll land on him and he'll announce he's Napoleon, or Joan of Arc, and they'll hustle him off to the nearest asylum. Are you prepared for the possibility, Jim, that you're going to spend your entire time in the future sitting in a loony-bin undergoing therapy?"

"Or exorcism," Mortenson suggested. "If there's been some kind of reversion to barbarism. Christ, you might even get your host burned at the stake!"

"I don't think so," McCulloch said quietly. "I'm a lot more optimistic than you guys. I don't expect to land in a world of witch-doctors and mumbo-jumbo, and I don't expect to find myself in a place that locks people up in Bedlam because they suddenly start acting a little strange. The chances are that I am going to unsettle my host when I enter him, but that he'll simply get two sanity-stabilizer pills from his medicine chest and take them with a glass of water and feel better in five minutes. And then I'll explain what's happening to him."

"More than likely no explanations will be necessary," said Maggie Caldwell. "By the time you arrive, time travel will have been a going proposition for three or four generations, after all. Having a traveler from the past turn up in your head will be old stuff to them. Your host will probably know exactly what's going on from the moment you hit him."

"Let's hope so," Bleier said. He looked across the laboratory to Rodrigues. "What's the count, Bob?"

"T minus eighteen minutes."

"I'm not worried about a thing," McCulloch said.

Caldwell took his hand in hers. "Neither am I, Jim."

"Then why is your hand so cold?" he asked.

"So I'm a little worried," she said.

McCulloch grinned. "So am I. A little. Only a little."

"You're human, Jim. No one's ever done this before."

"It'll be a can of corn!" Ybarra said.

Bleier looked at him blankly. "What the hell does that mean, Jake?"

Ybarra said, "Archaic twentieth-century slang. It means it's going to be a lot easier than we think."

"I told you," said McCulloch, "I'm not worried."

"I'm still worried about the impact on the host," said Bleier.

"All those Napoleons and Joans of Arc that have been cluttering the asylums for the last few hundred years," Maggie Caldwell said. "Could it be that they're really hosts for time-travelers going backward in time?"

"You can't go backward," said Mortenson. "You know that. The round trip has to begin with a forward leap."

"Under present theory," Caldwell said. "But present theory's only five years old. It may turn out to be incomplete. We may have had all sorts of travelers out of the future jumping through history, and never even knew it. All the nuts, lunatics, inexplicable geniuses, idiot-savants—"

"Save it, Maggie," Bleier said. "Let's stick to what we understand right now."

"Oh? Do we understand anything?" McCulloch asked.

Bleier gave him a sour look. "I thought you said you weren't worried."

"I'm not. Not much. But I'd be a fool if I thought we really had a firm handle on what we're doing. We're shooting in the dark, and let's never kid ourselves about it."

"T minus fifteen," Rodrigues called.

"Try to make the landing easy on your host, Jim," Bleier said.

"I've got no reason not to want to," said McCulloch.

He realized that he had been wandering. Bleier, Maggie, Mortenson, Ybarra—for a moment they had been more real to him than the congregation of lobsters. He had heard their voices, he had seen their faces, Bleier plump and perspiring and serious, Ybarra dark and lean, Maggie with her crown of short upswept red hair blazing in the laboratory light— and yet they were all dead, a hundred million years dead, two hundred million, back there with the triceratops and the trilobite in the drowned former world, and here he was among the lobster-people. How futile all those discussions of what the world of the early twenty-second century was going to be like! Those speculations on population density, religious belief, attitudes toward science, level of technological achievement, all those late-night sessions in the final months of the project, designed to prepare him for any eventuality he might encounter while he was visiting the future—what a waste, what a needless exercise. As was all that fretting about upsetting the mental stability of the person who would receive his transtemporalized consciousness. Such qualms, such moral delicacy—all unnecessary, McCulloch knew now.

But of course they had not anticipated sending him so eerily far across the dark abysm of time, into a world in which humankind and all its works were not even legendary memories, and the host who would receive him was a calm and thoughtful crustacean capable of taking him in with only the most mild and brief disruption of its serenity.

The lobsters, he noticed now, had reconfigured themselves while his mind had been drifting. They had broken up their circle and were arrayed in a long line stretching over the ocean floor, with his host at the end of the procession. The queue was a close one, each lobster so close to the one before it that it could touch it with the tips of its antennae, which from time to time they seemed to be doing; and they all were moving in a weird kind of quasi-military lockstep, every lobster swinging the same set of walking-legs forward at the same time.

—Where are we going? McCulloch asked his host.

—The pilgrimage has begun.

—What pilgrimage is that?

—To the dry place, said the host. To the place of no water. To the land.

—Why?

—It is the custom. We have decided that the time of the Molting of the World is soon to come; and therefore we must make the pilgrimage. It is the end of all things. It is the coming of a newer world. You are the herald: so we have agreed.

—Will you explain? I have a thousand questions. I need to know more about all this, McCulloch said.

—Soon. Soon. This is not a time for explanations.

McCulloch felt a firm and unequivocal closing of contact, an emphatic withdrawal. He sensed a hard ringing silence that was almost an absence of the host, and knew it would be inappropriate to transgress against it. That was painful, for he brimmed now with an overwhelming rush of curiosity. The Molting of the World? The end of all things? A pilgrimage to the land? What land? Where? But he did not ask. He could not ask. The host seemed to have vanished from him, disappearing utterly into this pilgrimage, this migration, moving in its lockstep way with total concentration and a kind of mystic intensity. McCulloch did not intrude. He felt as though he had been left alone in the body they shared.

As they marched, he concentrated on observing, since he could not interrogate. And there was much to see; for the longer he dwelled within his host, the more accustomed he grew to the lobster's sensory mechanisms. The compound eyes, for instance. Enough of his former life had returned to him now so that he remembered human eyes clearly, those two large gleaming ovals, so keen, so subtle of focus, set beneath protecting ridges of bone. His host's eyes were nothing like that: they were two clusters of tiny lenses rising on jointed, movable stalks, and what they showed was an intricately dissected view, a mosaic of isolated points of light. But he was learning somehow to translate those complex and baffling images into a single clear one, just as, no doubt, a creature accustomed to compound-lens vision would sooner or later learn to see through human eyes, if need be. And McCulloch found now that he could not only make more sense out of the views he received through his host's eyes, but that he was seeing farther, into quite distant dim recesses of this sunless undersea realm.

Not that the stalked eyes seemed to be a very important part of the lobster's perceptive apparatus. They provided nothing more than a certain crude awareness of the immediate terrain. But apparently the real work of perceiving was done mainly by the thousands of fine bristles, so minute that they were all but invisible, that sprouted on every surface of his host's body. These seemed to send a constant stream of messages to the lobster's brain: information on the texture and topography of the ocean floor, on tiny shifts in the flow and temperature of the water, of the proximity of obstacles, and much else. Some of the small hairlike filaments were sensitive to touch and others, it appeared, to chemicals; for whenever the lobster approached some other life-form, it received data on its scent—or the underwater equivalent—long before the creature itself was within visual range. The quantity and richness of these inputs astonished McCulloch. At every moment came a torrent of data corresponding to the landside senses he remembered, smell, taste, touch; and some central processing unit within the lobster's brain handled everything in the most effortless fashion.

But there was no sound. The ocean world appeared to be wholly silent. McCulloch knew that that was untrue, that sound waves propagated through water as persistently as through air, if somewhat more rapidly. Yet the lobster seemed neither to possess nor to need any sort of auditory equipment. The sensory bristles brought in all the data it required. The "speech" of these creatures, McCulloch had long ago realized, was effected not by voice but by means of spurts of chemicals released into the water, hormones, perhaps, or amino acids, something of a distinct and readily recognizable identity, emitted in some high-redundancy pattern that permitted easy recognition and decoding despite the difficulties caused by currents and eddies. It was, McCulloch thought, like trying to communicate by printing individual letters on scraps of paper and hurling them into the wind. But it did somehow seem to work, however clumsy a concept it might be, because of the extreme sensitivity of the lobster's myriad chemoreceptors.

The antennae played some significant role also. There were two sets of them, a pair of three-branched ones just behind the eyes and a much longer single-branched pair behind those. The long ones restlessly twitched and probed inquisitively and most likely, he suspected, served as simple balancing and coordination devices much like the whiskers of a cat. The purpose of the smaller antennae eluded him, but it was his guess that they were involved in the process of communication between one lobster and another, either by some semaphore system or in a deeper communion beyond his still awkward comprehension.

McCulloch regretted not knowing more about the lobsters of his own era. But he had only a broad general knowledge of natural history, extensive, fairly deep, yet not good enough to tell him whether these elaborate sensory functions were characteristic of all lobsters or had evolved during the millions of years it had taken to create the water-world. Probably some of each, he decided. Very likely even the lobsters of the former world had had much of this scanning equipment, enough to allow them to locate their prey, to find their way around in the dark suboceanic depths, to undertake their long and unerring migrations. But he found it hard to believe that they could have had much "speech" capacity, that they gathered in solemn sessions to discuss abstruse questions of theology and mythology, to argue gently about omens and heralds and the end of all things. That was something that the patient and ceaseless unfoldings of time must have wrought.

The lobsters marched without show of fatigue: not scampering in that dancelike way that his host had adopted while summoning its comrades to save it from the swimming creature, but moving nevertheless in an elegant and graceful fashion, barely touching the ground with the tips of their legs, going onward step by step by step steadily and fairly swiftly.

McCulloch noticed that new lobsters frequently joined the procession, cutting in from left or right just ahead of his host, who always remained at the rear of the line; that line now was so long, hundreds of lobsters long, that it was impossible to see its beginning. Now and again one would reach out with its bigger claw to seize some passing animal, a starfish or urchin or small crab, and without missing a step would shred and devour it, tossing the unwanted husk to the cloud of planktonic scavengers that always hovered nearby. This foraging on the march was done with utter lack of self-consciousness; it was almost by reflex that these creatures snatched and gobbled as they journeyed.

And yet all the same they did not seem like mere marauding mouths. From this long line of crustaceans there emanated, McCulloch realized, a mysterious sense of community, a wholeness of society, that he did not understand but quite sharply sensed. This was plainly not a mere migration but a true pilgrimage. He thought ruefully of his earlier condescending view of these people, incapable of achieving the Taj Mahal or the Sistine Chapel, and felt abashed: for he was beginning to see that they had other accomplishments of a less tangible sort that were only barely apparent to his displaced and struggling mind.

"When you come back," Maggie said, "you'll be someone else. There's no escaping that. It's the one thing I'm frightened of. Not that you'll die making the hop, or that you'll get into some sort of terrible trouble in the future, or that we won't be able to bring you back at all, or anything like that. But that you'll have become someone else."

"I feel pretty secure in my identity," McCulloch told her.

"I know you do. God knows, you're the most stable person in the group, and that's why you're going. But even so. Nobody's ever done anything like this before. It can't help but change you. When you return, you're going to be unique among the human race."

"That sounds very awesome. But I'm not sure it'll matter that much, Mag. I'm just taking a little trip. If I were going to Paris, or Istanbul, or even Antarctica, would I come back totally transformed? I'd have had some new experiences, but–"

"It isn't the same," she said. "It isn't even remotely the same." She came across the room to him and put her hands on his shoulders, and stared deep into his eyes, which sent a little chill through him, as it always did; for when she looked at him that way there was a sudden flow of energy between them, a powerful warm rapport rushing from her to him and from him to her as though through a huge conduit, that delighted and frightened him both at once. He could lose himself in her. He had never let himself feel that way about anyone before. And this was not the moment to begin. There was no room in him for such feelings, not now, not when he was within a couple of hours of leaping off into the most unknown of unknowns. When he returned—if he returned—he might risk allowing something at last to develop with Maggie. But not on the eve of departure, when everything in his universe was tentative and conditional. "Can I tell you a little story, Jim?" she asked.

"Sure."

"When my father was on the faculty at Cal, he was invited to a reception to meet a couple of the early astronauts, two of the Apollo men—I don't remember which ones, but they were from the second or third voyage to the Moon. When he showed up at the faculty club, there were two or three hundred people there, milling around having cocktails, and most of them were people he didn't know. He walked in and looked around and within ten seconds he had found the astronauts. He didn't have to be told. He just knew. And this is my father, remember, who doesn't believe in ESP or anything like that. But he said they were impossible to miss, even in that crowd. You could see it on their faces, you could feel the radiance coming from them, there was an aura, there was something about their eyes. Something that said, I have walked on the Moon, I have been to that place which is not of our world and I have come back, and now I am someone else. I am who I was before, but I am someone else also."

"But they went to the Moon, Mag!"

"And you're going to the future, Jim. That's even weirder. You're going to a place that doesn't exist. And you may meet yourself there—ninety-nine years old, and waiting to shake hands with you—or you might meet me, or your grandson, or find out that everyone on Earth is dead, or that everyone has turned into a disembodied spirit, or that they're all immortal superbeings, or—or—Christ, I don't know. You'll see a world that nobody alive today is supposed to see. And when you come back, you'll have that aura. You'll be transformed."

"Is that so frightening?"

"To me it is," she said.

"Why is that?"

"Dummy," she said. "Dope. How explicit do I have to be, anyway? I thought I was being obvious enough."

He could not meet her eyes. "This isn't the best moment to talk about—"

"I know. I'm sorry, Jim. But you're important to me, and you're going somewhere and you're going to become someone else, and I'm scared. Selfish and scared."

"Are you telling me not to go?"

"Don't be absurd. You'd go no matter what I told you, and I'd despise you if you didn't. There's no turning back now."

"No."

"I shouldn't have dumped any of this on you today. You don't need it right this moment."

"It's okay," he said softly. He turned until he was looking straight at her, and for a long moment he simply stared into her eyes and did not speak, and then at last he said, "Listen, I'm going to take a big fantastic improbable insane voyage, and I'm going to be a witness to God knows what, and then I'm going to come back and yes, I'll be changed—only an ox wouldn't be changed, or maybe only a block of stone—but I'll still be me, whoever me is. Don't worry, okay? I'll still be me. And we'll still be us."

"Whoever us is."

"Whoever. Jesus, I wish you were going with me, Mag!"

"That's the silliest schoolboy thing I've ever heard you say."

"True, though."

"Well, I can't go. Only one at a time can go, and it's

you. I'm not even sure I'd want to go. I'm not as crazy as
you are, I suspect. You go, Jim, and come back and tell me
all about it."

"Yes."

"And then we'll see what there is to see about you and
me."

"Yes," he said.

She smiled. "Let me show you a poem, okay? You must
know it, because it's Eliot, and you know all the Eliot there
is. But I was reading him last night—thinking of you, reading him—and I found this, and it seemed to be the right
words, and I wrote them down. From one of the Quartets."

"I think I know," he said:

> *"Time past and time future*
> *Allow but a little consciousness—' "*

"That's a good one too," Maggie said. "But it's not the
one I had in mind." She unfolded a piece of paper. "It's this:

> *'We shall not cease from exploration*
> *And the end of all our exploring*
> *Will be to arrive where we started—' "*

" '—And know the place for the first time,' " he completed.
"Yes. Exactly. To arrive where we started. And know the
place for the first time."

The lobsters were singing as they marched. That was the only
word, McCulloch thought, that seemed to apply. The line of
pilgrims now was immensely long—there must have been
thousands in the procession by this time, and more were join-
ing constantly—and from them arose an outpouring of chemical signals, within the narrowest of tonal ranges, that

mingled in a close harmony and amounted to a kind of sustained chant on a few notes, swelling, filling all the ocean with its powerful and intense presence. Once again he had an image of them as monks, but not Benedictines, now: these were Buddhist, rather, an endless line of yellow-robed holy men singing a great Om as they made their way up some Tibetan slope. He was awed and humbled by it—by the intensity, and by the wholeheartedness of the devotion. It was getting hard for him to remember that these were crustaceans, no more than ragged claws scuttling across the floors of silent seas; he sensed minds all about him, whole and elaborate minds arising out of some rich cultural matrix, and it was coming to seem quite natural to him that these people should have armored exoskeletons and jointed eye-stalks and a dozen busy legs.

His host had still not broken its silence, which must have extended now over a considerable period. Just how long a period, McCulloch had no idea, for there were no significant alternations of light and dark down here to indicate the passing of time, nor did the marchers ever seem to sleep, and they took their food, as he had seen, in a casual and random way without breaking step. But it seemed to McCulloch that he had been effectively alone in the host's body for many days.

He was not minded to try to re-enter contact with the other just yet—not until he received some sort of signal from it. Plainly the host had withdrawn into some inner sanctuary to undertake a profound meditation; and McCulloch, now that the early bewilderment and anguish of his journey through time had begun to wear off, did not feel so dependent upon the host that he needed to blurt his queries constantly into his companion's consciousness. He would watch, and wait, and attempt to fathom the mysteries of this place unaided.

The landscape had undergone a great many changes since the beginning of the march. That gentle bottom of fine white sand had yielded to a terrain of rough dark gravel, and that to one of a pale sedimentary stuff made up of tiny shells, the mortal remains, no doubt, of vast hordes of diatoms and foraminifera, that rose like clouds of snowflakes at the lobsters' lightest steps. Then came a zone where a stratum of thick red clay spread in all directions. The clay held embedded in it an odd assortment of rounded rocks and clamshells and bits of chitin, so that it had the look of some complex paving material from a fashionable terrace. And after that they entered a region where slender spires of a sharp black stone, faceted like worked flint, sprouted stalagmite-fashion at their feet. Through all of this the lobster-pilgrims marched unperturbed, never halting, never breaking their file, moving in a straight line whenever possible and making only the slightest of deviations when compelled to it by the harshness of the topography.

Now they were in a district of coarse yellow sandy globules, out of which two types of coral grew: thin angular strands of deep jet, and supple, almost mobile fingers of a rich lovely salmon hue. McCulloch wondered where on Earth such stuff might be found, and chided himself at once for the foolishness of the thought: the seas he knew had been swallowed long ago in the great all-encompassing ocean that swathed the world, and the familiar continents, he supposed, had broken from their moorings and slipped to strange parts of the globe well before the rising of the waters. He had no landmarks. There was an equator somewhere, and there were two poles, but down here beyond the reach of direct sunlight, in this warm changeless uterine sea, neither north nor south nor east held any meaning. He remembered other lines:

Sand-strewn caverns, cool and deep
Where the winds are all asleep;
Where the spent lights quiver and gleam;
Where the salt weed sways in the stream;
Where the sea-beasts rang'd all round
Feed in the ooze of their pasture-ground . . .

What was the next line? Something about great whales coming sailing by, sail and sail with unshut eye, round the world for ever and aye. Yes, but there were no great whales here, if he understood his host correctly, no dolphins, no sharks, no minnows; there were only these swarming lower creatures, mysteriously raised on high, lords of the world. And mankind? Birds and bats, horses and bears? Gone. Gone. And the valleys and meadows? The lakes and streams? Taken by the sea. The world lay before him like a land of dreams, transformed. But was it, as the poet had said, a place which hath really neither joy, nor love, nor light, nor certitude, nor peace, nor help for pain? It did not seem that way. For light there was merely that diffuse faint glow, so obscure it was close to nonexistent, that filtered down through unknown fathoms. But what was that lobster-song, that ever-swelling crescendo, if not some hymn to love and certitude and peace, and help for pain? He was overwhelmed by peace, surprised by joy, and he did not understand what was happening to him. He was part of the march, that was all. He was a member of the pilgrimage.

He had wanted to know if there was any way he could signal to be pulled back home: a panic button, so to speak. Bleier was the one he asked, and the question seemed to drive the man into an agony of uneasiness. He scowled, he tugged at his jowls, he ran his hands through his sparse strands of hair.

"No," he said finally. "We weren't able to solve that one, Jim. There's simply no way of propagating a signal backward in time."

"I didn't think so," McCulloch said. "I just wondered."

"Since we're not actually sending your physical body, you shouldn't find yourself in any real trouble. Psychic discomfort, at the worst—disorientation, emotional upheaval, at the worst a sort of terminal homesickness. But I think you're strong enough to pull your way through any of that. And you'll always know that we're going to be yanking you back to us at the end of the experiment."

"How long am I going to be gone?"

"Elapsed time will be virtually nil. We'll throw the switch, off you'll go, you'll do your jaunt, we'll grab you back, and it'll seem like no time at all, perhaps a thousandth of a second. We aren't going to believe that you went anywhere at all, until you start telling us about it."

McCulloch sensed that Bleier was being deliberately evasive, not for the first time since McCulloch had been selected as the time-traveler. "It'll seem like no time at all to the people watching in the lab," he said. "But what about for me?"

"Well, of course for you it'll be a little different, because you'll have had a subjective experience in another time-frame."

"That's what I'm getting at. How long are you planning to leave me in the future? An hour? A week?"

"That's really hard to determine, Jim."

"What does that mean?"

"You know, we've sent only rabbits and stuff. They've come back okay, beyond much doubt—"

"Sure. They still munch on lettuce when they're hungry, and they don't tie their ears together in knots before they hop. So I suppose they're none the worse for wear."

"Obviously we can't get much of a report from a rabbit."

"Obviously."

"You're sounding awfully goddamned hostile today, Jim. Are you sure you don't want us to scrub the mission and start training another volunteer?" Bleier asked.

"I'm just trying to elicit a little hard info," McCulloch said. "I'm not trying to back out. And if I sound hostile, it's only because you're dancing all around my questions, which is becoming a considerable pain in the ass."

Bleier looked squarely at him and glowered. "All right. I'll tell you anything you want to know that I'm capable of answering. Which is what I think I've been doing all along. When the rabbits come back, we test them and we observe no physiological changes, no trace of ill effects as a result of having separated the psyche from the body for the duration of a time-jaunt. Christ, we can't even tell the rabbits have been on a time-jaunt, except that our instruments indicate the right sort of thermodynamic drain and entropic reversal, and for all we know we're kidding ourselves about that, which is why we're risking our reputations and your neck to send a human being who can tell us what the fuck happens when we throw the switch. But you've seen the rabbits jaunting. You know as well as I do that they come back okay."

Patiently McCulloch said, "Yes. As okay as a rabbit ever is, I guess. But what I'm trying to find out from you, and what you seem unwilling to tell me, is how long I'm going to be up there in subjective time."

"We don't know, Jim," Bleier said.

"You don't know? What if it's ten years? What if it's a thousand? What if I'm going to live out an entire life-span, or whatever is considered a life-span a hundred years from now, and grow old and wise and wither away and die and then wake up a thousandth of a second later on your lab table?"

"We don't know. That's why we have to send a human subject."

"There's no way to measure subjective jaunt-time?"

"Our instruments are here. They aren't there. You're the only instrument we'll have there. For all we know, we're sending you off for a million years, and when you come back here you'll have turned into something out of H. G. Wells. Is that straight-forward enough for you, Jim? But I don't think it's going to happen that way, and Mortenson doesn't think so either, or Ybarra for that matter. What we think is that you'll spend something between a day and a couple of months in the future, with the outside possibility of a year. And when we give you the hook, you'll be back here with virtually nil elapsed time. But to answer your first question again, there's no way you can instruct us to yank you back. You'll just have to sweat it out, however long it may be. I thought you knew that. The hook, when it comes, will be virtually automatic, a function of the thermodynamic homeostasis, like the recoil of a gun. An equal and opposite reaction: or maybe more like the snapping back of a rubber band. Pick whatever metaphor you want. But if you don't like the way any of this sounds, it's not too late for you to back out, and nobody will say a word against you. It's never too late to back out. Remember that, Jim."

McCulloch shrugged. "Thanks for leveling with me. I appreciate that. And no, I don't want to drop out. The only thing I wonder about is whether my stay in the future is going to seem too long or too goddamned short. But I won't know that until I get there, will I? And then the time I have to wait before coming home is going to be entirely out of my hands. And out of yours too, is how it seems. But that's all right. I'll take my chances. I just wondered what I'd do if I got there and found that I didn't much like it there."

"My bet is that you'll have the opposite problem," said Bleier. "You'll like it so much you won't want to come back."

Again and again, while the pilgrims traveled onward, McCulloch detected bright flares of intelligence gleaming like brilliant pinpoints of light in the darkness of the sea. Each creature seemed to have a characteristic emanation, a glow of neural energy. The simple ones—worms, urchins, starfish, sponges—emitted dim gentle signals; but there were others as dazzling as beacons. The lobster-folk were not the only sentient life-forms down here.

Occasionally he saw, as he had in the early muddled moments of the jaunt, isolated colonies of the giant sea anemones: great flowery-looking things, rising on thick pedestals. From them came a soft alluring lustful purr, a siren crooning calculated to bring unwary animals within reach of their swaying tentacles and the eager mouths hidden within the fleshy petals. Cemented to the floor on their swaying stalks, they seemed like somber philosophers, lost in the intervals between meals in deep reflections on the purpose of the cosmos. McCulloch longed to pause and try to speak with them, for their powerful emanation appeared plainly to indicate that they possessed a strong intelligence, but the lobsters moved past the anemones without halting.

The squid-like beings that frequently passed in flotillas overhead seemed even keener of mind: large animals, sleek and arrogant of motion, with long turquoise bodies that terminated in hawser-like arms, and enormous bulging eyes of a startling scarlet color. He found them ugly and repugnant, and did not quite know why. Perhaps it was some attitude of his host's that carried over subliminally to him; for there was an unmistakable chill among the lobsters whenever the squids appeared, and the chanting of the marchers grew more vehement, as though betokening a warning.

That some kind of frosty detente existed between the two kinds of life-forms was apparent from the regard they showed one another and from the distances they maintained. Never did the squids descend into the ocean-floor zone that was the chief domain of the lobsters, but for long spans of time they would soar above, in a kind of patient aerial surveillance, while the lobsters, striving ostentatiously to ignore them, betrayed discomfort by quickened movements of their antennae.

Still other kinds of high-order intelligence manifested themselves as the pilgrimage proceeded. In a zone of hard and rocky terrain McCulloch felt a new and distinctive mental pulsation, coming from some creature that he must not have encountered before. But he saw nothing unusual: merely a rough grayish landscape pockmarked by dense clumps of oysters and barnacles, some shaggy outcroppings of sponges and yellow seaweeds, a couple of torpid anemones. Yet out of the midst of all that unremarkable clutter came clear strong signals, produced by minds of considerable force. Whose? Not the oysters and barnacles, surely. The mystery intensified as the lobsters, without pausing in their march, interrupted their chant to utter words of greeting, and had greetings in return, drifting toward them from that tangle of marine underbrush.

"Why do you march?" the unseen speakers asked, in a voice that rose in the water like a deep slow groaning.

"We have had an Omen," answered the lobsters.

"Ah, is it the Time?"

"The Time will surely be here," the lobsters replied.

"Where is the herald, then?"

"The herald is within me," said McCulloch's host, breaking its long silence at last.

—To whom do you speak? McCulloch asked.

—Can you not see? There. Before us.

McCulloch saw only algae, barnacles, sponges, oysters.

—Where?

—In a moment you will see, said the host.

The column of pilgrims had continued all the while to move forward, until now it was within the thick groves of seaweed. And now McCulloch saw who the other speakers were. Huge crabs were crouched at the bases of many of the larger rock formations, creatures far greater in size than the largest of the lobsters; but they were camouflaged so well that they were virtually invisible except at the closest range. On their broad arching backs whole gardens grew: brilliantly colored sponges, algae in somber reds and browns, fluffy many-branched crimson things, odd complex feathery growths, even a small anemone or two, all jammed together in such profusion that nothing of the underlying crab showed except beady long-stalked eyes and glinting claws. Why beings that signalled their presence with potent telepathic outputs should choose to cloak themselves in such elaborate concealments, McCulloch could not guess: perhaps it was to deceive a prey so simple that it was unable to detect the emanations of these crabs' minds.

As the lobsters approached, the crabs heaved themselves up a little way from the rocky bottom, and shifted themselves ponderously from side to side, causing the intricate streamers and filaments and branches of the creatures growing on them to stir and wave about. It was like a forest agitated by a sudden hard gust of wind from the north.

"Why do you march, why do you march?" called the crabs. "Surely it is not yet the Time. Surely!"

"Surely it is," the lobsters replied. "So we all agree. Will you march with us?"

"Show us your herald!" the crabs cried. "Let us see the Omen!"

—Speak to them, said McCulloch's host.

—But what am I to say?

—The truth. What else can you say?

—I know nothing. Everything here is a mystery to me.

—I will explain all things afterward. Speak to them now.

—Without understanding?

—Tell them what you told us.

Baffled, McCulloch said, speaking through the host, "I have come from the former world as an emissary. Whether I am a herald, whether I bring an Omen, is not for me to say. In my own world I breathed air and carried my shell within my body."

"Unmistakably a herald," said the lobsters.

To which the crabs replied, "That is not so unmistakable to us. We sense a wanderer and a revenant among you. But what does that mean? The Molting of the World is not a small thing, good friends. Shall we march, just because this strangeness is come upon you? It is not enough evidence. And to march is not a small thing either, at least for us."

"We have chosen to march," the lobsters said, and indeed they had not halted at all throughout this colloquy; the vanguard of their procession was far out of sight in a black-walled canyon, and McCulloch's host, still at the end of the line, was passing now through the last few crouching-places of the great crabs. "If you mean to join us, come now."

From the crabs came a heavy outpouring of regret. "Alas, alas, we are large, we are slow, the way is long, the path is dangerous."

"Then we will leave you."

"If it is the Time, we know that you will perform the offices on our behalf. If it is not the Time, it is just as well that we do not make the pilgrimage. We are—not—certain. We—cannot—be—sure—it—is—an—Omen—"

McCulloch's host was far beyond the last of the crabs. Their words were faint and indistinct, and the final few were lost in the gentle surgings of the water.

—They make a great error, said McCulloch's host to him. If it is truly the Time, and they do not join the march, it might happen that their souls will be lost. That is a severe risk: but they are a lazy folk. Well, we will perform the offices on their behalf.

And to the crabs the host called, "We will do all that is required, have no fear!" But it was impossible, McCulloch thought, that the words could have reached the crabs across such a distance.

He and the host now were entering the mouth of the black canyon. With the host awake and talkative once again, McCulloch meant to seize the moment at last to have some answers to his questions.

—Tell me now—he began.

But before he could complete the thought, he felt the sea roil and surge about him as though he had been swept up in a monstrous wave. That could not be, not at this depth; but yet that irresistible force, booming toward him out of the dark canyon and catching him up, hurled him into a chaos as desperate as that of his moment of arrival. He sought to cling, to grasp, but there was no purchase; he was loose of his moorings; he was tossed and flung like a bubble on the winds.

—Help me! he called. What's happening to us?

—To you, friend human McCulloch. To you alone. Can I aid you?

What was that? Happening only to him? But certainly

he and the lobster both were caught in this undersea tempest, both being thrown about, both whirled in the same maelstrom—

Faces danced around him. Charlie Bleier, pudgy, earnest-looking. Maggie, tender-eyed, troubled. Bleier had his hand on McCulloch's right wrist, Maggie on the other, and they were tugging, tugging—

But he had no wrists. He was a lobster.

"Come, Jim—"

"No! Not yet!"

"Jim—Jim—"

"Stop—pulling—you're hurting—"

"Jim—"

McCulloch struggled to free himself from their grasp. As he swung his arms in wild circles, Maggie and Bleier, still clinging to them, went whipping about like tethered balloons. "Let go," he shouted. "You aren't here! There's nothing for you to hold on to! You're just hallucinations! Let—go—!"

And then, as suddenly as they had come, they were gone.

The sea was calm. He was in his accustomed place, seated somewhere deep within his host's consciousness. The lobster was moving forward, steady as ever, into the black canyon, following the long line of its companions.

McCulloch was too stunned and dazed to attempt contact for a long while. Finally, when he felt some measure of composure return, he reached his mind into his host's:

—What happened?

—I cannot say. What did it seem like to you?

—The water grew wild and stormy. I saw faces out of the former world. Friends of mine. They were pulling at my arms. You felt nothing?

—Nothing, said the host, except a sense of your own turmoil. We are deep here: beyond the reach of storms.

—Evidently I'm not.

—Perhaps your homefaring-time is coming. Your world is summoning you.

Of course! The faces, the pulling at his arms—the plausibility of the host's suggestion left McCulloch trembling with dismay. Homefaring-time! Back there in the lost and inconceivable past, they had begun angling for him, casting their line into the vast gulf of time—

—I'm not ready, he protested. I've only just arrived here! I know nothing yet! How can they call me so soon?

—Resist them, if you would remain.

—Will you help me?

—How would that be possible?

—I'm not sure, McCulloch said. But it's too early for me to go back. If they pull on me again, hold me! Can you?

—I can try, friend human McCulloch.

—And you have to keep your promise to me now.

—What promise is that?

—You said you would explain things to me. Why you've undertaken this pilgrimage. What it is I'm supposed to be the Omen of. What happens when the Time comes. The Molting of the World.

—Ah, said the host.

But that was all it said. In silence it scrabbled with busy legs over a sharply creviced terrain. McCulloch felt a fierce impatience growing in him. What if they yanked him again, now, and this time they succeeded? There was so much yet to learn! But he hesitated to prod the host again, feeling abashed. Long moments passed. Two more squids appeared: the radiance of their probing minds was like twin searchlights overhead. The ocean floor sloped downward gradually but perceptibly here. The squids vanished, and another of the predatory big-mouthed swimming-things, looking as immense as a whale and, McCulloch supposed, filling the same ecological niche, came cruising down into the level where the lobsters marched, considered their numbers in what appeared to be some surprise, and swam slowly upward again and out of sight. Something else of great size, flapping enormous wings somewhat like those of a stingray but clearly just a boneless mass of chitin-strutted flesh, appeared next, surveyed the pilgrims with equally bland curiosity, and flew to the front of the line of lobsters, where McCulloch lost it in the darkness. While all of this was happening the host was quiet and inaccessible, and McCulloch did not dare attempt to penetrate its privacy. But then, as the pilgrims were moving through a region where huge, dim-witted scallops with great bright eyes nestled everywhere, waving gaudy pink and blue mantles, the host unexpectedly resumed the conversation as though there had been no interruption, saying:

—What we call the Time of the Molting of the World is the time when the world undergoes a change of nature, and is purified and reborn. At such a time, we journey to the place of dry land, and perform certain holy rites.

—And these rites bring about the Molting of the World? McCulloch asked.

—Not at all. The Molting is an event wholly beyond our control. The rites are performed for our own sakes, not for the world's.

—I'm not sure I understand.

—We wish to survive the Molting, to travel onward into the world to come. For this reason, at a Time of Molting, we must make our observances, we must demonstrate our worth. It is the responsibility of my people. We bear the duty for all the peoples of the world.

—A priestly caste, is that it? McCulloch said. When this cataclysm comes, the lobsters go forth to say the prayers for everyone, so that everyone's soul will survive?

The host was silent again: pondering McCulloch's terms, perhaps, translating them into more appropriate equivalents. Eventually it replied:

—That is essentially correct.

—But other peoples can join the pilgrimage if they want. Those crabs. The anemones. The squids, even?

—We invite all to come. But we do not expect anyone but ourselves actually to do it.

—How often has there been such a ceremony? McCulloch asked.

—I cannot say. Never, perhaps.

—Never?

—The Molting of the World is not a common event. We think it has happened only twice since the beginning of time.

In amazement McCulloch said:

—Twice since the world began, and you think it's going to happen again in your own lifetimes?

—Of course we cannot be sure of that. But we have had an Omen, or so we think, and we must abide by that. It was foretold that when the end is near, an emissary from the former world would come among us. And so it has come to pass. Is that not so?

—Indeed.

—Then we must make the pilgrimage, for if you have not brought the Omen we have merely wasted some effort, but if you are the true herald we will have for-

feited all of eternity if we let your message go un-
heeded.

It sounded eerily familiar to McCulloch: a messianic
prophecy, a cult of the millennium, an apocalyptic transfig-
uration. He felt for a moment as though he had landed in
the tenth century instead of in some impossibly remote future epoch. And yet the host's tone was so calm and rational, the sense of spiritual obligation that the lobster
conveyed was so profound, that McCulloch found nothing
absurd in these beliefs. Perhaps the world did end from time
to time, and the performing of certain rituals did in fact
permit its inhabitants to transfer their souls onward into
whatever unimaginable environment was to succeed the
present one. Perhaps.

—Tell me, said McCulloch. What were the former worlds
like, and what will the next one be?

—You should know more about the former worlds than
I, friend human McCulloch. And as for the world to
come, we may only speculate.

—But what are your traditions about those worlds?

—The first world, the lobster said, was a world of fire.

—You can understand fire, living in the sea?

—We have heard tales of it from those who have been
to the dry place. Above the water there is air, and in
the air there hangs a ball of fire, which gives the world
warmth. Is this not the case?

McCulloch, hearing a creature of the ocean floor speak
of things so far beyond its scope and comprehension, felt a
warm burst of delight and admiration.

—Yes! We call that ball of fire the sun.

—Ah, so that is what you mean, when you think of the
sun! The word was a mystery to me, when first you
used it. But I understand you much better now, do you
not agree?

—You amaze me, McCulloch said.

—The first world, so we think, was fire: it was like the sun. And when we dwelled upon that world, we were fire also. It is the fire that we carry within us to this day, that glow, that brightness, which is our life, and which goes from us when we die. After a span of time so long that we could never describe its length, the Time of the Molting came upon the fire-world and it grew hard, and gathered a cloak of air about itself, and creatures lived upon the land and breathed the air. I find that harder to comprehend, in truth, than I do the fire-world. But that was the first Molting, when the air-world emerged: that world from which you have come to us. I hope you will tell me of your world, friend human McCulloch, when there is time.

—So I will, said McCulloch. But there is so much more I need to hear from you first!

—Ask it.

—The second Molting—the disappearance of my world, the coming of yours—

—The tradition is that the sea existed, even in the former world, and that it was not small. At the Time of the Molting it rose and devoured the land and all that was upon it, except for one place that was not devoured, which is sacred. And then all the world was covered by water, and that was the second Molting, which brought forth the third world.

—How long ago was that?

—How can I speak of the passing of time? There is no way to speak of that. Time passes, and lives end, and worlds are transformed. But we have no words for that. If every grain of sand in the sea were one lifetime, then it would be as many life-times ago as there are grains of sand in the sea. But does that help you? Does that tell you anything? It happened. It was very long ago. And now our world's turn has come, or so we think.

—And the next world? What will that be like? McCulloch asked.

—There are those who claim to know such things, but I am not one of them. We will know the next world when we have entered it, and I am content to wait until then for the knowledge.

McCulloch had a sense then that the host had wearied of this sustained contact, and was withdrawing once again from it; and, though his own thirst for knowledge was far from sated, he chose once again not to attempt to resist that withdrawal.

All this while the pilgrims had continued down a gentle incline into the great bowl of a sunken valley. Once again now the ocean floor was level, but the water was notably deeper here, and the diffused light from above was so dim that only the most rugged of algae could grow, making the landscape bleak and sparse. There were no sponges here, and little coral, and the anemones were pale and small, giving little sign of the potent intelligence that infused their larger cousins in the shallower zones of the sea.

But there were other creatures at this level that McCulloch had not seen before. Platoons of alert, mobile oysters skipped over the bottom, leaping in agile bounds on columns of water that they squirted like jets from tubes in their dark green mantles: now and again they paused in mid-leap and their shells quickly opened and closed, snapping shut, no doubt, on some hapless larval thing of the plankton too small for McCulloch, via the lobster's imperfect vision, to detect. From these oysters came bright darting blurts of mental activity, sharp and probing: they must be as intelligent, he thought, as cats or dogs. Yet from time to time a lobster, swooping with an astonishingly swift claw, would seize one of these oysters and deftly, almost instaneously, shuck and devour it. Appetite was no respecter of intelligence in this world of needful carnivores, McCulloch realized.

Intelligent, too, in their way, were the hordes of nearly invisible little crustaceans—shrimp of some sort, he imagined—that danced in shining clouds just above the line of march. They were ghostly things perhaps an inch long, virtually transparent, colorless, lovely, graceful. Their heads bore two huge glistening black eyes; their intestines, glowing coils running the length of their bodies, were tinged with green; the tips of their tails were an elegant crimson. They swam with the aid of a horde of busy fin-like legs, and seemed almost to be mocking their stolid, plodding cousins as they marched; but these sparkling little creatures also occasionally fell victim to the lobsters' inexorable claws, and each time it was like the extinguishing of a tiny brilliant candle.

An emanation of intelligence of a different sort came from bulky animals that McCulloch noticed roaming through the gravelly foothills flanking the line of march. These seemed at first glance to be another sort of lobster, larger even than McCulloch's companions: heavily armored things with many-segmented abdomens and thick paddle-shaped arms. But then, as one of them drew nearer, McCulloch saw the curved tapering tail with its sinister spike, and realized he was in the presence of the scorpions of the sea.

They gave off a deep, almost somnolent mental wave: slow thinkers but not light ones, Teutonic ponderers, grapplers with the abstruse. There were perhaps two dozen of them, who advanced upon the pilgrims and in quick one-sided struggles pounced, stung, slew. McCulloch watched in amazement as each of the scorpions dragged away a victim and, no more than a dozen feet from the line of march, began to gouge into its armor to draw forth tender chunks of pale flesh, without drawing the slightest response from the impassive, steadily marching column of lobsters.

They had not been so complacent when the great-mouthed swimming thing had menaced McCulloch's host; then, the lobsters had come in hordes to tear the attacker apart. And whenever one of the big squids came by, the edgy hostility of the lobsters, their willingness to do battle if necessary, was manifest. But they seemed indifferent to the scorpions. The lobsters accepted their onslaught as placidly as though it were merely a toll they must pay in order to pass through this district. Perhaps it was. McCulloch was only beginning to perceive how dense and intricate a fabric of ritual bound this submarine world together.

The lobsters marched onward, chanting in unfailing rhythm as though nothing untoward had happened. The scorpions, their hungers evidently gratified, withdrew and congregated a short distance off, watching without much show of interest as the procession went by them. By the time McCulloch's host, bringing up the rear, had gone past the scorpions, they were fighting among themselves in a lazy, half-hearted way, like playful lions after a successful hunt. Their mental emanation, sluggishly booming through the water, grew steadily more blurred, more vague, more toneless.

And then it was overlaid and entirely masked by the pulsation of some new and awesome kind of mind ahead: one of enormous power, whose output beat upon the water with what was almost a physical force, like some massive metal chain being lashed against the surface of the ocean. Apparently the source of this gigantic output still lay at a considerable distance, for, strong as it was, it grew stronger still as the lobsters advanced toward it, until at last it was an overwhelming clangor, terrifying, bewildering. McCulloch could no longer remain quiescent under the impact of that monstrous sound. Breaking through to the sanctuary of his host, he cried:

—What is it?

—We are approaching a god, the lobster replied.

—A god, did you say?

—A divine presence, yes. Did you think we were the rulers of this world?

In fact McCulloch had, assuming automatically that his time-jaunt had deposited him within the consciousness of some member of this world's highest species, just as he would have expected to have landed, had he reached the twenty-second century as intended, in the consciousness of a human rather than in a frog or a horse. But obviously the division between humanity and all sub-sentient species in his own world did not have an exact parallel here; many races, perhaps all of them, had some sort of intelligence, and it was becoming clear that the lobsters, though a high life-form, were not the highest. He found that dismaying and even humbling; for the lobsters seemed quite adequately intelligent to him, quite the equals—for all his early condescension to them—of mankind itself. And now he was to meet one of their gods? How great a mind was a god likely to have?

The booming of that mind grew unbearably intense, nor was there any way to hide from it. McCulloch visualized himself doubled over in pain, pressing his hands to his ears, an image that drew a quizzical shaft of thought from his host. Still the lobsters pressed forward, but even they were responding now to the waves of mental energy that rippled outward from that unimaginable source. They had at last broken ranks, and were fanning out horizontally on the broad dark plain of the ocean floor, as though deploying themselves before a place of worship. Where was the god? McCulloch, striving with difficulty to see in this nearly lightless place, thought he made out some vast shape ahead, some dark entity, swollen and fearsome, that rose like a colossal boulder in the midst of the suddenly diminutive-looking lobsters. He saw eyes like bright yellow platters, gleaming furiously; he saw a huge frightful beak; he saw what he thought at first to be a nest of writhing serpents, and then realized to be tentacles, dozens of them, coiling and uncoiling with a terrible restless energy. To the host he said:

—Is that your god?

But he could not hear the reply, for an agonizing new force suddenly buffeted him, one even more powerful than that which was emanating from the giant creature that sat before him. It ripped upward through his soul like a spike. It cast him forth, and he tumbled over and over, helpless in some incomprehensible limbo, where nevertheless he could still hear the faint distant voice of his lobster host:

—Friend human McCulloch? Friend human McCulloch?

He was drowning. He had waded incautiously into the surf, deceived by the beauty of the transparent tropical water and the shimmering white sand below, and a wave had caught him and knocked him to his knees, and the next wave had come before he could arise, pulling him under. And now he tossed like a discarded doll in the suddenly turbulent sea, struggling to get his head above water and failing, failing, failing.

Maggie was standing on the shore, calling in panic to him, and somehow he could hear her words even through the tumult of the crashing waves: "This way, Jim, swim toward me! Oh, please, Jim, this way, this way!"

Bleier was there too, Mortenson, Bob Rodrigues, the whole group, ten or fifteen people, running about worriedly, beckoning to him, calling his name. It was odd that he could see them, if he was under water. And he could hear them so clearly, too, Bleier telling him to stand up and walk ashore, the water wasn't deep at all, and Rodrigues saying to come in on hands and knees if he couldn't manage to get up, and Ybarra yelling that it was getting late, that they couldn't wait all the goddamned afternoon, that he had been swimming long enough. McCulloch wondered why they didn't come after him, if they were so eager to get him to shore. Obviously he was in trouble. Obviously he was unable to help himself.

"Look," he said, "I'm drowning, can't you see? Throw me a line, for Christ's sake!" Water rushed into his mouth as he spoke. It filled his lungs, it pressed against his brain.

"We can't hear you, Jim!"

"Throw me a line!" he cried again, and felt the torrents pouring through his body. "I'm—drowning—drowning—"

And then he realized that he did not at all want them to rescue him, that it was worse to be rescued than to drown. He did not understand why he felt that way, but he made no attempt to question the feeling. All that concerned him now was preventing those people on the shore, those humans, from seizing him and taking him from the water. They were rushing about, assembling some kind of machine to pull him in, an arm at the end of a great boom. McCulloch signalled to them to leave him alone.

"I'm okay," he called. "I'm not drowning after all! I'm fine right where I am!"

But now they had their machine in operation, and its long metal arm was reaching out over the water toward him.

He turned and dived, and swam as hard as he could away from the shore, but it was no use: the boom seemed to extend over an infinite distance, and no matter how fast he swam the boom moved faster, so that it hovered just above him now, and from its tip some sort of hook was descending—

"No—no—let me be! I don't want to go ashore!"

Then he felt a hand on his wrist: firm, reassuring, taking control. All right, he thought. They've caught me after all, they're going to pull me in. There's nothing I can do about it. They have me, and that's all there is to it. But he realized, after a moment, that he was heading not toward shore but out to sea, beyond the waves, into the calm warm depths. And the hand that was on his wrist was not a hand; it was a tentacle, thick as heavy cable, a strong sturdy tentacle lined on one side by rounded suction cups that held him in an unbreakable grip.

That was all right. Anything to be away from that wild crashing surf. It was much more peaceful out here. He could rest, catch his breath, get his equilibrium. And all the while that powerful tentacle towed him steadily seaward. He could still hear the voices of his friends on shore, but they were as faint as the cries of distant sea-birds now, and when he looked back he saw only tiny dots, like excited ants, moving along the beach. McCulloch waved at them. "See you some other time," he called. "I didn't want to come out of the water yet anyway." Better here. Much much better. Peaceful. Warm. Like the womb. And that tentacle around his wrist: so reassuring, so steady.

—Friend human McCulloch? Friend human McCulloch?

—This is where I belong. Isn't it?

—Yes. This is where you belong. You are one of us, friend human McCulloch. You are one of us.

* * *

Gradually the turbulence subsided, and he found himself regaining his balance. He was still within the lobster; the whole horde of lobsters was gathered around him, thousands upon thousands of them, a gentle solicitous community; and right in front of him was the largest octopus imaginable, a creature that must have been fifteen or twenty feet in diameter, with tentacles that extended an implausible distance on all sides. Somehow he did not find the sight frightening.

"He is recovered now," his host announced.

—What happened to me? McCulloch asked.

—Your people called you again. But you did not want to make your homefaring, and you resisted them. And when we understood that you wanted to remain, the god aided you, and you broke free of their pull.

—The god?

His host indicated the great octopus.

—There.

It did not seem at all improbable to McCulloch now. The infinite fullness of time brings about everything, he thought: even intelligent lobsters, even a divine octopus. He still could feel the mighty telepathic output of the vast creature, but though it had lost none of its power it no longer caused him discomfort; it was like the roaring thunder of some great waterfall, to which one becomes accustomed, and which, in time, one begins to love. The octopus sat motionless, its immense yellow eyes trained on McCulloch, its scarlet mantle rippling gently, its tentacles weaving in intricate patterns. McCulloch thought of an octopus he had once seen when he was diving in the West Indies: a small shy scuttling thing, hurrying to slither behind a gnarled coral head. He felt chastened and awed by this evidence of the magnifications wrought by the eons. A hundred million years? Half a billion? The numbers were without meaning.

But that span of years had produced this creature. He sensed a serene intelligence of incomprehensible depth, benign, tranquil, all-penetrating: a god indeed. Yes. Truly a god. Why not?

The great cephalopod was partly sheltered by an over-hanging wall of rock. Clustered about it were dozens of the scorpion-things, motionless, poised: plainly a guard force. Overhead swam a whole army of the big squids, doubtless guardians also, and for once the presence of those creatures did not trigger any emotion in the lobsters, as if they re-garded squids in the service of the god as acceptable ones. The scene left McCulloch dazed with awe. He had never felt farther from home.

—The god would speak with you, said his host.

—What shall I say?

—Listen, first.

McCulloch's lobster moved forward until it stood vir-tually beneath the octopus' huge beak. From the octopus, then, came an outpouring of words that McCulloch did not immediately comprehend, but which, after a moment, he understood to be some kind of benediction that enfolded his soul like a warm blanket. And gradually he perceived that he was being spoken to.

"Can you tell us why you have come all this way, hu-man McCulloch?"

"It was an error. They didn't mean to send me so far— only a hundred years or less, that was all we were trying to cross. But it was our first attempt. We didn't really know what we were doing. And I suppose I wound up halfway across time—a hundred million years, two hundred, maybe a billion—who knows?"

"It is a great distance. Do you feel no fear?"

"At the beginning I did. But not any longer. This world is alien to me, but not frightening."

"Do you prefer it to your own?"

"I don't understand," McCulloch said.

"Your people summoned you. You refused to go. You appealed to us for aid, and we aided you in resisting your homecalling, because it was what you seemed to require from us."

"I'm—not ready to go home yet," he said. "There's so much I haven't seen yet, and that I want to see. I want to see everything. I'll never have an opportunity like this again. Perhaps no one ever will. Besides, I have services to perform here. I'm the herald; I bring the Omen; I'm part of this pilgrimage. I think I ought to stay until the rites have been performed. I want to stay until then."

"Those rites will not be performed," said the octopus quietly.

"Not performed?"

"You are not the herald. You carry no Omen. The Time is not at hand."

McCulloch did not know what to reply. Confusion swirled within him. No Omen? Not the Time?

—It is so, said the host. We were in error. The god has shown us that we came to our conclusion too quickly. The Time of the Molting may be near, but it is not yet upon us. You have many of the outer signs of a herald, but there is no Omen upon you. You are merely a visitor. An accident.

McCulloch was assailed by a startlingly keen pang of disappointment. It was absurd; but for a time he had been the central figure in some apocalyptic ritual of immense significance, or at least had been thought to be, and all that suddenly was gone from him, and he felt strangely diminished, irrelevant, bereft of his bewildering grandeur. A visitor. An accident.

—In that case I feel great shame and sorrow, he said. To

have caused so much trouble for you. To have sent you off on this pointless pilgrimage.

—No blame attaches to you, said the host. We acted of our free choice, after considering the evidence.

"Nor was the pilgrimage pointless," the octopus declared. "There are no pointless pilgrimages. And this one will continue."

"But if there's no Omen—if this is not the Time—"

"There are other needs to consider," replied the octopus, "and other observances to carry out. We must visit the dry place ourselves, from time to time, so that we may prepare ourselves for the world that is to succeed ours, for it will be very different from ours. It is time now for such a visit, and well past time. And also we must bring you to the dry place, for only there can we properly make you one of us."

"I don't understand," said McCulloch.

"You have asked to stay among us; and if you stay, you must become one of us, for your sake, and for ours. And that can best be done at the dry place. It is not necessary that you understand that now, human McCulloch."

—Make no further reply, said McCulloch's host. The god has spoken. We must proceed.

Shortly the lobsters resumed their march, chanting as before, though in a more subdued way, and, so it seemed to McCulloch, singing a different melody. From the context of his conversation with it, McCulloch had supposed that the octopus now would accompany them, which puzzled him, for the huge unwieldy creature did not seem capable of any extensive journey. That proved to be the case: the octopus did not go along, though the vast booming resonances of its mental output followed the procession for what must have been hundreds of miles.

Once more the line was a single one, with McCulloch's

host at the end of the file. A short while after departure it said:

> —I am glad, friend human McCulloch, that you chose to continue with us. I would be sorry to lose you now.
>
> —Do you mean that? Isn't it an inconvenience for you, to carry me around inside your mind?
>
> —I have grown quite accustomed to it. You are part of me, friend human McCulloch. We are part of one another. At the place of the dry land we will celebrate our sharing of this body.
>
> —I was lucky, said McCulloch, to have landed like this in a mind that would make me welcome.
>
> —Any of us would have made you welcome, responded the host.

McCulloch pondered that. Was it merely a courteous turn of phrase, or did the lobster mean him to take the answer literally? Most likely the latter: the host's words seemed always to have only a single level of meaning, a straightforwardly literal one. So any of the lobsters would have taken him in uncomplainingly? Perhaps so. They appeared to be virtually interchangeable beings, without distinctive individual personalities, without names, even. The host had remained silent when McCulloch had asked him its name, and had not seemed to understand what kind of a label McCulloch's own name was. So powerful was their sense of community, then, that they must have little sense of private identity. He had never cared much for that sort of hive-mentality, where he had observed it in human society. But here it seemed not only appropriate but admirable.

> —How much longer will it be, McCulloch asked, before we reach the place of dry land?
>
> —Long.
>
> —Can you tell me where it is?

—It is in the place where the world grows narrower, said the host.

McCulloch had realized, the moment he asked the question, that it was meaningless: what useful answer could the lobster possibly give? The old continents were gone and their names long forgotten. But the answer he had received was meaningless too: where, on a round planet, is the place where the world grows narrower? He wondered what sort of geography the lobsters understood. If I live among them a hundred years, he thought, I will probably just begin to comprehend what their perceptions are like.

Where the world grows narrower. All right. Possibly the place of the dry land was some surviving outcropping of the former world, the summit of Mount Everest, perhaps, Kilimanjaro, whatever. Or perhaps not: perhaps even those peaks had been ground down by time, and new ones had arisen—one of them, at least, tall enough to rise above the universal expanse of sea. It was folly to suppose that any shred at all of his world remained accessible: it was all down there beneath tons of water and millions of years of sediments, the old continents buried, hidden, rearranged by time like pieces scattered about a board.

The pulsations of the octopus' mind could no longer be felt. As the lobsters went tirelessly onward, moving always in that lithe skipping stride of theirs and never halting to rest or to feed, the terrain rose for a time and then began to dip again, slightly at first and then more than slightly. They entered into waters that were deeper and significantly darker, and somewhat cooler as well. In this somber zone, where vision seemed all but useless, the pilgrims grew silent for long spells for the first time, neither chanting nor speaking to one another, and McCulloch's host, who had become increasingly quiet, disappeared once more into its impenetrable inner domain and rarely emerged.

In the gloom and darkness there began to appear a strange red glow off to the left, as though someone had left a lantern hanging midway between the ocean floor and the surface of the sea. The lobsters, when that mysterious light came into view, at once changed the direction of their line of march to go veering off to the right; but at the same time they resumed their chanting, and kept one eye trained on the glowing place as they walked.

The water felt warmer here. A zone of unusual heat was spreading outward from the glow. And the taste of the water, and what McCulloch persisted in thinking of as its smell, were peculiar, with a harsh choking salty flavor. Brimstone? Ashes?

McCulloch realized that what he was seeing was an undersea volcano, belching forth a stream of red-hot lava that was turning the sea into a boiling bubbling cauldron. The sight stirred him oddly. He felt that he was looking into the pulsing ancient core of the world, the primordial flame, the geological link that bound the otherwise vanished former worlds to this one. There awakened in him a powerful tide of awe, and a baffling unfocused yearning that he might have termed homesickness, except that it was not, for he was no longer sure where his true home lay.

—Yes, said the host. It is a mountain on fire. We think it is a part of the older of the two former worlds that has endured both of the Moltings. It is a very sacred place.

—An object of pilgrimage? McCulloch asked.

—Only to those who wish to end their lives. The fire devours all who approach it.

—In my world we had many such fiery mountains, McCulloch said. They often did great destruction.

—How strange your world must have been!

—It was very beautiful, said McCulloch.

—Surely. But strange. The dry land, the fire in the air—
the sun, I mean—the air-breathing creatures—yes,
strange, very strange. I can scarcely believe it really
existed.

—There are times, now, when I begin to feel the same
way, McCulloch said.

The volcano receded in the distance; its warmth could no
longer be felt; the water was dark again, and cold, and
growing colder, and McCulloch could no longer detect any
trace of that sulphurous aroma. It seemed to him that they
were moving now down an endless incline, where scarcely
any creatures dwelled.

And then he realized that the marchers ahead had
halted, and were drawn up in a long row as they had been
when they came to the place where the octopus held its
court. Another god? No. There was only blackness ahead.

—Where are we? he asked.

—It is the shore of the great abyss.

Indeed what lay before them looked like the pit itself:
lightless, without landmark, an empty landscape. McCulloch
understood now that they had been marching all this while
across some sunken continent's coastal plain, and at last
they had come to—what?—the graveyard where one of
Earth's lost oceans lay buried in ocean?

—Is it possible to continue? he asked.

—Of course, said the host. But now we must swim.

Already the lobsters before them were kicking off from
shore with vigorous strokes of their tails and vanishing into
the open sea beyond. A moment later McCulloch's host
joined them. Almost at once there was no sense of a bottom
beneath them—only a dark and infinitely deep void. Swimming across this, McCulloch thought, is like falling through
time—an endless descent and no safety net.

The lobsters, he knew, were not true swimming creatures: like the lobsters of his own era they were bottom-dwellers, who walked to get where they needed to go. But they could never cross this abyss that way, and so they were swimming now, moving steadily by flexing their huge abdominal muscles and their tails. Was it terrifying to them to be setting forth into a place without landmarks like this? His host remained utterly calm, as though this were no more than an afternoon stroll.

McCulloch lost what little perception of the passage of time that he had had. Heave, stroke, forward, heave, stroke, forward, that was all, endless repetition. Out of the depths there occasionally came an upwelling of cold water, like a dull, heavy river miraculously flowing upward through air, and in that strange surging from below rose a fountain of nourishment, tiny transparent struggling creatures and even smaller flecks of some substance that must have been edible, for the lobsters, without missing a stroke, sucked in all they could hold. And swam on and on. McCulloch had a sense of being involved in a trek of epic magnitude, a once-in-many generations thing that would be legendary long after.

Enemies roved this open sea: the free-swimming creatures that had evolved out of God only knew which kinds of worms or slugs to become the contemporary equivalents of sharks and whales. Now and again one of these huge beasts dived through the horde of lobsters, harvesting it at will. But they could eat only so much; and the survivors kept going onward.

Until at last—months, years later?—the far shore came into view; the ocean floor, long invisible, reared up beneath them and afforded support; the swimmers at last put their legs down on the solid bottom, and with something that sounded much like gratitude in their voices began once again to chant in unison as they ascended the rising flank of a new continent.

The first rays of the sun, when they came into view an unknown span of time later, struck McCulloch with an astonishing, overwhelming impact. He perceived them first as a pale greenish glow resting in the upper levels of the sea just ahead, striking downward like illuminated wands; he did not then know what he was seeing, but the sight engendered wonder in him all the same, and later, when that radiance diminished and was gone and in a short while returned, he understood that the pilgrims were coming up out of the sea. So they had reached their goal: the still point of the turning world, the one remaining unsubmerged scrap of the former Earth.

—Yes, said the host. This is it.

In that same instant McCulloch felt another tug from the past: a summons dizzying in its imperative impact. He thought he could hear Maggie Caldwell's voice crying across the time-winds: "Jim, Jim, come back to us!" And Bleier, grouchy, angered, muttering, "For Christ's sake, McCulloch, stop holding on up there! This is getting expensive!" Was it all his imagination, that fantasy of hands on his wrists, familiar faces hovering before his eyes?

"Leave me alone," he said. "I'm still not ready."

"Will you ever be?" That was Maggie. "Jim, you'll be marooned. You'll be stranded there if you don't let us pull you back now."

"I may be marooned already," he said, and brushed the voices out of his mind with surprising ease.

He returned his attention to his companions and saw that they had halted their trek a little way short of that zone of light which now was but a quick scramble ahead of them. Their linear formation was broken once again. Some of the lobsters, marching blindly forward, were piling up in confused-looking heaps in the shallows, forming mounds fifteen or twenty lobsters deep. Many of the others had begun a bizarre convulsive dance: a wild twitchy cavorting, rearing up on their back legs, waving their claws about, flicking their antennae in frantic circles.

—What's happening? McCulloch asked his host. Is this the beginning of a rite?

But the host did not reply. The host did not appear to be within their shared body at all. McCulloch felt a silence far deeper than the host's earlier withdrawals; this seemed not a withdrawal but an evacuation, leaving McCulloch in sole possession. That new solitude came rolling in upon him with a crushing force. He sent forth a tentative probe, found nothing, found less than nothing. Perhaps it's meant to be this way, he thought. Perhaps it was necessary for him to face this climactic initiation unaided, unaccompanied.

Then he noticed that what he had taken to be a weird jerky dance was actually the onset of a mass molting prodrome. Hundreds of the lobsters had been stricken simultaneously, he realized, with that strange painful sense of inner expansion, of volcanic upheaval and stress: that heaving and rearing about was the first stage of the splitting of the shell.

And all of the molters were females.

Until that instant McCulloch had not been aware of any division into sexes among the lobsters. He had barely been able to tell one from the next; they had no individual character, no shred of uniqueness. Now, suddenly, strangely, he knew without being told that half of his companions were females, and that they were molting now because they were fertile only when they had shed their old armor, and that the pilgrimage to the place of the dry land was the appropriate time to engender the young. He had asked no questions of anyone to learn that; the knowledge was simply within him; and, reflecting on that, he saw that the host was absent from him because the host was wholly fused with him; he was the host, the host was Jim McCulloch.

He approached a female, knowing precisely which one was the appropriate one, and sang to her, and she acknowledged his song with a song of her own, and raised her third pair of legs to him, and let him plant his gametes beside her oviducts. There was no apparent pleasure in it, as he remembered pleasure from his days as a human. Yet it brought him a subtle but unmistakable sense of fulfillment, of the completion of biological destiny, that had a kind of orgasmic finality about it, and left him calm and anchored at the absolute dead center of his soul: yes, truly the still point of the turning world, he thought.

His mate moved away to begin her new Growing and the awaiting of her motherhood. And McCulloch, unbidden, began to ascend the slope that led to the land.

The bottom was fine sand here, soft, elegant. He barely touched it with his legs as he raced shoreward. Before him lay a world of light, radiant, heavenly, a bright irresistible beacon. He went on until the water, pearly-pink and transparent, was only a foot or two deep, and the domed upper curve of his back was reaching into the air. He felt no fear. There was no danger in this. Serenely he went forward—the leader, now, of the trek—and climbed out into the hot sunlight.

It was an island, low and sandy, so small that he imagined he could cross it in a day. The sky was intensely blue and the sun, hanging close to a noon position, looked swollen and fiery. A little grove of palm trees clustered a few hundred yards inland, but he saw nothing else, no birds, no insects, no animal life of any sort. Walking was difficult here—his breath was short, his shell seemed to be too tight, his stalked eyes were stinging in the air—but he pulled himself forward, almost to the trees. Other male lobsters, hundreds of them, thousands of them, were following. He felt himself linked to each of them: his people, his nation, his community, his brothers.

Now, at that moment of completion and communion, came one more call from the past.

There was no turbulence in it this time. No one was yanking at his wrists, no surf boiled and heaved in his mind and threatened to dash him on the reefs of the soul. The call was simple and clear: This is the moment of coming back, Jim.

Was it? Had he no choice? He belonged here. These were his people. This was where his loyalties lay.

And yet, and yet: he knew that he had been sent on a mission unique in human history, that he had been granted a vision beyond all dreams, that it was his duty to return and report on it. There was no ambiguity about that. He owed it to Bleier and Maggie and Ybarra and the rest to return, to tell them everything.

How clear it all was! He belonged here, and he belonged there, and an unbreakable net of loyalties and responsibilities held him to both places. It was a perfect equilibrium; and therefore he was tranquil and at ease. The pull was on him; he resisted nothing, for he was at last beyond all resistance to anything. The immense sun was a drumbeat in the heavens; the fiery warmth was a benediction; he had never known such peace.

"I must make my homefaring now," he said, and released himself, and let himself drift upward, light as a bubble, toward the sun.

Strange figures surrounded him, tall and narrow-bodied, with odd fleshy faces and huge moist mouths and bulging staring eyes, and their kind of speech was a crude hubbub of sound-waves that bashed and battered against his sensibilities with painful intensity. "We were afraid the signal wasn't reaching you, Jim," they said. "We tried again and again, but there was no contact, nothing. And then just as we were giving up, suddenly your eyes were opening, you were stirring, you stretched your arms—"

He felt air pouring into his body, and dryness all about him. It was a struggle to understand the speech of these creatures who were bending over him, and he hated the reek that came from their flesh and the booming vibrations that they made with their mouths. But gradually he found himself returning to himself, like one who has been lost in a dream so profound that it eclipses reality for the first few moments of wakefulness.

"How long was I gone?" he asked.

"Four minutes and eighteen seconds," Ybarra said.

McCulloch shook his head. "Four minutes? Eighteen seconds? It was more like forty months, to me. Longer. I don't know how long."

"Where did you go, Jim? What was it like?"

"Wait," someone else said. "He's not ready for debriefing yet. Can't you see, he's about to collapse?"

McCulloch shrugged. "You sent me too far."

"How far? Five hundred years?" Maggie asked.

"Millions," he said.

Someone gasped.

"He's dazed," a voice said at his left ear.

"Millions of years," McCulloch said in a slow, steady, determinedly articulate voice. "Millions. The whole earth was covered by the sea, except for one little island. The people are lobsters. They have a society, a culture. They worship a giant octopus."

Maggie was crying. "Jim, oh, Jim—"

"No. It's true. I went on migration with them. Intelligent lobsters is what they are. And I wanted to stay with them forever. I felt you pulling at me, but I—didn't—want—to—go—"

"Give him a sedative, Doc," Bleier said.

"You think I'm crazy? You think I'm deranged? They were lobsters, fellows. Lobsters."

After he had slept and showered and changed his clothes they came to see him again, and by that time he realized that he must have been behaving like a lunatic in the first moments of his return, blurting out his words, weeping, carrying on, crying out what surely had sounded like gibberish to them. Now he was rested, he was calm, he was at home in his own body once again.

He told them all that had befallen him, and from their faces he saw at first that they still thought he had gone around the bend: but as he kept speaking, quietly, straightforwardly, in rich detail, they began to acknowledge his report in subtle little ways, asking questions about the geography, about the ecological balance in a manner that showed him they were not simply humoring him. And after that, as it sank in upon them that he really had dwelled for a period of many months at the far end of time, beyond the span of the present world, they came to look upon him—it was unmistakable—as someone who was now wholly unlike them. In particular he saw the cold glassy stare in Maggie Caldwell's eyes.

Then they left him, for he was tiring again; and later Maggie came to see him alone, and took his hand and held it between hers, which were cold.

She said, "What do you want to do now, Jim?"

"To go back there."

"I thought you did."

"It's impossible, isn't it?" he said.

"We could try. But it couldn't ever work. We don't know what we're doing, yet, with that machine. We don't know where we'd send you. We might miss by a million years. By a billion."

"That's what I figured too."

"But you want to go back?"

He nodded. "I can't explain it. It was like being a member of some Buddhist monastery, do you see? Feeling absolutely sure that this is where you belong, that everything fits together perfectly, that you're an integral part of it. I've never felt anything like that before. I never will again."

"I'll talk to Bleier, Jim, about sending you back."

"No. Don't. I can't possibly get there. And I don't want to land anywhere else. Let Ybarra take the next trip. I'll stay here."

"Will you be happy?"

He smiled. "I'll do my best," he said.

When the others understood what the problem was, they saw to it that he went into reentry therapy—Bleier had already foreseen something like that, and made preparations for it—and after a while the pain went from him, that sense of having undergone a violent separation, of having been ripped untimely from the womb. He resumed his work in the group and gradually recovered his mental balance and took an active part in the second transmission, which sent a young anthropologist named Ludwig off for two minutes and eight seconds. Ludwig did not see lobsters, to McCulloch's intense disappointment. He went sixty years into the future and came back glowing with wondrous tales of atomic fusion plants.

That was too bad, McCulloch thought. But soon he decided that it was just as well, that he preferred being the only one who had encountered the world beyond this world, probably the only human being who ever would.

He thought of that world with love, wondering about his mate and her millions of larvae, about the journey of his friends back across the great abyss, about the legends that were being spun about his visit in that unimaginably distant epoch. Sometimes the pain of separation returned, and Maggie found him crying in the night, and held him until he was whole again. And eventually the pain did not return. But still he did not forget, and in some part of his soul he longed to make his homefaring back to his true kind, and he rarely passed a day when he did not think he could hear the inaudible sound of delicate claws, scurrying over the sands of silent seas.

THOMAS THE
PROCLAIMER

THOMAS THE PROCLAIMER

AN INTRODUCTION

In the 1970s I assembled a number of "triplet" theme anthologies, in which some well-known science-fiction writer was asked to provide a provocative idea that would be used as the basis for novella-length stories by the chosen contributors. Sometimes I provided the theme idea myself, sometimes I asked other writers— among them Isaac Asimov and Arthur C. Clarke—to set the theme.

For the 1972 book I invited Lester del Rey to provide the literary challenge. In much of his own work del Rey had taken iconoclastic views of conventional religious ideas, and that was precisely what he did here. We read in the Book of Joshua how the Israelite warrior Joshua, not wanting night to fall while he was in the midst of battle, cried out, "Sun, stand thou still," and the Lord complied: "The sun stood still in the midst of heaven, and hasted not to go down about a whole day," and Joshua was victorious.

What Lester del Rey asked was what would happen if, in our own era of widespread disbelief, the same miracle were to take place: that a great leader would appear and cry out to God for a sign in the heavens so that the unbelieving should heed, and God would comply, so that "for a day and a night the Earth moved not around the Sun, neither did it rotate. And the laws of momentum were confounded." And the question that Lester propounded to the three writers was, "What kind of world might exist were the basis of faith replaced by certain knowledge?"

I named the anthology *The Day the Sun Stood Still* (though of course it was the Earth that would cease to move), asked Poul Anderson and Gordon R. Dickson to write stories for the book, and chose to write the third one myself. They came through magnificently, Anderson with a novella called "A Chapter of Revelation," and Dickson with "Things Which Are Caesar's."

My own story, which I wrote in April of 1971, was "Thomas the Proclaimer." It was a fertile creative period for me. I had just finished the novel *The Book of Skulls* and the short story "Good News from the Vatican," which would win a Nebula, and I was about to start on *Dying Inside*. I chose to set "Thomas the Proclaimer" at the very edge of what we later would come to call Y2K: the miracle occurs on June 6, 1999, and the story moves inexorably along to the apocalyptic end of December.

I've never felt that science fiction should be taken as literal prophecy, and that belief is confirmed again here. We know now that neither the Sun nor the Earth stood still on June 6, 1999, and no wild-eyed hordes of religious fanatics were rampaging through our cities as December 31 approached. Nor did such events as the Children's Crusade for Sanity, the Nine Weeks' War, or the Night of the Lasers occur during the 1980s. But the future looked plenty chaotic to me in 1971 as I wrote the story, and much of that chaos did unfold in one form and another, and though "Thomas the Proclaimer" is in no way literally prophetic, I think you will find that it quite accurately prefigured much of what would occur in the world in the generation just ended.

THOMAS THE PROCLAIMER

1.

Moonlight, Starlight, Torchlight

How long will this night last? The blackness, though moon-pierced, star-pierced, torch-pierced, is dense and tangible. They are singing and chanting in the valley Bitter smoke from their firebrands rises to the hilltop where Thomas stands, flanked by his closest followers. Fragments of old hymns dance through the trees. "Rock of Ages, Cleft for Me. "O God, Our Help in Ages Past." "Jesus, Lover of My Soul Let Me to Thy Bosom Fly." Thomas is the center of all attention. A kind of invisible aura surrounds his blocky, powerful figure, an unseen crackling electrical radiance. Saul Kraft, at his side, seems eclipsed and obscured, a small, fragile-looking man, overshadowed now but far from unimportant in the events of this night. "Nearer, My God, to Thee." Thomas begins to hum the tune, then to sing. His voice, though deep and magical, the true charismatic voice, tumbles randomly from key to key: the prophet has no ear for music. Kraft smiles sourly at Thomas' dismal sounds.

> Watchman, tell us of the night,
> What its signs of promise are.
> Traveler, o'er yon mountain's height,
> See that glory-beaming star!

Ragged shouts from below. Occasional sobs and loud coughs. What is the hour? The hour is late. Thomas runs his hands through his long, tangled hair, tugging, smoothing, pulling the strands down toward his thick shoulders. The familiar gesture, beloved by the multitudes. He wonders if he should make an appearance. They are calling his name; he hears the rhythmic cries punching through the snarl of clashing hymns. *Tho-mas! Tho-mas! Tho-mas!* Hysteria in their voices. They want him to come forth and stretch out his arms and make the heavens move again, just as he caused them to stop. But Thomas resists that grand but hollow gesture. How easy it is to play the prophet's part! He did not cause the heavens to stop, though, and he knows that he cannot make them move again. Not of his own will alone, at any rate.

"What time is it?" he asks.

"Quarter to ten," Kraft tells him. Adding, after an instant's thought: "P.M."

So the twenty-four hours are nearly up. And still the sky hangs frozen. Well, Thomas? Is this not what you asked for? Go down on your knees, you cried, and beg Him for a Sign, so that we may know He is still with us, in this our time of need. And render up to Him a great shout. And the people knelt throughout all the lands. And begged. And shouted. And the Sign was given. Why, then, this sense of foreboding? Why these fears? Surely this night will pass.

Look at Kraft. Smiling serenely. Kraft has never known any doubts. Those cold eyes, those thin wide lips, the fixed expression of tranquillity.

"You ought to speak to them," Kraft says.

"I have nothing to say."

"A few words of comfort for them."

"Let's see what happens, first. What can I tell them now?"

"Empty of words, Thomas? You, who have had so much to proclaim?"

Thomas shrugs. There are times when Kraft infuriates him: the little man needling him, goading, scheming, never letting up, always pushing this Crusade toward some appointed goal grasped by Kraft alone. The intensity of Kraft's faith exhausts Thomas. Annoyed, the prophet turns away from him. Thomas sees scattered fires leaping on the horizon. Prayer meetings? Or are they riots? Peering at those distant blazes, Thomas jabs idly at the tuner of the radio before him.

". . . rounding out the unprecedented span of twenty-four hours of continuous daylight in much of the Eastern Hemisphere, an endless daybreak over the Near East and an endless noon over Siberia, eastern China, the Philippines, and Indonesia. Meanwhile western Europe and the Americas remain locked in endless night. . . ."

". . . then spake Joshua to the Lord in the day when the Lord delivered up the Amorites before the children of Israel, and he said in the sight of Israel, Sun, stand thou still upon Gibeon; and thou, Moon, in the valley of Ajalon. And the sun stood still, and the moon stayed, until the people had avenged themselves upon their enemies. Is this not written in the book of Jasher? So the sun stood still in the midst of heaven, and hasted not to go down about a whole day. . . ."

". . . an astonishing culmination, apparently, to the campaign led by Thomas Davidson of Reno, Nevada, known popularly as Thomas the Proclaimer. The shaggy-bearded, long-haired, self-designated Apostle of Peace brought his Crusade of Faith to a climax yesterday with the worldwide program of simultaneous prayer that appears to have been the cause of..."

> *Watchman, does its beauteous ray*
> *Aught of joy or hope foretell?*
> *Traveler, yes; it brings the day,*
> *Promised day of Israel.*

Kraft says sharply, "Do you hear what they're singing, Thomas? You've got to speak to them. You got them into this; now they want you to tell them you'll get them out of it."

"Not yet, Saul."

"You mustn't let your moment slip by. Show them that God still speaks through you!"

"When God is ready to speak again," Thomas says frostily, "I'll let His words come forth. Not before." He glares at Kraft and punches for another change of station.

"... continued meetings in Washington, but no communiqué as yet. Meanwhile, at the United Nations..."

"... Behold, He cometh with clouds; and every eye shall see Him, and they also which pierced Him: and all kindreds of the Earth shall wail because of Him. Even so, Amen..."

"... outbreaks of looting in Caracas, Mexico City, Oakland, and Vancouver. But in the daylight half of the world, violence and other disruption has been slight, though an unconfirmed report from Moscow..."

"... and when, brethren, when did the sun cease in its course? At six in the morning, brethren, six in the morning, Jerusalem time! And on what day, brethren? Why, the sixth of June, the sixth day of the sixth month! *Six—six—six!* And what does Holy Writ tell us, my dearly beloved ones, in the thirteenth chapter of Revelations? That a beast shall rise up out of the sea, having seven heads and ten horns, and upon his horns ten crowns, and upon his heads the name of blasphemy. And the Holy Book tells us the number of the beast, beloved, and the number is six hundred three score and six, wherein we see again the significant digits, *six—six—six!* Who then can deny that these are the last days, and that the Apocalypse must be upon us? Thus in this time of woe and fire as we sit upon this stilled planet awaiting His judgment, we must..."

"... latest observatory report confirms that no appreciable momentum effects could be detected as the Earth shifted to its present period of rotation. Scientists agree that the world's abrupt slowing on its axis should have produced a global catastrophe leading, perhaps, to the destruction of all life. However, nothing but minor tidal disturbances have been recorded so far. Two hours ago, we interviewed Presidential Science Adviser Raymond Bartell, who made this statement:

" 'Calculations now show that the Earth's period of rotation and its period of revolution have suddenly become equal; that is, the day and the year now have the same length. This locks the Earth into its present position relative to the sun, so that the side of the Earth now enjoying daylight will continue indefinitely to do so, while the other side will remain permanently in night. Other effects of the slowdown that might have been expected include the flooding of coastal areas, the collapse of most buildings, and a series of earthquakes and volcanic eruptions, but none of these things seem to have happened. For the moment we have no rational explanation of all this, and I must admit it's a great temptation to say that Thomas the Proclaimer must have managed to get his miracle, because there isn't any other apparent way of...' "

"...I am Alpha and Omega, the beginning and the ending, saith the Lord, which is, and which was, and which is to come, the Almighty...."

With a fierce fingerthrust Thomas silences all the radio's clamoring voices. Alpha and Omega! Apocalyptist garbage! The drivel of hysterical preachers pouring from a thousand transmitters, poisoning the air! Thomas despises all these criers of doom. None of them knows anything. No one understands. His throat fills with a turbulence of angry incoherent words, almost choking him. A coppery taste of denunciations. Kraft again urges him to speak. Thomas glowers. Why doesn't Kraft do the speaking himself, for once? He's a truer believer than I am. He's the real prophet. But of course the idea is ridiculous. Kraft has no eloquence, no fire. Only ideas and visions. He'd bore everybody to splinters. Thomas succumbs. He beckons with his fingertips. "The microphone," he mutters. "Let me have the microphone."

Among his entourage there is fluttery excitement. "He wants the mike!" they murmur. "Give him the mike!" Much activity on the part of the technicians. Kraft presses a plaque of cold metal into the Proclaimer's hand. Grins, winks. "Make their hearts soar," Kraft whispers. "Send them on a trip!" Everyone waits. In the valley the torches bob and weave; have they begun dancing down there? Overhead the pocked moon holds its corner of the sky in frosty grasp. The stars are chained to their places. Thomas draws a deep breath and lets the air travel inward, upward, surging to the recesses of his skull. He waits for the good lightheadedness to come upon him, the buoyancy that liberates his tongue. He thinks he is ready to speak. He hears the desperate chanting: *"Tho-mas! Tho-mas! Tho-mas!"* It is more than half a day since his last public statement. He is tense and hollow; he has fasted throughout this Day of the Sign, and of course he has not slept. No one has slept.

"Friends," he begins. "Friends, this is Thomas."

The amplifiers hurl his voice outward. A thousand loud-speakers drifting in the air pick up his words and they bounce across the valley, returning as jagged echoes. He hears cries, eerie shrieks; his own name ascends to him in blurry distortions. *Too-mis! Too-mis! Too-mis!*

"Nearly a full day has passed," he says, "since the Lord gave us the Sign for which we asked. For us it has been a long day of darkness, and for others it has been a day of strange light, and for all of us there has been fear. But this I say to you now: BE . . . NOT . . . AFRAID. For the Lord is good and we are the Lord's."

Now he pauses. Not only for effect; his throat is raging. He signals furiously and Kraft, scowling, hands him a flask. Thomas takes a deep gulp of the good red wine, cool, strong. Ah. He glances at the screen beside him: the video pickup relayed from the valley. What lunacy down there! Wild-eyed, sweaty madmen, half naked and worse, jumping up and down! Crying out his name, invoking him as though he were divine. *Too-mis! Too-mis!*

"There are those who tell you now," Thomas goes on, "that the end of days is at hand, that judgment is come. They talk of apocalypses and the wrath of God. And what do I say to that? I say: BE . . . NOT . . . AFRAID. The Lord God is a God of mercy. We asked Him for a Sign, and a Sign was given. Should we not therefore rejoice? Now we may be certain of His presence and His guidance. Ignore the doom-sayers. Put away your fears. We live now in God's love!"

Thomas halts again. For the first time in his memory he has no sense of being in command of his audience. Is he

reaching them at all? Is he touching the right chords? Or
has he begun already to lose them? Maybe it was a mistake
to let Kraft nag him into speaking so soon. He thought he
was ready; maybe not. Now he sees Kraft staring at him,
aghast, pantomiming the gestures of speech, silently telling
him, *Get with it, you've got to keep talking now!* Thomas'
self-assurance momentarily wavers, and terror floods his
soul, for he knows that if he falters at this point he may
well be destroyed by the forces he has set loose. Teetering
at the brink of an abyss, he searches frantically for his customary confidence. Where is that steely column of words
that ordinarily rises unbidden from the depths of him? Another gulp of wine, fast. Good. Kraft, nervously rubbing
hands together, essays a smile of encouragement. Thomas
tugs at his hair. He pushes back his shoulders, thrusts out
his chest. Be not afraid! He feels control returning after the
frightening lapse. They are his, all those who listen. They
have always been his. What are they shouting in the valley
now? No longer his name, but some new cry. He strains to
hear. Two words. What are they? *De-dum! De-dum! De-
dum!* What? *De-dum! De-dum! De-dum, Too-mis, de-dum!*
What? What? "The sun," Kraft says. The sun? Yes. They
want the sun. "The sun! The sun! The sun!"

"The sun," Thomas says. "Yes. This day the sun stands
still, as our Sign from Him. BE NOT AFRAID! A long dawn
over Jerusalem has He decreed, and a long night for us, but
not so very long, and soon sped." Thomas feels the power
surging at last. Kraft nods to him, and Thomas nods back
and spits a stream of wine at Kraft's feet. He is aware of
that consciousness of risk in which the joy of prophecy lies:
I will bring forth what I see, and trust to God to make it
real. That feeling of risk accepted, of triumph over doubt.
Calmly he says, "The Day of the Sign will end in a few
minutes. Once more the world will turn, and moon and stars

will move across the sky. So put down your torches, and go to your homes, and offer up joyful prayers of thanksgiving to Him, for this night will pass, and dawn will come at the appointed hour."

How do you know, Thomas? Why are you so sure?

He hands the microphone to Saul Kraft and calls for more wine. Around him are tense faces, rigid eyes, clamped jaws. Thomas smiles. He goes among them, slapping backs, punching shoulders, laughing, embracing, winking ribaldly, poking his fingers playfully into their ribs. Be of good cheer, ye who follow my way! Share ye not my faith in Him? He asks Kraft how he came across. Fine, Kraft says, except for that uneasy moment in the middle. Thomas slaps Kraft's back hard enough to loosen teeth. Good old Saul. My inspiration, my counselor, my beacon. Thomas pushes his flask toward Kraft's face. Kraft shakes his head. He is fastidious about drinking, about decorum in general, as fastidious as Thomas is disreputable. You disapprove of me, don't you, Saul? But you need my charisma. You need my energy and my big loud voice. Too bad, Saul, that prophets aren't as neat and house-broken as you'd like them to be. "Ten o'clock," someone says. "It's now been going on for twenty-four hours."

A woman says, "The moon! Look! Didn't the moon just start to move again?"

From Kraft: "You wouldn't be able to see it with the naked eye. Not possibly. No way."

"Ask Thomas! Ask him!"

One of the technicians cries, "I can feel it! The Earth is turning!"

"Look, the stars!"

"Thomas! Thomas!"

They rush to him. Thomas, benign, serene, stretching forth his huge hands to reassure them, tells them that he has felt it too. Yes. There is motion in the universe again. Perhaps the turnings of the heavenly bodies are too subtle to be detected in a single glance, perhaps an hour or more will be needed for verification, and yet he knows, he is sure, he is absolutely sure. The Lord has withdrawn His Sign. The Earth turns. "Let us sleep now," Thomas says joyfully, "and greet the dawn in happiness."

2.

The Dance of the Apocalyptists

In late afternoon every day a band of Apocalyptists gathers by the stinking shore of Lake Erie to dance the sunset in. Their faces are painted with grotesque nightmare stripes; their expressions are wild; they fling themselves about in jerky, lurching steps, awkward and convulsive, the classic death-dance. Two immense golden loudspeakers, mounted like idols atop metal spikes rammed into the soggy soil, bellow abstract rhythms at them from either side. The leader of the group stands thigh-deep in the fouled waters, chanting, beckoning, directing them with short blurted cries: "People . . . holy people . . . chosen people . . . blessed people . . . persecuted people. . . . Dance! . . . Dance! . . . The end . . . is near. . . ." And they dance. Fingers shooting electrically into the air, elbows ramming empty space, knees rising high, they scramble toward the lake, withdraw, advance, withdraw, advance, three steps forward and two steps back, a will-you-won't-you-will-you-won't-you approach to salvation.

They have been doing this seven times a week since the beginning of the year, this fateful, terminal year, but only in the week since the Day of the Sign have they drawn much of an audience. At the outset, in frozen January, no one would bother to come to watch a dozen madmen capering on the windswept ice. Then the cult began getting sporadic television coverage, and that brought a few curiosity seekers. On the milder nights of April perhaps thirty dancers and twenty onlookers could be found at the lake. But now it is June, apocalyptic June, when the Lord in all His Majesty has revealed Himself, and the nightly dances are an event that brings thousands out of Cleveland's suburbs. Police lines hold the mob at a safe distance from the performers. A closed-circuit video loop relays the action to those on the outskirts of the crowd, too far away for a direct view. Network copters hover, cameras ready in case something unusual happens—the death of a dancer, the bursting loose of the mob, mass conversions, another miracle, anything. The air is cool tonight. The sun, delicately blurred and purpled by the smoky haze that perpetually thickens this region's sky, drops toward the breast of the lake. The dancers move in frenzied patterns, those in the front rank approaching the water, dipping their toes, retreating. Their leader, slapping the lake, throwing up fountaining spumes, continues to exhort them in a high, strained voice.

"People . . . holy people . . . chosen people . . ."

"Hallelujah! Hallelujah!"

"Come and be sealed! Blessed people . . . persecuted people . . . Come! Be! Sealed! Unto! The! Lord!"

"Hallelujah!"

The spectators shift uneasily. Some nudge and snigger. Some, staring fixedly, lock their arms and glower. Some move their lips in silent prayer or silent curses. Some look tempted to lurch forward and join the dance. Some will. Each night, there are a few who go forward. Each night, also, there are some who attempt to burst the police lines and attack the dancers. In June alone seven spectators have suffered heart seizures at the nightly festival: five fatalities.

"Servants of God!" cries the man in the water.

"Hallelujah!" reply the dancers.

"The year is speeding! The time is coming!"

"Hallelujah!"

"The trumpet shall sound! And we shall be saved!"

"Yes! Yes! Yes! Yes!"

Oh, the fervor of the dance! The wildness of the faces! The painted stripes swirl and run as sweat invades the thick greasy pigments. One could strew hot coals on the shore, now, and the dancers would advance all the same, oblivious, blissful. The choreography of their faith absorbs them wholly at this moment and they admit of no distractions. There is so little time left, after all, and such a great output of holy exertion is required of them before the end! June is almost half spent. The year itself is almost half spent. January approaches: the dawning of the new millennium, the day of the final trump, the moment of apocalypse. January 1, 2000: six and a half months away. And already He has given the Sign that the end of days is at hand. They dance. Through ecstatic movement comes salvation.

"Fear God, and give glory to Him; for the hour of His Judgment is come!"

"Hallelujah! Amen!"

"And worship Him that made heaven, and earth, and the sea, and the fountains of waters!"

"Hallelujah! Amen!"

They dance. The music grows more intense: prickly blurts of harsh tone flickering through the air. Spectators begin to clap hands and sway. Here comes the first convert of the night, now, a woman, middle-aged, plump, beseeching her way through the police cordon. An electronic device checks her for concealed weapons and explosive devices;

she is found to be harmless; she passes the line and runs, stumbling, to join the dance.

"For the great day of His wrath is come; and who shall be able to stand?"

"Amen!"

"Servants of God! Be sealed unto Him, and be saved!"

"Sealed . . . sealed . . . We shall be sealed. . . . We shall be saved. . . ."

"And I saw four angels standing on the four corners of the Earth, holding the four winds of the Earth, that the wind should not blow on the Earth, nor on the sea, nor on any tree," roars the man in the water. "And I saw another angel ascending from the east, having the seal of the living God: and he cried with a loud voice to the four angels, to whom it was given to hurt the Earth and the sea, saying, Hurt not the Earth, neither the sea, nor the trees, till we have sealed the servants of our God in their foreheads."

"Sealed! Hallelujah! Amen!"

"And I heard the number of them which were sealed: and there were sealed an hundred and forty and four thousand of all the tribes of the children of Israel."

"Sealed! Sealed!"

"Come to me and be sealed! Dance and be sealed!"

The sun drops into the lake. The purple stain of sunset spreads across the horizon. The dancers shriek ecstatically and rush toward the water. They splash one another; they offer frantic baptisms in the murky lake; they drink, they spew forth what they have drunk, they drink again. Surrounding their leader. Seeking his blessing. An angry thick mutter from the onlookers. They are disgusted by this hectic show of faith. A menagerie, they say. A circus sideshow. These freaks. These godly freaks. Whom we have come to watch, so that we may despise them.

And if they are right? And if the world *does* end next January 1, and we go to hellfire, while *they* are saved? Impossible. Preposterous. Absurd. But yet, who's to say? Only last week the Earth stood still a whole day. We live under His hand now. We always have, but now we have no liberty to doubt it. We can no longer deny that He's up there, watching us, listening to us, thinking about us. And if the end is really coming, as the crazy dancers think, what should I do to prepare for it? Should I join the dance? God help me. God help us all. Now the darkness falls. Look at the lunatics wallowing in the lake.

"Hallelujah! Amen!"

3.

The Sleep of Reason Produces Monsters

When I was about seven years old, which is to say somewhere in the late 1960's, I was playing out in front of the house on a Sunday morning, perhaps stalking some ladybirds for my insect collection, when three freckle-faced Irish kids who lived on the next block came wandering by. They were on their way home from church. The youngest one was my age, and the other two must have been eight or nine. To me they were Big Boys: ragged, strong, swaggering, alien. My father was a college professor and theirs was probably a bus conductor or a coal miner, and so they were as strange to me as a trio of tourists from Patagonia would have been. They stopped and watched me for a minute, and then the biggest one called me out into the street, and he asked me how it was that they never saw me in church on Sundays.

The simplest and most tactful thing for me to tell them would have been that I didn't happen to be Roman Catholic.

That was true. I think that all they wanted to find out was what church I *did* go to, since I obviously didn't go to theirs. Was I Jewish, Moslem, Presbyterian, Baptist, what? But I was a smug little snot then, and instead of handling the situation diplomatically I cheerfully told them that I didn't go to church because I didn't believe in God.

They looked at me as though I had just blown my nose on the American flag.

"Say that again?" the biggest one demanded.

"I don't believe in God," I said. "Religion's just a big fake. My father says so, and I think he's right."

They frowned and backed off a few paces and conferred in low, earnest voices, with many glances in my direction. Evidently I was their first atheist. I assumed we would now have a debate on the existence of the Deity: they would explain to me the motives that led them to use up so many valuable hours on their knees inside the Church of Our Lady of the Sorrows, and then I would try to show them how silly it was to worry so much about an invisible old man in the sky. But a theological disputation wasn't their style. They came out of their huddle and strolled toward me, and I suddenly detected menace in their eyes, and just as the two smaller ones lunged at me I slipped past them and started to run. They had longer legs, but I was more agile; besides, I was on my home block and knew the turf better. I sprinted halfway down the street, darted into an alley, slipped through the open place in the back of the Allertons' garage, doubled back up the street via the rear lane, and made it safely into our house by way of the kitchen door. For the next couple of days I stayed close to home after school and kept a wary watch, but the pious Irish lads never came around again to punish the blasphemer. After that I learned to be more careful about expressing my opinions on religious matters.

But I never became a believer. I had a natural predisposition toward skepticism. *If you can't measure it, it isn't there.* That included not only Old Whiskers and His Only Begotten Son, but all the other mystic baggage that people liked to carry around in those tense credulous years: the flying saucers, Zen Buddhism, the Atlantis cult, Hare Krishna, macrobiotics, telepathy and other species of extrasensory perception, theosophy, entropy-worship, astrology, and such. I was willing to accept neutrinos, quasars, the theory of continental drift, and the various species of quarks, because I respected the evidence for their existence; I couldn't buy the other stuff, the irrational stuff, the assorted opiates of the masses. When the Moon is in the seventh house, etc., etc.—sorry, no. I clung to the path of reason as I made my uneasy journey toward maturity, and hardheaded little Billy Gifford, smartypants bug collector, remained unchurched as he ripened into Professor William F. Gifford, Ph.D., of the Department of Physics, Harvard. I wasn't *hostile* to organized religion, I just ignored it, as I might ignore a newspaper account of a jai-alai tournament in Afghanistan.

I envied the faithful their faith, oh, yes. When the dark times got darker, how sweet it must have been to be able to rush to Our Lady of the Sorrows for comfort! *They* could pray, *they* had the illusion that a divine plan governed this best of all possible worlds, while I was left in bleak, stormy limbo, dismally aware that the universe makes no sense and that the only universal truth there is is that Entropy Eventually Wins.

There were times when I wanted genuinely to be able to pray, when I was weary of operating solely on my own existential capital, when I wanted to grovel and cry out, *Okay, Lord, I give up, You take it from here.* I had favors to ask of Him. God, let my little girl's fever go down. Let my plane not crash. Let them not shoot this President too. Let the races learn how to live in peace before the blacks get around to burning down my street. Let the peace-loving enlightened students not bomb the computer center this semester. Let the next kindergarten drug scandal not erupt in my boy's school. Let the lion lie down with the lamb. As we zoomed along on the Chaos Express, I was sometimes tempted toward godliness the way the godly are tempted toward sin. But my love of divine reason left me no way to opt for the irrational. Call it stiffneckedness, call it rampant egomania: no matter how bad things got, Bill Gifford wasn't going to submit to the tyranny of a hobgoblin. Even a benevolent one. Even if I had favors to ask of Him. So much to ask; so little faith. Intellectual honesty *über alles*, Gifford! While every year things were a little worse than the last.

When I was growing up, in the 1970's, it was fashionable for educated and serious-minded people to get together and tell each other that Western civilization was collapsing. The Germans had a word for it, *Schadenfreude*, the pleasure one gets from talking about catastrophes. And the 1970's were shadowed by catastrophes, real or expected: the pollution escalation, the population explosion, Vietnam and all the little Vietnams, the supersonic transport, black separatism, white backlash, student unrest, extremist women's lib, the neofascism of the New Left, the neonihilism of the New Right, a hundred other varieties of dynamic irrationality going full blast, yes, ample fuel for the *Schadenfreude* syndrome. Yes, my parents and their civilized friends said solemnly, sadly, gleefully, it's all blowing up, it's all going smash, it's all whooshing down the drain. Through the fumes of the Saturday-night pot came the inevitable portentous quotes from Yeats: *Things fall apart; the center cannot hold; mere anarchy is loosed upon the world.* Well, what shall we do about it? Perhaps it's really beyond our control now. Brethren, shall we pray? Lift up your voices unto Him! But I can't. I'd feel like a damned fool. Forgive me, God, but I must deny You! *The best lack all conviction, while the worst are full of passionate intensity.*

And of course everything got much more awful than the doomsayers of the 1970's really expected. Even those who most dearly relished enumerating the calamities to come still thought, beneath their grim joy, that somehow reason ultimately would triumph. The most gloomy Jeremiah entertained secret hopes that the noble ecological resolutions would eventually be translated into meaningful environmental action, that the crazy birth spiral would be checked in time, that the strident rhetoric of the innumerable protest groups would be tempered and modulated as time brought them the beginning of a fulfillment of their revolutionary goals—but no. Came the 1980's, the decade of my young manhood, and all the hysteria jumped to the next-highest energy level. That was when we began having the Gas Mask Days. The programmed electrical shutdowns. The elegantly orchestrated international chaos of the Third World People's Prosperity Group. The airport riots. The black rains. The Computer Purge. The Brazilian Pacification Program. The Claude Harkins Book List with its accompanying library-burnings. The Ecological Police Action. The Genetic Purity League and its even more frightening black counterpart. The Children's Crusade for Sanity. The Nine Weeks' War. The Night of the Lasers. The center had long ago ceased to hold; now we were strapped to a runaway wheel. Amidst the furies I studied, married, brought forth young, built a career, fought off daily terror, and, like everyone else, waited for the inevitable final calamity.

Who could doubt that it would come? Not you, not I. And not the strange wild-eyed folk who emerged among us like dark growths pushing out of rotting logs, the Apocalyptists, who raised *Schadenfreude* to the sacramental level and organized an ecstatic religion of doom. The end of the world, they told us, was scheduled for January 1, A.D. 2000, and upon that date, 144,000 elite souls, who had "sealed" themselves unto God by devotion and good works, would be saved; the rest of us poor sinners would be hauled before the Judge. I could see their point. Although I rejected their talk of the Second Coming, having long ago rejected the First, and although I shared neither their confidence in the exact date of the apocalypse nor their notions of how the survivors would be chosen, I agreed with them that the end was close at hand. The fact that for a quarter of a century we had been milking giddy cocktail-party chatter out of the impending collapse of Western civilization didn't of itself guarantee that Western civilization wasn't going to collapse; some of the things people like to say at cocktail parties can hit the target. As a physicist with a decent understanding of the entropic process I found all the signs of advanced societal decay easy to identify: for a century we had been increasing the complexity of society's functions so that an ever-higher level of organization was required in order to make things run, and for much of that time we had simultaneously been trending toward total universal democracy, toward a world consisting of several billion self-governing republics with a maximum of three citizens each. Any closed system which experiences simultaneous sharp increases in mechanical complexity and in entropic diffusion is going to go to pieces long before the maximum distribution of energy is reached. The pattern of consents and contracts on which civilization is based is destroyed; every social interaction, from parking your car to settling an international boundary dispute, becomes a problem that can be handled only by means of force, since all "civilized" techniques of reconciling disagreement have been suspended as irrelevant; when the delivery of mail is a matter of private negotiation between the citizen and his postman, what hope is there for the rule of reason? Somewhere, somehow, we had passed a point of no return—in 1984, 1972, maybe even that ghastly day in November of 1963—and nothing now could save us from plunging over the brink.

Nothing?

Out of Nevada came Thomas, shaggy Thomas, Thomas the Proclaimer, rising above the slot machines and the roulette wheels to cry, If ye have faith, ye shall be saved! An anti-Apocalyptist prophet, no less, whose message was that civilization still might be preserved, that it was not yet too late. The voice of hope, the enemy of entropy, the new Apostle of Peace. Though to people like me he looked just as wild-eyed and hairy and dangerous and terrifyingly psychotic as the worshipers of the holocaust, for he, like the Apocalyptists, dealt in forces operating outside the realm of sanity. By rights he should have come out of the backwoods of Arkansas or the crazier corners of California, but he didn't, he was a desert rat, a Nevadan, a sand-eating latter-day John the Baptist. A true prophet for our times, too, seedy, disreputable, a wine-swiller, a cynic. Capable of beginning a global telecast sermon with a belch. An ex-soldier who had happily napalmed whole provinces during the Brazilian Pacification Program. A part-time dealer in bootlegged hallucinogens. An expert at pocket-picking and computer-jamming. He had gone into the evangelism business because he thought he could make an easy buck that way, peddling the Gospels and appropriating the collection box, but a funny thing had happened to him, he claimed: he had seen the Lord, he had discovered the error of his ways, he had become inflamed with righteousness. Hiding not his grimy past, he now offered himself as a walking personification of redemption: *Look ye, if I can be saved from sin, there's hope for everyone!* The media picked him up. That magnificent voice of his, that great mop of hair, those eyes, that hypnotic self-confidence-perfect. He walked from California to Florida to proclaim the coming millennium. And gathered followers, thousands, millions, all those who weren't yet ready to let Armageddon begin, and he made them pray and pray and pray, he held revival meetings that were beamed to Karachi and Katmandu and Addis Ababa and Shanghai, he preached no particular theology and no particular scripture, but only a smooth ecumenical theism that practically anybody could swallow, whether he be Confucianist or Moslem or Hindu. Listen, Thomas said, there is a God, some kind of all-powerful being out there whose divine plan guides the universe, and He watches over us, and don't you believe otherwise! And He is good and will not let us come to harm if we hew to His path. And He has tested us with all these troubles, in order to measure the depth of our faith in Him. So let's show Him, brethren! Let's all pray together and send up a great shout unto Him! For He would certainly give a Sign, and the unbelievers would at last be converted, and the epoch of purity would commence. People said, Why not give it a try? We've got a lot to gain and nothing to lose. A vulgar version of the old Pascal wager: if He's really there, He may help us, and if He's not, we've only wasted a little time. So the hour of beseeching was set.

In faculty circles we had a good deal of fun with the whole idea, we brittle worldly rational types, but sometimes there was a nervous edge to our jokes and a forced heartiness to our laughter, as if some of us suspected that Pascal might have been offering pretty good odds, or that Thomas might just have hit on something. Naturally I was among the skeptics, though as usual I kept my doubts to myself. (The lesson learned so long ago, the narrow escape from the

Irish lads.) I hadn't really paid much attention to Thomas and his message, any more than I did to football scores or children's video programs: not my sphere, not my concern. But as the day of prayer drew near, the old temptation beset me. *Give in at last, Gifford. Bow your head and offer homage. Even if He's the myth you've always known He is, do it. Do it!* I argued with myself. I told myself not to be an idiot, not to yield to the age-old claims of superstition. I reminded myself of the holy wars, the Inquisition, the lascivious Renaissance popes, all the crimes of the pious. *So what, Gifford? Can't you be an ordinary humble God-fearing human being for once in your life? Down on your knees beside your brethren? Read your Pascal. Suppose He exists and is listening, and suppose your refusal is the one that tips the scales against mankind? We're not asking so very much.* Still I fought the sly inner voice. To believe is absurd, I cried. I must not let despair stampede me into the renunciation of reason, even in this apocalyptic moment. Thomas is a cunning ruffian and his followers are hysterical grubby fools. *And you're an arrogant elitist, Gifford. Who may live long enough to repent his arrogance.* It was psychological warfare, Gifford vs. Gifford, reason vs. faith.

In the end reason lost. I was jittery, off balance, demoralized. The most astonishing people were coming out in support of Thomas the Proclaimer, and I felt increasingly isolated, a man of ice, heart of stone, the village atheist scowling at Christmas wreaths. Up until the final moment I wasn't sure what I was going to do, but then the hour struck and I found myself in my study, alone, door locked, safely apart from wife and children—who had already, all of them, somewhat defiantly announced their intentions of participating—and there I was on my knees, feeling foolish, feeling preposterous, my cheeks blazing, my lips moving, saying the words. *Saying the words.* Around the world the billions of believers prayed, and I also. I too prayed, embarrassed by my weakness, and the pain of my shame was a stone in my throat.

And the Lord heard us, and He gave a Sign. And for a day and a night (less 1×12^{-4} sidereal day) the Earth moved not around the sun, neither did it rotate. And the laws of momentum were confounded, as was I. Then Earth again took up its appointed course, as though nothing out of the ordinary had occurred. Imagine my chagrin. I wish I knew where to find those Irish boys. I have some apologies to make.

4.

Thomas Preaches in the Marketplace

I hear what you're saying. You tell me I'm a prophet. You tell me I'm a saint. Some of you even tell me I'm the Son of God come again. You tell me I made the sun stand still over Jerusalem. Well, no, I didn't do that, the Lord Almighty did that, the Lord of Hosts. Through His divine Will, in response to your prayers. And I'm only the vehicle through which your prayers were channeled. I'm not any kind of saint, folks. I'm not the Son of God reborn, or any of the other crazy things you've been saying I am. I'm only Thomas.

Who am I?

I'm just a voice. A spokesman. A tool through which His will was made manifest. I'm not giving you the old humility act, friends, I'm trying to make you see the truth about me.

Who am I?

I'll tell you who I was, though you know it already. I

was a bandit, I was a man of evil, I was a defiler of the law. A killer, a liar, a drunkard, a cheat! I did what I damned pleased. I was a law unto myself. If I ever got caught, you bet I wouldn't have whined for mercy. I'd have spit in the judge's face and taken my punishment with my eyes open. Only I never got caught, because my luck was running good and because this is a time when a really bad man can flourish, when the wicked are raised high and the virtuous are ground into the mud. Outside the law, that was me! Thomas the criminal! Thomas the brigand, thumbing his nose! Doing bad was my religion, all the time—when I was down there in Brazil with those flamethrowers, or when I was free-lancing your pockets in our cities, or when I was ringing up funny numbers on the big computers. I belonged to Satan if ever a man did, that's the truth, and then what happened? The Lord came along to Satan and said to him, Satan, give me Thomas, I have need of him. And Satan handed me over to Him, because Satan is God's servant too.

And the Lord took me and shook me and knocked me around and said, Thomas, you're nothing but trash!

And I said, I know that, Lord, but who was it who made me that way?

And the Lord laughed and said, You've got guts, Thomas, talking back to me like that. I like a man with guts. But you're wrong, fellow. I made you with the potential to be a saint or a sinner, and you chose to be a sinner, yes, your own free will! You think I'd bother to create people to be wicked? I'm not interested in creating puppets, Thomas, I set out to make me a race of *human beings*. I gave you your options and you opted for evil, eh, Thomas? Isn't that the truth?

And I said, Well, Lord, maybe it is; I don't know.

And the Lord God grew annoyed with me and took me again and shook me again and knocked me around some more, and when I picked myself up I had a puffed lip and a bloody nose, and He asked me how I would do things if I could live my life over again from the start. And I looked Him right in the eye and said, Well, Lord, I'd say that being evil paid off pretty well for me. I lived a right nice life and I had all my happies and I never spent a day behind bars, oh, no. So tell me, Lord, since I got away with everything the first time, why shouldn't I opt to be a sinner again?

And He said, Because you've done that already, and now it's time for you to do something else.

I said, What's that, Lord?

He said, I want you to do something important for me, Thomas. There's a world out there full of people who've lost all faith, people without hope, people who've made up their minds it's no use trying any more, the world's going to end. I want to reach those people somehow, Thomas, and tell them that they're wrong. And show them that they can shape their own destiny, that if they have faith in themselves and in me they can build a good world.

I said, That's easy, Lord. Why don't You just appear in the sky and say that to them, like You just did to me?

He laughed again and said, Oh, no, Thomas, that's much too easy. I told you, I don't run a puppet show. They've got to *want* to lift themselves up out of despair. They've got to take the first step by themselves. You follow me, Thomas?

Yes, Lord, but where do I come in?

And He said, You go to them, Thomas, and you tell them all about your wasted, useless, defiant life, and then tell them how the Lord gave you a chance to do something worthwhile for a change, and how you rose up above your evil self and accepted the opportunity. And then tell them to gather and pray and restore their faith, and ask for a Sign from on high. Thomas, if they listen to you, if they pray and it's sincere prayer, I promise you I *will* give them a Sign,

I *will* reveal myself to them, and all doubt will drop like scales from their eyes. Will you do that thing for me, Thomas?

Friends, I listened to the Lord, and I discovered myself shaking and quivering and bursting into sweat, and in a moment, in the twinkling of an eye, I wasn't the old filthy Thomas any more, I was somebody new and clean, I was a man with a high purpose, a man with a belief in something bigger and better than his own greedy desires. And I went down among you, changed as I was, and I told my tale, and all of you know the rest of the story, how we came freely together and offered up our hearts to Him, and how He vouchsafed us a miracle these two and a half weeks past, and gave us a Sign that He still watches over us.

But what do I see now, in these latter days after the giving of the Sign? What do I see?

Where is that new world of faith? Where is that new dream of hope? Where is mankind shoulder to shoulder, praising Him and working together to reach the light?

What do I see? I see this rotting planet turning black inside and splitting open at the core. I see the cancer of doubt. I see the virus of confusion. I see His Sign misinterpreted on every hand, and its beauty trampled on and destroyed.

I still see painted fools dancing and beating on drums and screaming that the world is going to be destroyed at the end of this year of nineteen hundred and ninety-nine. What madness is this? Has God not spoken? Has He not told us joyful news? God is with us! God is good! Why do these Apocalyptists not yet accept the truth of His Sign?

Even worse! Each day new madnesses take form! What are these cults sprouting up among us? Who are these people who demand of God that He return and spell out His intentions, as though the Sign wasn't enough for them? And who are these cowardly blasphemers who say we must lie down in fear and weep piteous tears, because we have invoked not God but Satan, and destruction is our lot? Who are these men of empty souls who bleat and mumble and snivel in our midst? And look at your lofty churchmen, in their priestly robes and glittering tiaras, trying to explain away the Sign as some accident of nature! What talk is this from God's own ministers? And behold the formerly godless ones, screeching like frightened monkeys now that their godlessness has been ripped from them! What do I see? I see madness and terror on all sides, where I should see only joy abounding!

I beg you, friends, have care, take counsel with your souls. I beg you, think clearly now if you ever have thought at all. Choose a wise path, friends, or you will throw away all the glory of the Day of the Sign and lay waste to our great achievement. Give no comfort to the forces of darkness. Keep away from these peddlers of lunatic creeds. Strive to recapture the wonder of that moment when all mankind spoke with a single voice. I beg you—how can you have doubt of Him now?—I beg you—faith—the triumph of faith—let us not allow—let us—not allow—not—allow—

(Jesus, my throat! All this shouting, it's like swallowing fire. Give me that bottle, will you? Come on, give it here! The wine. The wine. Now. Ah. Oh, that's better! Much better, oh, yes. No, wait, give it back—good, good—stop looking at me like that, Saul. Ah. *Ah*.)

And so I beseech you today, brothers and sisters in the Lord—brothers and sisters (what was I saying, Saul? what did I start to say?)—I call upon you to rededicate yourselves—to pledge yourselves to—to (is that it? I can't remember)—to a new Crusade of Faith, that's what we need, a purging of all our doubts and all our hesitations and all our (oh, Jesus, Saul, I'm lost, I don't remember where the hell

I'm supposed to be. Let the music start playing. Quick. That's it. Good and loud. Louder.) Folks, let's all sing! Raise your voices joyously unto Him!

> *I shall praise the Lord my God,*
> *Fountain of all power . . .*

That's the way! Sing! Everybody sing!

5.

Ceremonies of Innocence

Throughout the world the quest for an appropriate response to the event of June 6 continues. No satisfactory interpretation of that day's happenings has yet been established, though many have been proposed. Meanwhile passions run high; tempers easily give way; a surprising degree of violence has entered the situation. Clearly the temporary slowing of the earth's axial rotation must have imposed exceptional emotional stress on the entire global population, creating severe strains that have persisted and even intensified in the succeeding weeks. Instances of seemingly motiveless crimes, particularly arson and vandalism, have greatly increased. Government authorities in Brazil, India, the United Arab Republic, and Italy have suggested that clandestine revolutionary or counterrevolutionary groups are behind much of this activity, taking advantage of the widespread mood of uncertainty to stir discontent. No evidence of this has thus far been made public. Much hostility has been directed toward the organized religions, a phenomenon for which there is as yet no generally accepted explanation, although several sociologists have asserted that this pattern of violent anticlerical behavior is a reaction to the failure of most established religious bodies as of this time to provide official interpretations of the so-called "miracle" of June 6. Reports of the destruction by mob action of houses of worship of various faiths, with accompanying injuries or fatalities suffered by ecclesiastical personnel, have come from Mexico, Denmark, Burma, Puerto Rico, Portugal, Hungary, Ethiopia, the Philippines, and, in the United States, Alabama, Colorado, and New York. Statements are promised shortly by leaders of most major faiths. Meanwhile a tendency has developed in certain ecclesiastical quarters toward supporting a mechanistic or rationalistic causation for the June 6 event; thus on Tuesday the Archbishop of York, stressing that he was speaking as a private citizen and not as a prelate of the Church of England, declared that we should not rule out entirely the possibility of a manipulation of the Earth's movements by superior beings native to another planet, intent on spreading confusion preparatory to conquest. Modern theologians, the Archbishop said, see no inherent impossibility in the doctrine of a separate act of creation that brought forth an intelligent species on some extraterrestrial or extragalactic planet, nor is it inconceivable, he went on, that it might be the Lord's ultimate purpose to cause a purging of sinful mankind at the hands of that other species. Thus the slowing of the Earth's rotation may have been an attempt by these enemies from space to capitalize on the emotions generated by the recent campaign of the so-called prophet Thomas the Proclaimer. A spokesman for the Coptic Patriarch of Alexandria, commenting favorably two days later on the Archbishop's theory, added that in the private view of the Patriarch it seems less implausible that such an alien species should exist than that a divine miracle of the June 6 sort could be invoked by popular demand. A number of other religious leaders, similarly speaking unofficially, have cautioned against too rapid acceptance of the divine origin of the June 6 event, without as yet going so far as to embrace the Archbishop of York's suggestion. On Friday Dr. Nathan F. Scharf, President of the Central Conference of American Rabbis, urgently appealed to American and Israeli scientists to produce a computer-generated mathematical schema capable of demonstrating how a unique but natural conjunction of astronomical forces might have resulted in the June 6 event. The only reply to this appeal thus far has come from Ssu-ma Hsiang-ju, Minister of Science of the People's Republic of China, who has revealed that a task force of several hundred Chinese astronomers is already at work on such a project. But his Soviet counterpart, Academician N. V. Posilippov, has on the contrary called for a revision of Marxist-Leninist astronomical theory to take into account what he terms "the possibility of intervention by as yet undefined forces, perhaps of supernatural aspect, in the motions of the heavenly bodies." We may conclude, therefore, that the situation remains in flux. Observers agree that the chief beneficiaries of the June 6 event at this point have been the various recently founded apocalyptic sects, who now regard the so-called Day of the Sign as an indication of the imminent destruction of life on Earth. Undoubtedly much of the current violence and other irrational behavior can be traced to the increased activity of such groups. A related manifestation is the dramatic expansion in recent weeks of older millenarian sects, notably the Pentecostal churches. The Protestant world in general has experienced a rebirth of the Pentecostal-inspired phenomenon known as glossolalia, or "speaking in tongues," a technique for penetrating to revelatory or prophetic levels by means of unreined ecstatic outbursts *illalum gha ghollim ve illalum ghollim ghaznim kroo! Aiha! Kroo illalum nildaz sitamon ghaznim* of seemingly random syllables in no language known to the speaker; the value of this practice has *mehigioo camaleelee honistar zam* been a matter of controversy in religious circles for many centuries.

6.

The Woman Who Is Sore at Heart Reproaches Thomas

I knew he was in our county and I had to get to see him because he was the one who made all this trouble for me. So I went to his headquarters, the place where the broadcasts were being made that week, and I saw him standing in the middle of a group of his followers. A very handsome man, really, somewhat too dirty and wild-looking for my tastes, but you give him a shave and a haircut and he'd be quite attractive in my estimation. Big and strong he is, and when you see him you want to throw yourself into his arms, though of course I was in no frame of mind to do any such thing just then and in any case I'm not that sort of woman. I went right toward him. There was a tremendous crowd in the street, but I'm not discouraged easily, my husband likes to call me his "little bulldog" sometimes, and I just bulled my way through that mob, a little kicking and some elbowing and I think I bit someone's arm once and I got through. There was Thomas and next to him that skinny little man who's always with him, that Saul Kraft, who I guess is his press agent or something. As I got close, three of his bodyguards looked at me and then at each other, probably saying oh-oh, here comes another crank dame, and they started to surround me and move me away, and Thomas wasn't even looking at me, and I began to yell, saying I had to talk to Thomas, I had something important to say. And then this Saul Kraft told them to let go of me and bring me forward. They checked me out for concealed weapons and then Thomas asked me what I wanted.

I felt nervous before him. Such a famous man. But I planted my feet flat on the ground and stuck my jaw up the way Dad taught me, and I said, "You did all this. You've wrecked me, Thomas. You've got me so I don't know if I'm standing on my head or right side up."

He gave me a funny sideways smile. "I did?"

"Look," I said, "I'll tell you how it was. I went to Mass every week, my whole family, Church of the Redeemer on Wilson Avenue. We put money in the plate, we did everything the fathers told us to do, we tried to live good Christian lives, right? Not that we really thought much about God. Whether He was actually up there listening to me saying my paternoster. I figured He was too busy to worry much about me, and I couldn't be too concerned about Him, because He surpasses my understanding, you follow? Instead I prayed to the fathers. To me Father McDermott was like God Himself, in a way, not meaning any disrespect. What I'm trying to say is that the average ordinary person, they don't have a very close relationship with God, you follow? With the church, yes, with the fathers, but not with God. Okay. Now you come along and say the world is in a mess, so let's pray to God to show Himself like in the olden times. I ask Father McDermott about it and he says it's all right, it's permitted even though it isn't an idea that came from Rome, on such-and-such day we'll have this world moment of prayer. So I pray, and the sun stands still. June 6, you made the sun stand still."

"Not me. *Him*." Thomas was smiling again. And looking at me like he could read everything in my soul.

I said, "You know what I mean. It's a miracle, anyway. The biggest miracle since, I don't know, since the Resurrection. The next day we need help, guidance, right? My husband and I, we go to church. *The church is closed.* Locked tight. We go around back and try to find the fathers. Nobody there but a housekeeper and she's scared. Won't open up. Why is the church shut? They're afraid of rioters, she says. Where's Father McDermott? He's gone to the Archdiocese for a conference. So have all the other fathers. Go away, she says. Nobody's here. You follow me, Thomas? Biggest miracle since the Resurrection, *and they close the church the next day.*"

Thomas said, "They got nervous, I guess."

"Nervous? Sure they were nervous. That's my whole point. Where were the fathers when we needed them? Conferring at the Archdiocese. The Cardinal was holding a special meeting about the crisis. *The crisis*, Thomas! God Himself works a miracle, and to the church it's a crisis! What am I supposed to do? Where does it leave me? I need the church, the church has always been telling me that, and all of a sudden the church locks its doors and says to me, Go figure it out by yourself, lady, we won't have a bulletin for a couple of days. The church was scared! I think they were afraid the Lord was going to come in and say we don't need priests any more, we don't need churches, all this organized-religion stuff hasn't worked out so well anyway, so let's forget it and move right into the Millennium."

"Anything big and strange always upsets the people in power," Thomas said, shrugging. "But the church opened again, didn't it?"

"Sure, four days later. Business as usual, except we aren't supposed to ask any questions about June 6 yet. Because they don't have The Word from Rome yet, the interpretation, the official policy." I had to laugh. "Three weeks, almost, since it happened, and the College of Cardinals is still in special consistory, trying to decide what position the church ought to take. Isn't that crazy, Thomas? If the Pope can't recognize a miracle when he sees one, what good is the whole church?"

"All right," Thomas said, "but why blame me?"

"Because you took my church away from me. I can't trust those people any more. I don't know what to believe. We've got God right here beside us, and the church isn't giving any leadership. What do we do now? How do we handle this thing?"

"Have faith, my child," he said, "and pray for salvation, and remain steadfast in your righteousness." He said a lot of other stuff like that too, rattling it off like he was a computer programmed to deliver blessings. I could tell he wasn't sincere. He wasn't trying to answer me, just to calm me down and get rid of me.

"No," I said, breaking in on him. "That stuff isn't good enough. *Have faith. Pray a lot.* I've been doing that all my life. Okay, we prayed and we got God to show Himself. What now? What's your program, Thomas? Tell me that. What do you want us to do? You took our church away—what will you give us to replace it?"

I could tell he didn't have any answers.

His face turned red and he tugged on the ends of his hair and looked at Saul Kraft in a sour way, almost like he was saying I-told-you-so with his eyes. Then he looked back at me and I saw either sorrow or fear in his face, I don't know which, and I realized right then that this Thomas is just a human being like you and me, a scared human being, who doesn't really understand what's happening and doesn't know how to go on from this point. He tried to fake it. He told me again to pray, never underestimate the power of prayer, et cetera, et cetera, but his heart wasn't in his words.

He was stuck. *What's your program, Thomas?* He doesn't
have any. He hasn't thought things through past the point
of getting the Sign from God. He can't help us now. There's
your Thomas for you, the Proclaimer, the prophet. He's
scared. We're all scared, and he's just one of us, no different,
no wiser. And last night the Apocalyptists burned the shop-
ping center. You know, if you had asked me six months ago
how I'd feel if God gave us a Sign that He was really watching over us, I'd have told you that I thought it would be the
most wonderful thing that had ever happened since Jesus
in the manger. But now it's happened. And I'm not so sure
how wonderful it is. I walk around feeling that the ground
might open up under my feet any time. I don't know what's
going to happen to us all. God has come, and it ought to
be beautiful, and instead it's just scary. I never imagined it
would be this way. Oh, God. God I feel so lost. God I feel
so empty.

7.

An Insight of Discerners

Speaking before an audience was nothing new for me, of
course. Not after all the years I've spent in classrooms, patiently instructing each season's hairy new crop of young
in the mysteries of tachyon theory, anterior-charge particles, and time-reversal equations. Nor was this audience a
particularly alien or frightening one: it was made up mainly
of faculty people from Harvard and M.I.T., some graduate
students, and a sprinkling of lawyers, psychologists, and
other professional folk from Cambridge and the outskirts.
All of us part of the community of scholarship, so to speak.
The sort of audience that might come together to protest the

latest incident of ecological rape or of preventive national liberation. But one aspect of my role this evening was unsettling to me. This was in the truest sense a religious gathering; that is, we were meeting to discuss the nature of God and to arrive at some comprehension of our proper relationship to Him. And I was the main speaker, me, old Bill Gifford, who for nearly four decades had regarded the Deity as an antiquated irrelevance. I was this flock's pastor. How strange that felt.

"But I believe that many of you are in the same predicament," I told them. "Men and women to whom the religious impulse has been something essentially foreign. Whose lives were complete and fulfilled although prayer and ritual were wholly absent from them. Who regarded the concept of a supreme being as meaningless and who looked upon the churchgoing habits of those around them as nothing more than lower-class superstitiousness on the one hand and middle-class pietism on the other. And then came the great surprise of June 6—forcing us to reconsider doctrines we had scorned, forcing us to reexamine our basic philosophical constructs, forcing us to seek an acceptable explanation of a phenomenon that we had always deemed impossible and implausible. All of you, like myself, suddenly found yourselves treading very deep metaphysical waters."

The nucleus of this group had come together on an *ad hoc* basis the week after It happened, and since then had been meeting two or three times a week. At first there was no formal organizational structure, no organizational name, no policy; it was merely a gathering of intelligent and sophisticated New Englanders who felt unable to cope individually with the altered nature of reality and who needed mutual reassurance and reinforcement. That was why I started going, anyway. But within ten days we were groping toward a more positive purpose: no longer simply to learn how to *accept* what had befallen humanity, but to find some way of turning it to a useful purpose. I had begun articulating some ideas along those lines in private conversation, and abruptly I was asked by several of the leaders of the group to make my thoughts public at the next meeting.

"An astonishing event has occurred," I went on. "A good many ingenious theories have been proposed to account for it—as, for example, that the Earth was brought to a halt through the workings of an extrasensory telekinetic force generated by the simultaneous concentration of the entire world population. We have also heard the astrological explanations—that the planets or the stars were lined up in a certain once-in-a-universe's-lifetime way to bring about such a result. And there have been the arguments, some of them coming from quite surprising places, in favor of the notion that the June 6 event was the doing of malevolent creatures from outer space. The telekinesis hypothesis has a certain superficial plausibility, marred only by the fact that experimenters in the past have never been able to detect even an iota of telekinetic ability in any human being or combination of human beings. Perhaps a simultaneous worldwide effort might generate forces not to be found in any unit smaller than the total human population, but such reasoning requires an undesirable multiplication of hypotheses. I believe that most of you here agree with me that the other explanations of the June 6 event beg one critical question: Why did the slowing of the Earth occur so promptly, in seemingly direct response to Thomas the Proclaimer's campaign of global prayer? Can we believe that a unique alignment of astrological forces just happened to occur the day after that hour of prayer? Can we believe that the extragalactic fiends just happened to meddle with the Earth's rotation on that particular day? The element of coincidence necessary to sustain these and other arguments is fatal to them, I think.

"What are we left with, then? Only with the explanation that the Lord Almighty, heeding mankind's entreaties, performed a miracle so that we should be confirmed in our faith in Him.

"So I conclude. So do many of you. But does it necessarily follow that mankind's sorry religious history, with all of its holy wars, its absurd dogmas, its childish rituals, its fastings and flagellations, is thereby justified? Because you and you and you and I were bowled over on June 6, blasted out of our skepticism by an event that has no rational explanation, should we therefore rush to the churches and synagogues and mosques and enroll immediately in the orthodoxy of our choice? I think not. I submit that our attitudes of skepticism and rationalism were properly held, although our aim was misplaced. In scorning the showy, trivial trappings of organized faith, in walking past the churches where our neighbors devoutly knelt, we erred by turning away also from the matter that underlay their faith: the existence of a supreme being whose divine plan guides the universe. The spinning of prayer wheels and the mumbling of credos seemed so inane to us that, in our revulsion for such things, we were led to deny all notions of a higher order, of a teleological universe, and we embraced the concept of a wholly random cosmos. And then the Earth stood still for a day and a night.

"How did it happen? We admit it was God's doing, you and I, amazed though we are to find ourselves saying so. We have been hammered into a posture of belief by that inexplicable event. But what do we mean by 'God'? Who is He? An old man with long white whiskers? Where is He to be found? Somewhere between the orbits of Mars and Jupiter? Is He a supernatural being, or merely an extraterrestrial one? Does He too acknowledge a superior authority? And so on, an infinity of new questions. We have no valid knowledge of His nature, though now we have certain knowledge of His existence.

"Very well. A tremendous opportunity now exists for us the discerning few, for us who are in the habit of intellectual activity. All about us we see a world in frenzy. The Apocalyptists swoon with joy over the approaching catastrophe, the glossolaliacs chatter in maniac glee, the heads of entrenched churchly hierarchies are aghast at the possibility that the Millennium may really be at hand; everything is in flux, everything is new and strange. New cults spring up. Old creeds dissolve. And this is our moment. Let us step in and replace credulity and superstition with reason. An end to cults; an end to theology; an end to blind faith. Let it be our goal to relate the events of that awesome day to some principle of reason, and develop a useful, dynamic, *rational* movement of rebirth and revival—not a religion per se but rather a cluster of belief, based on the concept that a divine plan exists, that we live under the authority of a supreme or at least superior being, and that we must strive to come to some kind of rational relationship with this being.

"We've already had the moral strength to admit that our old intuitive skepticism was an error. Now let us provide an attractive alternate for those of us who still find ritualistic orthodoxy unpalatable, but who fear a total collapse into apocalyptic disarray if no steps are taken to strengthen mankind's spiritual insight. Let us create, if we can, a purely secular movement, a nonreligious religion, which offers the hope of establishing a meaningful dialogue between Us and Him. Let us make plans. Let us find powerful symbols with which we may sway the undecided and the confused. Let us march forth as crusaders in a dramatic effort to rescue humanity from unreason and desperation."

And so forth. I think it was a pretty eloquent speech, especially coming from someone who isn't in the habit of delivering orations. A transcript of it got into the local paper the next day and was reprinted all over. My "us the discerning few" line drew a lot of attention, and spawned an instant label for our previously unnamed movement. We became known as the Discerners. Once we had a name, our status was different. We weren't simply a group of concerned citizens any longer. Now we constituted a cult—a skeptical, rational, antisuperstitious cult, true, but nevertheless a cult, a sect, the newest facet of the world's furiously proliferating latter-day craziness.

8.

An Expectation of Awaiters

I know it hasn't been fashionable to believe in God these last twenty thirty forty years people haven't been keeping His path much but I always did even when I was a little boy I believed truly and I loved Him and I wanted to go to church all the time even in the middle of the week I'd say to Mother let's go to church I genuinely enjoyed kneeling and praying and feeling Him near me but she'd say no Davey you've got to wait till Sunday for that it's only Wednesday now. So as they say I'm no stranger to His ways and of course when they called for that day of prayer I prayed with all my heart that He might give us a Sign but even so I'm no fool I mean I don't accept everything on a silver platter I ask questions I have doubts I test things and probe a little I'm not one of your ordinary country bumpkins that takes everything on faith. In a way I suppose I could be said to belong to the discerning few although I don't want any of you to get the idea I'm a Discerner oh no I have no sympathy whatever with that atheistic bunch. Anyway we all prayed and the Sign came and my first reaction was joy I don't mind telling you I wept for joy when the sun stood still feeling that all the faith of a lifetime had been confirmed and the godless had better shiver in their boots but then a day or so later I began to think about it and I asked myself how do we know that the Sign really came from God? How can we be sure that the being we have invoked is really on our side I asked myself and of course I had no good answer to that. For all I knew we had conjured up Satan the Accursed and what we imagined was a miracle was really a trick out of the depths of hell designed to lead us all to perdition. Here are these Discerners telling us that they repent their atheism because they know now that God is real and God is with us but how naive they are they aren't even allowing for the possibility that the Sign is a snare and a delusion I tell you we can't be sure the thing is we absolutely *can't be sure*. The Sign might have been from God or from the Devil and we don't know we won't know until we receive a second Sign which I await which I believe will be coming quite soon. And what will that second Sign tell us? I maintain that that has not yet been decided on high it may be a Sign announcing our utter damnation or it may be a Sign welcoming us to the Earthly Paradise and we must await it humbly and prayerfully my friends we must pray and purify ourselves and prepare for the worst as well as for the best. I like to think that in a short while God Himself will present Himself to us not in a any indirect way like stopping the sun but rather in a direct manifestation either as God the Father or as God the Son and we will all be saved but this will come about *only if we remain righteous*. If we succumb to error and evil we will bring it to pass that the Devil's advent will descend on us for as Thomas has said himself our destiny is in our hands as well as in His and I believe the first Sign was only the start of a process that will be decided for good or for evil in the days just ahead. Therefore I Davey Strafford call upon you my friends to keep the way of the faith for we must not waver in our hope that He Who Comes will be lovingly inclined toward us and I say that this is our time of supreme test and if we fail it we may discover that it is Satan who shows up to claim our souls. I say once more we cannot interpret the first Sign we can only have faith that it is truly from God and we must pray that this is so while we await the ultimate verdict of heaven therefore we have obtained the rental of a vacant grocery store on Coshocton Avenue which we have renamed the First Church of the Awaiters of Redemption and we will pray round the clock there are seventeen of us now and we will pray in three-hour shifts five of us at a time in rotation the numbers increasing as our expected rapid growth takes place I trust you will come to us and swell our voices for we must pray we've got to there's no other hope now just pray a lot in order that He Who Comes may be benevolent and I ask you to keep praying and have a trusting heart in this our time of waiting.

9.

A Crying of Proclaimers

Kraft enters the room as Thomas puts down the telephone. "Who were you talking to?" Kraft asks.

"Gifford the Discerner, calling from Boston."

"Why are you answering the phone yourself?"

"There was no one else here."

"There were three apostles in the outer office who could have handled the call, Thomas."

Thomas shrugs. "They would have had to refer it to me eventually. So I answered. What's wrong with that?"

"You've got to maintain distance between yourself and ordinary daily routines. You've got to stay up there on your pedestal and not go around answering telephones."

"I'll try, Saul," says Thomas heavily.

"What did Gifford want?"

"He'd like to merge his group and ours."

Kraft's eyes flash. "To merge? *To merge?* What are we, some sort of manufacturing company? We're a movement. A spiritual force. To talk mergers is nonsense."

"He means that we should start working together, Saul. He says we should join forces because we're both on the side of sanity."

"Exactly what is that supposed to mean?"

"That we're both anti-Apocalyptist. That we're both working to preserve society instead of to bury it."

"An oversimplification," Kraft says. "We deal in faith and he deals in equations. We believe in a Divine Being and he believes in the sanctity of reason. Where's the meeting point?"

"The Cincinnati and Chicago fires are our meeting point, Saul. The Apocalyptists are going crazy. And now these Awaiters too, these spokesmen for Satan—no. We have to act. If I put myself at Gifford's disposal—"

"At his *disposal?*"

"He wants a statement from me backing the spirit if not the substance of the Discerner philosophy. He thinks it'll serve to calm things a little."

"He wants to co-opt you for his own purposes."

"For the purposes of mankind, Saul."

Kraft laughs harshly. "How naive you can be, Thomas!

Where's your sense? You can't make an alliance with athe-ists. You can't let them turn you into a ventriloquist's dummy who—"

"They believe in God just as much as—"

"You have power, Thomas. It's in your voice, it's in your eyes. They have none. They're just a bunch of professors. They want to borrow your power and make use of it to serve their own ends. They don't want you, Thomas, they want your charisma. I forbid this alliance."

Thomas is trembling. He towers over Kraft, but his entire body quivers and Kraft remains steady. Thomas says, "I'm so tired, Saul."

"Tired?"

"The uproar. The rioting. The fires. I'm carrying too big a burden. Gifford can help me. With planning with ideas. That's a clever bunch, those people."

"I can give you all the help you need."

"No, Saul! What have you been telling me all along? That prayer is sufficient unto every occasion! Faith! Faith! Faith! Faith! Faith moves mountains! Well? You were right, yes, you channeled your faith through me and I spoke to the people and we got ourselves a miracle, but what now? What have we really accomplished? Everything's falling apart, and we need strong souls to build and rebuild, and you aren't offering anything new. You—"

"The Lord will provide for—"

"Will He? Will He, Saul? How many thousands dead already, since June 6? How much property damage? Gov-ernment paralyzed. Transportation breaking down. New cults. New prophets. Here's Gifford saying, Let's join hands, Thomas, let's try to work together, and you tell me—"

"I forbid this," Kraft says.

"It's all agreed. Gifford's going to take the first plane west, and—"

"I'll call him. He mustn't come. If he does I won't let him see you. I'll notify the apostles to bar him."

"No, Saul."

"We don't need him. We'll be ruined if we let him near you."

"Why?"

"Because he's godless and our movement's strength proceeds from the Lord!" Kraft shouts. "Thomas, what's happened to you? Where's you fire? Where's your zeal? Where's my old swaggering Thomas who talked back to God? Belch, Thomas. Spit on the floor, scratch your belly, curse a little. I'll get you some wine. It shocks me to see you sniveling like this. Telling me how tired you are, how scared."

"I don't feel like swaggering much these days, Saul."

"Damn you, swagger anyway! The whole world is watching you! Here, listen—I'll rough out a new speech for you that you'll deliver on full hookup tomorrow night. We'll outflank Gifford and his bunch. We'll co-opt *him*. What you'll do, Thomas, is call for a new act of faith, some kind of mass demonstration, something symbolic and powerful, something to turn people away from despair and destruction. We'll follow the Discerner line *plus* our own element of faith. You'll denounce all the false new cults and urge everyone to—to—let me think—to make a pilgrimage of some kind?—a coming together—a mass baptism, that's it, a march to the sea, everybody bathing in God's own sea, washing away doubt and sin. Right? A rededication to faith." Kraft's face is red. His forehead gleams. Thomas scowls at him. Kraft goes on, "Stop pulling those long faces. You'll do it and it'll work. It'll pull people back from the abyss of Apocalypticism. Positive goals, that's our approach. Thomas the Proclaimer cries out that we must work together under God. Yes? Yes. We'll get this thing under control in ten days, I promise you. Now go have yourself a drink. Relax. I've got to call Gifford, and then I'll start blocking in your new appeal. Go on. And stop looking so glum, Thomas! We hold a mighty power in our hands. We're wielding the sword of the Lord. You want to turn all that over to Gifford's crowd? Go. Go. Get some rest, Thomas."

10.

A Prostration of Propitiators

ALL PARISH CHAIRMEN PLEASE COPY AND DISTRIBUTE. The Reverend August Hammacher to his dearly beloved brothers and sisters in Christ, members of the Authentic Church of the Doctrine of Propitiation, this message from Central Shrine: greetings and blessings. Be you hereby advised that we have notified Elder Davey Strafford of the First Church of the Awaiters of Redemption that as of this date we no longer consider ourselves in communion with his church, on grounds of irremediable doctrinal differences. It is now forbidden for members of the Authentic Church to participate in the Awaiter rite or to have any sacramental contact with the instrumentalities of the Awaiter creed, although we shall continue to remember the Awaiters in our prayers and to strive for their salvation as if they were our own people.

The schism between ourselves and the Awaiters, which has been in the making for more than a week, arises from a fundamental disagreement over the nature of the Sign. It is of course our belief, greatly strengthened by the violent events of recent days, that the Author of the Sign was Satan and that the Sign foretells a coming realignment in heaven, the probable beneficiaries of which are to be the Diabolical Forces. In expectation of the imminent establishment of the

Dark Powers on Earth, we therefore direct our most humble homage to Satan the Second Incarnation of Christ, hoping that when He comes among us He will take cognizance of our obeisance and spare us from the ultimate holocaust.

Now the Awaiters hold what is essentially an agnostic position, saying that we cannot know whether the Sign proceeds from God or from Satan, and that pending further revelation we must continue to pray as before to the Father and the Son, so that perhaps through our devotions we may stave off the advent of Satan entirely. There is one point of superficial kinship between their ideas and ours, which is an unwillingness to share the confidence of Thomas the Proclaimer on the one hand, and the Discerners on the other, that the Sign is God's work. But it may be seen that a basic conflict of doctrine exists between ourselves and the Awaiters, for they refuse to comprehend our teachings concerning the potential benevolence of Satan, and cling to an attitude that may be deemed dangerously offensive by Him. Unwilling to commit themselves finally to one side or the other, they hope to steer a cautious middle course, not realizing that when the Dark One comes He will chastise all those who failed to accept the proper meaning of the revelation of June 6. We have hoped to sway the Awaiters to our position, but their attitude has grown increasingly abusive as we have exposed their doctrinal inconsistencies, and now we have no option but to pronounce excommunication upon them. For what does Revelation say? "I know thy works, that thou art neither cold nor hot: I would thou wert cold or hot. So then because thou art lukewarm, and neither cold nor hot, I will spue thee out of my mouth." We cannot risk being tainted by these lukewarm Awaiters who will not bow the knee to the Dark One, though they admit the possibility (but not the inevitability) of His Advent.

However, dearly loved friends in Christ, I am happy to reveal that we have this day established preliminary communion with the United Diabolist Apocalyptic Pentecostal Church of the United States, the headquarters of which is in Los Angeles, California. I need not here recapitulate the deep doctrinal chasms separating us from the Apocalyptist sects in general; but although we abhor certain teachings even of this Diabolist faction, we recognize large areas of common belief linking us, and hope to wean the United Diabolist Apocalytics entirely from their errors in the course of time. This is by no means to be interpreted as presently authorizing communicants of the Authentic Church of the Doctrine of Propitiation to take part in Apocalyptist activities, even those which are nondestructive, but I do wish to advise you of the possibility of a deeper relationship with at least one Apocalyptist group even as we sever our union with the Awaiters. Our love goes out to all of you, from all of us at Central Shrine. We prostrate ourselves humbly before the Dark One whose triumph is ordained. In the name of the Father, the Son, the Holy Ghost, and He Who Comes. Amen.

11.

The March to the Sea

It was the most frightening thing ever. Like an army invading us. Like a plague of locusts. They came like the locusts came up upon the land of Egypt when Moses stretched out his hand. Exodus 10:15 tells it: *For they covered the face of the whole earth, so that the land was darkened; and they did eat every herb of the land, and all the fruit of the trees which the hail had left: and there remained not any green thing in the trees, or in the herbs of the field, through all the land of*

Egypt. Like a nightmare. Lucy and me were the Egyptians and all of Thomas' people, they were the locusts.

Lucy wanted to be in the middle of it all along. To her Thomas was like a holy prophet of God from the moment he first started to preach, although I tried to tell her back then that he was a charlatan and a dangerous lunatic with a criminal record. Look at his face, I said, look at those eyes! A lot of good it did me. She kept a scrapbook of him like he was a movie star and she was a fifteen-year-old girl instead of a woman of seventy-four. Pictures of him, texts of all his speeches. She got angry at me when I called him crazy or unscrupulous: we had our worst quarrel in maybe thirty years when she wanted to send him $500 to help pay for his television expenses and I absolutely refused. Naturally after the Day of the Sign she came to look upon him as being right up there in the same exalted category as Moses and Elijah and John the Baptist one of the true anointed voices of the Lord, and I guess I was starting to think of him that way too, despite myself. Though I didn't like him or trust him I sensed he had a special power. When everybody was praying for the Sign I prayed too, not so much because I thought it would come about but just to avoid trouble with Lucy, but I did put my heart into the prayer, and when the Earth stopped turning a shiver ran all through me and I got such a jolt of amazement that I thought I might be having a stroke. So I apologized to Lucy for all I had said about Thomas. I still suspected he was a madman and a charlatan, but I couldn't deny that he had something of the saint and prophet about him too. I suppose it's possible for a man to be a saint and a charlatan both. Anything's possible. I understand that one of these new religions is saying that Satan is actually an incarnation of Jesus, or the fourth member of the Trinity, or something like that. Honestly.

Well then all the riotings and burnings began when the hot weather came and the world seemed to be going crazy with things worse not better after God had given His Sign, and Thomas called for this Day of Rededication, everybody to go down to the sea and wash off his sins, a real oldtime total-immersion revival meeting where we'd all get together and denounce the new cults and get things back on the right track again.

And Lucy came to me all aglow and said, Let's go, let's be part of it. I think there were supposed to be ten gathering-places all around the United States, New York and Houston and San Diego and Seattle and Chicago and I don't remember which else, but Thomas himself was going to attend the main one at Atlantic City, which is just a little ways down the coast from us, and the proceedings would be beamed by live telecast to all the other meetings being held here and overseas. She hadn't ever seen Thomas in person. I told her it was crazy for people our age to get mixed up in a mob of the size Thomas always attracts. We'd be crushed, we'd be trampled, we'd die sure as anything. Look, I said, we live right here by the seashore anyway, the ocean is fifty steps from our front porch; so why ask for trouble? We'll stay here and watch the praying on television, and then when everybody goes down into the sea to be purified we can go right here on our own beach and we'll be part of things in a way without taking the risks. I could see that Lucy was disappointed about not seeing Thomas in person but after all she's a sensible woman and I'm going to be eighty next November and there had already been some pretty wild scenes at each of Thomas' public appearances.

The big day dawned and I turned on the television and then of course we got the news that Atlantic City had banned Thomas' meeting at the last minute on the grounds of public safety. A big oil tanker had broken up off shore the night before and an oil slick was heading toward the beach, the mayor said. If there was a mass meeting on the beach that day it would interfere with the city's pollution-prevention procedures, and also the oil would endanger the health of anybody who went into the water, so the whole Atlantic City waterfront was being cordoned off, extra police brought in from out of town, laser lines set up, and so forth. Actually the oil slick wasn't anywhere near Atlantic City and was drifting the other way, and when the mayor talked about public safety he really meant the safety of his city, not wanting a couple of million people ripping up the boardwalk and breaking windows. So there was Atlantic City sealed off and Thomas had this immense horde of people already collected, coming from Philadelphia and Trenton and Wilmington and even Baltimore, a crowd so big it couldn't be counted, five, six, maybe ten million people. They showed it from a helicopter view and everybody was standing shoulder to shoulder for about twenty miles in this direction and fifty miles in that direction, that's how it seemed, anyway, and about the only open place was where Thomas was, a clearing around fifty yards across with his apostles forming a tight ring protecting him.

Where was this mob going to go, since it couldn't get into Atlantic City? Why, Thomas said, everybody would just march up the Jersey coast and spread out along the shore from Long Beach Island to Sandy Hook. When I heard that I wanted to jump into the car and start heading for maybe Montana, but it was too late: the marchers were already on their way, all the mainland highways were choked with them. I went up on the sundeck with our binoculars and I could see the first of them coming across the causeway, walking seventy or eighty abreast, and a sea of faces behind them going inland on and on back toward Manahawkin and beyond. Well it was like the Mongol hordes of Genghis

Khan. One swarm went south toward Beach Haven and the other came up through Surf City and Loveladies and Harvey Cedars in our direction. Thousands and thousands and thousands of them. Our island is long and skinny like any coastal sandspit, and it's pretty well built up both on the beach side and on the bay side, no open space except the narrow streets, and there wasn't *room* for all those people. But they kept on coming, and as I watched through the binoculars I thought I was getting dizzy because I imagined some of the houses on the beach side were moving too, and then I realized that the houses *were* moving, some of the flimsier ones, they were being pushed right off their foundations by the press of humanity. Toppling and being ground underfoot, entire houses, can you imagine? I told Lucy to pray, but she was already doing it, and I got my shotgun ready because I felt I had to try at least to protect us, but I said to her that this was probably going to be our last day alive and I kissed her and we told each other how good it had been, all of it, fifty-three years together. And then the mob came spilling through our part of the island. Rushing down to the beach. A berserk crazy multitude.

And Thomas was there, right close to our place. Bigger than I thought he'd be, and his hair and beard were all tangled up, and his face was red and peeling some from sunburn—he was that close, I could see the sunburn—and he was still in the middle of his ring of apostles, and he was shouting through a bullhorn, but no matter how much amplification they gave him from the copter-borne speakers overhead it was impossible to understand anything he was saying. Saul Kraft was next to him. He looked pale and frightened. People were rushing into the water, some of them fully clothed and some stark naked, until the whole shoreline was packed right out to where the breakers begin. As more and more people piled into the water the ones in front were pushed beyond their depth, and I think this was when the drownings started. I know I saw a number of people waving and kicking and yelling for help and getting swept out to sea. Thomas remained on shore, shouting through the bullhorn. He must have realized it was all out of control, but there was nothing he could do. Until this point the thrust of the mob was all forward, toward the sea, but now there was a change in the flow: some of those in the water tried to force their way back up onto land, and smashed head on into those going the other way. I thought they were coming up out of the water to avoid being drowned, but then I saw the black smears on their clothing and I thought, *the oil slick!* and yes, there it was, not down by Atlantic City but up here by us, right off the beach and moving shoreward. People in the water were getting bogged down in it, getting it all over their hair and faces, but they couldn't reach the shore because of the rush still heading in the opposite direction. This was when the tramplings started as the ones coming out of the water, coughing and choking and blinded with oil, fell under the feet of those still trying to get into the sea.

I looked at Thomas again and he was like a maniac. His face was wild and he had thrown the bullhorn away and he was just screaming, with angry cords standing out on his neck and forehead. Saul Kraft went up to him and said something and Thomas turned like the wrath of God, turned and rose up and brought his hands down like two clubs on Saul Kraft's head, and you know Kraft is a small man and he went down like he was dead, with blood all over his face. Two or three apostles picked him up and carried him into one of the beachfront houses. Just then somebody managed to slip through the cordon of apostles and went running toward Thomas. He was a short, plump man wearing the robes of one of the new religions, an Awaiter or Propitiator or I don't know what, and he had a laser-hatchet in his hand. He shouted something at Thomas and lifted the hatchet. But Thomas moved toward him and stood so tall that the assassin almost seemed to shrink, and the man was so afraid that he couldn't do a thing. Thomas reached out and plucked the hatchet from his hand and threw it aside. Then he caught the man and started hitting him, tremendous close-range punches, slam slam slam, all but knocking the man's head off his shoulders. Thomas didn't look human while he was doing that. He was some kind of machine of destruction. He was bellowing and roaring and running foam from his mouth, and he was into this terrible deadly rhythm of punching, slam slam slam. Finally he stopped and took the man by both hands and flung him across the beach, like you'd fling a rag doll. The man flew maybe twenty feet and landed and didn't move. I'm certain Thomas beat him to death. There's your holy prophet for you, your saint of God. Suddenly Thomas' whole appearance changed: he became terribly calm, almost frozen, standing there with his arms dangling and his shoulders hunched up and his chest heaving from all that hitting. And he began to cry. His face broke up like winter ice on a spring pond and I saw the tears. I'll never forget that: Thomas the Proclaimer all alone in the middle of that madhouse on the beach, sobbing like a new widow.

I didn't see anything after that. There was a crash of glass from downstairs and I grabbed my gun and went down to see, and I found maybe fifteen people piled up on the livingroom floor who had been pushed right through the picture window by the crowd outside. The window had cut them all up and some were terribly maimed and there was blood on everything, and more and more and more people kept flying through the place where the window had been, and I heard Lucy screaming and my gun went off and I don't know what happened after that. Next I remember it was the middle of the night and I was sitting in our completely wrecked house and I saw a helicopter land on the beach, and a tactical squad began collecting bodies. There were hundreds of dead just on our strip of beach. Drowned, trampled, chocked by oil, heart attacks, everything. The corpses are gone now but the island's is a ruin. We're asking the government for disaster aid. I don't know: is a religious meeting a proper disaster? It was for us. That was your Day of Rededication, all right: a disaster. Prayer and purification to bring us all together under the banner of the Lord. May I be struck dead for saying this if I don't mean it with all my heart: I wish the Lord and all his prophets would disappear and leave us alone. We've had enough religion for one season.

12.

The Voice from the Heavens

Saul Kraft, hidden behind nine thousand dollars' worth of security devices, an array of scanners and sensors and shunt-gates and trip-vaults, wonders why everything is going so badly. Perhaps his choice of Thomas as the vehicle was an error. Thomas, he has come to realize, is too complicated, too unpredictable—a dual soul, demon and angel inextricably merged. Nevertheless the Crusade had begun promisingly enough. Working through Thomas, he had coaxed God Almighty into responding to the prayers of mankind, hadn't he? How much better than that do you need to do?

But now. This nightmarish carnival atmosphere everywhere. These cults, these other prophets. A thousand interpretations of an event whose meaning should have been crystal clear. The bonfires. Madness crackling like lightning across the sky. Maybe the fault was in Thomas. The Proclaimer had been deficient in true grace all along. Possibly any mass movement centered on a prophet who had Thomas' faults of character was inherently doomed to slip into chaos.

Or maybe the fault was mine, O Lord.

Kraft has been in seclusion for many days, perhaps for several weeks; he is no longer sure when he began this retreat. He will see no one, not even Thomas, who is eager to make amends. Kraft's injuries have healed and he holds no grievance against Thomas for striking him: the fiasco of the Day of Rededication had driven all of them a little insane there on the beach, and Thomas' outburst of violence was understandable if not justifiable. It may even have been of divine inspiration, God inflicting punishment on Kraft through the vehicle of Thomas for his sins. The sin of pride, mainly. To turn Gifford away, to organize the Day of Rededication for such cynical motives—

Kraft fears for his soul, and for the soul of Thomas.

He dares not see Thomas now, not until he has regained his own spiritual equilibrium; Thomas is too turbulent, too tempestuous, emits such powerful emanations of self-will; Kraft must first recapture his moral strength. He fasts much of the time. He tries to surrender himself fully in prayer. But prayer will not come: he feels cut off from the Almighty, separated from Him as he has never been before. By bungling this holy Crusade he must have earned the Lord's displeasure. A gulf, a chasm, parts them; Kraft is earthbound and helpless. He abandons his efforts to pray. He prowls his suite restlessly, listening for intruders, constantly running security checks. He switches on his closed-circuit video inputs, expecting to see fires in the streets, but all is calm out

there. He listens to news bulletins on the radio: chaos, turmoil, everywhere. Thomas is said to be dead; Thomas is
reported on the same day to be in Istanbul, Karachi, Johannesburg, San Francisco; the Propitiators have announced
that on the twenty-fourth of November, according to their
calculations, Satan will appear on Earth to enter into his
sovereignty; the Pope, at last breaking his silence, has declared that he has no idea what power might have been
responsible for the startling happenings of June 6, but
thinks it would be rash to attribute the event to God's direct
intervention without some further evidence. So the Pope has
become an Awaiter too. Kraft smiles. Marvelous! Kraft wonders if the Archbishop of Canterbury is attending Propitiator
services. Or the Dalai Lama consorting with the Apocalyptists. Anything can happen now. Gog and Magog are let
loose upon the world. Kraft no longer is surprised by anything. He feels no astonishment even when he turns the
radio on late one afternoon and finds that God Himself
seems to be making a broadcast.

God's voice is rich and majestic. It reminds Kraft somewhat of the voice of Thomas, but God's tone is less fervid,
less evangelical; He speaks in an easy but serious-minded
way, like a Senator campaigning for election to his fifth
term of office. There is a barely perceptible easternness to
God's accent: He could be a Senator from Pennsylvania,
maybe, or Ohio. He has gone on the air, He explains, in the
hope of restoring order to a troubled world. He wishes to reassure everyone: no apocalypse is planned, and those who
anticipate the imminent destruction of the world are most
unwise. Nor should you pay heed to those who claim that the
recent Sign was the work of Satan. It certainly was not, God
says, not at all, and propitiation of the Evil One is uncalled
for. By all means let's give the Devil his due, but nothing be-

yond that. All I intended when I stopped the Earth's rotation, God declares, was to let you know that I'm here, looking after your interests. I wanted you to be aware that in the event of really bad trouble down there I'll see to it—

Kraft, lips clamped tautly, changes stations. The resonant baritone voice pursues him.

—that peace is maintained and the forces of justice are strengthened in—

Kraft turns on his television set. The screen shows nothing but the channel insignia. Across the top of the screen gleams a bright-green title:

ALLEGED VOICE OF GOD

and across the bottom, in frantic scarlet, is a second caption:

BY LIVE PICKUP FROM THE MOON

The Deity, meanwhile, has moved smoothly on to new themes. All the problems of the world, He observes, can be attributed to the rise and spread of atheistic socialism. The false prophet Karl Marx, aided by the Antichrist Lenin and the subsidiary demons Stalin and Mao, have set loose in the world a plague of godlessness that has tainted the entire twentieth century and, here at the dawn of the twenty-first, must at last be eradicated. For a long time the zealous godly folk of the world resisted the pernicious Bolshevik doctrines, God continues, His voice still lucid and reasonable; but in the past twenty years an accommodation with the powers of darkness has come into effect, and this has allowed spreading corruption to infect even such splendidly righteous lands as Japan, Brazil, the German Federal Republic, and God's own beloved United States of America. The foul philosophy of coexistence has led to a step-by-step entrapment of the forces of good, and as a result—

Kraft finds all of this quite odd. Is God speaking to every nation in English, or is He speaking Japanese to the Japanese, Hebrew to the Israelis, Croatian to the Croats, Bulgarian to the Bulgars? And when did God become so staunch a defender of the capitalist ethic? Kraft recalls something about driving money-changers out of the temple, long ago. But now the voice of God appears to be demanding a holy war against Communism. Kraft hears Him calling on the legions of the sanctified to attack the Marxist foe wherever the red flag flies. Sack embassies and consulates, burn the houses of ardent left-wingers, destroy libraries and other sources of dangerous propaganda, the Lord advises. He says everything in a level, civilized tone.

Abruptly, in midsentence, the voice of the Almighty vanishes from the airwaves. A short time later an announcer, unable to conceal his chagrin, declares that the broadcast was a hoax contrived by bored technicians in a satellite relay station. Investigations have begun to determine how so many radio and television stations let themselves be persuaded to transmit it as a public-interest item. But for many godless Marxists the revelation comes too late. The requested sackings and lootings have occurred in dozens of cities. Hundreds of diplomats, guards, and clerical workers have been slain by maddened mobs bent on doing the Lord's work. Property losses are immense. An international crisis is developing, and there are scattered reports of retribution against American citizens in several Eastern European countries. We live in strange times, Kraft tells himself. He prays. For himself. For Thomas. For all mankind. Lord have mercy. Amen. Amen. Amen.

13.

The Burial of Faith

The line of march begins at the city line and runs westward out of town into the suburban maze. The marchers, at least a thousand of them, stride vigorously forward even though a dank, oppressive heat enfolds them. On they go, past the park dense with the dark-green leaves of late summer, past the highway cloverleaf, past the row of burned motels and filling stations, past the bombed reservoir, past the cemeteries, heading for the municipal dumping-grounds.

Gifford, leading the long sober procession, wears ordinary classroom clothes: a pair of worn khaki trousers, a loose-fitting gray shirt, and old leather sandals. Originally there had been some talk of having the most important Discerners come garbed in their academic robes, but Gifford had vetoed that on the grounds that it wasn't in keeping with the spirit of the ceremony. Today all of the old superstitions and pomposities were to be laid to rest; why then bedeck the chief iconoclasts in hieratic costume as though they were priests, as though this new creed were going to be just as full of mummery as the outmoded religious it hoped to supplant?

Because the marchers are so simply dressed, the contrast is all the more striking between the plain garments they wear and the elaborate, rich-textured ecclesiastical paraphernalia they carry. No one is empty-handed; each has some vestment, some sacred artifact, some work of scripture. Draped over Gifford's left arm is a large white linen alb, ornately embroidered, with a dangling silken cincture. The man behind him carries a deacon's dalmatic; the third marcher has a handsome chasuble; the fourth, a splendid cope. The rest of the priestly gear is close behind: amice, stole, maniple, vimpa. A frosty-eyed woman well along in years waves a crozier aloft; the man beside her wears a mitre at a mockingly rakish angle. Here are cassocks, surplices, hoods, tippets, cottas, rochets, mozzettas, mantellettas, chimeres, and much more: virtually everything, in fact, save the papal tiara itself. Here are chalices, crucifixes, thuribles, fonts; three men struggle beneath a marvelously carved fragment of a pulpit; a little band of marchers displays Greek Orthodox outfits, the rhason and the sticharion, the epitrachelion and the epimanikia, the sakkos, the epigonation, the zone, the omophorion; they brandish ikons and enkolpia, dikerotikera and dikanikion. Austere Presbyterian gowns may be seen, and rabbinical yarmulkes and tallithim and tfilin. Farther back in the procession one may observe more exotic holy objects, prayer wheels and tonkas, sudras and kustis, idols of fifty sorts, things sacred to Confucianists, Shintoists, Parsees, Buddhists both Mahayana and Hinayana, Jains, Sikhs, animists of no formal rite, and others. The marchers have shofars, mezuzahs, candelabra, communion trays, even collection plates; no portable element of faith has been ignored. And of course the holy books of the new world are well represented: an infinity of Old and New Testaments, the Koran, the Bhagavad-Gita, the Upanishads, the Tao-te-ching, the Vedas, the Vedanta Sutra, the Talmud, the Book of the Dead, and more. Gifford has been queasy about destroying books, for that is an act with ugly undertones; but these are extreme times, and extreme measures are required. Therefore he has given his consent even for that.

Much of the material the marchers carry was freely contributed, mostly by disgruntled members of congregations, some of it given by disaffected clergymen themselves. The other objects come mostly from churches or museums plundered during the civil disturbances. But the Discerners have done no plundering of their own; they have merely accepted donations and picked up some artifacts that rioters had scattered in the streets. On this point Gifford was most strict: acquisition of material by force was prohibited. Thus the robes and emblems of the newly founded creeds are seen but sparsely today, since Awaiters and Propitiators and their like would hardly have been inclined to contribute to Gifford's festival of destruction.

They have reached the municipal dump now. It is a vast flat wasteland, surprisingly aseptic-looking: there are large areas of meadow, and the unreclaimed regions of the dump have been neatly graded and mulched, in readiness for the scheduled autumn planting of grass. The marchers put down their burdens and the chief Discerners come forward to take spades and shovels from a truck that has accompanied them. Gifford looks up; helicopters hover and television cameras bristle in the sky. This event will have extensive coverage. He turns to face the others and intones, "Let this ceremony mark the end of all ceremonies. Let this rite usher in a time without rites. Let reason rule forevermore."

Gifford lifts the first shovelful of soil himself. Now the rest of the diggers set to work, preparing a trench three feet deep, ten to twelve feet wide. The topsoil comes off easily, revealing strata of cans, broken toys, discarded television sets, automobile tires, and garden rakes. A mound of debris begins to grow as the digging team does its task; soon a shallow opening gapes. Though it is now late afternoon, the heat has not diminished, and those who dig stream with sweat. They rest frequently, panting, leaning on their tools. Meanwhile those who are not digging stand quietly, not putting down that which they carry.

Twilight is near before Gifford decides that the trench

is adequate. Again he looks up at the cameras, again he turns to face his followers.

He says, "On this day we bury a hundred thousand years of superstition. We lay to rest the old idols, the old fantasies, the old errors, the old lies. The time of faith is over and done with; the era of certainty opens. No longer do we need theologians to speculate on the proper way of worshiping the Lord; no longer do we need priests to mediate between ourselves and Him; no longer do we need man-made scriptures that pretend to interpret His nature. We have all of us felt His hand upon our world, and the time has come to approach Him with clear eyes, with an alert, open mind. Hence we give to the earth these relics of bygone epochs, and we call upon discerning men and woman everywhere to join us in this ceremony of renunciation."

He signals. One by one the Discerners advance to the edge of the pit. One by one they cast their burdens in: albs, chasubles, copes, mitres, Korans, Upanishads, yarmulkes, crucifixes. No one hurries; the Burial of Faith is serious business. As it proceeds, a drum roll of dull distant thunder reverberates along the horizon. A storm on the way? Just heat lightning, perhaps, Gifford decides. The ceremony continues. In with the maniple. In with the shofar. In with the cassock. Thunder again: louder, more distinct. The sky darkens. Gifford attempts to hasten the tempo of the ceremony, beckoning the Discerners forward to drop their booty. A blade of lightning slices the heavens and this time the answering thunderclap comes almost instantaneously, *ka-thock*. A few drops of rain. The forecast had been in error. A nuisance, but no real harm. Another flash of lightning. A tremendous crash. That one must have struck only a few hundred yards away. There is some nervous laughter. "We've annoyed Zeus," someone says. "He's throwing thunderbolts." Gifford is not amused; he enjoys ironies, but not

now, not now. And he realizes that he has become just credulous enough, since the sixth of June, to be at least mar-
ginally worried that the Almighty might indeed be about to
punish this sacrilegious band of Discerners. A flash again.
Ka-thock! The clouds now split asunder and torrents of rain
abruptly descend. In moments, shirts are pasted to skins, the
floor of the pit turns to mud, rivulets begin to stream across
the dump.

And then, as though they had scheduled the storm for
their own purposes, a mob of fierce-faced people in gaudy
robes bursts into view. They wield clubs, pitchforks, rake
handles, cleavers, and other improvised weapons; they
scream incoherent, unintelligible slogans; and they rush into
the midst of the Discerners, laying about them vigorously.
"Death to the godless blasphemers!" is what they are shriek-
ing, and similar phrases. Who are they, Gifford wonders?
Awaiters. Propitiators. Diabolists. Apocalyptists. Perhaps a
coalition of all cultists. The television helicopters descend
to get a better view of the melee, and hang just out of reach,
twenty or thirty feet above the struggle. Their powerful
floodlights provide apocalyptic illumination. Gifford finds
hands at his throat: a crazed woman, howling, grotesque.
He pushes her away and she tumbles into the pit, landing
on a stack of mud-crusted Bibles. A frantic stampede has
begun; his people are rushing in all directions, followed by
the vengeful servants of the Lord, who wield their weapons
with vindictive glee. Gifford sees his friends fall, wounded,
badly hurt, perhaps slain. Where are the police? Why are
they giving no protection? "Kill all the blasphemers!" a maniac voice shrills near him. He whirls, ready to defend himself. A pitchfork. He feels a strange cold clarity of thought
and moves swiftly in, feinting, seizing the handle of the
pitchfork, wresting it from his adversary. The rain redoubles
its force; a sheet of water comes between Gifford and the

other, and when he can see again, he is alone at the edge of the pit. He hurls the pitchfork into the pit and instantly wishes he had kept it, for three of the robed ones are coming toward him. He breaks into a cautious trot, tries to move past them, puts on a sudden spurt of speed, and slips in the mud. He lands in a puddle; the taste of mud is in his mouth; he is breathless, terrified, unable to rise. They fling themselves upon him. "Wait," he says. "This is madness!" One of them has a club. "No," Gifford mutters. "No. No. No. No."

14.

The Seventh Seal

1. And when he had opened the seventh seal, there was silence in heaven about the space of half an hour.

2. And I saw the seven angels which stood before God; and to them were given seven trumpets.

3. And another angel came and stood at the altar, having a golden censer; and there was given unto him much incense, that he should offer it with the prayers of all saints upon the golden altar which was before the throne.

4. And the smoke of the incense, which came with the prayers of the saints, ascended up before God out of the angel's hand.

5. And the angel took the censer, and filled it with fire of the altar, and cast it into the earth: and there were voices, and thunderings, and lightnings, and an earthquake.

6. And the seven angels which had the seven trumpets prepared themselves to sound.

7. The first angel sounded, and there followed hail and fire mingled with blood, and they were cast upon the earth:

and the third part of trees was burnt up, and all green grass was burnt up.

8. And the second angel sounded, and as it were a great mountain burning with fire was cast into the sea: and the third part of the sea became blood;

9. And the third part of the creatures which were in the sea, and had life, died; and the third part of the ships were destroyed.

10. And the third angel sounded, and there fell a great star from heaven, burning as it were a lamp, and it fell upon the third part of the rivers, and upon the fountains of waters;

11. And the name of the star is called Wormwood: and the third part of the waters became wormwood; and many men died of the waters, because they were made bitter.

12. And the fourth angel sounded, and the third part of the sun was smitten, and the third part of the moon, and the third part of the stars; so as the third part of them was darkened, and the day shone not for a third part of it, and the night likewise.

13. And I beheld, and heard an angel flying through the midst of heaven, saying with a loud voice, Woe, woe, woe, to the inhabiters of the earth by reason of the other voices of the trumpet of the three angels, which are yet so sound!

15.

The Flight of the Prophet

All, all over. Thomas weeps. The cities burn. The very lakes are afire. So many thousands dead. The Apocalyptists dance, for though the year is not yet sped the end seems plainly in view. The Church of Rome has pronounced anathema on Thomas, denying his miracle: he is the Anti-christ, the Pope has said. Signs and portents are seen everywhere. This is the season of two-headed calves and dogs with cats' faces. New prophets have arisen. God may shortly return, or He may not; revelations differ. Many people now pray for an end to all such visitations and miracles. The Awaiters no longer Await, but now ask that we be spared from His next coming; even the Diabolists and the Propitiators cry, Come not, Lucifer. Those who begged a Sign from God in June would be content now only with God's renewed and prolonged absence. Let Him neglect us; let Him dismiss us from His mind. It is a time of torches and hymns. Rumors of barbaric warfare come from distant continents. They say the neutron bomb has been used in Bolivia. Thomas' last few followers have asked him to speak with God once more, in the hope that things can still be set to rights, but Thomas refuses. The lines of communication to the Deity are closed. He dares not reopen them: see, see how many plagues and evils he has let loose as it is! He renounces his prophethood. Others may dabble in charismatic mysticism if they so please. Others may kneel before the burning bush or sweat in the glare of the pillar of fire. Not Thomas. Thomas' vocation is gone. All over. All, all, all over.

He hopes to slip into anonymity. He shaves his beard and docks his hair; he obtains a new wardrobe, bland and undistinguished; he alters the color of his eyes; he practices walking in a slouch to lessen his great height. Perhaps he has not lost his pocket-picking skills. He will go silently into the cities, head down, fingers on the ready, and thus he will make his way. It will be a quieter life.

Disguised, alone, Thomas goes forth. He wanders unmolested from place to place, sleeping in odd corners, eating in dim rooms. He is in Chicago for the Long Sabbath, and he is in Milwaukee for the Night of Blood, and he is in St. Louis for the Invocation of Flame. These events leave him unaffected. He moves on. The year is ebbing. The leaves have fallen. If the Apocalyptists tell us true, mankind has but a few weeks left. God's wrath, or Satan's, will blaze over the land as the year 2000 sweeps in on December's heels. Thomas scarcely minds. Let him go unnoticed and he will not mind if the universe tumbles about him.

"What do you think?" he is asked on a street corner in Los Angeles. "Will God come back on New Year's Day?"

A few idle loungers, killing time. Thomas slouches among them. They do not recognize him, he is sure. But they want an answer. "Well? What do you say?"

Thomas makes his voice furry and thick, and mumbles, "No, not a chance. He's never going to mess with us again. He gave us a miracle and look what we made out of it."

"That so? You really think so?"

Thomas nods. "God's turned His back on us. He said, Here, I give you proof of My existence, now pull yourselves together and get somewhere. And instead we fell apart all the faster. So that's it. We've had it. The end is coming."

"Hey, you might be right!" Grins. Winks.

This conversation makes Thomas uncomfortable. He starts to edge away, elbows out, head bobbing clumsily, shoulders hunched. His new walk, his camouflage.

"Wait," one of them says. "Stick around. Let's talk a little."

Thomas hesitates.

"You know, I think you're right, fellow. We made a royal mess. I tell you something else: we never should have started all that stuff. Asking for a Sign. Stopping the Earth. Would have been a lot better off if that Thomas had stuck to picking pockets, let me tell you."

"I agree three hundred percent," Thomas says, flashing a quick smile, on-off. "If you'll excuse me—"

Again he starts to shuffle away. Ten paces. An office

building's door opens. A short, slender man steps out. *Oh, God! Saul!* Thomas covers his face with his hand and turns away. Too late. No use. Kraft recognizes him through all the alterations. His eyes gleam. "Thomas!" he gasps.

"No. You're mistaken. My name is—"

"Where have you been?" Kraft demands. "Everyone's searching for you, Thomas. Oh, it was wicked of you to run away, to shirk your responsibilities. You dumped everything into our hands, didn't you? But you were the only one with the strength to lead people. You were the only one who—"

"Keep your voice down," Thomas says hoarsely. No use pretending. "For the love of God, Saul, stop yelling at me! Stop saying my name! Do you want everyone to know that I'm—"

"That's exactly what I want," Kraft says. By now a fair crowd has gathered, ten people, a dozen. Kraft points. "Don't you know him? That's Thomas the Proclaimer! He's shaved and cut his hair, but can't you see his face all the same? There's your prophet! There's the thief who talked with God!"

"No, Saul!"

"Thomas?" someone says. And they all begin to mutter it. "Thomas? Thomas? Thomas?" They nod heads, point, rub chins, nod heads again. "Thomas? Thomas?"

Surrounding him. Staring. Touching him. He tries to push them away. Too many of them, and no apostles, now. Kraft is at the edge of the crowd, smiling, the little Judas! "Keep back," Thomas says. "You've got the wrong man. I'm not Thomas. I'd like to get my hands on him myself. I—I—" *Judas! Judas!* "Saul!" he screams. And then they swarm over him.

WE ARE FOR
THE DARK

WE ARE FOR THE DARK

AN INTRODUCTION

Where do story ideas come from? the non-writer often asks. And the writer's usual answer is a bemused shrug. But in this instance I can reply very precisely.

My wife and I were visiting London in September of 1987 and of course we were spending virtually every evening at the theatre and some afternoons besides. On the next to last day of our stay we were at the National Theatre, on the south side of the Thames, to see Anthony Hopkins and Judi Dench in *Antony and Cleopatra*, a wondrous, magical matinee performance. Act Five came around, Cleopatra's great catastrophe, and her serving-maid Iras signalled the beginning of the final act with lines long familiar to me:

> *Finish, good lady; the bright day is done.*
> *And we are for the dark.*

A mysterious shiver ran through me at those words, *we are for the dark*. I had seen the play half a dozen times or more over the years, and they had never seemed unusual to me before; but, hearing them now, I suddenly saw great vistas of black space opening before me. Later that splendid afternoon, strolling back across the bridge toward the heart of the city under brilliant summer sunshine, I found myself contnuing to dwell on the vistas that Shakespeare's five words had evoked for me, and soon I was taking notes for a story that had absolutely nothing to do with the travails of Cleopatra or Antony.

That was the engendering point. The other details followed quickly enough, all but the mechanism of the matter-transmission system around which the interstellar venture of the story was to be built. That had to wait until January of the following year. Now I was in Los Angeles, resting and reading before going out to dinner, and suddenly I found myself scribbling down stuff about the spontaneous conversion of matter into antimatter and a necessary balancing conversion in the opposite direction. Whether any such thing is actually the case is beyond my own scientific expertise, but the idea seemed plausible enough to work with, and very quickly I had built an entire method of faster-than-light travel out of it, one which is probably utterly unfeasible in the real universe but would serve well enough in my fictional one. I wrote the story in March of 1988 and Gardner Dozois published it in *Isaac Asimov's Science Fiction Magazine*. For me it had some of the sweep and grandeur that first had drawn me to science fiction as a reader more than forty years before, and it pleased me greatly on that account. I thought that it might attract some attention among readers, but, oddly, it seemed to pass almost unnoticed—no awards nominations, no year's-best selection. Which puzzled me; but eventually I put the matter out of mind. Stories of mine that I had thought of as quite minor indeed had gone on to gain not only awards nominations but, more than once, the awards themselves; stories that had seemed to me to be failures when I wrote them had been reprinted a dozen times over in later years; and, occasionally, a story that moved me profoundly as I composed it had gone straight from publication to oblivion almost as if it had never existed at all. "We Are for the Dark" seems to have been one of those, though I still have hope for its rediscovery.

But the moral is clear, at least to me: write what satisfies you and let the awards and anthologizations take care of themselves, because there's no way of predicting what kind of career a story will have. Strive always to do your best, and, when you believe that you have, allow yourself the pleasure of your own approval. If readers happen to share your delight in your own work, that's a bonus in which to rejoice, but it's folly ever to expect others to respond to your work in the same way you do yourself.

WE ARE FOR
THE DARK

Great warmth comes from him, golden cascades of bright, nurturing energy. The Master is often said to be like a sun, and so he is, a luminous creature, a saint, a sun indeed. But warmth is not the only thing that emanates from suns. They radiate at many frequencies of the spectrum, hissing and crackling and glaring like furnaces as they send forth the angry power that withers, the power that kills. The moment I enter the Master's presence I feel that other force, that terrible one, flowing from him. The air about him hums with it, though the warmth of him, the benevolence, is evident also. His power is frightful. And yet all he is is a man, a very old one at that, with a smooth round hairless head and pale, mysteriously gentle eyes. Why should I fear him? My faith is strong. I love the Master. We all love him.

This is only the fifth time I have met him. The last was seven years ago, at the time of the Altair launch. We of the other House rarely have reason to come to the Sanctuary, or they to us. But he recognizes me at once, and calls me by name, and pours cool clear golden wine for me with his own hand. As I expect, he says nothing at first about his reason for summoning me. He talks instead of his recent visit to the Capital, where great swarms of ragged hungry people trotted tirelessly alongside his palanquin as he was borne in procession, begging him to send them into the Dark. "Soon, soon, my children," is what he tells me now that he told them then. "Soon we will all go to our new dwelling-places in the stars." And he wept, he says, for sheer joy, feeling the intensity of their love for him, feeling their longing for the new worlds to which we alone hold the keys. It seems to me that he is quietly weeping now, telling me these things.

Behind his desk is a star-map of extraordinary vividness and detail, occupying the rear wall of his austere chamber. Indeed, it is the rear wall: a huge curving shield of some gleaming dark substance blacker than night, within which I can see our galaxy depicted, its glittering core, its spiralling arms. Many of the high-magnitude stars shine forth clearly in their actual colors. Beyond, sinking into the depths of the dark matrix in a way that makes the map seem to stretch outward to infinity, are the neighboring galaxies, resting in clouds of shimmering dust. More distant clusters and nebulae are visible still farther from the map's center. As I stare, I feel myself carried on and on to the outermost ramparts of the universe. I compliment him on the ingenuity of the map, and on its startling realism.

But that seems to be a mistake. "Realism? This map?" the Master cries, and the energies flickering around him grow fierce and sizzling once again. "This map is nothing: a crazy hodgepodge. A lunacy. Look, this star sent us its light twelve billion years ago, and that one six billion years ago, and this other one twenty-three years ago, and we're seeing them all at once. But this one didn't even exist when that one started beaming its light at us. And this one may have died five billion years ago, but we won't know it for five billion more." His voice, usually so soft, is rising now and there is a dangerous edge on it. I have never seen him this angry. "So what does this map actually show us? Not the absolute reality of the universe but only a meaningless ragbag of subjective impressions. It shows the stars as they happen to appear to us just at this minute and we pretend that that is the actual cosmos, the true configuration." His face has grown flushed. He pours more wine. His hand is trembling, suddenly, and I think he will miss the rim of the glass, but no: his control is perfect. We drink in silence. Another moment and he is calm again, benign as the Buddha, bathing me in the glow and lustre of his spirit.

"Well, we must do the best we can within our limitations," he says gently. "For the closer spans the map is not so useless." He touches something on his desk and the starmap undergoes a dizzying shift, the outer clusters dropping away and the center of our own galaxy coming up until it fills the whole screen. Another flick of his finger and the inner realm of the galaxy stands out in bright highlighting: that familiar sphere, a hundred light-years in diameter, which is the domain of our Mission. A network of brilliant yellow lines cuts across the heart of it from star to star, marking the places where we have chosen to place our first receiver stations. It is a pattern I could trace from memory, and, seeing it now, I feel a sense of comfort and well-being, as though I am looking at a map of my native city.

Now, surely, he will begin to speak of Mission matters, he will start working his way round to the reason for my being here. But no, no, he wants to tell me of a garden of aloes he has lately seen by the shores of the Mediterranean, twisted spiky green rosettes topped by flaming red torches of blooms, and then of his visit to a lake in East Africa where pink flamingos massed in millions, so that all the world seemed pink, and then of a pilgrimage he has undertaken in the highest passes of the Sierra Nevada, where gnarled little pines ten thousand years old endure the worst that winter can hurl at them. As he speaks, his face grows more animated, his eyes taken on an eager sparkle. His great age drops away from him: he seems younger by thirty, forty, fifty years. I had not realized he was so keen a student of nature. "The next time you are in my country," I tell him, "perhaps you will allow me to show you the place along the southern shore where the fairy penguins come to nest in summer. In all the world I think that is the place I love the best."

He smiles. "You must tell me more about that some time." But his tone is flat, his expression has gone slack. The effort of this little talk must have exhausted him. "This Earth of ours is so beautiful," he says. "Such marvels, such splendors."

What can he mean by that? Surely he knows that only a few scattered islands of beauty remain, rare fortunate places rising above the polluted seas or sheltered from the tainted air, and that everything else is soiled, stained, damaged, corroded beyond repair by one sort of human folly or another.

"Of course," he says, "I would leave it in a moment, if duty beckoned me into the Dark. I would not hesitate. That I could never return would mean nothing to me." For a time he is silent. Then he draws a disk from a drawer of his desk and slides it toward me. "This music has given me great pleasure. Perhaps it will please you also. We'll talk again in a day or two."

The map behind him goes blank. His gaze, though it still rests on me, is blank now also.

So the audience is over, and I have learned nothing.

Well, indirection has always been his method. I understand now that whatever has gone wrong with the Mission—for surely something has, why else would I be here?—is not only serious enough to warrant calling me away from my House and my work, but is so serious that the Master feels the need of more than one meeting to convey its nature to me. Of course I am calm. Calmness is inherent in the character of those who serve the Order. Yet there is a strangeness about all this that troubles me as I have never been troubled before in the forty years of my service.

Outside, the night air is warm, and still humid from earlier rain. The Master's lodge sits by itself atop a lofty stepped platform of pink granite, with the lesser buildings of the Order arrayed in a semi-circle below it on the side of the great curving hill. As I walk toward the hostelry where I am staying, novitiates and even some initiates stare at me as though they would like to prostrate themselves before me. They revere me as I revere the Master. They would touch the hem of my robe, if they could. I nod and smile. Their eyes are hungry, God-haunted, star-haunted.

"Lord Magistrate," they murmur. "God be with you, your grace. God be with you." One novitiate, a gaunt boy, all cheekbones and eyebrows, dares to run to my side and ask me if the Master is well. "Very well," I tell him. A girl, quivering like a bowstring, says my name over and over as though it alone can bring her salvation. A plump monkish-looking man in a gray robe much too heavy for this hot climate looks toward me for a blessing, and I give him a quick gesture and walk swiftly onward, sealing my attention now inward and heavenward to free myself of their sup-plications as I stride across the terraced platform to my lodging.

There is no moon tonight, and against the blackness of the highlands sky the stars shine forth resplendently by the tens of thousands. I feel those stars in all their multitudes pressing close about me, enclosing me, enfolding me, and I know that what I feel is the presence of God. I imagine even that I see the distant nebulas, the far-off island universes. I think of our little ships, patiently sailing across the great Dark toward the remote precincts of our chosen sphere of settlement, carrying with them the receivers that will, God willing, open all His heavens to us. My throat is dry. My eyes are moist. After forty years I have lost none of my ability to feel the wonder of it.

In my spacious and lavishly appointed room in the hostelry I kneel and make my devotions, and pray, as ever, to be brought ever closer to Him. In truth I am merely the vehicle by which others are allowed to approach Him, I know: the bridge through which they cross to Him. But in my way I serve God also, and to serve Him is to grow closer to Him. My task for these many years has been to send voyagers to the far worlds of His realm. It is not for me to go that way myself: that is my sacrifice, that is my glory. I have no regret over remaining Earthbound: far from it! Earth is our great mother. Earth is the mother of us all. Troubled as she is, blighted as she now may be, dying, even, I am content to stay here, and more than content. How could I leave? I have my task, and the place of my task is here, and here I must remain.

I meditate upon these things for a time.

Afterward I oil my body for sleep and pour myself a glass of the fine brandy I have brought with me from home. I go to the wall dispenser and allow myself thirty seconds of ecstasy. Then I remember the disk the Master gave me, and decide to play it before bed. The music, if that is what it is, makes no impression on me whatever. I hear one note, and the next, and the one after that, but I am unable to put them together into any kind of rhythmic or melodic pattern.

When it ends I play it again. Again I can hear only random sound, neither pleasant nor unpleasant, merely incomprehensible.

The next morning they conduct me on a grand tour of the Sanctuary complex to show me everything that has been constructed here since my last visit. The tropical sunlight is brilliant, dazzling, so strong that it bleaches the sky to a matte white, against which the colorful domes and pavilions and spires of the complex stand out in strange clarity and the lofty green bowl of surrounding hills, thick and lush with flowering trees bedecked in yellow and purple, takes on a heavy, looming quality.

Kastel, the Lord Invocator, is my chief guide, a burly, red-faced man with small, shrewd eyes and a deceptively hearty manner. With us also are a woman from the office of the Oracle and two sub-Adjudicators. They hurry me, though with the utmost tact, from one building to the next. All four of them treat me as though I were something extremely fragile, made of the most delicate spun glass—or, perhaps, as though I were a bomb primed to explode at the touch of a breath.

"Over here on the left," says Kastel, "is the new observatory, with the finest scanning equipment ever devised, providing continuous input from every region of the Mission. The scanner itself, I regret to say, Lord Magistrate, is out of service this morning. There, of course, is the shrine of the blessed Haakon. Here we see the computer core, and this, behind it under the opaque canopy, is the recently completed stellarium."

I see leaping fountains, marble pavements, alabaster walls, gleaming metallic facades. They are very proud of what they have constructed here. The House of the Sanctuary has evolved over the decades, and by now has come to combine in itself aspects of a pontifical capital, a major research facility, and the ultimate sybaritic resort. Everything is bright, shining, startlingly luxurious. It is at once a place of great symbolic power, a potent focus of spiritual authority as overwhelming in its grandeur as any great ceremonial center of the past—ranking with the Vatican, the Potala, the shrine at Delphi, the grand temple of the Aztecs—and an efficient command post for the systematic exploration of the universe. No one doubts that the Sanctuary is the primary House of the Order—how could it be anything else?—but the splendors of this mighty eyrie underscore that primacy beyond all question. In truth I prefer the starker, more disciplined surroundings of my own desert domain, ten thousand kilometers away. But the Sanctuary is certainly impressive in its way.

"And that one down there?" I ask, more for politeness' sake than anything else. "The long flat-roofed building near that row of palms?"

"The detention center, Lord Magistrate," replies one of the sub-Adjudicators.

I give him a questioning look.

"People from the towns below constantly come wandering in here," he explains. "Trespassers, I mean." His expression is cold. Plainly the intruders of which he speaks are annoyances to him; or is it my question that bothers him? "They hope they can talk us into shipping them out, you understand. Or think that the actual transmitters are somewhere on the premises and they can ship themselves out when nobody's looking. We keep them for a while, so that they'll learn that trying to break in here isn't acceptable. Not that it does much good. They keep on coming. We've caught at least twenty so far this week."

Kastel laughs. "We try to teach them a thing or two, all right! But they're too stupid to learn."

"They have no chance of getting past the perimeter screen," says the woman from the Oracle's office. "We pick them up right away. But as Joseph says, they keep on coming all the same." She shivers. "They look so dirty! And mean, and frightening. I don't think they want to be shipped out at all. I think they're just bandits who come up here to try to steal from us, and when they're caught they give us a story about wanting to be colonists. We're much too gentle with them, let me tell you. If we started dealing with them like the thieves they are, they wouldn't be so eager to come creeping around in here."

I find myself wondering just what does happen to the detainees in the detention center. I suspect that they are treated a good deal less gently than the woman from the Oracle's office thinks, or would have me believe. But I am only a guest here. It's not my place to make inquiries into their security methods.

It is like another world up here above the clouds. Below is the teeming Earth, dark and troubled, cult-ridden, doom-ridden, sweltering and stewing in its own corruption and decay; while in this airy realm far above the crumbling and sweltering cities of the plain these votaries of the Order, safe behind their perimeter screen, go quietly about their task of designing and clarifying the plan that is carrying mankind's best outward into God's starry realm. The contrast is vast and jarring: pink marble terraces and fountains here, disease and squalor and despair below.

And yet, is it any different at my own headquarters on the Australian plains? In our House we do not go in for these architectural splendors, no alabaster, no onyx, just plain green metal shacks to house our equipment and ourselves. But we keep ourselves apart from the hungry sweaty multitudes in hieratic seclusion, a privileged caste, living simply but well, undeniably well, as we perform our own task of selecting those who are to go to the stars and sending them forth on their unimaginable journeys. In our own way we are as remote from the pressures and torments of mankind as these coddled functionaries of the Sanctuary. We know nothing of the life beyond our own Order. Nothing. Nothing.

The Master says, "I was too harsh yesterday, and even blasphemous." The map behind him is aglow once again, displaying the inner sphere of the galaxy and the lines marking the network of the Mission, as it had the day before. The Master himself is glowing too, his soft skin ruddy as a baby's, his eyes agleam. How old is he? A hundred fifty? Two hundred? "The map, after all, shows us the face of God," he says. "If the map is inadequate, it simply reveals the inadequacies of our own perceptions. But should we condemn it, then? Hardly, any more than we should condemn ourselves for not being gods. We should revere it, rather, flawed though it may be, because it is the best approximation that we can ever make of the reality of the Divine."

"The face of God?"

"What is God, if not the Great Totality? And how can we expect to see and comprehend the Totality of the Totality in a single glance?" The Master smiles. These are not thoughts that he has just had for the first time, nor can his complete reversal of yesterday's outburst be a spontaneous one. He is playing with me. "God is eternal motion through infinite space. He is the cosmos as it was twelve billion years ago and as it was twelve billion years from now, all in the same instant. This map you see here is our pitiful attempt at a representation of something inherently incapable of being represented; but we are to be praised for making an attempt, however foredoomed, at doing that which cannot be done."

I nod. I stare. What could I possibly say?

"When we experience the revelation of God," the Master continues softly, "what we receive is not the communication of a formula about a static world, which enables us to be at rest, but rather a sense of the power of the Creator, which sets us in motion even as He is in motion."

I think of Dante, who said, "In His will is our peace." Is there a contradiction here? How can "motion" be "peace"? Why is the Master telling me all this? Theology has never been my specialty, nor the specialty of my House in general, and he knows that. The abstruse nature of this discussion is troublesome to me. My eyes rest upon the Master, but their focus changes, so that I am looking beyond him, to red Antares and blue Rigel and fiery blue-white Vega, blazing at me from the wall.

The Master says, "Our Mission, you must surely agree, is an aspect of God's great plan. It is His way of enabling us to undertake the journey toward Him."

"Of course."

"Then whatever thwarts the design of the Mission must be counter to the will of God, is that not so?"

It is not a question. I am silent again, waiting.

He gestures toward the screen. "I would think that you know this pattern of lights and lines better than you do that of the palm of your hand."

"So I do."

"What about this one?"

The Master touches a control. The pattern suddenly changes: the bright symmetrical network linking the inner stars is sundered, and streaks of light now skid wildly out of the center toward the far reaches of the galaxy, like errant particles racing outward in a photomicrograph of an atomic reaction. The sight is a jarring one: balance overthrown, the sky untuned, discordancy triumphant. I wince and lean back from it as though he has slapped my face.

"Ah. You don't like it, eh?"

"Your pardon. It seems like a desecration."

"It is," he says. "Exactly so."

I feel chilled. I want him to restore the screen to its proper state. But he leaves the shattered image where it is.

He says, "This is only a probability projection, you understand. Based on early fragmentary reports from the farther outposts, by way of the Order's relay station on Lalande 21185. We aren't really sure what's going on out there. What we hope, naturally, is that our projections are inaccurate and that the plan is being followed after all. Harder data will be here soon."

"Some of those lines must reach out a thousand light-years!"

"More than that."

"Nothing could possibly have gotten so far from Earth in just the hundred years or so that we've been—"

"These are projections. Those are vectors. But they seem to be telling us that some carrier ships have been aimed beyond the predetermined targets, and are moving through the Dark on trajectories far more vast than anything we intend."

"But the plan—the Mission—"

His voice begins to develop an edge again. "Those whom we, acting through your House, have selected to implement the plan are very far from home, Lord Magistrate. They are no longer subject to our control. If they choose to do as they please once they're fifty light-years away, what means do we have of bringing them into check?"

"I find it very hard to believe that any of the colonists we've sent forth would be capable of setting aside the ordinances of Darklaw," I say, with perhaps too much heat in my voice.

What I have done, I realize, is to contradict him. Contradicting the Master is never a good idea. I see the lightnings playing about his head, though his expression remains mild and he continues to regard me benignly. Only the faintest of flushes on his ancient face betrays his anger. He makes no reply. I am getting into deep waters very quickly.

"Meaning no disrespect," I say, "but if this is, as you say, only a probability projection—"

"All that we have devoted our lives to is in jeopardy now," he says quietly. "What are we to do? What are we to do, Lord Magistrate?"

We have been building our highway to the stars for a century now and a little more, laying down one small pavingblock after another. That seems like a long time to those of us who measure our spans in tens of years, and we have nibbled only a small way into the great darkness; but though we often feel that progress has been slow, in fact we have achieved miracles already, and we have all of eternity to complete our task.

In summoning us toward Him, God did not provide us with magical chariots. The inflexible jacket of the relativistic equations constrains us as we work. The speed of light remains our limiting factor while we establish our network. Although the Velde Effect allows us to deceive it and in effect to sidestep it, we must first carry the Velde receivers to the stars, and for that we can use only conventional spacegoing vehicles. They can approach the velocity of light, they may virtually attain it, but they can never exceed it: a starship making the outward journey to a star forty lightyears from Earth must needs spend some forty years, and some beyond, in the doing of it. Later, when all the sky is linked by our receivers, that will not be a problem. But that is later.

The key to all that we do is the matter/antimatter relationship. When He built the universe for us, He placed all things in balance. The basic constituents of matter come in matched pairs: for each kind of particle there is an antiparticle, identical in mass but otherwise wholly opposite in all properties, mirror images in such things as electrical charge and axis of spin. Matter and antimatter annihilate one another upon contact, releasing tremendous energy. Conversely, any sufficiently strong energy field can bring about the creation of pairs of particles and antiparticles in equal quantities, though mutual annihilation will inevitably follow, converting the mass of the paired particles back into energy.

Apparently there is, and always has been since the Creation, a symmetry of matter and antimatter in the universe, equal quantities of each—a concept that has often been questioned by physicists, but which we believe now to be God's true design. Because of the incompatibility of matter and antimatter in the same vicinity, there is very little if any antimatter in our galaxy, which leads us to suppose that if symmetry is conserved, it must be through the existence of entire galaxies of antimatter, or even clusters of galaxies, at great distances from our own. Be that as it may: we will probably have no way of confirming or denying that for many thousands of years.

But the concept of symmetry is the essential thing. We base our work on Velde's Theorem, which suggests that the spontaneous conversion of matter into antimatter may occur at any time—though in fact it is an event of infinitesimal probability—but it must inescapably be accompanied by a simultaneous equal decay of antimatter into matter somewhere else, anywhere else, in the universe. About the same time that Velde offered this idea—that is, roughly a century and a half ago—Wilf demonstrated the feasibility of containment facilities capable of averting the otherwise inevitable mutual annihilation of matter and antimatter, thus making possible the controlled transformation of particles into their antiparticles. Finally came the work of Simtow, linking Wilf's technical achievements with Velde's theoretical work and giving us a device that not only achieved controlled matter/antimatter conversion but also coped with the apparent randomness of Velde symmetry-conservation.

Simtow's device tunes the Velde Effect so that conversion of matter into antimatter is accompanied by the requisite balancing transformation of antimatter into matter, not at some random site anywhere in the universe, but at a designated site. Simtow was able to induce particle decay at one pole of a closed system in such a way that a corresponding but opposite decay occurs at the other. Wilf containment fields were employed at both ends of the system to prevent annihilation of the newly converted particles by ambient particles of the opposing kind.

The way was open now, though it was some time before we realized it, for the effective instanteous transmission of matter across great distances. That was achieved by placing the receiving pole of a Simtow transformer at the intended destination. Then an intricate three-phase cycle carried out the transmission.

In the first phase, matter is converted into antimatter at the destination end in an untuned reaction, and stored in a Wilf containment vessel. This, following Velde's conservation equations, presumably would induce spontaneous transformation of an equivalent mass of antimatter into matter in one of the unknown remote antimatter galaxies, where it would be immediately annihilated.

In the second phase, matter is converted to antimatter

at the transmitting end, this time employing Simtow tuning so that the corresponding Velde-law transformation of the previously stored antimatter takes place not at some remote and random location but within the Wilf field at the designated receiving pole, which may be situated anywhere in the universe. What this amounts to, essentially, is the instantaneous particle-by-particle duplication of the transmitted matter at the receiving end.

The final step is to dispose of the unwanted antimatter that has been created at the transmission end. Since it is unstable outside the Wilf containment vessel, its continued existence in an all-matter system is pointless as well as untenable. Therefore it is annihilated under controlled circumstances, providing a significant release of energy that can be tapped to power a new cycle of the transmission process.

What is accomplished by all this? A certain quantity of matter at the transmission end of the system is destroyed; an exact duplicate of it is created, essentially simultaneously, at the receiving end. It made no difference, the early experimenters discovered, what was being put through the system: a stone, a book, a potted geranium, a frog. Whatever went in here came out there, an apparently perfect replica, indistinguishable in all respects from the original. Whether the two poles were situated at opposite ends of the same laboratory, or in different continents, or on Earth and Mars, the transmission was instant and total. What went forth alive came out alive. The geranium still bloomed and set seed; the frog still stared and leaped and gobbled insects. A mouse was sent, and thrived, and went on to live and die a full mouse-life. A pregnant cat made the journey and was delivered, three weeks later, of five healthy kittens. A dog— an ape—a man—

A man, yes. Has anyone ever made a bolder leap into the darkness than God's great servant Haakon Christiansen, the blessed Haakon whom we all celebrate and revere? He gambled everything on one toss of the dice, and won, and by his victory made himself immortal and gave us a gift beyond price.

His successful voyage opened the heavens. All we needed to do now was set up receiving stations. The Moon, Mars, the moons of Jupiter and Saturn, were only an eye-blink away. And then? Then? Why, of course, what remained but to carry our receivers to the stars?

For hours I wander the grounds of the Sanctuary, alone, undisturbed, deeply troubled. It is as if a spell of silence and solitude surrounds and protects me. No one dares approach me, neither as a supplicant of some sort nor to offer obei-sance nor merely to see if I am in need of any service. I suppose many eyes are studying me warily from a distance, but in some way it must be obvious to all who observe me that I am not to be intruded upon. I must cast a forbidding aura today. In the brilliance of the tropic afternoon a dark-ness and a chill have settled over my soul. It seems to me that the splendid grounds are white with snow as far as I can see, snow on the hills, snow on the lawns, snow piled high along the banks of the sparkling streams, a sterile whiteness all the way to the rim of the world.

I am a dour man, but not a melancholy or tormented one. Others mistake my disciplined nature for something darker, seeing in me an iciness of spirit, a somberness, a harshness that masks some pervasive anguish of the heart. It is not so. If I have renounced the privilege of going to the stars, which could surely have been mine, it is not be-cause I love the prospect of ending my days on this maimed and ravaged world of ours, but because I feel that God de-mands this service of me, that I remain here and help others to go forth. If I am hard and stern, it is because I can be nothing else, considering the choices I have made in shaping my course: I am a priest and a magistrate and a soldier of sorts, all in one. I have passed a dedicated and cloistered life. Yet I understand joy. There is a music in me. My senses are fully alive, all of them. From the outside I may appear unyielding and grim, but it is only because I have chosen to deny myself the pleasure of being ordinary, of being slothful, of being unproductive. There are those who misunderstand that in me, and see me as some kind of dismal monastic, narrow and fanatical, a gloomy man, a desolate man, one whom the commonplace would do well to fear and to shun. I think they are wrong. Yet this day, contemplating all that the Master has just told me and much that he has only implied, I am swept with such storms of foreboding and distress that I must radiate a frightful bleakness which warns others away. At any rate for much of this afternoon they all leave me alone to roam as I please.

The Sanctuary is a self-sufficient world. It needs nothing from outside. I stand near the summit of the great hill, looking down on children playing, gardeners setting out new plantings, novitiates sitting crosslegged at their studies on the lawn. I look toward the gardens and try to see color, but all color has leached away. The sun has passed beyond the horizon, here at this high altitude, but the sky is luminous. It is like a band of hot metal, glowing white. It devours everything: the edges of the world are slowly being engulfed by it. Whiteness is all, a universal snowy blanket.

For a long while I watch the children. They laugh, they shriek, they run in circles and fall down and rise again, still laughing. Don't they feel the sting of the snow? But the snow, I remind myself, is not there. It is illusionary snow, metaphorical snow, a trick of my troubled soul, a snowfall of the spirit. For the children there is no snow. I choose a little girl, taller and more serious than the others, standing somewhat to one side, and pretend that she is my own child. A strange idea, myself as a father, but pleasing. I could have had children. It might not have meant a very different life from the one I have had. But it was not what I chose. Now I toy with the fantasy for a time, enjoying it. I invent a name for the girl; I picture her running to me up the grassy slope; I see us sitting quietly together, poring over a chart of the sky. I tell her the names of the stars, I show her the constellations. The vision is so compelling that I begin to descend the slope toward her. She looks up at me while I am still some distance from her. I smile. She stares, solemn, uncertain of my intentions. Other children nudge her, point, and whisper. They draw back, edging away from me. It is as if my shadow has fallen upon them and chilled them as they played. I nod and move on, releasing them from its darkness.

A path strewn with glossy green leaves takes me to an overlook point at the cliff's edge, where I can see the broad bay far below, at the foot of Sanctuary Mountain. The water gleams like a burnished shield, or perhaps it is more like a huge shimmering pool of quicksilver. I imagine myself leaping from the stone balcony where I stand and soaring outward in a sharp smooth arc, striking the water cleanly, knifing down through it, vanishing without a trace.

Returning to the main Sanctuary complex, I happen to glance downslope toward the long narrow new building that I have been told is the detention center. A portcullis at its eastern end has been hoisted and a procession of prisoners is coming out. I know they are prisoners because they are roped together and walk in a sullen, slack way, heads down, shoulders slumped.

They are dressed in rags and tatters, or less than that. Even from fairly far away I can see cuts and bruises and scabs on them, and one has his arm in a sling, and one is bandaged so that nothing shows of his face but his glinting eyes. Three guards walk alongside them, carelessly dangling neural truncheons from green lanyards. The ropes that bind the prisoners are loosely tied, a perfunctory restraint. It would be no great task for them to break free and seize the truncheons from the captors. But they seem utterly beaten down; for them to make any sort of move toward freedom is probably as unlikely as the advent of an army of winged dragons swooping across the sky.

They are an incongruous and disturbing sight, these miserable prisoners plodding across this velvet landscape. Does the Master know that they are here, and that they are so poorly kept? I start to walk toward them. The Lord Invocator Kastel, emerging suddenly from nowhere as if he had been waiting behind a bush, steps across my path and says, "God keep you, your grace. Enjoying your stroll through the grounds?"

"Those people down there—"

"They are nothing, Lord Magistrate. Only some of our thieving rabble, coming out for a little fresh air."

"Are they well? Some of them look injured."

Kastel tugs at one ruddy fleshy jowl. "They are desperate people. Now and then they try to attack their guards. Despite all precautions we can't always avoid the use of force in restraining them."

"Of course. I quite understand," I say, making no effort to hide my sarcasm. "Is the Master aware that helpless prisoners are being beaten within a thousand meters of his lodge?"

"Lord Magistrate—!"

"If we are not humane in all our acts, what are we, Lord Invocator Kastel? What example do we set for the common folk?"

"It's these common folk of yours," Kastel says sharply—I

have not heard that tone from him before—"who ring this place like an army of filthy vermin, eager to steal anything they can carry away and destroy everything else. Do you realize, Lord Magistrate, that this mountain rises like a towering island of privilege above a sea of hungry people? That within a sixty-kilometer radius of these foothills there are probably thirty million empty bellies? That if our perimeter defenses were to fail, they'd sweep through here like locusts and clean the place out? And probably slaughter every last one of us, up to and including the Master."

"God forbid."

"God created them. He must love them. But if this House is going to carry out the work God intended for us, we have to keep them at bay. I tell you, Lord Magistrate, leave these grubby matters of administration to us. In a few days you'll go flying off to your secluded nest in the Outback, where your work is undisturbed by problems like these. Whereas we'll still be here, in our pretty little mountain paradise, with enemies on every side. If now and then we take some action that you might not consider entirely humane, I ask you to remember that we guard the Master here, who is the heart of the Mission." He allows me, for a moment, to see the contempt he feels for my qualms. Then he is all affability and concern again. In a completely different tone he says, "The observatory's scanning equipment will be back in operation again tonight. I want to invite you to watch the data come pouring in from every corner of space. It's an inspiring sight, Lord Magistrate."

"I would be pleased to see it."

"The progress we've made, Lord Magistrate—the way we've moved out and out, always in accordance with the divine plan—I tell you, I'm not what you'd call an emotional man, but when I see the track we're making across the Dark my eyes begin to well up, let me tell you. My eyes begin to well up."

His eyes, small and keen, study me for a reaction.

Then he says, "Everything's all right for you here?"

"Of course, Lord Invocator."

"Your conversations with the Master—have they met with your expectations?"

"Entirely so. He is truly a saint."

"Truly, Lord Magistrate. Truly."

"Where would the Mission be without him?"

"Where will it be," says Kastel thoughtfully, "when he is no longer here to guide us?"

"May that day be far from now."

"Indeed," Kastel says. "Though I have to tell you, in all confidence, I've started lately to fear—"

His voice trails off.

"Yes?"

"The Master," he whispers. "Didn't he seem different to you, somehow?"

"Different?"

"I know it's years since you last saw him. Perhaps you don't remember him as he was."

"He seemed lucid and powerful to me, the most commanding of men," I reply.

Kastel nods. He takes me by the arm and gently steers me toward the upper buildings of the Sanctuary complex, away from those ghastly prisoners, who are still shuffling about like walking corpses in front of their jail. Quietly he says, "Did he tell you that he thinks someone's interfering with the plan? That he has evidence that some of the receivers are being shipped far beyond the intended destinations?"

I look at him, wide-eyed.

"Do you really expect me to violate the confidential nature of the Master's audiences with me?"

"Of course not! Of course not, Lord Magistrate. But just between you and me—and we're both important men in the Order, it's essential that we level with each other at all times—I can admit to you that I'm pretty certain what the Master must have told you. Why else would he have sent for you? Why else pull you away from your House and interrupt what is now the key activity of the Mission? He's obsessed with this idea that there have been deviations from the plan. He's reading God knows what into the data. But I don't want to try to influence you. It's absurd to think that a man of your supreme rank in the second House of the Order can't analyze the situation unaided. You come tonight, you look at what the scanner says, you make up your own mind. That's all I ask. All right, Lord Magistrate? All right?"

He walks away, leaving me stunned and shocked. The Master insane? Or the Lord Invocator disloyal? Either one is unthinkable.

I will go to the observatory tonight, yes.

Kastel, by approaching me, seems to have broken the mysterious spell of privacy that has guarded me all afternoon. Now they come from all sides, crowding around me as though I am some archangel—staring, whispering, smiling hopefully at me. They gesture, they kneel. The bravest of them come right up to me and tell me their names, as though I will remember them when the time comes to send the next settlers off to the worlds of Epsilon Eridani, of Castor C, of Ross 154, of Wolf 359. I am kind with them, I am gracious, I am warm. It costs me nothing; it gives them happiness. I think of those bruised and slumpshouldered prisoners sullenly parading in front of the detention center. For them I can do nothing; for these, the maids and gardeners and acolytes and novitiates of the Sanctuary, I can at least provide a flicker of hope. And, smiling at them, reaching my hands toward them, my own mood lightens. All will be well. God will prevail, as ever. The Kastels of this world cannot dismay me.

I see the little girl at the edge of the circle, the one whom I had taken, for a strange instant, to be my daughter. Once again I smile at her. Once again she gives me a solemn stare, and edges away. There is laughter. "She means no disrespect," a woman says. "Shall I bring her to you, your grace?" I shake my head. "I must frighten her," I say. "Let her be." But the girl's stare remains to haunt me, and I see snow about me once more, thickening in the sky, covering the lush gardens of the Sanctuary, spreading to the rim of the world and beyond.

In the observatory they hand me a polarizing helmet to protect my eyes. The data flux is an overpowering sight: hot pulsing flares, like throbbing suns. I catch just a glimpse of it while still in the vestibule. The world, which has thawed for me, turns to snow yet again. It is a total white-out, a flash of photospheric intensity that washes away all surfaces and dechromatizes the universe.

"This way, your grace. Let me assist you."

Soft voices. Solicitous proximity. To them, I suppose, I am an old man. Yet the Master was old before I was born. Does he ever come here?

I hear them whispering: "The Lord Magistrate—the Lord Magistrate—"

The observatory, which I have never seen before, is one huge room, an eight-sided building as big as a cathedral, very dark and shadowy within, massive walls of some smooth moist-looking greenish stone, vaulted roof of burnished red metal, actually not a roof of all but an intricate antenna of colossal size and complexity, winding round and round and round upon itself. Spidery catwalks run everywhere to link the various areas of the great room. There is no telescope. This is not that sort of observatory. This is the central gathering-point for three rings of data-collectors, one on the Moon, one somewhere beyond the orbit of Jupiter, one eight light-years away on a world of the star Lalande 21185. They scan the heavens and pump a stream of binary digits toward this building, where the data arrives in awesome convulsive actinic spurts, like thunderbolts hurled from Olympus.

There is another wall-sized map of the Mission here, the same sort of device that I saw in the Master's office, but at least five times as large. It too displays the network of the inner stars illuminated in bright yellow lines. But it is the old pattern, the familiar one, the one we have worked with since the inception of the program. This screen shows none of the wild divagations and bizarre trajectories that marked the image the Master showed me in my last audience with him.

"The system's been down for four days," a voice at my elbow murmurs: one of the astronomers, a young one, who evidently has been assigned to me. She is dark-haired, snub-nosed, bright-eyed, a pleasant-faced girl. "We're just priming it now, bringing it up to realtime level. That's why the flares are so intense. There's a terrific mass of data backed up in the system and it's all trying to get in here at once."

"I see."

She smiles. "If you'll move this way, your grace—"

She guides me toward an inner balcony that hangs suspended over a well-like pit perhaps a hundred meters deep. In the dimness far below I see metal arms weaving in slow patterns, great gleaming disks turning rapidly, mirrors blinking and flashing. My astronomer explains that this is the main focal limb, or some such thing, but the details are lost on me. The whole building is quivering and trembling here, as though it is being pounded by a giant's hand. Colors are changing: the spectrum is being tugged far off to one side. Gripping the rail of the balcony, I feel a terrible vertigo coming over me. It seems to me that the expansion of the universe has suddenly been reversed, that all the galaxies are converging on this point, that I am standing in a vortex where floods of ultraviolet light, x-rays, and gamma rays come rushing in from all points of the cosmos at once. "Do you notice it?" I hear myself asking. "The violet-shift? Everything running backwards toward the center?"

"What's that, your grace?"

I am muttering incoherently. She has not understood a word, thank God! I see her staring at me, worried, perhaps shocked. But I pull myself together, I smile, I manage to offer a few rational-sounding questions. She grows calm. Making allowances for my age, perhaps, and for my ignorance of all that goes on in this building. I have my own area of technical competence, she knows—oh, yes, she certainly knows that!—but she realizes that it is quite different from hers.

From my vantage point overlooking the main focal limb I watch with more awe than comprehension as the data pours in, is refined and clarified, is analyzed, is synthesized, is registered on the various display units arrayed on the walls of the observatory. The young woman at my side keeps up a steady whispered flow of commentary, but I am distracted by the terrifying patterns of light and shadow all about me, by sudden and unpredictable bursts of high-pitched sound, by the vibrations of the building, and I miss some of the critical steps in her explanations and rapidly find myself lost. In truth I understand almost nothing of what is taking place around me. No doubt it is significant.

The place is crowded with members of the Order, and high ones at that, everyone at least an initiate, several wearing the armbands of the inner levels of the primary House, the red, the green, even a few amber. Lord Invocator Kastel is here, smiling smugly, embracing people like a politician, coming by more than once to make sure I appreciate the high drama of this great room. I nod, I smile, I assure him of my gratitude.

Indeed it is dramatic. Now that I have recovered from my vertigo I find myself looking outward rather than down, and my senses ride heavenward as though I myself am traveling to the stars.

This is the nerve-center of our Mission, this is the grand sensorium by which we keep track of our achievement.

The Alpha Centauri system was the starting-point, of course, when we first began seeding the stars with Velde receivers, and then Barnard's Star, Wolf 359, Lalande 21185, and so on outward and outward, Sirius, Ross 154, Epsilon Indi—who does not know the names?—to all the stars within a dozen light-years of Earth. Small unmanned starships, laser-powered robot drones, unfurling great lightsails and gliding starward on the urgent breath of photonic winds that we ourselves stirred up. Light was their propulsive force, and its steady pressure afforded constant acceleration, swiftly stepping up the velocity of our ships until it approached that of light.

Then, as they neared the stars that were their destinations, scanning for planets by one method or another, plotting orbital deviations or homing in on infrared radiation or measuring Doppler shifts—finding worlds, and sorting them to eliminate the unlivable ones, the gas giants, the ice-balls, the formaldehyde atmospheres—

One by one our little vessels made landfall on new Earths. Silently opened their hatches. Sent forth the robots who would set up the Velde receivers that would be our gateways. One by one, opening the heavens.

And then—the second phase, the fabricating devices emerging, going to work, tiny machines seeking out carbon, silicon, nitrogen, oxygen, and the rest of the necessary building-blocks, stacking up the atoms in the predesignated patterns, assembling new starships, new laser banks, new Velde receivers. Little mechanical minds giving the orders, little mechanical arms doing the work. It would take some fifteen years for one of our ships to reach a star twelve light-years away. But it would require much less than that for our automatic replicators to construct a dozen twins of that ship at the landing point and send them in a dozen directions, each bearing its own Velde receiver to be established on some farther star, each equipped to replicate itself just as quickly and send more ships onward. Thus we built our receiver network, spreading our highway from world to world across a sphere that by His will and our choice would encompass only a hundred light-years in the beginning. Then from our transmitters based on Earth we could begin to send—instantly, miraculously—the first colonists to the new worlds within our delimited sphere.

And so have we done. Standing here with my hands gripping the metal rail of the observatory balcony, I can in imagination send my mind forth to our colonies in the stars, to those tiny far-flung outposts peopled by the finest souls Earth can produce, men and women whom I myself have helped to choose and prepare and hurl across the gulf of night, pioneers sworn to Darklaw, bound by the highest of oaths not to repeat in the stars the errors we have made on Earth. And, thinking now of everything that our Order has achieved and all that we will yet achieve, the malaise that has afflicted my spirit since I arrived at the Sanctuary lifts, and a flood of joy engulfs me, and I throw my head back,

I stare toward the maze of data-gathering circuitry far above me, I let the full splendor of the Project invade my soul.

It is a wondrous moment, but short-lived. Into my ecstasies come intrusive sounds: mutterings, gasps, the scurrying of feet. I snap to attention. All about me, there is sudden excitement, almost a chaos. Someone is sobbing. Someone else is laughing. It is a wild, disagreeable laughter that is just this side of hysteria. A furious argument has broken out across the way: the individual words are blurred by echo but the anger of their inflection is unmistakable.

"What's happening?" I ask the astronomer beside me.

"The master chart," she says. Her voice has become thick and hoarse. There is a troubled gleam in her eyes. "It's showing the update now—the new information that's just come in—"

She points. I stare at the glowing star-map. The familiar pattern of the Mission network has been disrupted, now, and what I see, what they all see, is that same crazy display of errant tracks thrusting far out beyond our designated sphere of colonization that I beheld on the Master's own screen two days before.

The most tactful thing I can do, in the difficult few days that follow, is to withdraw to my quarters and wait until the Sanctuary people have begun to regain their equilibrium. My being here among them now must be a great embarrassment for them. They are taking this apparent deviation from the Mission's basic plan as a deep humiliation and a stinging rebuke upon their House. They find it not merely profoundly disquieting and improper, as I do, but a mark of shame, a sign that God himself has found inadequate the plan of which they are the designers and custodians, and has discarded it. How much more intense their loss of face must be for all this to be coming down upon them at a time when the Lord Magistrate of the Order's other high House is among them to witness their disgrace.

It would be even more considerate of me, perhaps, to return at once to my own House's headquarters in Australia and let the Sanctuary people sort out their position without my presence to distract and reproach them. But that I cannot do. The Master wants me here. He has called me all the way from Australia to be with him at the Sanctuary in this difficult time. Here I must stay until I know why.

So I keep out of the way. I ask for my meals in my chambers instead of going to the communal hall. I spend my days and nights in prayer and meditation and reading. I sip brandy and divert myself with music. I take pleasure from the dispenser when the need comes over me. I stay out of sight and await the unfolding of events.

But my isolation is shortlived. On the third day after my retreat into solitude Kastel comes to me, pale and shaken, all his hearty condescension gone from him now.

"Tell me," he says hoarsely, "what do you make of all this? Do you think the data's genuine?"

"What reason do I have to think otherwise?"

"But suppose"—he hesitates, and his eyes do not quite meet mine—"suppose the Master has rigged things somehow so that we're getting false information?"

"Would that be possible? And why would he do such a monstrous thing in the first place?"

"I don't know."

"Do you really have so little regard for the Master's honesty? Or is it his sanity that you question?"

He turns crimson.

"God forbid, either one!" he cries. "The Master is beyond all censure. I wonder only whether he has embarked upon some strange plan beyond our comprehension, absolutely beyond our understanding, which in the execution of his unfathomable purpose requires him to deceive us about the true state of things in the heavens."

Kastel's cautious, elaborately formal syntax offends my ear. He did not speak to me in such baroque turns and curlicues when he was explaining why it was necessary to beat the prisoners in the detention center. But I try not to let him see my distaste for him. Indeed he seems more to be pitied than detested, a frightened and bewildered man.

"Why don't you ask the Master?" I say.

"Who would dare? But in any case the Master has shut himself away from us all since the other night."

"Ah. Then ask the Oracle."

"The Oracle offers only mysteries and redundancies, as usual."

"I can't offer anything better," I tell him. "Have faith in the Master. Accept the data of your own scanner until you have solid reason to doubt it. Trust God."

Kastel, seeing I can tell him nothing useful, and obviously uneasy now over having expressed these all but sacrilegious suppositions about the Master to me, asks a blessing of me, and I give it, and he goes. But others come after him, one by one—hesitantly, even fearfully, as though expecting me to turn them away in scorn. High and low, haughty and humble, they seek audiences with me. I understand now what is happening. With the Master in seclusion, the community is leaderless in this difficult moment. On him they dare not intrude under any circumstances, if he has given the sign that he is not to be approached. I am the next highest ranking member of the hierarchy currently in residence at the Sanctuary. That I am of another House, and that between the Master and me lies an immense gulf of age and primacy, does not seem to matter to them just now. So it is to me that they come, asking for guidance, comfort, whatever. I give them what I can—platitudes, mainly—until I begin to feel hollow and cynical. Toward evening the young astronomer comes to me, she who had guided me through the observatory on the night of the great revelation. Her eyes are red and swollen, with dark rings below them. By now I have grown expert at offering these Sanctuary people the bland reassurances that are the best I can provide for them, but as I launch into what has become my standard routine I see that it is doing more harm to her than good—she begins to tremble, tears roll down her cheeks, she shakes her head and looks away, shivering—and suddenly my own facade of spiritual authority and philosophical detachment crumbles, and I am as troubled and confused as she is. I realize that she and I stand at the brink of the same black abyss. I begin to feel myself toppling forward into it. We reach for each other and embrace in a kind of wild defiance of our fears. She is half my age. Her skin is smooth, her flesh is firm. We each grasp for whatever comfort we can find. Afterward she seems stunned, numbed, dazed. She dresses in silence.

"Stay," I urge her. "Wait until morning."

"Please, your grace—no—no—"

But she manages a faint smile. Perhaps she is trying to tell me that though she is amazed by what we have done she feels no horror and perhaps not even regret. I hold the tips of her fingers in my hands for a moment, and we kiss quickly, a dry, light, chaste kiss, and she goes.

Afterward I experience a strange new clarity of mind. It is as if this unexpected coupling has burned away a thick fog of the soul and allowed me to think clearly once again.

In the night, which for me is a night of very little sleep, I contemplate the events of my stay at the House of Sanctuary and I come to terms, finally, with the obvious truth that I have tried to avoid for days. I remember the Master's casual phrase at my second audience with him, as he told me of his suspicion that certain colonists must be deviating from the tenets of Darklaw: "Those whom we, acting through your House, have selected. . . ." Am I being accused of some malfeasance? Yes. Of course. I am the one who chose the ones who have turned away from the plan. It has been decided that the guilt is to fall upon me. I should have seen it much earlier, but I have been distracted, I suppose, by troublesome emotions. Or else I have simply been unwilling to see.

I decide to fast today. When they bring me my morning meal-tray they will find a note from me, instructing them not to come to me again until I notify them.

I tell myself that this is not so much an act of penitence as one of purgation. Fasting is not something that the Order asks of us. For me it is a private act, one which I feel brings me closer to God. In any case my conscience is clear; it is simply that there are times when I think better on an empty stomach, and I am eager now to maintain and deepen that lucidity of perception that came upon me late the previous evening. I have fasted before, many times, when I felt a similar need. But then, when I take my morning shower, I dial it cold. The icy water burns and stings and flays; I have to compel myself to remain under it, but I do remain, and I hold myself beneath the shower head much longer than I might ordinarily have stayed there. That can only be penitence. Well, so be it. But penitence for what? I am guilty of no fault. Do they really intend to make me the scapegoat? Do I intend to offer myself to expiate the general failure? Why should I? Why do I punish myself now?

All that will be made known to me later. If I have chosen to impose a day of austerity and discomfort upon myself, there must be a good reason for it, and I will understand in good time.

Meanwhile I wear nothing but a simple linen robe of a rough texture, and savor the roughness against my skin. My stomach, by mid-morning, begins to grumble and protest, and I give it a glass of water, as though to mock its needs. A little later the vision of a fine meal assails me, succulent grilled fish on a shining porcelain plate, cool white wine in a sparkling crystal goblet. My throat goes dry, my head throbs. But instead of struggling against these tempting images I encourage them, I invite my traitor mind to do its worst: I add platters of gleaming red grapes to the imaginary feast, cheeses, loaves of bread fresh from the oven. The fish course is succeeded by roast lamb, the lamb by skewers of beef, the wine in the glass is now a fine red Coonawarra, there is rare old port to come afterward. I fantasize such gluttonies that they become absurd, and I lose my appetite altogether.

The hours go by and I begin to drift into the tranquility that for me is the first sign of the presence of God close at hand. Yet I find myself confronting a barrier. Instead of simply accepting His advent and letting Him engulf me, I trouble myself with finicky questions. Is He approaching me, I wonder? Or am I moving toward Him? I tell myself that the issue is an empty one. He is everywhere. It is the power of God which sets us in motion, yes, but He is motion incarnate. It is pointless to speak of my approaching Him, or His approaching me: those are two ways of describing the same thing. But while I contemplate such matters my mind itself holds me apart from Him.

I imagine myself in a tiny ship, drifting toward the stars. To make such a voyage is not what I desire; but it is a useful focus for my reverie. For the journey to the stars and the journey toward God are one thing and the same. It is the journey into reality.

Once, I know, these things were seen in a different light.

But it was inevitable that as we began to penetrate the depths of space we would come to see the metaphysical meaning of the venture on which we had embarked. And if we had not, we could not have proceeded. The curve of secular thought had extended as far as it could reach, from the seventeenth century to the twenty-first, and had begun to crack under its own weight; just when we were beginning to believe that we were God, we rediscovered the under-standing that we were not. The universe was too huge for us to face alone. That new ocean was so wide, and our boats so very small.

I urge my little craft onward. I set sail at last into the vastness of the Dark. My voyage has begun. God embraces my soul. He bids me be welcome in His kingdom. My heart is eased.

Under the Master's guidance we have all come to know that in our worldly lives we see only distortions—shadows on the cave wall. But as we penetrate the mysteries of the universe we are permitted to perceive things as they really are. The entry into the cosmos is the journey into the sublime, the literal attainment of heaven. It is a post-Christian idea: voyages must be undertaken, motion must never cease, we must seek Him always. In the seeking is the finding.

Gradually, as I reflect on these things yet again, the seeking ends for me and the finding begins, and my way becomes clear. I will resist nothing. I will accept everything. Whatever is required of me, that will I do, as always.

It is night, now. I am beyond any hunger and I feel no need for sleep. The walls of my chamber seem transparent to me and I can cast my vision outward to all the world, the heavy surging seas and the close blanket of the sky, the mountains and valleys, the rivers, the fields. I feel the nearness of billions of souls. Each human soul is a star: it glows with unique fire, and each has its counterpart in the heavens. There is one star that is the Master, and one that is Kastel, and one that is the young astronomer who shared my bed. And somewhere there is a star that is me. My spirit goes outward at last, it roves the distant blackness, it journeys on and on, to the ends of the universe. I soar above the Totality of the Totality. I look upon the face of God.

When the summons comes from the Master, shortly before dawn, I go to him at once. The rest of the House of Sanctuary sleeps. All is silent. Taking the garden path uphill, I experience a marvelous precision of sight: as though by great magnification I perceive the runnels and grooves on each blade of grass, the minute jagged teeth left by the mower as it bit it short, the glistening droplets of dew on the jade surface. Blossoms expand toward the pale new light now streaming out of the east as though they are coming awake. On the red earth of the path, strutting like dandies in a summer parade, are little shining scarlet-backed beetles with delicate black legs that terminate in intricate hairy feet. A fine mist rises from the ground. Within the silence I hear a thousand tiny noises.

The Master seems to be bursting with youthful strength, vitality, a mystic energy. He sits motionless, waiting for me to speak. The star-screen behind him is darkened, an ebony void, infinitely deep. I see the fine lines about his eyes and the corners of his mouth. His skin is pink, like a baby's. He could be six weeks old, or six thousand years.

His silence is immense.

"You hold me responsible?" I say at last.

He stares for a long while. "Don't you?"

"I am the Lord Magistrate of Senders. If there has been a failure, the fault must be mine."

"Yes. The fault must be yours."

He is silent again.

It is very easy, accepting this, far easier than I would have thought only the day before.

He says after a time, "What will you do?"

"You have my resignation."

"From your magistracy?"

"From the Order," I say. "How could I remain a priest, having been a Magistrate?"

"Ah. But you must."

The pale gentle eyes are inescapable.

"Then I will be a priest on some other world," I tell him. "I could never stay here. I respectfully request release from my vow of renunciation."

He smiles. I am saying exactly the things he hoped I would say.

"Granted."

It is done. I have stripped myself of rank and power. I will leave my House and my world; I will go forth into the Dark, although long ago I had gladly given that great privilege up. The irony is not lost on me. For all others it is heart's desire to leave Earth, for me it is merely the punishment for having failed the Mission. My penance will be my exile and my exile will be my penance. It is the defeat of all my work and the collapse of my vocation. But I must try not to see it that way. This is the beginning of the next phase of my life, nothing more. God will comfort me. Through my fall He has found a way of calling me to Him.

I wait for a gesture of dismissal, but it does not come.

"You understand," he says after a time, "that the Law of Return will hold, even for you?"

He means the prime tenet of Darklaw, the one that no one has ever violated. Those who depart from Earth may not come back to it. Ever. The journey is a one-way trip.

"Even for me," I say. "Yes. I understand."

*　　*　　*

I stand before a Velde doorway like any other, one that differs in no way from the one that just a short time before had carried me instantaneously halfway around the world, home from Sanctuary to the House of Senders. It is a cubicle of black glass, four meters high, three meters wide, three meters deep. A pair of black-light lenses face each other like owlish eyes on its inner sides. From the rear wall jut the three metal cones that are the discharge points.

How many journeys have I made by way of transmitting stations such as this one? Five hundred? A thousand? How many times have I been scanned, measured, dissected, stripped down to my component baryons, replicated: annihilated here, created there, all within the same moment? And stepped out of a receiver, intact, unchanged, at some distant point, Paris, Karachi, Istanbul, Nairobi, Dar-es-Salaam?

This doorway is no different from the ones through which I stepped those other times. But this journey will be unlike all those others. I have never left Earth before, not even to go to Mars, not even to the Moon. There has been no reason for it. But now I am to leap to the stars. Is it the scope of the leap that I fear? But I know better. The risks are not appreciably greater in a journey of twenty light-years than in one of twenty kilometers. Is it the strangeness of the new worlds which I will confront that arouses this uneasiness in me? But I have devoted my life to building those worlds. What is it, then? The knowledge that once I leave this House I will cease to be Lord Magistrate of the Senders, and become merely a wandering pilgrim?

Yes. Yes, I think that that is it. My life has been a comfortable one of power and assurance, and now I am entering the deepest unknown, leaving all that behind, leaving everything behind, giving up my House, relinquishing my magistracy, shedding all that I have been except for my essence itself, from which I can never be parted. It is a great severance. Yet why do I hesitate? I have asked so many others, after all, to submit to that severance. I have bound so many others, after all, by the unbending oaths of Darklaw. Perhaps it takes more time to prepare oneself than I have allowed. I have given myself very short notice indeed.

But the moment of uneasiness passes. All about me are friendly faces, men and women of my House, come to bid me a safe journey. Their eyes are moist, their smiles are tender. They know they will never see me again. I feel their love and their loyalty, and it eases my soul.

Ancient words drift through my mind.

Into thy hands, O Lord, I commend my spirit.

Yes. And my body also.

Lord, thou hast been our refuge: from one generation to another. Before the mountains were brought forth, or ever the earth and the world were made: thou art God from everlasting, and world without end.

Yes. And then:

The heavens declare the glory of God: and the firmament showeth His handiwork.

There is no sensation of transition. I was there; now I am here. I might have traveled no further than from Adelaide to Melbourne, or from Brisbane to Cairns. But I am very far from home now. The sky is amber, with swirls of blue. On the horizon is a great dull warm red mass, like a gigantic glowing coal, very close by. At the zenith is a smaller and brighter star, much more distant.

This world is called Cuchulain. It is the third moon of the subluminous star Gwydion, which is the dark companion of Lalande 21185. I am eight light-years from Earth. Cuchulain is the Order's prime outpost in the stars, the home of Second Sanctuary. Here is where I have chosen to spend my years of exile. The fallen magistrate, the broken vessel.

The air is heavy and mild. Crazy whorls of thick green ropy vegetation entangle everything, like a furry kelp that has infested the land. As I step from the Velde doorway I am confronted by a short, crisp little man in dark priestly robes. He is tonsured and wears a medallion of high office, though it is an office two or three levels down from the one that had been mine.

He introduces himself as Procurator-General Guardiano. Greeting me by name, he expresses his surprise at my most unexpected arrival in his diocese. Everyone knows that those who serve at my level of the Order must renounce all hope of emigration from Earth.

"I have resigned my magistracy," I tell him. "No," I say. "Actually I've been dismissed. For cause. I've been reassigned to the ordinary priesthood."

He stares, plainly shocked and stunned.

"It is still an honor to have you here, your grace," he says softly, after a moment.

I go with him to the chapter house, not far away. The gravitational pull here is heavier than Earth's, and I find myself leaning forward as I walk and pulling my feet after me as though the ground is sticky. But such incidental strangenesses as this are subsumed, to my surprise, by a greater familiarity: this place is not as alien as I had expected. I might merely be in some foreign land, and not on another world. The full impact of my total and final separation from Earth, I know, will not hit me until later.

We sit together in the refectory, sipping glass after glass of a sweet strong liqueur. Procurator-General Guardiano seems flustered by having someone of my rank appear without warning in his domain, but he is handling it well. He tries to make me feel at home. Other priests of the higher hierarchy appear—the word of my arrival must be traveling fast—and peer into the room. He waves them away. I tell him, briefly, the reasons for my downfall. He listens gravely and says, "Yes. We know that the outer worlds are in rebellion against Darklaw."

"Only the outer worlds?"

"So far, yes. It's very difficult for us to get reliable data."

"Are you saying that they've closed the frontier to the Order?"

"Oh, no, nothing like that. There's still free transit to every colony, and chapels everywhere. But the reports from the outer worlds are growing increasingly mysterious and bizarre. What we've decided is that we're going to have to send an Emissary Plenipotentiary to some of the rebel worlds to get the real story."

"A spy, you mean?"

"A spy? No. Not a spy. A teacher. A guide. A prophet, if you will. One who can bring them back to the true path." Guardiano shakes his head. "I have to tell you that all this disturbs me profoundly, this repudiation of Darklaw, these apparent breaches of the plan. It begins to occur to me— though I know the Master would have me strung up for saying any such thing—that we may have been in error from the beginning." He gives me a conspiratorial look. I smile encouragingly. He goes on, "I mean, this whole elitist approach of ours, the Order maintaining its monopoly over the mechanism of matter transmission, the Order deciding who will go to the stars and who will not, the Order attempting to create new worlds in our own image—" He seems to be talking half to himself. "Well, apparently it hasn't worked, has it? Do I dare say it? They're living just as they please, out there. We can't control them at long range. Your own personal tragedy is testimony to that. And yet, and yet—to think that we would be in such a shambles, and that a Lord Magistrate would be compelled to resign, and go into exile—exile, yes, that's what it is!—"

"Please," I say. His ramblings are embarrassing; and painful, too, for there may be seeds of truth in them. "What's over is over. All I want now is to live out my years quietly among the people of the Order on this world. Just tell me how I can be of use. Any work at all, even the simplest—"

"A waste, your grace. An absolute shameful waste."

"Please."

He fills my glass for the fourth or fifth time. A crafty look has come into his eyes. "You would accept any assignment I give you?"

"Yes. Anything."

"Anything?" he says.

I see myself sweeping the chapel house stairs, polishing sinks and tables, working in the garden on my knees.

"Even if there is risk?" he says. "Discomfort?"

"Anything."

He says, "You will be our Plenipotentiary, then."

There are two suns in the sky here, but they are not at all like Cuchulain's two, and the frosty air has a sharp sweet sting to it that is like nothing I have ever tasted before, and everything I see is haloed by a double shadow, a rim of pale red shading into deep, mysterious azure. It is very cold in this place. I am fourteen light-years from Earth.

A woman is watching me from just a few meters away. She says something I am unable to understand.

"Can you speak Anglic?" I reply.

"Anglic. All right." She gives me a chilly, appraising look. "What are you? Some kind of priest?"

"I was Lord Magistrate of the House of Senders, yes."

"Where?"

"Earth."

"On Earth? Really?"

I nod. "What is the name of this world?"

"Let me ask the questions," she says. Her speech is odd, not so much a foreign accent as a foreign intonation, a curious sing-song, vaguely menacing. Standing face to face just outside the Velde station, we look each other over. She is thick-shouldered, deep-chested, with a flat-featured face, close-cropped yellow hair, green eyes, a dusting of light red freckles across her heavy cheekbones. She wears a heavy blue jacket, fringed brown leggings, blue leather boots, and she is armed. Behind her I see a muddy road cut through a flat snowy field, some low rambling metal buildings with snow piled high on their roofs, and a landscape of distant jagged towering mountains whose sharp black spires are festooned with double-shadowed glaciers. An icy wind rips across the flat land. We are a long way from those two suns, the fierce blue-white one and its cooler crimson companion. Her eyes narrow and she says, "Lord Magistrate, eh? The House of Senders. Really?"

"This was my cloak of office. This medallion signified my rank in the Order."

"I don't see them."

"I'm sorry. I don't understand."

"You have no rank here. You hold no office here."

"Of course," I say. "I realize that. Except such power as Darklaw confers on me."

"Darklaw?"

I stare at her in some dismay. "Am I beyond the reach of Darklaw so soon?"

"It's not a word I hear very often. Shivering, are you? You come from a warmer place?"

"Earth," I say. "South Australia. It's warm there, yes."

"Earth. South Australia." She repeats the words as

though they are mere noises to her. "We have some Earth-born here, still. Not many. They'll be glad to see you, I suppose. The name of this world is Zima."

"Zima." A good strong sound. "What does that mean?"

"Mean?"

"The name must mean something. This planet wasn't named Zima just because someone liked the way it sounded."

"Can't you see why?" she asks, gesturing toward the far-off ice-shrouded mountains.

"I don't understand."

"Anglic is the only language you speak?"

"I know some Espanol and some Deutsch."

She shrugs. "Zima is Russkiye. It means Winter."

"And this is wintertime on Winter?"

"It is like this all the year round. And so we call the world Zima."

"Zima," I say. "Yes."

"We speak Russkiye here, mostly, though we know Anglic too. Everybody knows Anglic, everywhere in the Dark. It is necessary. You really speak no Russkiye?"

"Sorry."

"Ty shto, s pizdy sarvalsa?" she says, staring at me.

I shrug and am silent.

"Bros' dumat' zhopay!"

I shake my head sadly.

"Idi v zhopu!"

"No," I say. "Not a word."

She smiles, for the first time. "I believe you."

"What were you saying to me in Russkiye?"

"Very abusive things. I will not tell you what they were. If you understood, you would have become very angry. They were filthy tyhings, mockery. At least you would have laughed, hearing such vile words. I am named Marfa Ivanovna. You must talk with the boyars. If they think you are a spy, they will kill you."

I try to hide my astonishment, but I doubt that I succeed. Kill? What sort of world have we built here? Have these Zimans reinvented the middle ages?

"You are frightened?" she asks.

"Surprised," I say."

"You should lie to them, if you are a spy. Tell them you come to bring the Word of God, only. Or something else that is harmless. I like you. I would not want them to kill you."

A spy? No. As Guardiano would say, I am a teacher, a guide, a prophet, if you will. Or as I myself would say, I am a pilgrim, one who seeks atonement, one who seeks forgiveness.

"I'm not a spy, Marfa Ivanovna," I say.

"Good. Good. Tell them that." She puts her fingers in her mouth and whistles piercingly, and three burly bearded men in fur jackets appear as though rising out of the snowbanks. She speaks with them a long while in Russkiye. Then she turns to me. "These are the boyars Ivan Dimitrovich, Pyotr Pyotrovich, and Ivan Pyotrovich. They will conduct you to the voivode Ilya Alexandrovich, who will examine you. You should tell the voivode the truth."

"Yes," I say. "What else is there to tell?"

Guardiano had told me before I left Cuchulain, of course, that the world I was going to had been settled by emigrants from Russia. It was one of the first to be colonized, in the early years of the Mission. One would expect our Earthly ways to begin dropping away, and something like an indigenous culture to have begun evolving, in that much time. But I am startled, all the same, by how far they have drifted. At least Marfa Ivanova—who is, I imagine, a third-

generation Ziman—knows what Darklaw is. But is it observed? They have named their world Winter, at any rate,
and not New Russia or New Moscow or something like that,
which Darklaw would have forbidden. The new worlds in
the stars must not carry such Earthly baggage with them.
But whether they follow any of the other laws, I cannot say.
They have reverted to their ancient language here, but they
know Anglic as well, as they should. The robe of the Order
means something to her, but not, it would seem, a great
deal. She speaks of spies, of killing. Here at the outset of
my journey I can see already that there will be many surprises for me as I make my way through the Dark.

The voivode Ilya Alexandrovich is a small, agile-
looking man, brown-faced, weatherbeaten, with penetrating
blue eyes and a great shock of thick, coarse white hair. He
could be any age at all, but from his vigor and seeming
reserves of power I guess that he is about forty. In a harsh
climate the face is quickly etched with the signs of age, but
this man is probably younger than he looks.

Voivode, he tells me, means something like "mayor," or
"district chief." His office, brightly lit and stark, is a large
ground-floor room in an unassuming two-story aluminum
shack that is, I assume, the town hall. There is no place for
me to sit. I stand before him, and the three husky boyars,
who do not remove their fur jackets, stand behind me, arms
folded ominously across their breasts.

I see a desk, a faded wall map, a terminal. The only
other thing in the room is the immense bleached skull of
some alien beast on the floor beside his desk. It is an
astounding sight, two meters long and a meter high, with
two huge eye-sockets in the usual places and a third set
high between them, and a pair of colossal yellow tusks that
rise straight from the lower jaw almost to the ceiling. One
tusk is chipped at the tip, perhaps six centimeters broken

off. He sees me staring at it. "You ever see anything like that?" he asks, almost belligerently.

"Never. What is it?"

"We call it a bolshoi. Animal of the northern steppe, very big. You see one five kilometers away and you shit your trousers, I tell you for true." He grins. "Maybe we send one back to Earth some day to show them what we have here. Maybe."

His Anglic is much more heavily accented than Marfa Ivanovna's, and far less fluent. He seems unable to hold still very long. The district that he governs, he tells me, is the largest on Zima. It looks immense indeed on his map, a vast blue area, a territory that seems to be about the size of Brazil. But when I take a closer look I see three tiny dots clustered close together in the center of the blue zone. They are, I assume, the only villages. He follows my gaze and strides immediately across the room to tap the map. "This is Tyomni," he says. "That is this village. This one here, it is Doch. This one, Sin. In this territory we have six thousand people altogether. There are two other territories, here and here." He points to regions north and south of the blue zone. A yellow area and a pink one indicate the other settlements, each with two towns. The whole human population of this planet must be no more than ten thousand.

Turning suddenly toward me, he says, "You are big priest in the Order?"

"I was Lord Magistrate, yes. The House of Senders."

"Senders. Ah. I know Senders. The ones who choose the colonists. And who run the machinery, the transmitters."

"That's right."

"And you are the bolshoi Sender? The big man, the boss, the captain?"

"I was, yes. This robe, this medallion, those are signs of my office."

"A very big man. Only instead of sending, you are sent."

"Yes," I say.

"And you come here, why? Nobody from Earth comes here in ten, fifteen years." He no longer makes even an attempt to conceal his suspicions, or his hostility. His cold eyes flare with anger. "Being boss of Senders is not enough for you? You want to tell us how to run Zima? You want to run Zima yourself?"

"Nothing of that sort, believe me."

"Then what?"

"Do you have a map of the entire Dark?"

"The Dark," he says, as though the word is unfamiliar to him. Then he says something in Russkiye to one of the boyars. The man leaves the room and returns, a few moments later, with a wide, flat black screen that turns out to be a small version of the wall screen in the Master's office. He lights it and they all look expectantly at me.

The display is a little different from the one I am accustomed to, since it centers on Zima, not on Earth, but the glowing inner sphere that marks the location of the Mission stars is easy enough to find. I point to that sphere and I remind them, apologizing for telling them what they already know, that the great plan of the Mission calls for an orderly expansion through space from Earth in a carefully delimited zone a hundred light-years in diameter. Only when that sphere has been settled are we to go farther, not because there are any technical difficulties in sending our carrier ships a thousand light-years out, or ten thousand, but because the Master has felt from the start that we must assimilate our first immense wave of outward movement, must pause and come to an understanding of what it is like to have created a galactic empire on so vast a scale, before we attempt to go onward into the infinity that awaits us. Otherwise, I say, we risk falling victim to a megalomaniacal centrifugal dizziness from which we may never recover. And so Darklaw forbids journeys beyond the boundary.

They watch me stonily throughout my recital of these overfamiliar concepts, saying nothing.

I go on to tell them that Earth now is receiving indications that voyages far beyond the hundred-light-year limit have taken place.

Their faces are expressionless.

"What is that to us?" the voivode asks.

"One of the deviant tracks begins here," I say.

"Our Anglic is very poor. Perhaps you can say that another way."

"When the first ship brought the Velde receiver to Zima, it built replicas of itself and of the receiver, and sent them onward to other stars farther from Earth. We've traced the various trajectories that lead beyond the Mission boundaries, and one of them comes out of a world that received its Velde equipment from a world that got its equipment from here. A granddaughter world, so to speak."

"This has nothing to do with us, nothing at all," the voivode says coolly.

"Zima is only my starting point," I say. "It may be that you are in contact with these outer worlds, that I can get some clue from you about who is making these voyages, and why, and where he's setting out from."

"We have no knowledge of any of this."

I point out, trying not to do it in any overbearing way, that by the authority of Darklaw vested in me as a Plenipotentiary of the Order he is required to assist me in my inquiry. But there is no way to brandish the authority of Darklaw that is not overbearing, and I see the voivode stiffen at once, I see his face grow black, I see very clearly that he regards himself as autonomous and his world as independent of Earth.

That comes as no surprise to me. We were not so naive, so innocent of historical precedent, as to think we could maintain control over the colonies. What we wanted was quite the opposite, new Earths free of our grasp—cut off, indeed, by an inflexible law forbidding all contact between mother world and colony once the colony has been established—and free, likewise, of the compulsion to replicate the tragic mistakes that the old Earth had made. But because we had felt the hand of God guiding us in every way as we led mankind forth into the Dark, we believed that God's law as we understood it would never be repudiated by those whom we had given the stars. Now, seeing evidence that His law is subordinate out here to the will of wilful men, I fear for the structure that we have devoted our lives to building.

"If this is why you really have come," the voivode says, "then you have wasted your time. But perhaps I misunderstand everything you say. My Anglic is not good. We must talk again." He gestures to the boyars and says something in Russiye that is unmistakably a dismissal. They take me away and give me a room in some sort of dreary lodging-house overlooking the plaza at the center of town. When they leave, they lock the door behind them. I am a prisoner.

It is a harsh land. In the first few days of my internment there is a snowstorm every afternoon. First the sky turns metal-gray, and then black. Then hard little pellets of snow, driven by the rising wind, strike the window. Then it comes down in heavy fluffy flakes for several hours. Afterwards machines scuttle out and clear the pathways. I have never before been in a place where they have snow. It seems quite beautiful to me, a kind of benediction, a cleansing cover.

This is a very small town, and there is wilderness all

around it. On the second day and again on the third, packs of wild beasts go racing through the central plaza. They look something like huge dogs, but they have very long legs, almost like those of horses, and their tails are tipped with three pairs of ugly-looking spikes. They move through the town like a whirlwind, prowling in the trash, butting their heads against the closed doors, and everyone gets quickly out of their way.

Later on the third day there is an execution in the plaza, practically below my window. A jowly, heavily bearded man clad in furs is led forth, strapped to a post, and shot by five men in uniforms. For all I can tell, he is one of the three boyars who took me to the voivode on my first day. I have never seen anyone killed before, and the whole event has such a strange, dreamlike quality for me that the shock and horror and revulsion do not strike me until perhaps half an hour later.

It is hard for me to say which I find the most alien, the snowstorms, the packs of fierce beasts running through the town, or the execution.

My food is shoved through a slot in the door. It is rough, simple stuff, stews and soups and a kind of gritty bread. That is all right. Not until the fourth day does anyone come to see me. My first visitor is Marfa Ivanovna, who says, "They think you're a spy. I told you to tell them the truth."

"I did."

"Are you a spy?"

"You know that I'm not."

"Yes," she says. "I know. But the voivode is troubled. He thinks you mean to overthrow him."

"All I want is for him to give me some information. Then I'll be gone from here and won't ever return."

"He is a very suspicious man."

"Let him come here and pray with me, and see what my

nature is like. All I am is a servant of God. Which I hope is true of the voivode as well."

"He is thinking of having you shot," Marfa Ivanovna says.

"Let him come to me and pray with me," I tell her.

The voivode comes to me, not once but three times. We do no praying—in truth, any mention of God, or Darklaw, or even the Mission, seems to make him uncomfortable—but gradually we begin to understand each other. We are not that different. He is a hard, dedicated, cautious man governing a harsh troublesome land. I have been called hard and dedicated and cautious myself. My nature is not as suspicious as his, but I have not had to contend with snowstorms and wild beasts and the other hazards of this place. Nor am I Russian. They seem to be suspicious from birth, these Russians. And they have lived apart from Earth a long while. That too is Darklaw: we would not have the new worlds contaminated with our plagues of the spirit or of the flesh, nor do we want alien plagues of either kind carried back from them to us. We have enough of our own already.

I am not going to be shot. He makes that clear. "We talked of it, yes. But it would be wrong."

"The man who was? What did he do?"

"He took that which was not his," says the voivode, and shrugs. "He was worse than a beast. He could not be allowed to live among us."

Nothing is said of when I will be released. I am left alone for two more days. The coarse dull food begins to oppress me, and the solitude. There is another snowstorm, worse than the last. From my window I see ungainly birds something like vultures, with long naked yellow necks and drooping reptilian tails, circling in the sky. Finally the voivode comes a second time, and simply stares at me as though expecting me to blurt out some confession. I look at him in puzzlement, and after long silence he laughs explosively and summons an aide, who brings in a bottle of a clear fiery liquor. Two or three quick gulps and he becomes expansive, and tells me of his childhood. His father was voivode before him, long ago, and was killed by a wild animal while out hunting. I try to imagine a world that still has dangerous animals roaming freely. To me it is like a world where the gods of primitive man are real and alive, and go disguised among mortals, striking out at them randomly and without warning.

Then he asks me about myself, wanting to know how old I was when I became a priest of the Order, and whether I was as religious as a boy as I am now. I tell him what I can, within the limits placed on me by my vows. Perhaps I go a little beyond the limits, even. I explain about my early interest in technical matters, my entering the Order at seventeen, my life of service.

The part about my religious vocation seems odd to him. He appears to think I must have undergone some sudden conversion midway through my adolescence. "There has never been a time when God has not been present at my side," I say.

"How very lucky you are," he says.

"Lucky?"

He touches his glass to mine.

"Your health," he says. We drink. Then he says, "What does your Order really want with us, anyway?"

"With you? We want nothing with you. Three generations ago we gave you your world; everything after that is up to you."

"No. You want to dictate how we shall live. You are people of the past, and we are people of the future, and you are unable to understand our souls."

"Not so," I tell him. "Why do you think we want to dictate to you? Have we interfered with you up till now?"

"You are here now, though."

"Not to interfere. Only to gain information."

"Ah. Is this so?" He laughs and drinks. "Your health," he says again.

He comes a third time a couple of days later. I am restless and irritable when he enters; I have had enough of this imprisonment, these groundless suspicions, this bleak and frosty world; I am ready to be on my way. It is all I can do to keep from bluntly demanding my freedom. As it is I am uncharacteristically sharp and surly with him, answering in quick snarling monosyllables when he asks me how I have slept, whether I am well, is my room warm enough. He gives me a look of surprise, and then one of thoughtful appraisal, and then he smiles. He is in complete control, and we both know it.

"Tell me once more," he says, "why you have come to us."

I calm myself and run through the whole thing one more time. He nods. Now that he knows me better, he tells me, he begins to think that I may be sincere, that I have not come to spy, that I actually would be willing to chase across the galaxy this way in pursuit of an ideal. And so on in that vein for a time, both patronizing and genuinely friendly almost in the same breath.

Then he says, "We have decided that it is best to send you onward."

"Where?"

"The name of the world is Entrada. It is one of our daughter worlds, eleven light-years away, a very hot place. We trade our precious metals for their spices. Someone came from there not long ago and told us of a strange man named Oesterreich, who passed through Entrada and spoke of undertaking journeys to new and distant places. Perhaps he can provide you with the answers that you seek. If you can find him."

"Oesterreich?"

"That is the name, yes."

"Can you tell me any more about him than that?"

"What I have told you is all that I know."

He stares at me truculently, as if defying me to show that he is lying. But I believe him.

"Even for that much assistance, I am grateful," I say.

"Yes. Never let it be said that we have failed to offer aid to the Order." He smiles again. "But if you ever come to this world again, you understand, we will know that you were a spy after all. And we will treat you accordingly."

Marfa Ivanovna is in charge of the Velde equipment. She positions me within the transmitting doorway, moving me about this way and that to be certain that I will be squarely within the field. When she is satisfied, she says, "You know, you ought not ever come back this way."

"I understand that."

"You must be a very virtuous man. Ilya Alexandrovitch came very close to putting you to death, and then he changed his mind. This I know for certain. But he remains suspicious of you. He is suspicious of everything the Order does."

"The Order has never done anything to injure him or anyone else on this planet, and never will."

"That may be so," says Marfa Ivanovna. "But still, you are lucky to be leaving here alive. You should not come back. And you should tell others of your sort to stay away from Zima too. We do not accept the Order here."

I am still pondering the implications of that astonishing statement when she does something even more astonishing.

Stepping into the cubicle with me, she suddenly opens her fur-trimmed jacket, revealing full round breasts, very pale, dusted with the same light red freckles that she has on her face. She seizes me by the hair and presses my head against her breasts, and holds it there a long moment. Her skin is very warm. It seems almost feverish.

"For luck," she says, and steps back. Her eyes are sad and strange. It could almost be a loving look, or perhaps a pitying one, or both. Then she turns away from me and throws the switch.

Entrada is torrid and moist, a humid sweltering hothouse of a place so much the antithesis of Zima that my body rebels immediately against the shift from one world to the other. Coming forth into it, I feel the heat rolling toward me like an implacable wall of water. It sweeps up and over me and smashes me to my knees. I am sick and numb with displacement and dislocation. It seems impossible for me to draw a breath. The thick, shimmering, golden-green atmosphere here is almost liquid; it crams itself into my throat, it squeezes my lungs in an agonizing grip. Through blurring eyes I see a tight green web of jungle foliage rising before me, a jumbled vista of corrugated-tin shacks, a patch of sky the color of shallow sea-water, and, high above, a merciless, throbbing, weirdly elongated sun shaped like no sun I have ever imagined. Then I sway and fall forward and see nothing more.

I lie suspended in delirium a long while. It is a pleasing restful time, like being in the womb. I am becalmed in a great stillness, lulled by soft voices and sweet music. But gradually consciousness begins to break through. I swim upward toward the light that glows somewhere above me, and my eyes open, and I see a serene friendly face, and a voice says, "It's nothing to worry about. Everyone who comes here the way you did has a touch of it, the first time. At your age I suppose it's worse than usual."

Dazedly I realize that I am in mid-conversation.

"A touch of what?" I ask.

The other, who is a slender gray-eyed woman of middle years wearing a sort of Indian sari, smiles and says, "Of the Falling. It's a lambda effect. But I'm sorry. We've been talking for a while, and I thought you were awake. Evidently you weren't."

"I am now," I tell her. "But I don't think I've been for very long."

Nodding, she says, "Let's start over. You're in Traveler's Hospice. The humidity got you, and the heat, and the lightness of the gravity. You're all right now."

"Yes."

"Do you think you can stand?"

"I can try," I say.

She helps me up. I feel so giddy that I expect to float away. Carefully she guides me toward the window of my room. Outside I see a veranda and a close-cropped lawn. Just beyond, a dark curtain of dense bush closes everything off. The intense light makes everything seem very near; it is as if I could put my hand out the window and thrust it into the heart of that exuberant jungle.

"So bright—the sun—" I whisper.

In fact there are two whitish suns in the sky, so close to each other that their photospheres overlap and each is distended by the other's gravitational pull, making them nearly oval in shape. Together they seem to form a single egg-shaped mass, though even the one quick dazzled glance I can allow myself tells me that this is really a binary system, discrete bundles of energy forever locked together.

Awed and amazed, I touch my fingertips to my cheek

in wonder, and feel a thick coarse beard there that I had not had before.

The woman says, "Two suns, actually. Their centers are only about a million and a half kilometers apart, and they revolve around each other every seven and a half hours. We're the fourth planet out, but we're as far from them as Neptune is from the Sun."

But I have lost interest for the moment in astronomical matters. I rub my face, exploring its strange new shagginess. The beard covers my cheeks, my jaws, much of my throat.

"How long have I been unconscious?" I ask.

"About three weeks."

"Your weeks or Earth weeks?"

"We use Earth weeks here."

"And that was just a light case? Does everybody who gets the Falling spend three weeks being delirious?"

"Sometimes much more. Sometimes they never come out of it."

I stare at her. "And it's just the heat, the humidity, the lightness of the gravity? They can knock you down the moment you step out of the transmitter and put you under for weeks? I would think it should take something like a stroke to do that."

"It is something like a stroke," she says. "Did you think that traveling between stars is like stepping across the street? You come from a low-lambda world to a high-lambda one without doing your adaptation drills and of course the change is going to knock you flat right away. What did you expect?"

High-lambda? Low-lambda?

"I don't know what you're talking about," I say.

"Didn't they tell you on Zima about the adaptation drills before they shipped you here?"

"Not a thing."

"Or about lambda differentials?"

"Nothing," I say.

Her face grows very solemn. "Pigs, that's all they are. They should have prepared you for the jump. But I guess they didn't care whether you lived or died."

I think of Marfa Ivanovna, wishing me luck as she reached for the switch. I think of that strange sad look in her eyes. I think of the voivode Ilya Alexandrovitch, who might have had me shot but decided instead to offer me a free trip off his world, a one-way trip. There is much that I am only now beginning to understand, I see, about this empire that Earth is building in what we call the Dark. We are building it in the dark, yes, in more ways than one.

"No," I say. "I guess they didn't care."

They are friendlier on Entrada, no question of that. Interstellar trade is important here and visitors from other worlds are far more common than they are on wintry Zima. Apparently I am free to live at the hospice as long as I wish. The weeks of my stay have stretched now into months, and no one suggests that it is time for me to be moving along.

I had not expected to stay here so long. But gathering the information I need has been a slow business, with many a maddening detour and delay.

At least I experience no further lambda problems. Lambda, they tell me, is a planetary force that became known only when Velde jumps between solar systems began. There are high-lambda worlds and low-lambda worlds, and anyone going from one kind to the other without proper preparation is apt to undergo severe stress. It is all news to me. I wonder if the Order on Earth is aware at all of these difficulties. But perhaps they feel that matters which may arise during journeys between worlds of the Dark are of no concern to us of the mother world.

They have taken me through the adaptation drills here at the hospice somehow while I was still unconscious, and I am more or less capable now of handling Entradan conditions. The perpetual steambath heat, which no amount of air conditioning seems really to mitigate, is hard to cope with, and the odd combination of heavy atmosphere and light gravity puts me at risk of nausea with every breath, though after a time I get the knack of pulling shallow nips of air. There are allergens borne on every breeze, too, pollen of a thousand kinds and some free-floating alkaloids, against which I need daily medication. My face turns red under the force of the double sun, and the skin of my cheeks gets strangely soft, which makes my new beard an annoyance. I rid myself of it. My hair acquires an unfamiliar silver sheen, not displeasing, but unexpected. All this considered, though, I can manage here.

Entrada has a dozen major settlements and several hundred thousand people. It is a big world, metal-poor and light, on which a dozen small continents and some intricate archipelagoes float in huge warm seas. The whole planet is tropical, even at the poles: distant though it is from its suns, it would probably be inhospitable to human life if it were very much closer. The soil of Entrada has the lunatic fertility that we associate with the tropics, and agriculture is the prime occupation here. The people, drawn from many regions of Earth, are attractive and outgoing, with an appealingly easy manner.

It appears that they have not drifted as far from Darklaw here as the Zimans have.

Certainly the Order is respected. There are chapels everywhere and the people use them. Whenever I enter one there is a little stir of excitement, for it is generally known that I was Lord Magistrate of the Senders during my time on Earth, and that makes me a celebrity, or a curiosity, or both. Many of the Entradans are Earthborn themselves—emigration to this world was still going on as recently as eight or ten years ago—and the sight of my medallion inspires respect and even awe in them. I do not wear my robe of office, not in this heat. Probably I will never wear it again, no matter what climate I find myself in when I leave here. Someone else is Lord Magistrate of the House of Senders now, after all. But the medallion alone is enough to win me a distinction here that I surely never had on Zima.

I think, though, that they pick and choose among the tenets of Darklaw to their own satisfaction on Entrada, obeying those which suit them and casting aside anything that seems too constricting. I am not sure of this, but it seems likely. To discuss such matters with anyone I have come to know here is, of course, impossible. The people I have managed to get to know so far, at the hospice, at the chapel house in town, at the tavern where I have begun to take my meals, are pleasant and sociable. But they become uneasy, even evasive, whenever I speak of any aspect of Earth's migration into space. Let me mention the Order, or the Master, or anything at all concerning the Mission, and they begin to moisten their lips and look uncomfortable. Clearly things are happening out here, things never envisioned by the founders of the Order, and they are unwilling to talk about them with anyone who himself wears the high medallion.

It is a measure of the changes that have come over me since I began this journey that I am neither surprised nor dismayed by this.

Why should we have believed that we could prescribe a single code of law that would meet the needs of hundreds of widely varying worlds? Of course they would modify our teachings to fit their own evolving cultures, and some would probably depart entirely from that which we had created for them. It was only to be expected. Many things have become clear to me on this journey that I did not see before, that, indeed, I did not so much as pause to consider. But much else remains mysterious.

I am at the busy waterfront esplanade, leaning over the rail, staring out toward Volcano Isle, a dim gray peak far out to sea. It is mid-morning, before the full heat of noon has descended. I have been here long enough so that I think of this as the cool time of the day.

"Your grace?" a voice calls. "Lord Magistrate?"

No one calls me those things here.

I glance down to my left. A dark-haired man in worn seaman's clothes and a braided captain's hat is looking up at me out of a rowboat just below the sea-wall. He is smiling and waving. I have no idea who he is, but he plainly wants to talk with me, and anything that helps me break the barrier that stands between me and real knowledge of this place is to be encouraged.

He points to the far end of the harbor, where there is a ramp leading from the little beach to the esplanade, and tells me in pantomime that he means to tie up his boat and go ashore. I wait for him at the head of the ramp, and after a few moments he comes trudging up to greet me. He is perhaps fifty years old, trim and sun-bronzed, with a lean weatherbeaten face.

"You don't remember me," he says.

"I'm afraid not."

"You personally interviewed me and approved my application to emigrate, eighteen years ago. Sandys. Lloyd Sandys." He smiles hopefully, as though his name alone will open the floodgates of my memory.

When I was Lord Magistrate I reviewed five hundred

emigrant dossiers a week, and interviewed ten or fifteen applicants a day myself, and forgot each one the moment I approved or rejected them. But for this man the interview with the Lord Magistrate of the Senders was the most significant moment of his life.

"Sorry," I say. "So many names, so many faces—"

"I would have recognized you even if I hadn't already heard you were here. After all these years, you've hardly changed at all, your grace." He grins. "So now you've come to settle on Entrada yourself?"

"Only a short visit."

"Ah." He is visibly disappointed. "You ought to think of staying. It's a wonderful place, if you don't mind a little heat. I haven't regretted coming here for a minute."

He takes me to a seaside tavern where he is obviously well known, and orders lunch for both of us: skewers of small corkscrew-shaped creatures that look and taste a little like squid, and a flask of a strange but likable emerald-colored wine with a heavy, musky, spicy flavor. He tells me that he has four sturdy sons and four strapping daughters, and that he and his wife run a harbor ferry, short hops to the surrounding islands of this archipelago, which is Entrada's main population center. There still are traces of Melbourne in his accent. He seems very happy. "You'll let me take you on a tour, won't you?" he asks. "We've got some very beautiful islands out there, and you can't get to see them by Velde jumps."

I protest that I don't want to take him away from his work, but he shrugs that off. Work can always wait, he says. There's no hurry, on a world where anyone can dip his net in the sea and come up with a good meal. We have another flask of wine. He seems open, genial, trustworthy. Over cheese and fruit he asks me why I've come here.

I hesitate.

"A fact-finding mission," I say.

"Ah. Is that really so? Can I be of any help, d'ye think?"

It is several more winy lunches, and a little boat-trip to some nearby islands fragrant with masses of intoxicating purple blooms, before I am willing to begin taking Sandys into my confidence. I tell him that the Order has sent me into the Dark to study and report on the ways of life that are evolving on the new worlds. He seems untroubled by that, though Ilya Alexandrovitch might have had me shot for such an admission.

Later, I tell him about the apparent deviations from the planned scope of the Mission that are the immediate reason for my journey.

"You mean, going out beyond the hundred-light-year zone?"

"Yes."

"That's pretty amazing, that anyone would go there."

"We have indications that it's happening."

"Really," he says.

"And on Zima," I continue, "I picked up a story that somebody here on Entrada has been preaching ventures into the far Dark. You don't know anything about that, do you?"

His only overt reaction is a light frown, quickly erased. Perhaps he has nothing to tell me. Or else we have reached the point, perhaps, beyond which he is unwilling to speak.

But some hours later he revives the topic himself. We are on our way back to harbor, sunburned and a little tipsy from an outing to one of the prettiest of the local islands, when he suddenly says, "I remember hearing something about that preacher you mentioned before."

I wait, not saying anything.

"My wife told me about him. There was somebody going around talking about far voyages, she said." New color comes to his face, a deep red beneath the bronze. "I must have forgotten about it when we were talking before." In fact he must know that I think him disingenuous for withholding this from me all afternoon. But I make no attempt to call him on that. We are still testing each other.

I ask him if he can get more information for me, and he promises to discuss it with his wife. Then he is absent for a week, making a circuit of the outer rim of the archipelago to deliver freight. When he returns, finally, he brings with him an unusual golden brandy from one of the remote islands as a gift for me, but my cautious attempt to revive our earlier conversation runs into a familiar sort of Entradan evasiveness. It is almost as though he doesn't know what I'm referring to.

At length I say bluntly, "Have you had a chance to talk to your wife about that preacher?"

He looks troubled. "In fact, it slipped my mind."

"Ah."

"Tonight, maybe—"

"I understand that the man's name is Oesterreich," I say. His eyes go wide.

"You know that, do you?"

"Help me, will you, Sandys? I'm the one who sent you to this place, remember? Your whole life here wouldn't exist but for me."

"That's true. That's very true."

"Who's Oesterreich?"

"I never knew him. I never had any dealings with him."

"Tell me what you know about him."

"A crazy man, he was."

"Was?"

"He's not here any more."

I uncork the bottle of rare brandy, pour a little for myself, a more generous shot for Sandys.

"Where'd he go?" I ask.

He sips, reflectively. After a time he says, "I don't know, your grace. That's God's own truth. I haven't seen or heard of him in a couple of years. He chartered one of the other captains here, a man named Feraud, to take him to one of the islands, and that's the last I know."

"Which island?"

"I don't know."

"Do you think Feraud remembers?"

"I could ask him," Sandys says.

"Yes. Ask him. Would you do that?"

"I could ask him, yes," he says.

So it goes, slowly. Sandys confers with his friend Feraud, who hesitates and evades, or so Sandys tells me; but eventually Feraud finds it in him to recall that he had taken Oesterreich to Volcano Isle, three hours' journey to the west. Sandys admits to me, now that he is too deep in to hold back, that he himself actually heard Oesterreich speak several times, that Oesterreich claimed to be in possession of some secret way of reaching worlds immensely remote from the settled part of the Dark.

"And do you believe that?"

"I don't know. He seemed crazy to me."

"Crazy how?"

"The look in his eye. The things he said. That it's our destiny to reach the rim of the universe. That the Order holds us back out of its own timidity. That we must follow the Goddess Avatar, who beckons us onward to—"

"Who?"

His face flushes bright crimson. "The Goddess Avatar. I don't know what she is, your grace. Honestly. It's some cult he's running, some new religion he's made up. I told you he's crazy. I've never believed any of this."

There is a pounding in my temples, and a fierce ache

behind my eyes. My throat has gone dry and not even Sandys' brandy can soothe it.

"Where do you think Oesterreich is now?"

"I don't know." His eyes are tormented. "Honestly. Honestly. I think he's gone from Entrada."

"Is there a Velde transmitter station on Volcano Isle?"

He thinks for a moment. "Yes. Yes, there is."

"Will you do me one more favor?" I ask. "One thing,
and then I won't ask any more."

"Yes?"

"Take a ride over to Volcano Isle tomorrow. Talk with
the people who run the Velde station there. See if you can
find out where they sent Oesterreich."

"They'll never tell me anything like that."

I put five shining coins in front of him, each one worth
as much as he can make in a month's ferrying.

"Use these," I say. "If you come back with the answer,
there are five more for you."

"Come with me, your grace. You speak to them."

"No."

"You ought to see Volcano Isle. It's a fantastic place.
The center of it blew out thousands of years ago, and people
live up on the rim, around a lagoon so deep nobody's been
able to find the bottom. I was meaning to take you there
anyway, and—"

"You go," I say. "Just you."

After a moment he pockets the coins. In the morning I
watch him go off in one of his boats, a small hydrofoil skiff.
There is no word from him for two days, and then he comes
to me at the hospice, looking tense and unshaven.

"It wasn't easy," he says.

"You found out where he went?"

"Yes."

"Go on," I urge, but he is silent, lips working but nothing coming out. I produce five more of the coins and lay them before him. He ignores them. This is some interior struggle.

He says, after a time, "We aren't supposed to reveal anything about anything of this. I told you what I've already told you because I owe you. You understand that?"

"Yes."

"You mustn't ever let anyone know who gave you the information."

"Don't worry," I say.

He studies me for a time. Then he says, "The name of the planet where Oesterreich went is Eden. It's a seventeen-light-year hop. You won't need lambda adjustment, coming from here. There's hardly any differential. All right, your grace? That's what all I can tell you." He stares at the coins and shakes his head. Then he runs out of the room, leaving them behind.

Eden turns out to be no Eden at all. I see a spongy, marshy landscape, a gray sodden sky, a raw, half-built town. There seem to be two suns, a faint yellow-white one and a larger reddish one. A closer look reveals that the system here is like the Lalande one: the reddish one is not really a star but a glowing substellar mass about the size of Jupiter. Eden is one of its moons. What we like to speak of in the Order as the new Earths of the Dark are in fact scarcely Earthlike at all, I am coming to realize: all they have in common with the mother world is a tolerably breathable atmosphere and a manageable gravitational pull. How can we speak of a world as an Earth when its sun is not yellow but white or red or green, or there are two or three or even four suns in the sky all day and all night, or the primary source of warmth is not even a sun but a giant planet-like ball of hot gas?

"Settler?" they ask me, when I arrive on Eden.

"Traveler," I reply. "Short-term visit."

They scarcely seem to care. This is a difficult world and they have no time for bureaucratic formalities. So long as I have money, and I do—at least these strange daughter worlds of ours still honor our currency—I am, if not exactly welcome, then at least permitted.

Do they observe Darklaw here? When I arrive I am wearing neither my robe of office nor my medallion, and it seems just as well. The Order appears not to be in favor, this far out. I can find no sign of our chapels or other indications of submission to our rule. What I do find, as I wander the rough streets of this jerry-rigged town on this cool, rain-swept world, is a chapel of some other kind, a white geodesic dome with a mysterious symbol—three superimposed six-pointed stars—painted in black on its door.

"Goddess save you," a woman coming out says brusquely to me, and shoulders past me in the rain.

They are not even bothering to hide things, this far out on the frontier.

I go inside. The walls are white and an odd, disturbing mural is painted on one of them. It shows what seems to be a windowless ruined temple drifting in blue starry space, with all manner of objects and creatures floating near it, owls, skulls, snakes, masks, golden cups, bodiless heads. It is like a scene viewed in a dream. The temple's alabaster walls are covered with hieroglyphics. A passageway leads inward and inward and inward, and at its end I can see a tiny view of an eerie landscape like a plateau at the end of time.

There are half a dozen people in the room, each facing in a different direction, reading aloud in low murmurs. A slender dark-skinned man looks up at me and says, "Goddess save you, father. How does your journey go?"

"I'm trying to find Oesterreich. They said he's here."

A couple of the other readers look up. A woman with straw-colored hair says, "He's gone Goddessward."

"I'm sorry. I don't under—"

Another woman, whose features are tiny and delicately modeled in the center of a face vast as the map of Russia, breaks in to tell me, "He was going to stop off on Phosphor first. You may be able to catch up with him there. Goddess save you, father."

I stare at her, at the mural of the mural of the stone temple, at the other woman.

"Thank you," I say. "Goddess save you," my voice adds.

I buy passage to Phosphor. It is sixty-seven light-years from Earth. The necessary lambda adjustment costs nearly as much as the transit fee itself, and I must spend three days going through the adaptation process before I can leave.

Then, Goddess save me, I am ready to set out from Eden for whatever greater strangeness awaits me beyond.

As I wait for the Simtow reaction to annihilate me and reconstruct me in some unknown place, I think of all those who passed through my House over the years as I selected the outbound colonists—and how I and the Lord Magistrates before me had clung to the fantasy that we were shaping perfect new Earths out there in the Dark, that we were composing exquisite symphonies of human nature, filtering out all of the discordances that had marred all our history up till now. Without ever going to the new worlds ourselves to view the results of our work, of course, because to go would mean to cut ourselves off forever, by Darklaw's own constricting terms, from our House, from our task, from Earth itself. And now, catapulted into the Dark in a moment's convulsive turn, by shame and guilt and the need to try to repair that which I had evidently made breakable instead of imperishable, I am learning that I have been wrong all along, that the symphonies of human nature that I had composed were built out of the same old tunes, that people will do what they will do unconstrained by abstract regulations laid down for them a priori by others far away. The tight filter of which the House of Senders is so proud is no filter at all. We send our finest ones to the stars and they turn their backs on us at once. And, pondering these things, it seems to me that my soul is pounding at the gates of my mind, that madness is pressing close against the walls of my spirit—a thing which I have always dreaded, the thing which brought me to the cloisters of the Order in the first place.

Black light flashes in my eyes and once more I go leaping through the Dark.

"He isn't here," they tell me on Phosphor. There is a huge cool red sun here, and a hot blue one a couple of hundred solar units away, close enough to blaze like a brilliant beacon in the day sky. "He's gone on to Entropy. Goddess save you."

"Goddess save you," I say.

There are triple-triangle signs on every doorfront in Phosphor's single city. The city's name is Jerusalem. To name cities or worlds for places on Earth is forbidden. But I know that I have left Darklaw far behind here.

Entropy, they say, is ninety-one light-years from Earth. I am approaching the limits of the sphere of settlement.

Oesterreich has a soft, insinuating voice. He says, "You should come with me. I really would like to take a Lord Magistrate along when I go to her."

"I'm no longer a Lord Magistrate."

"You can't ever stop being a Lord Magistrate. Do you think you can take the Order off just by putting your medallion in your suitcase?"

"Who is she, this Goddess Avatar everybody talks about?"

Oesterreich laughs. "Come with me and you'll find out."

He is a small man, very lean, with broad, looming shoulders that make him appear much taller than he is when he is sitting down. Maybe he is forty years old, maybe much older. His face is paper-white, with perpetual bluish stubble, and his eyes have a black troublesome gleam that strikes me as a mark either of extraordinary intelligence or of pervasive insanity, or perhaps both at once. It was not difficult at all for me to find him, only hours after my arrival on Entropy. The planet has a single village, a thousand settlers. The air is mild here, the sun yellow-green. Three huge moons hang just overhead in the daytime sky, as though dangling on a clothesline.

I say, "Is she real, this goddess of yours?"

"Oh, she's real, all right. As real as you or me."

"Someone we can walk up to and speak with?"

"Her name used to be Margaret Benevente. She was born in Geneva. She emigrated to a world called Three Suns about thirty years ago."

"And now she's a goddess."

"No. I never said that."

"What is she, then?"

"She's the Goddess Avatar."

"Which means what?"

He smiles. "Which means she's a holy woman in whom certain fundamental principles of the universe have been incarnated. You want to know any more than that, you come with me, eh? Your grace."

"And where is she?"

"She's on an uninhabited planet about five thousand light-years from here right now."

I am dealing with a lunatic, I tell myself. That gleam is the gleam of madness, yes.

"You don't believe that, do you?" he asks.

"How can it be possible?"

"Come with me and you'll find out."

"Five thousand light-years—" I shake my head. "No. No."

He shrugs. "So don't go, then."

There is a terrible silence in the little room. I feel impaled on it. Thunder crashes outside, finally, breaking the tension. Lightning has been playing across the sky constantly since my arrival, but there has been no rain.

"Faster-than-light travel is impossible," I say inanely. "Except by way of Velde transmission. You know that. If we've got Velde equipment five thousand light-years from here, we would have had to start shipping it out around the time the Pyramids were being built in Egypt."

"What makes you think we get there with Velde equipment?" Oesterreich asks me.

He will not explain. Follow me and you'll see, he tells me. Follow me and you'll see.

The curious thing is that I like him. He is not exactly a likable man—too intense, too tightly wound, the fanaticism carried much too close to the surface—but he has a sort of charm all the same. He travels from world to world, he tells me, bringing the new gospel of the Goddess Avatar. That is exactly how he says it, "the new gospel of the Goddess Avatar," and I feel a chill when I hear the phrase. It seems absurd and frightening both at once. Yet I suppose those who brought the Order to the world a hundred fifty years

ago must have seemed just as strange and just as preposterous to those who first heard our words.

Of course, we had the Velde equipment to support our
philosophies.

But these people have—what? The strength of insanity?
The clear cool purposefulness that comes from having put
reality completely behind them?

"You were in the Order once, weren't you?" I ask him.

"You know it, your grace."

"Which House?"

"The Mission," he says.

"I should have guessed that. And now you have a new
mission, is that it?"

"An extension of the old one. Mohammed, you know,
didn't see Islam as a contradiction of Judaism and Christi-
anity. Just as the next level of revelation, incorporating the
previous ones."

"So you would incorporate the Order into your new belief?"

"We would never repudiate the Order, your grace."

"And Darklaw? How widely is that observed, would you
say, in the colony worlds?"

"I think we've kept much of it," Oesterreich says. "Certainly we keep the part about not trying to return to Earth.
And the part about spreading the Mission outward."

"Beyond the boundaries decreed, it would seem."

"This is a new dispensation," he says.

"But not a repudiation of the original teachings?"

"Oh, no," he says, and smiles. "Not a repudiation at all,
your grace."

He has that passionate confidence, that unshakable assurance, that is the mark of the real prophet and also of the
true madman. There is something diabolical about him, and

irresistible. In these conversations with him I have so far managed to remain outwardly calm, even genial, but the fact is that I am quaking within. I really do believe he is insane. Either that or an utter fraud, a cynical salesman of the irrational and the unreal, and though he is flippant he does not seem at all cynical. A madman, then. Is his condition infectious? As I have said, the fear of madness has been with me all my life; and so my harsh discipline, my fierce commitment, my depth of belief. He threatens all my defenses.

"When do you set out to visit your Goddess Avatar?" I ask.

"Whenever you like, your grace."

"You really think I'm going with you?"

"Of course you are. How else can you find out what you came out here to learn?"

"I've learned that the colonies have fallen away from Darklaw. Isn't that enough?"

"But you think we've all gone crazy, right?"

"When did I say that?"

"You didn't need to say it."

"If I send word to Earth of what's happened, and the Order chooses to cut off all further technical assistance and all shipments of manufactured goods—?"

"They won't do that. But even if they do—well, we're pretty much self-sufficient out here now, and getting more so every year—"

"And further emigration from Earth?"

"That would be your loss, not ours, your grace. Earth needs the colonies as a safety valve for her population surplus. We can get along without more emigrants. We know how to reproduce, out here." He grins at me. "This is foolish talk. You've come this far. Now go the rest of the way with me."

I am silent.

"Well?"

"Now, you mean?"

"Right now."

There is only one Velde station on Entropy, about three hundred meters from the house where I have been talking with Oesterreich. We go to it under a sky berserk with green lightning. He seems not even to notice.

"Don't we have to do lambda drills?" I ask.

"Not for this hop," Oesterreich says. "There's no differential between here and there." He is busy setting up co-ordinates. "Get into the chamber, your grace."

"And have you send me God knows where by myself?"

"Don't be foolish. Please."

It may be the craziest thing I have ever done. But I am the servant of the Order; and the Order has asked this of me. I step into the chamber. No one else is with us. He continues to press keys, and I realize that he is setting up an automatic transfer, requiring no external operator. When he is done with that he joins me, and there is the moment of flash.

We emerge into a cool, dry world with an Earthlike sun, a sea-green sky, a barren, rocky landscape. Ahead of us stretches an empty plateau broken here and there by small granite hillocks that rise like humped islands out of the flatness.

"Where are we?" I ask.

"Fifty light-years from Entropy, and about eighty-five light-years from Earth."

"What's the name of this place?"

"It doesn't have one. Nobody lives here. Come, now we walk a little."

We start forward. The ground has the look that comes of not having felt rain for ten or twenty years, but tough little tussocks of a grayish jagged-looking grass are pushing up somehow through the hard, stony red soil. When we have gone a hundred meters or so the land begins to drop away sharply on my left, so that I can look down into a broad, flat valley about three hundred meters below us. A solitary huge beast, somewhat like an elephant in bulk and manner, is grazing quietly down there, patiently prodding at the ground with its rigid two-pronged snout.

"Here we are," Oesterreich says.

We have reached the nearest of the little granite islands. When we walk around it, I see that its face on the farther side is fissured and broken, creating a sort of cave. Oesterreich beckons and we step a short way into it.

To our right, against the wall of the cave, is a curious narrow three-sided framework, a kind of tapering doorway, with deep darkness behind it. It is made of an odd glossy metal, or perhaps a plastic, with a texture that is both sleek and porous at the same time. There are hieroglyphs inscribed on it that seem much like those I saw on the wall of the stone temple in the mural in the Goddess-chapel on Phosphor, and to either side of it, mounted in the cave wall, are the triple six-pointed stars that are the emblem of Oesterreich's cult.

"What is this here?" I say, after a time.

"It's something like a Velde transmitter."

"It isn't anything like a Velde transmitter."

"It works very much like a Velde transmitter," he says. "You'll see when we step into its field. Are you ready?"

"Wait."

He nods. "I'm waiting."

"We're going to let this thing send us somewhere?"

"That's right, your grace."

"What is it? Who built it?"

"I've already told you what it is. As for who built it, I don't have any idea. Nobody does. We think it's five or ten million years old, maybe. It could be older than that by a factor of ten. Or a factor of a hundred. We have no way of judging."

After a long silence I say, "You're telling me that it's an alien device?"

"That's right."

"We've never discovered any sign of intelligent alien life anywhere in the galaxy."

"There's one right in front of you," Oesterreich says. "It isn't the only one."

"You've found aliens?"

"We've found their matter-transmitters. A few of them, anyway. They still work. Are you ready to jump now, your grace?"

I stare blankly at the three-sided doorway.

"Where to?"

"To a planet about five hundred light-years from here, where we can catch the bus that'll take us to the Goddess Avatar."

"You're actually serious?"

"Let's go, your grace."

"What about lambda effects?"

"There aren't any. Lambda differentials are a flaw in the Velde technology, not in the universe itself. This system gets us around without any lambda problems at all. Of course, we don't know how it works. Are you ready?"

"All right," I say helplessly.

He beckons to me and together we step toward the doorway and simply walk through it, and out the other side into a such astonishing beauty that I want to fall down and give praise. Great feathery trees rise higher than sequoias, and a milky waterfall comes tumbling down the flank of an ebony mountain that fills half the sky, and the air quivers with a diamond-bright haze. Before me stretches a meadow like a scarlet carpet, vanishing into the middle distance. There is a Mesozoic richness of texture to everything: it gleams, it shimmers, it trembles in splendor.

A second doorway, identical to the first, is mounted against an enormous boulder right in front of us. It too is flanked by the triple star emblem.

"Put your medallion on," Oesterreich tells me.

"My medallion?" I say, stupidly.

"Put it on. The Goddess Avatar will wonder why you're with me, and that'll tell her."

"Is she here?"

"She's on the next world. This is just a way station. We had to stop here first. I don't know why. Nobody does. Ready?"

"I'd like to stay here longer."

"You can come back some other time," he says. "She's waiting for you. Let's go."

"Yes," I say, and fumble in my pocket and find my medallion, and put it around my throat. Oesterreich winks and puts his thumb and forefinger together approvingly. He takes my hand and we step through.

She is a lean, leathery-looking woman of sixty or seventy years with hard bright blue eyes. She wears a khaki jacket, an olive-drab field hat, khaki shorts, heavy boots. Her graying hair is tucked behind her in a tight bun. Standing in front of a small tent, tapping something into a hand terminal, she looks like an aging geology professor out on a field trip in Wyoming. But next to her tent the triple emblem of the Goddess is displayed on a sandstone plaque.

This is a Mesozoic landscape too, but much less lush than the last one: great red-brown cliffs sparsely peppered with giant ferns and palms, four-winged insects the size of dragons zooming overhead, huge grotesque things that look very much like dinosaurs warily circling each other in a stony arroyo out near the horizon. I see some other tents out there too. There is a little colony here. The sun is reddish-yellow, and large.

"Well, what do we have here?" she says. "A Lord Magistrate, is it?"

"He was nosing around on Zima and Entrada, trying to find out what was going on."

"Well, now he knows." Her voice is like flint. I feel her contempt, her hostility, like something palpable. I feel her strength, too, a cold, harsh, brutal power. She says, "What was your house, Lord Magistrate?"

"Senders."

She studies me as if I were a specimen in a display case. In all my life I have known only one other person of such force and intensity, and that is the Master. But she is nothing like him.

"And now the Sender is sent?"

"Yes," I say. "There were deviations from the plan. It became necessary for me to resign my magistracy."

"We weren't supposed to come out this far, were we?" she asks. "The light of that sun up there won't get to Earth until the seventy-third century, do you know that? But here we are. Here we are!" She laughs, a crazed sort of cackle. I begin to wonder if they intend to kill me. The aura that comes from her is terrifying. The geology professor I took her for at first is gone: what I see now is something strange and fierce, a prophet, a seer. Then suddenly the fierceness vanishes too and something quite different comes from her: tenderness, pity, even love. The strength of it catches me unawares and I gasp at its power. These shifts of hers are managed without apparent means; she has spoken only a few words, and all the rest has been done with movement, with posture, with expression. I know that I am in the presence of some great charismatic. She walks over to me and with her face close to mine says, "We spoiled your plan, I know. But we too follow the divine rule. We discovered things that nobody had supected, and everything changed for us. Everything."

"Do you need me, Lady?" Oesterreich asks.

"No. Not now." She touches the tips of her fingers to my medallion of office, rubbing it lightly as though it is a magic talisman. Softly she says, "Let me take you on a tour of the galaxy, Lord Magistrate."

One of the alien doorways is located right behind her tent. We step through it hand in hand, and emerge on a dazzling green hillside looking out over a sea of ice. Three tiny blue-white suns hang like diamonds in the sky. In the trembling air they look like the three six-pointed stars of the emblem. "One of their capital cities was here once," she says. "But it's all at the bottom of that sea now. We ran a scan on it and saw the ruins, and some day we'll try to get down there." She beckons and we step through again, and out onto a turbulent desert of iron-hard red sand, where heavily armored crabs the size of footballs go scuttling sullenly away as we appear. "We think there's another city under here," she says. Stooping, she picks up a worn sherd of gray pottery and puts it in my hand. "That's an artifact millions of years old. We find them all over the place." I stare at it as if she has handed me a small fragment of the core of a star. She touches my medallion again, just a light grazing stroke, and leads me on into the next doorway, and out onto a world of billowing white clouds and soft dewy hills, and onward from there to one where trees hang like ropes from the sky, and onward from there, and onward from there—

"How did you find all this?" I ask, finally.

"I was living on Three Suns. You know where that is?

We were exploring the nearby worlds, trying to see if there was anything worthwhile, and one day I stepped out of a Velde unit and found myself looking at a peculiar three-sided kind of doorway right next to it, and I got too close and found myself going through into another world entirely. That was all there was to it."

"And you kept on going through one doorway after another?"

"Fifty of them. I didn't know then how to tune for destination, so I just kept jumping, hoping I'd get back to my starting point eventually. There wasn't any reason in the world why I should. But after six months I did. The Goddess protects me."

"The Goddess," I say.

She looks at me as though awaiting a challenge. But I am silent.

"These doorways link the whole galaxy together like the Paris Metro," she says after a moment. "We can go everywhere with them. Everywhere."

"And the Goddess? Are the doorways Her work?"

"We hope to find that out some day."

"What about this emblem?" I ask, pointing to the six-pointed stars beside the gateway. "What does that signify?"

"Her presence," she says. "Come. I'll show you."

We step through once more, and emerge into night. The sky on this world is the blackest black I have ever seen, with comets and shooting stars blazing across it in almost comic profusion. There are two moons, bright as mirrors. A dozen meters to one side is the white stone temple of the chapel mural I saw on Eden, marked with the same hieroglyphs that are shown on the painting there and that are inscribed on all the alien doorways. It is made of cyclopean slabs of white stone that look as if they were carved billions of years ago. She takes my arm and guides me through its squared-off doorway into a high-vaulted inner chamber where the triple six-pointed triangle, fashioned out of the glossy door-way material, is mounted on a stone altar.

"This is the only building of theirs we've ever found," she says. Her eyes are gleaming. "It must have been a holy place. Can you doubt it? You can feel the power."

"Yes."

"Touch the emblem."

"What will happen to me if I do?"

"Touch it," she says. "Are you afraid?"

"Why should I trust you?"

"Because the Goddess has used me to bring you to this place. Go on. Touch."

I put my hand to the smooth cool alien substance, and instantly I feel the force of revelation flowing through me, the unmistakable power of the Godhead. I see the multi-plicity of worlds, an infinity of them circling an infinity of suns. I see the Totality. I see the face of God clear and plain. It is what I have sought all my life and thought that I had already found; but I know at once that I am finding it for the first time. If I had fasted for a thousand years, or prayed for ten thousand, I could not have felt anything like that. It is the music out of which all things are built. It is the ocean in which all things float. I hear the voice of every god and goddess that ever had worshippers, and it is all one voice, and it goes coursing through me like a river of fire.

After a moment I take my hand away. And step back, trembling, shaking my head. This is too easy. One does not reach God by touching a strip of smooth plastic.

She says, "We mean to find them. They're still alive somewhere. How could they not be? And who could doubt that we were meant to follow them and find them? And kneel before them, for they are Whom we seek. So we'll go on and on, as far as we need to go, in search of them. To the farthest reaches, if we have to. To the rim of the universe and then beyond. With these doorways there are no limits. We've been handed the key to everywhere. We are for the Dark, all of it, on and on and on, not the little hundred-light-year sphere that your Order preaches, but the whole galaxy and even beyond. Who knows how far these door-ways reach? The Magellanic Clouds? Andromeda? M33? They're waiting for us out there. As they have waited for a billion years."

So she thinks she can hunt Him down through doorway after doorway. Or Her. Whichever. But she is wrong. He who made the universe made the makers of the doorways also.

"And the Goddess—?" I say.

"The Goddess is the Unknown. The Goddess is the Mystery toward which we journey. You don't feel Her presence?"

"I'm not sure."

"You will. If not now, then later. She'll greet us when we arrive. And embrace us, and make us all gods."

I stare a long while at the six-pointed stars. It would be simple enough to put forth my hand again and drink in the river of revelation a second time. But there is no need. That fire still courses through me. It always will, drawing me onward toward itself. Whatever it may be, there is no denying its power.

She says, "I'll show you one more thing, and then we'll leave here."

We continue through the temple and out the far side, where the wall has toppled. From a platform amid the rubble we have an unimpeded view of the heavens. An immense array of stars glitters above us, set out in utterly unfamiliar patterns. She points straight overhead, where a Milky Way in two whirling strands spills across the sky.

"That's Earth right up there," she says. "Can you see it?

Going around that little yellow sun, only a hundred thousand light-years away? I wonder if they ever paid us a visit. We won't know, will we, until we turn up one of their doorways somewhere in the Himalayas, or under the Antarctic ice, or somewhere like that. I think that when we finally reach them, they'll recognize us. It's interesting to think about it, isn't it." Her hand rests lightly on my wrist. "Shall we go back now, Lord Magistrate?"

So we return, in two or three hops, to the world of the dinosaurs and the giant dragonflies. There is nothing I can say. I feel storms within my skull. I feel myself spread out across half the universe.

Oesterreich waits for me now. He will take me back to Phosphor, or Entropy, or Entrada, or Zima, or Cuchulain, or anywhere else I care to go.

"You could even go back to Earth," the Goddess Avatar says. "Now that you know what's happening out here. You could go back home and tell the Master all about it."

"The Master already knows, I suspect. And there's no way I can go home. Don't you understand that?"

She laughs lightly. "Darklaw, yes. I forgot. The rule is that no one goes back. We've been catapulted out here to be cleansed of original sin, and to return to Mother Earth would be a crime against the laws of thermodynamics. Well, as you wish. You're a free man."

"It isn't Darklaw," I say. "Darklaw doesn't bind anyone any more."

I begin to shiver. Within my mind shards and fragments are falling from the sky: the House of Senders, the House of the Sanctuary, the whole Order and all its laws, the mountains and valleys of Earth, the body and fabric of Earth. All is shattered; all is made new; I am infinitely small against the infinite greatness of the cosmos. I am dazzled by the light of an infinity of suns.

And yet, though I must shield my eyes from that fiery glow, though I am numbed and humbled by the vastness of that vastness, I see that there are no limits to what may be attained, that the edge of the universe awaits me, that I need only reach and stretch, and stretch and reach, and ultimately I will touch it.

I see that even if she has made too great a leap of faith, even if she has surrendered herself to assumptions without basis, she is on the right path. The quest is unattainable because its goal is infinite. But the way leads ever outward. There is no destination, only a journey. And she has traveled farther on that journey than anyone.

And me? I had thought I was going out into the stars to spin out the last of my days quietly and obscurely, but I realize now that my pilgrimage is nowhere near its end. Indeed it is only beginning. This is not any road that I ever thought I would take. But this is the road that I am taking, all the same, and I have no choice but to follow it, though I am not sure yet whether I am wandering deeper into exile or finding my way back at last to my true home.

What I cannot help but see now is that our Mission is ended and that a new one has begun; or, rather, that this new Mission is the continuation and culmination of ours. Our Order has taught from the first that the way to reach God is to go to the stars. So it is. And so we have done. We have been too timid, limiting ourselves to that little ball of space surrounding Earth. But we have not failed. We have made possible everything that is to follow after.

I hand her my medallion. She looks at it the way I looked at that bit of alien pottery on the desert world, and then she starts to hand it back to me, but I shake my head.

"For you," I say. "A gift. An offering. It's of no use to me now."

She is standing with her back to the great reddish-yellow sun of this place, and it seems to me that light is streaming from her as it does from the Master, that she is aglow, that she is luminous, that she is herself a sun.

"Goddess save you, Lady," I say quietly.

All the worlds of the galaxy are whirling about me. I will take this road and see where it leads, for now I know there is no other.

"Goddess save you," I say. "Goddess save you, Lady."

THE SECRET SHARER

THE SECRET SHARER

AN INTRODUCTION

I make no secret of my admiration for the work of Joseph Conrad. (Or for Conrad himself, the tough, stubborn little man who, although English was only his third language, after Polish and French, not only was able to pass the difficult oral qualifying exam to become a captain in the British merchant marine, but then, a decade or so later, transformed himself into one of the greatest figures in twentieth-century English literature.) Most of what I owe to Conrad as a writer is buried deep in the substructure of my stories— a way of looking at narrative, a way of understanding character. But occasionally I've made the homage more visible. My novel *Downward to the Earth* of 1969 is a kind of free transposition of his novella "Heart of Darkness" to science fiction, a borrowing that I signalled overtly by labeling my most tormented character with the name of Kurtz. "Heart of Darkness," when I first encountered it as a reader almost fifty years ago, had been packaged as half of a two-novella paperback collection, the other story being Conrad's "The Secret Sharer." And some time late in 1986, I felt the urge, I know not why—a love of symmetry? A compulsion toward completion?—to finish what I had begun in *Downward to the*

Earth by writing a story adapted from the other great novella of that paperback of long ago.

This time I was less subtle than before, announcing my intentions not by using one of Conrad's character names but by appropriating his story's actual title. (This produced a pleasantly absurd result when my story was published in *Isaac Asimov's Science Fiction Magazine* and a reader wrote to the editor, somewhat indignantly, to ask whether I knew that the title had already been used by Joseph Conrad. I swiped not only the title but Conrad's basic story situation, that of the ship captain who finds a stowaway on board and eventually is drawn into a strange alliance with him. (Her, in my story.) But otherwise I translated the Conrad into purely science-fictional terms and produced something that I think represents completely original work, however much it may owe to the structure of a classic earlier story.

"Translate" is perhaps not the appropriate term for what I did. A "translation," in the uncompromising critical vocabulary set forth by Damon Knight and James Blish in the 1950s upon which I based much of my own fiction-writing esthetic, is defined as an adaptation of a stock format of mundane fiction into s-f by the simple one-for-one substitution of science-fiction noises for the artifacts of the mundane genre. That is, change "Colt .44" to "laser pistol" and "horse" to "greeznak" and "Comanche" to "Sloogl" and you can easily generate a sort of science fiction out of a standard western story, complete with cattle rustlers, scalpings, and cavalry rescues. But you don't get real science fiction; you don't get anything new and intellectually stimulating, just a western story that has greeznaks and Sloogls in it. Change "Los Angeles Police Department" to "Dry-lands Patrol" and "crack dealer" to "canal-dust dealer" and you've got a crime story set on Mars, but so what? Change "the canals of Venice" to "the marshy streets of Venusburg" and the sinister agents of S.M.E.R.S.H. to the sinister agents of A.A.A.A.R.G.H. and you've got a James Bond story set on the second planet, but it's still a James Bond story.

I don't think that that's what I've done here. The particular way in which Vox stows away aboard the *Sword of Orion* is nothing that Joseph Conrad could have understood, and arises, I think, purely out of the science-fictional inventions at the heart of the story. The way she leaves the ship is very different from anything depicted in Conrad's maritime fiction. The starwalk scene provides visionary possibilities quite unlike those afforded by a long stare into the vastness of the trackless Pacific. And so on. "The Secret Sharer" by Robert Silverberg is, or so I believe, a new and unique science-fiction story set, for reasons of the author's private amusement, within the framework of a well-known century-old masterpiece of the sea by Joseph Conrad.

"The Secret Sharer"—mine, not Conrad's—was a Nebula and Hugo nominee in 1988 as best novella of the year, but didn't get the trophies. It did win the third of the major s-f honors, the *Locus* award. Usually most of the *Locus* winners go on to get Hugo as well, but that year it didn't happen. I regretted that. But Joseph Conrad's original version of the story didn't win a Hugo or a Nebula either, and people still read it admiringly to this day. You take your lumps in this business, and you go bravely onward: it's the only way. Conrad would have understood that philosophy.

THE SECRET SHARER

It was my first time to heaven and I was no one at all, no one at all, and this was the voyage that was supposed to make me someone.

But though I was no one at all I dared to look upon the million worlds and I felt a great sorrow for them. There they were all about me, humming along on their courses through the night, each of them believing it was actually going somewhere. And each one wrong, of course, for worlds go nowhere, except around and around and around, pathetic monkeys on a string, forever tethered in place. They seem to move, yes. But really they stand still. And I—I who stared at the worlds of heaven and was swept with compassion for them—I knew that though I seemed to be standing still, I was in fact moving. For I was aboard a ship of heaven, a ship of the Service, that was spanning the light-years at a speed so incomprehensibly great that it might as well have been no speed at all.

I was very young. My ship, then as now, was the *Sword of Orion*, on a journey out of Kansas Four bound for Cul-de-Sac and Strappado and Mangan's Bitch and several other worlds, via the usual spinarounds. It was my first voyage and I was in command.

I thought for a long time that I would lose my soul on that voyage; but now I know that what was happening aboard that ship was not the losing of a soul but the gaining of one. And perhaps of more than one.

2.

Roacher thought I was sweet. I could have killed him for that; but of course he was dead already.

You have to give up your life when you go to heaven. What you get in return is for me to know and you, if you care, to find out; but the inescapable thing is that you leave behind anything that ever linked you to life on shore, and you become something else. We say that you give up the body and you get your soul. Certainly you can keep your body too, if you want it. Most do. But it isn't any good to you any more, not in the ways that you think a body is good to you. I mean to tell you how it was for me on my first voyage aboard the *Sword of Orion*, so many years ago.

I was the youngest officer on board, so naturally I was captain.

They put you in command right at the start, before you're anyone. That's the only test that means a damn: they throw you in the sea and if you can swim you don't drown, and if you can't you do. The drowned ones go back in the tank and they serve their own useful purposes, as push-cells or downloaders or mind-wipers or Johnny-scrub-and-scour or whatever. The ones that don't drown go on to other commands. No one is wasted. The Age of Waste has been over a long time.

On the third virtual day out from Kansas Four, Roacher told me that I was the sweetest captain he had ever served under. And he had served under plenty of them, for Roacher had gone up to heaven at least two hundred years before, maybe more.

"I can see it in your eyes, the sweetness. I can see it in the angle you hold your head."

He didn't mean it as a compliment.

"We can put you off ship at Ultima Thule," Roacher said. "Nobody will hold it against you. We'll put you in a bottle and send you down, and the Thuleys will catch you and decant you and you'll be able to find your way back to Kansas Four in twenty or fifty years. It might be the best thing."

Roacher is small and parched, with brown skin and eyes that shine with the purple luminescence of space. Some of the worlds he has seen were forgotten a thousand years ago.

"Go bottle yourself, Roacher," I told him.

"Ah, captain, captain! Don't take it the wrong way. Here, captain, give us a touch of the sweetness." He reached out a claw, trying to stroke me along the side of my face. "Give us a touch, captain, give us just a little touch!"

"I'll fry your soul and have it for breakfast, Roacher. There's sweetness for you. Go scuttle off, will you? Go jack yourself to the mast and drink hydrogen, Roacher. Go. Go."

"So sweet," he said. But he went. I had the power to hurt him. He knew I could do it, because I was captain. He also knew I wouldn't; but there was always the possibility he was wrong. The captain exists in that margin between certainty and possibility. A crewman tests the width of that margin at his own risk. Roacher knew that. He had been a captain once himself, after all.

There were seventeen of us to heaven that voyage, staffing a ten-kilo Megaspore-class ship with full annexes and extensions and all virtualities. We carried a bulging cargo of the things regarded in those days as vital in the distant colonies: pre-read vapor chips, artificial intelligences, climate nodes, matrix jacks, mediq machines, bone banks, soil converters, transit spheres, communication bubbles, skin-and-organ synthesizers, wildlife domestication plaques, gene replacement kits, a sealed consignment of obliteration sand and other proscribed weapons, and so on. We also had fifty billion dollars in the form of liquid currency pods, central-bank-to-central-bank transmission. In addition there was a passenger load of seven thousand colonists. Eight hundred of these were on the hoof and the others were stored in matrix form for body transplant on the worlds of destination. A standard load, in other words. The crew worked on commission, also as per standard, one percent of bill-of-lading value divided in customary lays. Mine was the 50th lay—that is, two percent of the net profits of the voyage—and that included a bonus for serving as captain; otherwise I would have had the 100th lay or something even longer. Roacher had the 10th lay and his jackmate Bulgar the 14th, although they weren't even officers. Which demonstrates the value of seniority in the Service. But seniority is the same thing as survival, after all, and why should survival not be rewarded? On my most recent voyage I drew the 19th lay. I will have better than that on my next.

3.

You have never seen a starship. We keep only to heaven; when we are to worldward, shoreships come out to us for the downloading. The closest we ever go to planetskin is a million shiplengths. Any closer and we'd be shaken apart by that terrible strength which emanates from worlds.

We don't miss landcrawling, though. It's a plague to us. If I had to step to shore now, after having spent most of my lifetime in heaven, I would die of the drop-death within an hour. That is a monstrous way to die; but why would I ever go ashore? The likelihood of that still existed for me at the time I first sailed the *Sword of Orion*, you understand, but I have long since given it up. That is what I mean when I say that you give up your life when you go to heaven. But of course what also goes from you is any feeling that to be ashore has anything to do with being alive. If you could ride a starship, or even see one as we see them, you would understand. I don't blame you for being what you are.

Let me show you the *Sword of Orion*. Though you will never see it as we see it.

What would you see, if you left the ship as we sometimes do to do the starwalk in the Great Open?

The first thing you would see was the light of the ship. A starship gives off a tremendous insistent glow of light that splits heaven like the blast of a trumpet. That great light both precedes and follows. Ahead of the ship rides a luminescent cone of brightness bellowing in the void. In its wake the ship leaves a photonic track so intense that it could be gathered up and weighed. It is the stardrive that issues this light: a ship eats space, and light is its offthrow.

Within the light you would see a needle ten kilometers long. That is the ship. One end tapers to a sharp point and the other has the Eye, and it is several days' journey by foot from end to end through all the compartments that lie between. It is a world self-contained. The needle is a flattened one. You could walk about easily on the outer surface of the ship, the skin of the top deck, what we call Skin Deck. Or just as easily on Belly Deck, the one on the bottom side. We call one the top deck and the other the bottom, but when you are outside the ship these distinctions have no meaning. Between Skin and Belly lie Crew Deck, Passenger Deck, Cargo Deck, Drive Deck. Ordinarily no one goes from one deck to another. We stay where we belong. The engines are in the Eye. So are the captain's quarters.

That needle is the ship, but it is not the whole ship. What you will not be able to see are the annexes and extensions and virtualities. These accompany the ship, enfolding it in a webwork of intricate outstructures. But they are of a subordinate level of reality and therefore they defy vision. A ship tunnels into the void, spreading far and wide to find room for all that it must carry. In these outlying zones are kept our supplies and provisions, our stores of fuel, and all cargo traveling at second-class rates. If the ship transports prisoners, they will ride in an annex. If the ship expects to encounter severe probability turbulence during the course of the voyage, it will arm itself with stabilizers, and those will be carried in the virtualities, ready to be brought into being if needed. These are the mysteries of our profession. Take them on faith, or ignore them, as you will: they are not meant for you to know.

A ship takes forty years to build. There are two hundred seventy-one of them in service now. New ones are constantly under construction. They are the only link binding the Mother Worlds and the eight hundred ninety-eight Colonies and the colonies of the Colonies. Four ships have been lost since the beginning of the Service. No one knows why. The loss of a starship is the worst disaster I can imagine. The last such event occurred sixty virtual years ago.

A starship never returns to the world from which it was launched. The galaxy is too large for that. It makes its voyage and it continues onward through heaven in an endless open circuit. That is the service of the Service. There would be no point in returning, since thousands of worldward years sweep by behind us as we make our voyages. We live outside of time. We must, for there is no other way. That is our burden and our privilege. That is the service of the Service.

4.

On the fifth virtual day of the voyage I suddenly felt a tic, a nibble, a subtle indication that something had gone wrong. It was a very trifling thing, barely perceptible, like the scatter of eroded pebbles that tells you that the palaces and towers of a great ruined city lie buried beneath the mound on which you climb. Unless you are looking for such signals you will not see them. But I was primed for discovery that day. I was eager for it. A strange kind of joy came over me when I picked up that fleeting signal of wrongness.

I keyed the intelligence on duty and said, "What was that tremor on Passenger Deck?"

The intelligence arrived instantly in my mind, a sharp gray-green presence with a halo of tingling music.

"I am aware of no tremor, sir."

"There was a distinct tremor. There was a data-spurt just now."

"Indeed, sir? A data-spurt, sir?" The intelligence sounded aghast, but in a condescending way. It was humoring me. "What action shall I take, sir?"

I was being invited to retreat.

The intelligence on duty was a 49 Henry Henry. The Henry series affects a sort of slippery innocence that I find disingenuous. Still, they are very capable intelligences. I wondered if I had misread the signal. Perhaps I was too eager for an event, any event, that would confirm my relationship with the ship.

There is never a sense of motion or activity aboard a starship: we float in silence on a tide of darkness, cloaked in our own dazzling light. Nothing moves, nothing seems to live in all the universe. Since we had left Kansas Four I had felt that great silence judging me. Was I really captain of this vessel? Good: then let me feel the weight of duty upon my shoulders.

We were past Ultima Thule by this time, and there could be no turning back. Borne on our cloak of light, we would roar through heaven for week after virtual week until we came to worldward at the first of our destinations, which was Cul-de-Sac in the Vainglory Archipelago, out by the Spook Clusters. Here in free space I must begin to master the ship, or it would master me.

"Sir?" the intelligence said.

"Run a data uptake," I ordered. "All Passenger Deck input for the past half hour. There was movement. There was a spurt."

I knew I might be wrong. Still, to err on the side of caution may be naive, but it isn't a sin. And I knew that at this stage in the voyage nothing I could say or do would make me seem other than naive to the crew of the *Sword of Orion*. What did I have to lose by ordering a recheck, then? I was hungry for surprises. Any irregularity that 49 Henry Henry turned up would be to my advantage; the absence of one would make nothing worse for me.

"Begging your pardon, sir," 49 Henry Henry reported after a moment, "but there was no tremor, sir."

"Maybe I overstated it, then. Calling it a tremor. Maybe it was just an anomaly. What do you say, 49 Henry Henry?" I wondered if I was humiliating myself, negotiating like this with an intelligence. "There was something. I'm sure of that. An unmistakable irregular burst in the data-flow. An anomaly, yes. What do you say, 49 Henry Henry?"

"Yes, sir."

"Yes what?"

"The record does show an irregularity, sir. Your observation was quite acute, sir."

"Go on."

"No cause for alarm, sir. A minor metabolic movement, nothing more. Like turning over in your sleep." You bastard, what do you know about sleep? "Extremely unusual, sir, that you should be able to observe anything so small. I commend you, sir. The passengers are all well, sir."

"Very good," I said. "Enter this exchange in the log, 49 Henry Henry."

"Already entered, sir," the intelligence said. "Permission to decouple, sir?"

"Yes, you can decouple," I told it.

The shimmer of music that signalled its presence grew tinny and was gone. I could imagine it smirking as it went about its ghostly flitting rounds deep in the neural conduits of the ship. Scornful software, glowing with contempt for its putative master. The poor captain, it was thinking. The poor hopeless silly boy of a captain. A passenger sneezes and he's ready to seal all bulkheads.

Well, let it smirk, I thought. I have acted appropriately and the record will show it.

I knew that all this was part of my testing.

You may think that to be captain of such a ship as the *Sword of Orion* in your first voyage to heaven is an awesome responsibility and an inconceivable burden. So it is, but not for the reason you think.

In truth the captain's duties are the least significant of anyone's aboard the ship. The others have well-defined tasks that are essential to the smooth running of the voyage, although the ship could, if the need arose, generate virtual replacements for any and every crew member and function adequately on its own. The captain's task, though, is fundamentally abstract. His role is to witness the voyage, to embody it in his own consciousness, to give it coherence, continuity, by reducing it to a pattern of decisions and responses. In that sense the captain is simply so much software: he is the coding through which the voyage is expressed as a series of linear functions. If he fails to perform that duty adequately, others will quietly see to it that the voyage proceeds as it should. What is destroyed, in the course of a voyage that is inadequately captained, is the captain himself, not the voyage. My pre-flight training made that absolutely clear. The voyage can survive the most feeble of captains. As I have said, four starships have been lost since the Service began, and no one knows why. But there is no reason to think that any of those catastrophes were caused by failings of the captain. How could they have been? The captain is only the vehicle through which others act. It is not the captain who makes the voyage, but the voyage which makes the captain.

5.

Restless, troubled, I wandered the eye of the ship. Despite 49 Henry Henry's suave mockery I was still convinced there was trouble on board, or about to be.

Just as I reached Outerscreen Level I felt something strange touch me a second time. It was different this time, and deeply disturbing.

The Eye, as it makes the complete descent from Skin Deck to Belly Deck, is lined with screens that provide displays, actual or virtual, of all aspects of the ship both internal and external. I came up to the great black bevel-edged screen that provided our simulated view of the external realspace environment and was staring at the dwindling wheel of the Ultima Thule relay point when the new anomaly occurred. The other had been the merest of subliminal signals, a nip, a tickle. This was more like an attempted intrusion. Invisible fingers seemed to brush lightly over my brain, probing, seeking entrance. The fingers withdrew; a moment later there was a sudden stabbing pain in my left temple.

I stiffened. "Who's there?"

"Help me," a silent voice said.

I had heard wild tales of passenger matrixes breaking free of their storage circuits and drifting through the ship like ghosts, looking for an unguarded body that they might infiltrate. The sources were unreliable, old scoundrels like Roacher or Bulgar. I dismissed such stories as fables, the way I dismissed what I had heard of the vast tentacular krakens that were said to swim the seas of space, or the beckoning mermaids with shining breasts who danced along the force-lines at spinaround points. But I had felt this. The probing fingers, the sudden sharp pain. And the sense of someone frightened, frightened but strong, stronger than I, hovering close at hand.

"Where are you?"

There was no reply. Whatever it was, if it had been anything at all, had slipped back into hiding after that one furtive thrust.

But was it really gone?

"You're still here somewhere," I said. "I know that you are."

Silence. Stillness.

"You asked for help. Why did you disappear so fast?"

No response. I felt anger rising.

"Whoever you are. Whatever. Speak up."

Nothing. Silence. Had I imagined it? The probing, the voiceless voice?

No. No. I was certain that there was something invisible and unreal hovering about me. And I found it infuriating, not to be able to regain contact with it. To be toyed with this way, to be mocked like this.

This is my ship, I thought. I want no ghosts aboard my ship.

"You can be detected," I said. "You can be contained. You can be eradicated."

As I stood there blustering in my frustration, it seemed to me that I felt that touch against my mind again, a lighter one this time, wistful, regretful. Perhaps I invented it. Perhaps I have supplied it retroactively.

But it lasted only a part of an instant, if it happened at all, and then I was unquestionably alone again. The solitude was real and total and unmistakable. I stood gripping the rail of the screen, leaning forward into the brilliant blackness and swaying dizzily as if I were being pulled forward through the wall of the ship into space.

"Captain?"

The voice of 49 Henry Henry, tumbling out of the air behind me.

"Did you feel something that time?" I asked.

The intelligence ignored my question. "Captain, there's trouble on Passenger Deck. Hands-on alarm: will you come?"

"Set up a transit track for me," I said. "I'm on my way."

Lights began to glow in mid-air, yellow, blue, green. The interior of the ship is a vast opaque maze and moving about within it is difficult without an intelligence to guide you. 49 Henry Henry constructed an efficient route for me down the curve of the Eye and into the main body of the ship, and thence around the rim of the leeward wall to the elevator down to Passenger Deck. I rode an air-cushion tracker keyed to the lights. The journey took no more than fifteen minutes. Unaided I might have needed a week.

Passenger Deck is an echoing nest of coffins, hundreds of them, sometimes even thousands, arranged in rows three abreast. Here our live cargo sleeps until we arrive and decant the stored sleepers into wakefulness. Machinery sighs and murmurs all around them, coddling them in their suspension. Beyond, far off in the dim distance, is the place for passengers of a different sort—a spiderwebbing of sensory cables that holds our thousands of disembodied matrixes. Those are the colonists who have left their bodies behind when going into space. It is a dark and forbidding place, dimly lit by swirling velvet comets that circle overhead emitting sparks of red and green.

The trouble was in the suspension area. Five crewmen were there already, the oldest hands on board: Katkat, Dismas, Rio de Rio, Gavotte, Roacher. Seeing them all together, I knew this must be some major event. We move on distant orbits within the immensity of the ship: to see as many as three members of the crew in the same virtual month is extraordinary. Now here were five. I felt an oppressive sense of community among them. Each of these five had sailed the seas of heaven more years than I had been alive. For at least a dozen voyages now they had been together as a team. I was the stranger in their midst, unknown, untried, lightly regarded, insignificant. Already Roacher had indicted me for my sweetness, by which he meant, I knew, a basic incapacity to act decisively. I thought he was wrong. But perhaps he knew me better than I knew myself.

They stepped back, opening a path between them. Gavotte, a great hulking thick-shouldered man with a surprisingly delicate and precise way of conducting himself, gestured with open hands: Here, captain, see? See?

What I saw were coils of greenish smoke coming up

from a passenger housing, and the glass door of the housing half open, cracked from top to bottom, frosted by temperature differentials. I could hear a sullen dripping sound. Blue fluid fell in thick steady gouts from a shattered support line. Within the housing itself was the pale naked figure of a man, eyes wide open, mouth agape as if in a silent scream. His left arm was raised, his fist was clenched. He looked like an anguished statue.

They had body-salvage equipment standing by. The hapless passenger would be disassembled and all usable parts stored as soon as I gave the word.

"Is he irretrievable?" I asked.

"Take a look," Katkat said, pointing to the housing readout. All the curves pointed down. "We have nineteen percent degradation already, and rising. Do we disassemble?"

"Go ahead," I said. "Approved."

The lasers glinted and flailed. Body parts came into view, shining, moist. The coiling metallic arms of the body-salvage equipment rose and fell, lifting organs that were not yet beyond repair and putting them into storage. As the machine labored the men worked around it, shutting down the broken housing, tying off the disrupted feeders and refrigerator cables.

I asked Dismas what had happened. He was the mind-wiper for this sector, responsible for maintenance on the suspended passengers. His face was open and easy, but the deceptive cheeriness about his mouth and cheeks was mysteriously negated by his bleak, shadowy eyes. He told me that he had been working much farther down the deck, performing routine service on the Strappado-bound people, when he felt a sudden small disturbance, a quick tickle of wrongness.

"So did I," I said. "How long ago was that?"

"Half an hour, maybe. I didn't make a special note of

it. I thought it was something in my gut, captain. You felt it too, you say?"

I nodded. "Just a tickle. It's in the record." I heard the distant music of 49 Henry Henry. Perhaps the intelligence was trying to apologize for doubting me. "What happened next?" I asked.

"Went back to work. Five, ten minutes, maybe. Felt another jolt, a stronger one." He touched his forehead, right at the temple, showing me where. "Detectors went off, broken glass. Came running, found this Cul-de-Sac passenger here undergoing convulsions. Rising from his bindings, thrashing around. Pulled himself loose from everything, went smack against the housing window. Broke it. It's a very fast death."

"Matrix intrusion," Roacher said.

The skin of my scalp tightened. I turned to him.

"Tell me about that."

He shrugged. "Once in a long while someone in the storage circuits gets to feeling footloose, and finds a way out and goes roaming the ship. Looking for a body to jack into, that's what they're doing. Jack into me, jack into Katkat, even jack into you, captain. Anybody handy, just so they can feel flesh around them again. Jacked into this one here and something went wrong."

The probing fingers, yes. The silent voice. Help me.

"I never heard of anyone jacking into a passenger in suspension," Dismas said.

"No reason why not," said Roacher.

"What's the good? Still stuck in a housing, you are. Frozen down, that's no better than staying matrix."

"Five to two it was matrix intrusion," Roacher said, glaring.

"Done," Dismas said. Gavotte laughed and came in on the

bet. So too did sinuous little Katkat, taking the other side. Rio deRio, who had not spoken a word to anyone in his last six voyages, snorted and gestured obscenely at both factions.

I felt like an idle spectator. To regain some illusion of command I said, "If there's a matrix loose, it'll show up on ship inventory. Dismas, check with the intelligence on duty and report to me. Katkat, Gavotte, finish cleaning up this mess and seal everything off. Then I want your reports in the log and a copy to me. I'll be in my quarters. There'll be further instructions later. The missing matrix, if that's what we have on our hands, will be identified, located, and re-captured."

Roacher grinned at me. I thought he was going to lead a round of cheers.

I turned and mounted my tracker, and rode it following the lights, yellow, blue, green, back up through the maze of decks and out to the Eye.

As I entered my cabin something touched my mind and a silent voice said, "Please help me."

6.

Carefully I shut the door behind me, locked it, loaded the privacy screens. The captain's cabin aboard a Megaspore starship of the Service is a world in itself, serene, private, immense. In mine, spiral galaxies whirled and sparkled on the walls. I had a stream, a lake, a silver waterfall beyond it. The air was soft and glistening. At a touch of my hand I could have light, music, scent, color, from any one of a thousand hidden orifices. Or I could turn the walls trans-lucent and let the luminous splendor of starspace come flooding through.

Only when I was fully settled in, protected and insulated and comfortable, did I say, "All right. What are you?"

"You promise you won't report me to the captain?"

"I don't promise anything."

"You will help me, though?" The voice seemed at once frightened and insistent, urgent and vulnerable.

"How can I say? You give me nothing to work with."

"I'll tell you everything. But first you have to promise not to call the captain."

I debated with myself for a moment and opted for directness.

"I am the captain," I said.

"No!"

"Can you see this room? What do you think it is? Crew quarters? The scullery?"

I felt turbulent waves of fear coming from my invisible companion. And then nothing. Was it gone? Then I had made a mistake in being so forthright. This phantom had to be confined, sealed away, perhaps destroyed, before it could do more damage. I should have been more devious. And also I knew that I would regret it in another way if it had slipped away: I was taking a certain pleasure in being able to speak with someone—something—that was neither a member of my crew nor an omnipotent, contemptuous artificial intelligence.

"Are you still here?" I asked after a while.

Silence.

Gone, I thought. Sweeping through the *Sword of Orion* like a gale of wind. Probably down at the far end of the ship by this time.

Then, as if there had been no break in the conversation: "I just can't believe it. Of all the places I could have gone, I had to walk right into the captain's cabin."

"So it seems."

"And you're actually the captain?"

"Yes. Actually."

Another pause.

"You seem so young," it said. "For a captain."

"Be careful," I told it.

"I didn't mean anything by that, captain." With a touch of bravado, even defiance, mingling with uncertainty and anxiety. Captain sir."

Looking toward the ceiling, where shining resonator nodes shimmered all up and down the spectrum as slave-light leaped from junction to junction along the illuminator strands, I searched for a glimpse of it, some minute electro-magnetic clue. But there was nothing.

I imagined a web of impalpable force, a dancing will-o'-the-wisp, flitting erratically about the room, now perching on my shoulder, now clinging to some fixture, now extending itself to fill every open space: an airy thing, a sprite, playful and capricious. Curiously, not only was I un-afraid but I found myself strongly drawn to it. There was something strangely appealing about this quick vibrating spirit, so bright with contradictions. And yet it had caused the death of one of my passengers.

"Well?" I said. "You're safe here. But when are you go-ing to tell me what you are?"

"Isn't that obvious? I'm a matrix."

"Go on."

"A free matrix, a matrix on the loose. A matrix who's in big trouble. I think I've hurt someone. Maybe killed him."

"One of the passengers?" I said.

"So you know?"

"There's a dead passenger, yes. We're not sure what hap-pened."

"It wasn't my fault. It was an accident."

"That may be," I said. "Tell me about it. Tell me every-thing."

"Can I trust you?"

"More than anyone else on this ship."

"But you're the captain."

"That's why," I said.

7.

Her name was Leeleaine, but she wanted me to call her Vox. That means "voice," she said, in one of the ancient lan-guages of Earth. She was seventeen years old, from Jaana Head, which is an island off the coast of West Palabar on Kansas Four. Her father was a glass-farmer, her mother op-erated a gravity hole, and she had five brothers and three sisters, all of them much older than she was.

"Do you know what that's like, captain? Being the youngest of nine? And both your parents working all the time, and your cross-parents just as busy? Can you imag-ine? And growing up on Kansas Four, where it's a thousand kilometers between cities, and you aren't even in a city, you're on an island?"

"I know something of what that's like," I said.

"Are you from Kansas Four too?"

"No," I said. "Not from Kansas Four. But a place much like it, I think."

She spoke of a troubled, unruly childhood, full of lone-liness and anger. Kansas Four, I have heard, is a beautiful world, if you are inclined to find beauty in worlds: a wild and splendid place, where the sky is scarlet and the bare basalt mountains rise in the east like a magnificent black wall. But to hear Vox speak of it, it was squalid, grim, bleak. For her it was a loveless place where she led a loveless life.

And yet she told me of pale violet seas aglow with brilliant yellow fish, and trees that erupted with a shower of dazzling crimson fronds when they were in bloom, and warm rains that sang in the air like harps. I was not then so long in heaven that I had forgotten the beauty of seas or trees or rains, which by now are nothing but hollow words to me. Yet Vox had found her life on Kansas Four so hateful that she had been willing to abandon not only her native world but her body itself. That was a point of kinship between us: I too had given up my world and my former life, if not my actual flesh. But I had chosen heaven, and the Service. Vox had volunteered to exchange one landcrawling servitude for another.

"The day came," she said, "when I knew I couldn't stand it any more. I was so miserable, so empty: I thought about having to live this way for another two hundred years or even more, and I wanted to pick up the hills and throw them at each other. Or get into my mother's plummeter and take it straight to the bottom of the sea. I made a list of ways I could kill myself. But I knew I couldn't do it, not this way or that way or any way. I wanted to live. But I didn't want to live like that."

On that same day, she said, the soul-call from Cul-de-Sac reached Kansas Four. A thousand vacant bodies were available there and they wanted soul-matrixes to fill them. Without a moment's hesitation Vox put her name on the list.

There is a constant migration of souls between the worlds. On each of my voyages I have carried thousands of them, setting forth hopefully toward new bodies on strange planets.

Every world has a stock of bodies awaiting replacement souls. Most were the victims of sudden violence. Life is risky on shore, and death lurks everywhere. Salvaging and repairing a body is no troublesome matter, but once a soul has fled it can never be recovered. So the empty bodies of those who drown and those who are stung by lethal insects and those who are thrown from vehicles and those who are struck by falling branches as they work are collected and examined. If they are beyond repair they are disassembled and their usable parts set aside to be installed in others. But if their bodies can be made whole again, they are, and they are placed in holding chambers until new souls become available for them.

And then there are those who vacate their bodies voluntarily, perhaps because they are weary of them, or weary of their worlds, and wish to move along. They are the ones who sign up to fill the waiting bodies on far worlds, while others come behind them to fill the bodies they have abandoned. The least costly way to travel between the worlds is to surrender your body and go in matrix form, thus exchanging a discouraging life for an unfamiliar one. That was what Vox had done. In pain and despair she had agreed to allow the essence of herself, everything she had ever seen or felt or thought or dreamed, to be converted into a lattice of electrical impulses that the *Sword of Orion* would carry on its voyage from Kansas Four to Cul-de-Sac. A new body lay reserved for her there. Her own discarded body would remain in suspension on Kansas Four. Some day it might become the home of some wandering soul from another world; or, if there were no bids for it, it might eventually be disassembled by the body-salvagers, and its parts put to some worthy use. Vox would never know; Vox would never care.

"I can understand trading an unhappy life for a chance at a happy one," I said. "But why break loose on ship? What purpose could that serve? Why not wait until you got to Cul-de-Sac?"

"Because it was torture," she said.

"Torture? What was?"

"Living as a matrix." She laughed bitterly. "Living? It's worse than death could ever be!"

"Tell me."

"You've never done matrix, have you?"

"No," I said. "I chose another way to escape."

"Then you don't know. You can't know. You've got a ship full of maxtrixes in storage circuits but you don't understand a thing about them. Imagine that the back of your neck itches, captain. But you have no arms to scratch with. Your thigh starts to itch. Your chest. You lie there itching everywhere. And you can't scratch. Do you understand me?"

"How can a matrix feel an itch? A matrix is simply a pattern of electrical—"

"Oh, you're impossible! You're stupid! I'm not talking about actual literal itching. I'm giving you a suppose, a for-instance. Because you'd never be able to understand the real situation. Look: you're in the storage circuit. All you are is electricity. That's all a mind really is, anyway: electricity. But you used to have a body. The body had sensation. The body had feelings. You remember them. You're a prisoner. A prisoner remembers all sorts of things that used to be taken for granted. You'd give anything to feel the wind in your hair again, or the taste of cool milk, or the scent of flowers. Or even the pain of a cut finger. The saltiness of your blood when you lick the cut. Anything. I hated my body, don't you see? I couldn't wait to be rid of it. But once it was gone I missed the feelings it had. I missed the sense of flesh pulling at me, holding me to the ground, flesh full of nerves, flesh that could feel pleasure. Or pain."

"I understand," I said, and I think that I truly did. "But the voyage to Cul-de-Sac is short. A few virtual weeks and you'd be there, and out of storage and into your new body, and—"

"Weeks? Think of that itch on the back of your neck, Captain. The itch that you can't scratch. How long do you think you could stand it, lying there feeling that itch? Five minutes? An hour? Weeks?"

It seemed to me that an itch left unscratched would die of its own, perhaps in minutes. But that was only how it seemed to me. I was not Vox; I had not been a matrix in a storage circuit.

I said, "So you let yourself out? How?"

"It wasn't that hard to figure. I had nothing else to do but think about it. You align yourself with the polarity of the circuit. That's a matrix too, an electrical pattern holding you in crosswise bands. You change the alignment. It's like being tied up, and slipping the ropes around until you can slide free. And then you can go anywhere you like. You key into any bioprocessor aboard the ship and you draw your energy from that instead of from the storage circuit, and it sustains you. I can move anywhere around this ship at the speed of light. Anywhere. In just the time you blinked your eye, I've been everywhere. I've been to the far tip and out on the mast, and I've been down through the lower decks, and I've been in the crew quarters and the cargo places and I've even been a little way off into something that's right outside the ship but isn't quite real, if you know what I mean. Something that just seems to be a cradle of probability waves surrounding us. It's like being a ghost. But it doesn't solve anything. Do you see? The torture still goes on. You want to feel, but you can't. You want to be connected again, your senses, your inputs. That's why I tried to get into the passenger, do you see? But he wouldn't let me."

I began to understand at last.

Not everyone who goes to the worlds of heaven as a colonist travels in matrix form. Ordinarily anyone who can afford to take his body with him will do so; but relatively few can afford it. Those who do travel in suspension, the deepest of sleeps. We carry no waking passengers in the Service, not at any price. They would be trouble for us, poking here, poking there, asking questions, demanding to be served and pampered. They would shatter the peace of the voyage. And so they go down into their coffins, their housings, and there they sleep the voyage away, all life-processes halted, a death-in-life that will not be reversed until we bring them to their destinations.

And poor Vox, freed of her prisoning circuit and hungry for sensory data, had tried to slip herself into a passenger's body.

I listened, appalled and somber, as she told of her terrible odyssey through the ship. Breaking free of the circuit: that had been the first strangeness I felt, that tic, that nibble at the threshold of my consciousness.

Her first wild moment of freedom had been exhilarating and joyous. But then had come the realization that nothing really had changed. She was at large, but still she was incorporeal, caught in that monstrous frustration of bodilessness, yearning for a touch. Perhaps such torment was common among matrixes; perhaps that was why, now and then, they broke free as Vox had done, to roam ships like sad troubled spirits. So Roacher had said. Once in a long while someone in the storage circuits gets to feeling footloose, and finds a way out and goes roaming the ship. Looking for a body to jack into, that's what they're doing. Jack into me, jack into Katkat, even jack into you, captain. Anybody handy, just so they can feel flesh around them again. Yes.

That was the second jolt, the stronger one, that Dismas and I had felt, when Vox, selecting a passenger at random, suddenly, impulsively, had slipped herself inside his brain. She had realized her mistake at once. The passenger, lost in whatever dreams may come to the suspended, reacted to her intrusion with wild terror. Convulsions swept him; he rose, clawing at the equipment that sustained his life, trying desperately to evict the succubus that had penetrated him. In this frantic struggle he smashed the case of his housing and died. Vox, fleeing, frightened, careened about the ship in search of refuge, encountered me standing by the screen in the Eye, and made an abortive attempt to enter my mind. But just then the death of the passenger registered on 49 Henry Henry's sensors and when the intelligence made contact with me to tell me of the emergency Vox fled again, and hovered dolefully until I returned to my cabin. She had not meant to kill the passenger, she said. She was sorry that he had died. She felt some embarrassment, now, and fear. But no guilt. She rejected guilt for it almost defiantly. He had died? Well, so he had died. That was too bad. But how could she have known any such thing was going to happen? She was only looking for a body to take refuge in. Hearing that from her, I had a sense of her as someone utterly unlike me, someone volatile, unstable, perhaps violent. And yet I felt a strange kinship with her, even an identity. As though we were two parts of the same spirit; as though she and I were one and the same. I barely understood why.

"And what now?" I asked. "You say you want help. How?"

"Take me in."

"What?"

"Hide me. In you. If they find me, they'll eradicate me. You said so yourself, that it could be done, that I could be detected, contained, eradicated. But it won't happen if you protect me."

"I'm the captain," I said, astounded.

"Yes."

"How can I—"

"They'll all be looking for me. The intelligences, the crewmen. It scares them, knowing there's a matrix loose. They'll want to destroy me. But if they can't find me, they'll start to forget about me after a while. They'll think I've escaped into space, or something. And if I'm jacked into you, nobody's going to be able to find me."

"I have a responsibility to—"

"Please," she said. "I could go to one of the others, maybe. But I feel closest to you. Please. Please."

"Closest to me?"

"You aren't happy. You don't belong. Not here, not anywhere. You don't fit in, any more than I did on Kansas Four. I could feel it the moment I first touched your mind. You're a new captain, right? And the others on board are making it hard for you. Why should you care about them? Save me. We have more in common than you do with them. Please? You can't just let them eradicate me. I'm young. I didn't mean to hurt anyone. All I want is to get to Cul-de-Sac and be put in the body that's waiting for me there. A new start, my first start, really. Will you?"

"Why do you bother asking permission? You can simply enter me through my jack whenever you want, can't you?"

"The last one died," she said.

"He was in suspension. You didn't kill him by entering him. It was the surprise, the fright. He killed himself by thrashing around and wrecking his housing."

"Even so," said Vox. "I wouldn't try that again, an unwilling host. You have to say you'll let me, or I won't come in."

I was silent.

"Help me?" she said.

"Come," I told her.

8.

It was just like any other jacking: an electrochemical mind-to-mind bond, a linkage by way of the implant socket at the base of my spine. The sort of thing that any two people who wanted to make communion might do. There was just one difference, which was that we didn't use a jack. We skipped the whole intricate business of checking bandwiths and voltages and selecting the right transformer-adapter. She could do it all, simply by matching evoked potentials. I felt a momentary sharp sensation and then she was with me.

"Breathe," she said. "Breathe real deep. Fill your lungs. Rub your hands together. Touch your cheeks. Scratch behind your left ear. Please. Please. It's been so long for me since I've felt anything."

Her voice sounded the same as before, both real and unreal. There was no substance to it, no density of timbre, no sense that it was produced by the vibrations of vocal cords atop a column of air. Yet it was clear, firm, substantial in some essential way, a true voice in all respects except that there was no speaker to utter it. I suppose that while she was outside me she had needed to extend some strand of herself into my neural system in order to generate it. Now that was unnecessary. But I still perceived the voice as originating outside me, even though she had taken up residence within.

She overflowed with needs.

"Take a drink of water," she urged. "Eat something. Can you make your knuckles crack? Do it, oh, do it! Put your hand between your legs and squeeze. There's so much I want to feel. Do you have music here? Give me some music, will you? Something loud, something really hard."

I did the things she wanted. Gradually she grew more calm.

I was strangely calm myself. I had no special awareness then of her presence within me, no unfamiliar pressure in my skull, no slitherings along my spine. There was no mingling of her thought-stream and mine. She seemed not to have any way of controlling the movements or responses of my body. In these respects our contact was less intimate than any ordinary human jacking communion would have been. But that, I would soon discover, was by her choice. We would not remain so carefully compartmentalized for long.

"Is it better for you now?" I asked.

"I thought I was going to go crazy. If I didn't start feeling something again soon."

"You can feel things now?"

"Through you, yes. Whatever you touch, I touch."

"You know I can't hide you for long. They'll take my command away if I'm caught harboring a fugitive. Or worse."

"You don't have to speak out loud to me any more," she said.

"I don't understand."

"Just send it. We have the same nervous system now."

"You can read my thoughts?" I said, still aloud.

"Not really. I'm not hooked into the higher cerebral centers. But I pick up motor, sensory stuff. And I get subvocalizations. You know what those are? I can hear your thoughts if you want me to. It's like being in communion. You've been in communion, haven't you?"

"Once in a while."

"Then you know. Just open the channel to me. You can't go around the ship talking out loud to somebody invisible, you know. Send me something. It isn't hard."

"Like this?" I said, visualizing a packet of verbal information sliding through the channels of my mind.

"You see? You can do it!"

"Even so," I told her. "You still can't stay like this with me for long. You have to realize that."

She laughed. It was unmistakable, a silent but definite laugh. "You sound so serious. I bet you're still surprised you took me in the first place."

"I certainly am. Did you think I would?"

"Sure I did. From the first moment. You're basically a very kind person."

"Am I, Vox?"

"Of course. You just have to let yourself do it." Again the silent laughter. "I don't even know your name. Here I am right inside your head and I don't know your name."

"Adam."

"That's a nice name. Is that an Earth name?"

"An old Earth name, yes. Very old."

"And are you from Earth?" she asked.

"No. Except in the sense that we're all from Earth."

"Where, then?"

"I'd just as soon not talk about it," I said.

She thought about that. "You hated the place where you grew up that much?"

"Please, Vox—"

"Of course you hated it. Just like I hated Kansas Four. We're two of a kind, you and me. We're one and the same. You got all the caution and I got all the impulsiveness. But otherwise we're the same person. That's why we share so well. I'm glad I'm sharing with you, Adam. You won't make me leave, will you? We belong with each other. You'll let me stay until we reach Cul-de-Sac. I know you will."

"Maybe. Maybe not." I wasn't at all sure, either way.

"Oh, you will. You will, Adam. I know you better than you know yourself."

9.

So it began. I was in some new realm outside my established sense of myself, so far beyond my notions of appropriate behavior that I could not even feel astonishment at what I had done. I had taken her in, that was all. A stranger in my skull. She had turned to me in appeal and I had taken her in. It was as if her recklessness was contagious. And though I didn't mean to shelter her any longer than was absolutely necessary, I could already see that I wasn't going to make any move to eject her until her safety was assured.

But how was I going to hide her?

Invisible she might be, but not undetectable. And everyone on the ship would be searching for her.

There were sixteen crewmen on board who dreaded a loose matrix as they would a vampire. They would seek her as long as she remained at large. And not only the crew. The intelligences would be monitoring for her too, not out of any kind of fear but simply out of efficiency: they had nothing to fear from Vox but they would want the cargo manifests to come out in balance when we reached our destination.

The crew didn't trust me in the first place. I was too young, too new, too green, too sweet. I was just the sort who might be guilty of giving shelter to a secret fugitive. And it was altogether likely that her presence within me would be obvious to others in some way not apparent to me. As for the intelligences, they had access to all sorts of data as part of their routine maintenance operations. Perhaps they could measure tiny physiological changes, differences in my reaction times or circulatory efficiency or whatever, that would be a tipoff to the truth. How would I know? I would have to be on constant guard against discovery of the secret sharer of my consciousness.

The first test came less than an hour after Vox had entered me. The communicator light went on and I heard the far-off music of the intelligence on duty.

This one was 612 Jason, working the late shift. Its aura was golden, its music deep and throbbing. Jasons tend to be more brusque and less condescending than the Henry series, and in general I prefer them. But it was terrifying now to see that light, to hear that music, to know that the ship's intelligence wanted to speak with me. I shrank back at a tense awkward angle, the way one does when trying to avoid a face-to-face confrontation with someone.

But of course the intelligence had no face to confront. The intelligence was only a voice speaking to me out of a speaker grid, and a stew of magnetic impulses somewhere on the control levels of the ship. All the same, I perceived 612 Jason now as a great glowing eye, staring through me to the hidden Vox.

"What is it?" I asked.

"Report summary, captain. The dead passenger and the missing matrix."

Deep within me I felt a quick plunging sensation, and then the skin of my arms and shoulders began to glow as the chemicals of fear went coursing through my veins in a fierce tide. It was Vox, I knew, reacting in sudden alarm, opening the petcocks of my hormonal system. It was the thing I had dreaded. How could 612 Jason fail to notice that flood of endocrine response?

"Go on," I said, as coolly as I could.

But noticing was one thing, interpreting the data something else. Fluctuations in a human being's endocrine output might have any number of causes. To my troubled conscience everything was a glaring signal of my guilt. 612 Jason gave no indication that it suspected a thing.

The intelligence said, "The dead passenger was Hans Eger Olafssen, 54 years of age, a native of—"

"Never mind his details. You can let me have a printout on that part."

"The missing matrix," 612 Jason went on imperturbably. "Leeleaine Eliani, 17 years of age, a native of Kansas Four, bound for Cul-de-Sac, Vainglory Archipelago, under Transmission Contract No. D-14871532, dated the 27th day of the third month of—"

"Printout on that too," I cut in. "What I want to know is where she is now."

"That information is not available."

"That isn't a responsive answer, 612 Jason."

"No better answer can be provided at this time, captain. Tracer circuits have been activated and remain in constant search mode."

"And?"

"We have no data on the present location of the missing matrix."

Within me Vox reacted instantly to the intelligence's calm flat statement. The hormonal response changed from one of fear to one of relief. My blazing skin began at once to cool. Would 612 Jason notice that too, and from that small clue be able to assemble the subtext of my body's responses into a sequence that exposed my criminal violation of regulations?

"Don't relax too soon," I told her silently. "This may be some sort of trap."

To 612 Jason I said, "What data do you have, then?"

"Two things are known: the time at which the Eliani matrix achieved negation of its storage circuitry and the time of its presumed attempt at making neural entry into the suspended passenger Olafssen. Beyond that no data has been recovered."

"Its presumed attempt?" I said.

"There is no proof, captain."

"Olafssen's convulsions? The smashing of the storage housing?"

"We know that Olafssen responded to an electrical stimulus, captain. The source of the stimulus is impossible to trace, although the presumption is that it came from the missing matrix Eliani. These are matters for the subsequent inquiry. It is not within my responsibilities to assign definite causal relationships."

Spoken like a true Jason-series intelligence, I thought.

I said, "You don't have any effective way of tracing the movements of the Eliani matrix, is that what you're telling me?"

"We're dealing with extremely minute impedances, sir. In the ordinary functioning of the ship it is very difficult to distinguish a matrix manifestation from normal surges and pulses in the general electrical system."

"You mean, it might take something as big as the matrix trying to climb back into its own storage circuit to register on the monitoring system?"

"Very possibly, sir."

"Is there any reason to think the Eliani matrix is still on the ship at all?"

"There is no reason to think that it is not, captain."

"In other words, you don't know anything about anything concerning the Eliani matrix."

"I have provided you with all known data at this point. Trace efforts are continuing, sir."

"You still think this is a trap?" Vox asked me.

"It's sounding better and better by the minute. But shut up and don't distract me, will you?"

To the intelligence I said, "All right, keep me posted on the situation. I'm preparing for sleep, 612 Jason. I want the end-of-day status report, and then I want you to clear off and leave me alone."

"Very good, sir. Fifth virtual day of voyage. Position of ship sixteen units beyond last port of call, Kansas Four. Scheduled rendezvous with relay forces at Ultima Thule spinaround point was successfully achieved at the hour of—"

The intelligence droned on and on: the usual report of the routine events of the day, broken only by the novelty of an entry for the loss of a passenger and one for the escape of a matrix, then returning to the standard data, fuel levels and velocity soundings and all the rest. On the first four nights of the voyage I had solemnly tried to absorb all this torrent of ritualized downloading of the log as though my captaincy depended on committing it all to memory, but this night I barely listened, and nearly missed my cue when it was time to give it my approval before clocking out for the night. Vox had to prod me and let me know that the intelligence was waiting for something. I gave 612 Jason the confirm-and-clock-out and heard the welcome sound of its diminishing music as it decoupled the contact.

"What do you think?" Vox asked. "It doesn't know, does it?"

"Not yet," I said.

"You really are a pessimist, aren't you?"

"I think we may be able to bring this off," I told her. "But the moment we become overconfident, it'll be the end. Everyone on this ship wants to know where you are. The slightest slip and we're both gone."

"Okay. Don't lecture me."

"I'll try not to. Let's get some sleep now."

"I don't need to sleep."

"Well, I do."

"Can we talk for a while first?"

"Tomorrow," I said.

But of course sleep was impossible. I was all too aware of the stranger within me, perhaps prowling the most hidden places of my psyche at this moment. Or waiting to invade my dreams once I drifted off. For the first time I thought I could feel her presence even when she was silent: a hot node of identity pressing against the wall of my brain. Perhaps I imagined it. I lay stiff and tense, as wide awake as I have ever been in my life. After a time I had to call 612 Jason and ask it to put me under the wire; and even then my sleep was uneasy when it came.

10.

Until that point in the voyage I had taken nearly all of my meals in my quarters. It seemed a way of exerting my authority, such as it was, aboard ship. By my absence from the dining hall I created a presence, that of the austere and aloof captain; and I avoided the embarrassment of having to sit in the seat of command over men who were much my senior in all things. It was no great sacrifice for me. My quarters were more than comfortable, the food was the same as that which was available in the dining hall, the servo-steward that brought it was silent and efficient. The question of isolation did not arise. There has always been something solitary about me, as there is about most who are of the Service.

But when I awoke the next morning after what had seemed like an endless night, I went down to the dining hall for breakfast.

It was nothing like a deliberate change of policy, a decision that had been rigorously arrived at through careful reasoning. It wasn't a decision at all. Nor did Vox suggest it, though I'm sure she inspired it. It was purely automatic. I arose, showered, and dressed. I confess that I had forgotten all about the events of the night before. Vox was quiet within me. Not until I was under the shower, feeling the warm comforting ultrasonic vibration, did I remember her: there came a disturbing sensation of being in two places at once, and, immediately afterward, an astonishingly odd feeling of shame at my own nakedness. Both those feelings passed quickly. But they did indeed bring to mind that extraordinary thing which I had managed to suppress for some minutes, that I was no longer alone in my body.

She said nothing. Neither did I. After last night's astounding alliance I seemed to want to pull back into wordlessness, unthinkingness, a kind of automaton consciousness. The need for breakfast occurred to me and I called up a tracker to take me down to the dining hall. When I stepped outside the room I was surprised to encounter my servo-steward, already on its way up with my tray. Perhaps it was just as surprised to see me going out, though of course its blank metal face betrayed no feelings.

"I'll be having breakfast in the dining hall today," I told it.

"Very good, sir."

My tracker arrived. I climbed into its seat and it set out at once on its cushion of air toward the dining hall.

The dining hall of the *Sword of Orion* is a magnificent room at the Eye end of Crew Deck, with one glass wall providing a view of all the lights of heaven. By some whim of the designers we sit with that wall below us, so that the stars and their tethered worlds drift beneath our feet. The other walls are of some silvery metal chased with thin swirls of gold, everything shining by the reflected light of the passing star-clusters. At the center is a table of black stone, with places allotted for each of the seventeen members of the crew. It is a splendid if somewhat ridiculous place, a resonant reminder of the wealth and power of the Service.

Three of my shipmates were at their places when I entered. Pedregal was there, the supercargo, a compact, sullen man whose broad dome of a head seemed to rise directly from his shoulders. And there was Fresco, too, slender and elusive, the navigator, a lithe dark-skinned person of ambiguous sex who alternated from voyage to voyage, so I had been told, converting from male to female and back again according to some private rhythm. The third person was Raebuck, whose sphere of responsibility was communications, an older man whose flat, chilly gaze conveyed either boredom or menace, I could never be sure which.

"Why, it's the captain," said Pedregal calmly. "Favoring us with one of his rare visits."

All three stared at me with that curious testing intensity which I was coming to see was an inescapable part of my life aboard ship: a constant hazing meted out to any newcomer to the Service, an interminable probing for the place that was most vulnerable. Mine was a parsec wide and I was certain they would discover it at once. But I was determined to match them stare for stare, ploy for ploy, test for test.

"Good morning, gentlemen," I said. Then, giving Fresco a level glance, I added, "Good morning, Fresco."

I took my seat at the table's head and rang for service.

I was beginning to realize why I had come out of my cabin that morning. In part it was a reflection of Vox' presence within me, an expression of that new component of rashness and impulsiveness that had entered me with her. But mainly it was, I saw now, some stratagem of my own, hatched on some inaccessible subterranean level of my double mind. In order to conceal Vox most effectively, I would have to take the offensive: rather than skulking in my quarters and perhaps awakening perilous suspicions in the minds of my shipmates, I must come forth, defiantly, challengingly, almost flaunting the thing that I had done, and go among them, pretending that nothing unusual was afoot and forcing them to believe it. Such aggressiveness was not natural to my temperament. But perhaps I could draw on some reserves provided by Vox. If not, we both were lost.

Raebuck said, to no one in particular, "I suppose yesterday's disturbing events must inspire a need for companionship in the captain."

I faced him squarely. "I have all the companionship I require, Raebuck. But I agree that what happened yesterday was disturbing."

"A nasty business," Pedregal said, ponderously shaking his neckless head. "And a strange one, a matrix trying to get into a passenger. That's new to me, a thing like that. And to lose the passenger besides—that's bad. That's very bad."

"It does happen, losing a passenger," said Raebuck.

"A long time since it happened on a ship of mine," Pedregal rejoined.

"We lost a whole batch of them on the *Emperor of Callisto*," Fresco said. "You know the story? It was thirty years ago. We were making the run from Van Buren to the San Pedro Cluster. We picked up a supernova pulse and the intelligence on duty went into flicker. Somehow dumped a load of aluminum salts in the feed-lines and killed off fifteen, sixteen passengers. I saw the bodies before they went into the converter. Beyond salvage, they were."

"Yes," said Raebuck. "I heard of that one. And then there was the *Queen Astarte*, a couple of years after that. Tchelitchev was her captain, little green-eyed Russian woman from one of the Troika worlds. They were taking a routine inventory and two digits got transposed, and a faulty delivery signal slipped through. I think it was six dead, premature decanting, killed by air poisoning. Tchelitchev took it very badly. Very badly. Somehow the captain always does."

"And then that time on the *Hecuba*," said Pedregal. "No ship of mine, thank God. That was the captain who ran amok, thought the ship was too quiet, wanted to see some passengers moving around and started awakening them—"

Raebuck showed a quiver of surprise. "You know about that? I thought that was supposed to be hushed up."

"Things get around," Pedregal said, with something like a smirk. "The captain's name was Catania-Szu, I believe, a man from Mediterraneo, very high-strung, the way all of them are there. I was working the *Valparaiso* then, out of Mendax Nine bound for Scylla and Charybdis and neighboring points, and when we stopped to download some cargo in the Seneca system I got the whole story from a ship's clerk named—"

"You were on the *Valparaiso*?" Fresco asked. "Wasn't that the ship that had a free matrix, too, ten or eleven years back? A real soul-eater, so the report went—"

"After my time," said Pedregal, blandly waving his hand. "But I did hear of it. You get to hear about everything, when you're downloading cargo. Soul-eater, you say, reminds me of the time—"

And he launched into some tale of horror at a spinaround station in a far quadrant of the galaxy. But he was no more than halfway through it when Raebuck cut in with a gorier reminiscence of his own, and then Fresco, seething with impatience, broke in on him to tell of a ship infested by three free matrixes at once. I had no doubt that all this was being staged for my enlightenment, by way of showing me how seriously such events were taken in the Service, and how the captains under whom they occurred went down in the folklore of the starships with ineradicable black marks. But their attempts to unsettle me, if that is what they were, left me undismayed. Vox, silent within me, infused me with a strange confidence that allowed me to ignore the darker implications of these anecdotes.

I simply listened, playing my role: the neophyte fascinated by the accumulated depth of spacegoing experience that their stories implied.

Then I said, finally, "When matrixes get loose, how long do they generally manage to stay at large?"

"An hour or two, generally," said Raebuck. "As they drift around the ship, of course, they leave an electrical trail. We track it and close off access routes behind them and eventually we pin them down in close quarters. Then it's not hard to put them back in their bottles."

"And if they've jacked into some member of the crew?"

"That makes it even easier to find them."

Boldly I said, "Was there ever a case where a free matrix jacked into a member of the crew and managed to keep itself hidden?"

"Never," said a new voice. It belonged to Roacher, who had just entered the dining hall. He stood at the far end of the long table, staring at me. His strange luminescent eyes, harsh and probing, came to rest on mine. "No matter how clever the matrix may be, sooner or later the host will find some way to call for help."

"And if the host doesn't choose to call for help?" I asked.

Roacher studied me with great care.

Had I been too bold? Had I given away too much?

"But that would be a violation of regulations!" he said, in a tone of mock astonishment. "That would be a criminal act!"

11.

She asked me to take her starwalking, to show her the full view of the Great Open.

It was the third day of her concealment within me. Life aboard the *Sword of Orion* had returned to routine, or, to be more accurate, it had settled into a new routine in which the presence on board of an undetected and apparently undetectable free matrix was a constant element.

As Vox had suggested, there were some who quickly came to believe that the missing matrix must have slipped off into space, since the watchful ship-intelligences could find no trace of it. But there were others who kept looking over their shoulders, figuratively or literally, as if expecting the fugitive to attempt to thrust herself without warning into the spinal jacks that gave access to their nervous systems. They behaved exactly as if the ship were haunted. To placate those uneasy ones, I ordered round-the-clock circuit sweeps that would report every vagrant pulse and random surge. Each such anomalous electrical event was duly investigated, and, of course, none of these investigations led to anything significant. Now that Vox resided in my brain instead of the ship's wiring, she was beyond any such mode of discovery.

Whether anyone suspected the truth was something I had no way of knowing. Perhaps Roacher did; but he made no move to denounce me, nor did he so much as raise the issue of the missing matrix with me at all after that time in the dining hall. He might know nothing whatever; he might know everything, and not care; he might simply be keeping his own counsel for the moment. I had no way of telling.

I was growing accustomed to my double life, and to my daily duplicity. Vox had quickly come to seem as much a part of me as my arm, or my leg. When she was silent—and often I heard nothing from her for hours at a time—I was no more aware of her than I would be, in any special way, of my arm or my leg; but nevertheless I knew somehow that she was there. The boundaries between her mind and mine were eroding steadily. She was learning how to infiltrate me. At times it seemed to me that what we were were joint tenants of the same dwelling, rather than I the permanent occupant and she a guest. I came to perceive my own mind as something not notably different from hers, a mere web of electrical force which for the moment was housed in the soft moist globe that was the brain of the captain of the *Sword of Orion*. Either of us, so it seemed, might come and go within that soft moist globe as we pleased, flitting casually in or out after the wraithlike fashion of matrixes.

At other times it was not at all like that: I gave no thought to her presence and went about my tasks as if nothing had changed for me. Then it would come as a surprise when Vox announced herself to me with some sudden comment, some quick question. I had to learn to guard myself against letting my reaction show, if it happened when I was with other members of the crew. Though no one around us could hear anything when she spoke to me, or I to her, I knew it would be the end for our masquerade if anyone caught me in some unguarded moment of conversation with an unseen companion.

How far she had penetrated my mind began to become apparent to me when she asked to go on a starwalk.

"You know about that?" I said, startled, for starwalking is the private pleasure of the spacegoing and I had not known of it myself before I was taken into the Service.

Vox seemed amazed by my amazement. She indicated casually that the details of starwalking were common knowledge everywhere. But something rang false in her tone. Were the landcrawling folk really so familiar with our special pastime? Or had she picked what she knew of it out of the hitherto private reaches of my consciousness?

I chose not to ask. But I was uneasy about taking her with me into the Great Open, much as I was beginning to yearn for it myself. She was not one of us. She was planetary; she had not passed through the training of the Service.

I told her that.

"Take me anyway," she said. "It's the only chance I'll ever have."

"But the training—"

"I don't need it. Not if you've had it."

"What if that's not enough?"

"It will be," she said. "It know it will, Adam. There's nothing to be afraid of. You've had the training, haven't you? And I am you."

12.

Together we rode the transit track out of the Eye and down to Drive Deck, where the soul of the ship lies lost in throbbing dreams of the far galaxies as it pulls us ever onward across the unending night.

We passed through zones of utter darkness and zones of cascading light, through places where wheeling helixes of silvery radiance burst like auroras from the air, through passages so crazed in their geometry that they reawakened the terrors of the womb in anyone who traversed them. A starship is the mother of mysteries. Vox crouched, frozen with awe, within that portion of our brain that was hers. I felt the surges of her awe, one after another, as we went downward.

"Are you really sure you want to do this?" I asked.

"Yes!" she cried fiercely. "Keep going!"

"There's the possibility that you'll be detected," I told her.

"There's the possibility that I won't be," she said.

We continued to descend. Now we were in the realm of the three cyborg push-cells, Gabriel, Banquo, and Fleece. Those were three members of the crew whom we would never see at the table in the dining hall, for they dwelled here in the walls of Drive Deck, permanently jacked in, perpetually pumping their energies into the ship's great maw. I have already told you of our saying in the Service, that when you enter you give up the body and you get your soul. For most of us that is only a figure of speech: what we give up, when we say farewell forever to planetskin and take up our new lives in starships, is not the body itself but the body's trivial needs, the sweaty things so dear to shore people. But some of us are more literal in their renunciations. The flesh is a meaningless hindrance to them; they shed it entirely, knowing that they can experience starship life just as fully without it. They allow themselves to be transformed into extensions of the stardrive. From them comes the raw energy out of which is made the power that carries us hurtling through heaven. Their work is unending; their reward is a sort of immortality. It is not a choice I could make, nor, I think, you: but for them it is bliss. There can be no doubt about that.

"Another starwalk so soon, captain?" Banquo asked. For I had been here on the second day of the voyage, losing no time in availing myself of the great privilege of the Service.

"Is there any harm in it?"

"No, no harm," said Banquo. "Just isn't usual, is all."

"That's all right," I said. "That's not important to me."

Banquo is a gleaming metallic ovoid, twice the size of a human head, jacked into a slot in the wall. Within the ovoid is the matrix of what had once been Banquo, long ago on a world called Sunrise where night is unknown. Sunrise's golden dawns and shining days had not been good enough for Banquo, apparently. What Banquo had wanted was to be a gleaming metallic ovoid, hanging on the wall of Drive Deck aboard the *Sword of Orion.*

Any of the three cyborgs could set up a starwalk. But Banquo was the one who had done it for me that other time and it seemed best to return to him. He was the most congenial of the three. He struck me as amiable and easy. Gabriel, on my first visit, had seemed austere, remote, incomprehensible. He is an early model who had lived the equivalent of three human lifetimes as a cyborg aboard starships and there was not much about him that was human any more. Fleece, much younger, quick-minded and quirky, I mistrusted: in her weird edgy way she might just somehow be able to detect the hidden other who would be going along with me for the ride.

You must realize that when we starwalk we do not literally leave the ship, though that is how it seems to us. If we left the ship even for a moment we would be swept away and lost forever in the abyss of heaven. Going outside a starship of heaven is not like stepping outside an ordinary planet-launched shoreship that moves through normal space. But even if it were possible, there would be no point in leaving the ship. There is nothing to see out there. A starship moves through utter empty darkness.

But though there may be nothing to see, that does not mean that there is nothing out there. The entire universe is out there. If we could see it while we are traveling across the special space that is heaven we would find it flattened and curved, so that we had the illusion of viewing everything at once, all the far-flung galaxies back to the beginning of time. This is the Great Open, the totality of the continuum. Our external screens show it to us in simulated form, because we need occasional assurance that it is there.

A starship rides along the mighty lines of force which cross that immense void like the lines of the compass rose on an ancient mariner's map. When we starwalk, we ride those same lines, and we are held by them, sealed fast to the ship that is carrying us onward through heaven. We seem to step forth into space; we seem to look down on the ship, on the stars, on all the worlds of heaven. For the moment we become little starships flying along beside the great one that is our mother. It is magic; it is illusion; but it is magic that so closely approaches what we perceive as reality that there is no way to measure the difference, which means that in effect there is no difference.

"Ready?" I asked Vox.

"Absolutely."

Still I hesitated.

"Are you sure?"

"Go on," she said impatiently. "Do it!"

I put the jack to my spine myself. Banquo did the matching of impedances. If he were going to discover the passenger I carried, this would be the moment. But he showed no sign that anything was amiss. He queried me; I gave him the signal to proceed; there was a moment of sharp warmth at the back of my neck as my neural matrix, and Vox's traveling with it, rushed out through Banquo and hurtled downward toward its merger with the soul of the ship.

We were seized and drawn in and engulfed by the vast force that is the ship. As the coils of the engine caught us we were spun around and around, hurled from vector to vector, mercilessly stretched, distended by an unimaginable flux. And then there was a brightness all about us, a brightness that cried out in heaven with a mighty clamor. We were outside the ship. We were starwalking.

"Oh," she said. A little soft cry, a muted gasp of wonder.

The blazing mantle of the ship lay upon the darkness of heaven like a white shadow. That great cone of cold fiery light reached far out in front of us, arching awesomely toward heaven's vault, and behind us it extended beyond the limits of our sight. The slender tapering outline of the ship was clearly visible within it, the needle and its Eye, all ten kilometers of it easily apparent to us in a single glance.

And there were the stars. And there were the worlds of heaven.

The effect of the stardrive is to collapse the dimensions, each one in upon the other. Thus inordinate spaces are diminished and the galaxy may be spanned by human voyagers. There is no logic, no linearity of sequence, to heaven as it appears to our eyes. Wherever we look we see the universe bent back upon itself, revealing its entirety in an infinite series of infinite segments of itself. Any sector of stars contains all stars. Any demarcation of time encompasses all of time past and time to come. What we behold is altogether beyond our understanding, which is exactly as it should be; for what we are given, when we look through the Eye of the ship at the naked heavens, is a god's-eye view of the universe. And we are not gods.

"What are we seeing?" Vox murmured within me.

I tried to tell her. I showed her how to define her relative position so there would be an up and a down for her, a backward, a forward, a flow of time and event from beginning to end. I pointed out the arbitrary coordinate axes by which we locate ourselves in this fundamentally incomprehensible arena. I found known stars for her, and known worlds, and showed them to her.

She understood nothing. She was entirely lost.

I told her that there was no shame in that.

I told her that I had been just as bewildered, when I was undergoing my training in the simulator. That everyone was; and that no one, not even if he spent a thousand years aboard the starships that plied the routes of heaven, could ever come to anything more than a set of crude equivalents and approximations of understanding what starwalking shows us. Attaining actual understanding itself is beyond the best of us.

I could feel her struggling to encompass the impact of all that rose and wheeled and soared before us. Her mind was agile, though still only half-formed, and I sensed her working out her own system of explanations and assumptions, her analogies, her equivalencies. I gave her no more help. It was best for her to do these things by herself; and in any case I had no more help to give.

I had my own astonishment and bewilderment to deal with, on this my second starwalk in heaven.

Once more I looked down upon the myriad worlds turning in their orbits. I could see them easily, the little bright globes rotating in the huge night of the Great Open: red worlds, blue worlds, green ones, some turning their full faces to me, some showing mere slivers of a crescent. How they cleaved to their appointed tracks! How they clung to their parent stars!

I remembered that other time, only a few virtual days before, when I had felt such compassion for them, such sorrow. Knowing that they were condemned forever to follow the same path about the same star, a hopeless bondage, a meaningless retracing of a perpetual route. In their own eyes they might be footloose wanderers, but to me they had seemed the most pitiful of slaves. And so I had grieved for the worlds of heaven; but now, to my surprise, I felt no pity, only a kind of love. There was no reason to be sad for them.

They were what they were, and there was a supreme right-
ness in those fixed orbits and their obedient movements
along them. They were content with being what they were.
If they were loosed even a moment from that bondage, such
chaos would arise in the universe as could never be contained. Those circling worlds are the foundations upon
which all else is built; they know that and they take pride
in it; they are loyal to their tasks and we must honor them
for their devotion to their duty. And with honor comes love.

This must be Vox speaking within me, I told myself.

I had never thought such thoughts. Love the planets in
their orbits? What kind of notion was that? Perhaps no
stranger than my earlier notion of pitying them because
they weren't starships; but that thought had arisen from the
spontaneous depths of my own spirit and it had seemed to
make a kind of sense to me. Now it had given way to a
wholly other view.

I loved the worlds that moved before me and yet did
not move, in the great night of heaven.

I loved the strange fugitive girl within me who beheld
those worlds and loved them for their immobility.

I felt her seize me now, taking me impatiently onward,
outward, into the depths of heaven. She understood now;
she knew how it was done. And she was far more daring
than ever I would have allowed me to be. Together we
walked the stars. Not only walked but plunged and swooped
and soared, traveling among them like gods. Their hot
breath singed us. Their throbbing brightness thundered at
us. Their serene movements boomed a mighty music at us.
On and on we went, hand in hand, Vox leading, I letting
her draw me, deeper and deeper into the shining abyss that
was the universe. Until at last we halted, floating in mid-
cosmos, the ship nowhere to be seen, only the two of us
surrounded by a shield of suns.

In that moment a sweeping ecstasy filled my soul. I felt all eternity within my grasp. No, that puts it the wrong way around and makes it seem that I was seized by delusions of imperial grandeur, which was not at all the case. What I felt was myself within the grasp of all eternity, enfolded in the loving embrace of a complete and perfect cosmos in which nothing was out of place, or ever could be.

It is this that we go starwalking to attain. This sense of belonging, this sense of being contained in the divine perfection of the universe.

When it comes, there is no telling what effect it will have; but inner change is what it usually brings. I had come away from my first starwalk unaware of any transformation; but within three days I had impulsively opened myself to a wandering phantom, violating not only regulations but the nature of my own character as I understood it. I have always, as I think I have said, been an intensely private man. Even though I had given Vox refuge, I had been relieved and grateful that her mind and mine had remained separate entities within our shared brain.

Now I did what I could to break down whatever boundary remained between us.

I hadn't let her know anything, so far, of my life before going to heaven. I had met her occasional questions with coy evasions, with half-truths, with blunt refusals. It was the way I had always been with everyone, a habit of secrecy, an unwillingness to reveal myself. I had been even more secretive, perhaps, with Vox than with all the others, because of the very closeness of her mind to mine. As though I feared that by giving her any interior knowledge of me I was opening the way for her to take me over entirely, to absorb me into her own vigorous, undisciplined soul.

But now I offered my past to her in a joyous rush. We began to make our way slowly backward from that apoca-

lyptic place at the center of everything; and as we hovered
on the breast of the Great Open, drifting between the darkness and the brilliance of the light that the ship created, I
told her everything about myself that I had been holding
back.

I suppose they were mere trivial things, though to me
they were all so highly charged with meaning. I told her the
name of my home planet. I let her see it, the sea the color
of lead, the sky the color of smoke. I showed her the sparse
and scrubby gray headlands behind our house, where I
would go running for hours by myself, a tall slender boy
pounding tirelessly across the crackling sands as though demons were pursuing him.

I showed her everything: the somber child, the troubled
youth, the wary, overcautious young man. The playmates
who remained forever strangers, the friends whose voices
were drowned in hollow babbling echoes, the lovers whose
love seemed without substance or meaning. I told her of my
feeling that I was the only one alive in the world, that everyone about me was some sort of artificial being full of gears
and wires. Or that the world was only a flat colorless dream
in which I somehow had become trapped, but from which I
would eventually awaken into the true world of light and
color and richness of texture. Or that I might not be human
at all, but had been abandoned in the human galaxy by
creatures of another form entirely, who would return for me
some day far in the future.

I was lighthearted as I told her these things, and she
received them lightly. She knew them for what they were—
not symptoms of madness, but only the bleak fantasies of
a lonely child, seeking to make sense out of an incomprehensible universe in which he felt himself to be a stranger
and afraid.

"But you escaped," she said. "You found a place where you belonged!"

"Yes," I said. "I escaped."

And I told her of the day when I had seen a sudden light in the sky. My first thought then had been that my true parents had come back for me; my second, that it was some comet passing by. That light was a starship of heaven that had come to worldward in our system. And as I looked upward through the darkness on that day long ago, straining to catch a glimpse of the shoreships that were going up to it bearing cargo and passengers to be taken from our world to some unknowable place at the other end of the galaxy, I realized that that starship was my true home. I realized that the Service was my destiny.

And so it came to pass, I said, that I left my world behind, and my name, and my life, such as it had been, to enter the company of those who sail between the stars. I let her know that this was my first voyage, explaining that it is the peculiar custom of the Service to test all new officers by placing them in command at once. She asked me if I had found happiness here; and I said, quickly, Yes, I had, and then I said a moment later, Not yet, not yet, but I see at least the possibility of it.

She was quiet for a time. We watched the worlds turning and the stars like blazing spikes of color racing toward their far-off destinations, and the fiery white light of the ship itself streaming in the firmament as if it were the blood of some alien god. The thought came to me of all that I was risking by hiding her like this within me. I brushed it aside. This was neither the place nor the moment for doubt or fear or misgiving.

Then she said, "I'm glad you told me all that, Adam."

"Yes. I am too."

"I could feel it from the start, what sort of person you were. But I needed to hear it in your own words, your own thoughts. It's just like I've been saying. You and I, we're two of a kind. Square pegs in a world of round holes. You ran away to the Service and I ran away to a new life in somebody else's body."

I realized that Vox wasn't speaking of my body, but of the new one that waited for her on Cul-de-Sac.

And I realized too that there was one thing about herself that she had never shared with me, which was the nature of the flaw in her old body that had caused her to discard it. If I knew her more fully, I thought, I could love her more deeply: imperfections and all, which is the way of love. But she had shied away from telling me that, and I had never pressed her on it. Now, out here under the cool gleam of heaven, surely we had moved into a place of total trust, of complete union of soul.

I said, "Let me see you, Vox."

"See me? How could you—"

"Give me an image of yourself. You're too abstract for me this way. Vox. A voice. Only a voice. You talk to me, you live within me, and I still don't have the slightest idea what you look like."

"That's how I want it to be."

"Won't you show me how you look?"

"I won't look like anything. I'm a matrix. I'm nothing but electricity."

"I understand that. I mean how you looked before. Your old self, the one you left behind on Kansas Four."

She made no reply.

I thought she was hesitating, deciding; but some time went by, and still I heard nothing from her. What came from her was silence, only silence, a silence that had crashed down between us like a steel curtain.

"Vox?"

Nothing.

Where was she hiding? What had I done?

"What's the matter? Is it the thing I asked you?"

No answer.

"It's all right, Vox. Forget about it. It isn't important at all. You don't have to show me anything you don't want to show me."

Nothing. Silence.

"Vox? Vox?"

The worlds and stars wheeled in chaos before me. The light of the ship; roared up and down the spectrum from end to end. In growing panic I sought for her and found no trace of her presence within me. Nothing. Nothing.

"Are you all right?" came another voice. Banquo, from inside the ship. "I'm getting some pretty wild signals. You'd better come in. You've been out there long enough as it is."

Vox was gone. I had crossed some uncrossable boundary and I had frightened her away.

Numbly I gave Banquo the signal, and he brought me back inside.

13.

Alone, I made my way upward level by level through the darkness and mystery of the ship, toward the Eye. The crash of silence went on and on, like the falling of some colossal wave on an endless shore. I missed Vox terribly. I had never known such complete solitude as I felt now. I had not realized how accustomed I had become to her being there, nor what impact her leaving would have on me. In just those few days of giving her sanctuary, it had somehow come to seem to me that to house two souls within one brain was the normal condition of mankind, and that to be alone in one's skull as I was now was a shameful thing.

As I neared the place where Crew Deck narrows into the curve of the Eye a slender figure stepped without warning from the shadows.

"Captain."

My mind was full of the loss of Vox and he caught me unawares. I jumped back, badly startled.

"For the love of God, man!"

"It's just me. Bulgar. Don't be so scared, captain. It's only Bulgar."

"Let me be," I said, and brusquely beckoned him away.

"No. Wait, captain. Please, wait."

He clutched at my arm, holding me as I tried to go. I halted and turned toward him, trembling with anger and surprise.

Bulgar, Roacher's jackmate, was a gentle, soft-voiced little man, wide-mouthed, olive-skinned, with huge sad eyes. He and Roacher had sailed the skies of Heaven together since before I was born. They complemented each other. Where Roacher was small and hard, like fruit that has been left to dry in the sun for a hundred years, his jackmate Bulgar was small and tender, with a plump, succulent look about him. Together they seemed complete, an unassailable whole: I could readily imagine them lying together in their bunk, each jacked to the other, one person in two bodies, linked more intimately even than Vox and I had been.

With an effort I recovered my poise. Tightly I said, "What is it, Bulgar?"

"Can we talk a minute, captain?"

"We are talking. What do you want with me?"

"That loose matrix, sir."

My reaction must have been stronger than he was expecting. His eyes went wide and he took a step or two back from me.

Moistening his lips, he said, "We were wondering, captain—wondering how the search is going—whether you had any idea where the matrix might be—"

I said stiffly, "Who's we, Bulgar?"

"The men. Roacher. Me. Some of the others. Mainly Roacher, sir."

"Ah. So Roacher wants to know where the matrix is."

The little man moved closer. I saw him staring deep into me as though searching for Vox behind the mask of my carefully expressionless face. Did he know? Did they all? I wanted to cry out, She's not there any more, she's gone, she left me, she ran off into space. But apparently what was troubling Roacher and his shipmates was something other than the possibility that Vox had taken refuge with me.

Bulgar's tone was soft, insinuating, concerned. "Roacher's very worried, captain. He's been on ships with loose matrixes before. He knows how much trouble they can be. He's really worried, captain. I have to tell you that. I've never seen him so worried."

"What does he think the matrix will do to him?"

"He's afraid of being taken over," Bulgar said.

"Taken over?"

"The matrix coming into his head through his jack. Mixing itself up with his brain. It's been known to happen, captain."

"And why should it happen to Roacher, out of all the men on this ship? Why not you? Why not Pedregal? Or Rio de Rio? Or one of the passengers again?" I took a deep breath. "Why not me, for that matter?"

"He just wants to know, sir, what's the situation with the matrix now. Whether you've discovered anything about where it is. Whether you've been able to trap it."

There was something strange in Bulgar's eyes. I began to think I was being tested again. This assertion of Roacher's alleged terror of being infiltrated and possessed by the wandering matrix might simply be a roundabout way of finding out whether that had already happened to me.

"Tell him it's gone," I said.

"Gone, sir?"

"Gone. Vanished. It isn't anywhere on the ship any more. Tell him that, Bulgar. He can forget about her slithering down his precious jackhole."

"Her?"

"Female matrix, yes. But that doesn't matter now. She's gone. You can tell him that. Escaped. Flew off into heaven. The emergency's over." I glowered at him. I yearned to be rid of him, to go off by myself to nurse my new grief. "Shouldn't you be getting back to your post, Bulgar?"

Did he believe me? Or did he think that I had slapped together some transparent lie to cover my complicity in the continued absence of the matrix? I had no way of knowing. Bulgar gave me a little obsequious bow and started to back away.

"Sir," he said. "Thank you, sir. I'll tell him, sir."

He retreated into the shadows. I continued uplevel.

I passed Katkat on my way, and, a little while afterward, Raebuck. They looked at me without speaking. There was something reproachful but almost loving about Katkat's expression, but Raebuck's icy, baleful stare brought me close to flinching. In their different ways they were saying, Guilty, guilty, guilty. But of what?

Before, I had imagined that everyone whom I encountered aboard ship was able to tell at a single glance that I was harboring the fugitive, and was simply waiting for me to reveal myself with some foolish slip. Now everything was reversed. They looked at me and I told myself that they were thinking, He's all alone by himself in there, he doesn't have anyone else at all, and I shrank away, shamed by my solitude. I knew that this was the edge of madness. I was overwrought, overtired; perhaps it had been a mistake to go starwalking a second time so soon after my first. I needed to rest. I needed to hide.

I began to wish that there were someone aboard the *Sword of Orion* with whom I could discuss these things. But who, though? Roacher? 612 Jason? I was altogether isolated here. The only one I could speak to on this ship was Vox. And she was gone.

In the safety of my cabin I jacked myself into the mediq rack and gave myself a ten-minute purge. That helped. The phantom fears and intricate uncertainties that had taken possession of me began to ebb.

I keyed up the log and ran through the list of my captainly duties, such as they were, for the rest of the day. We were approaching a spinaround point, one of those nodes of force positioned equidistantly across heaven which a starship in transit must seize and use in order to propel itself onward through the next sector of the universe. Spinaround acquisition is performed automatically but at least in theory the responsibility for carrying it out successfully falls to the captain: I would give the commands, I would oversee the process from initiation through completion.

But there was still time for that.

I accessed 49 Henry Henry, who was the intelligence on duty, and asked for an update on the matrix situation.

"No change, sir," the intelligence reported at once.

"What does that mean?"

"Trace efforts continue as requested, sir. But we have not detected the location of the missing matrix."

"No clues? Not even a hint?"

"No data at all, sir. There's essentially no way to isolate

the minute electromagnetic pulse of a free matrix from the background noise of the ship's entire electrical system."

I believed it. 612 Jason Jason had told me that in nearly the same words.

I said, "I have reason to think that the matrix is no longer on the ship, 49 Henry Henry."

"Do you, sir?" said 49 Henry Henry in its usual aloof, half-mocking way.

"I do, yes. After a careful study of the situation, it's my opinion that the matrix exited the ship earlier this day and will not be heard from again."

"Shall I record that as an official position, sir?"

"Record it," I said.

"Done, sir."

"And therefore, 49 Henry Henry, you can cancel search mode immediately and close the file. We'll enter a debit for one matrix and the Service bookkeepers can work it out later."

"Very good, sir."

"Decouple," I ordered the intelligence.

49 Henry Henry went away. I sat quietly amid the splendors of my cabin, thinking back over my starwalk and reliving that sense of harmony, of love, of oneness with the worlds of heaven, that had come over me while Vox and I drifted on the bosom of the Great Open. And feeling once again the keen slicing sense of loss that I had felt since Vox' departure from me. In a little while I would have to rise and go to the command center and put myself through the motions of overseeing spinaround acquisition; but for the moment I remained where I was, motionless, silent, peering deep into the heart of my solitude.

"I'm not gone," said an unexpected quiet voice.

It came like a punch beneath the heart. It was a moment before I could speak.

"Vox?" I said at last. "Where are you, Vox?"

"Right here."

"Where?" I asked.

"Inside. I never went away."

"You never—"

"You upset me. I just had to hide for a while."

"You knew I was trying to find you?"

"Yes."

Color came to my cheeks. Anger roared like a stream in spate through my veins. I felt myself blazing.

"You knew how I felt, when you—when it seemed that you weren't there any more."

"Yes," she said, even more quietly, after a time.

I forced myself to grow calm. I told myself that she owed me nothing, except perhaps gratitude for sheltering her, and that whatever pain she had caused me by going silent was none of her affair. I reminded myself also that she was a child, unruly and turbulent and undisciplined.

After a bit I said, "I missed you. I missed you more than I want to say."

"I'm sorry," she said, sounding repentant, but not very. "I had to go away for a time. You upset me, Adam."

"By asking you to show me how you used to look?"

"Yes."

"I don't understand why that upset you so much."

"You don't have to," Vox said. "I don't mind now. You can see me, if you like. Do you still want to? Here. This is me. This is what I used to be. If it disgusts you don't blame me. Okay? Okay, Adam? Here. Have a look. Here I am."

14.

There was a wrenching within me, a twisting, a painful yanking sensation, as of some heavy barrier forcibly being pulled aside. And then the glorious radiant scarlet sky of Kansas Four blossomed on the screen of my mind.

She didn't simply show it to me. She took me there. I felt the soft moist wind on my face, I breathed the sweet, faintly pungent air, I heard the sly rustling of glossy leathery fronds that dangled from bright yellow trees. Beneath my bare feet the black soil was warm and spongy.

I was Leeleaine, who liked to call herself Vox. I was seventeen years old and swept by forces and compulsions as powerful as hurricanes.

I was her from within and also I saw her from outside.

My hair was long and thick and dark, tumbling down past my shoulders in an avalanche of untended curls and loops and snags. My hips were broad, my breasts were full and heavy: I could feel the pull of them, the pain of them. It was almost as if they were stiff with milk, though they were not. My face was tense, alert, sullen, aglow with angry intelligence. It was not an unappealing face. Vox was not an unappealing girl.

From her earlier reluctance to show herself to me I had expected her to be ugly, or perhaps deformed in some way, dragging herself about in a coarse, heavy, burdensome husk of flesh that was a constant reproach to her. She had spoken of her life on Kansas Four as being so dreary, so sad, so miserable, that she saw no hope in staying there. And had given up her body to be turned into mere electricity, on the promise that she could have a new body—any body—when she reached Cul-de-Sac. I hated my body, she had told me. I couldn't wait to be rid of it. She had refused even to give me a glimpse of it, retreating instead for hours into a desperate silence so total that I thought she had fled.

All that was a mystery to me now. The Leeleaine that I saw, that I was, was a fine sturdy-looking girl. Not beautiful, no, too strong and strapping for that, I suppose, but far from ugly: her eyes were warm and intelligent, her lips full, her nose finely modeled. And it was a healthy body, too, robust, vital. Of course she had no deformities; and why had I thought she had, when it would have been a simple matter of retrogenetic surgery to amend any bothersome defect? No, there was nothing wrong with the body that Vox had abandoned and for which she professed such loathing, for which she felt such shame.

Then I realized that I was seeing her from outside. I was seeing her as if by relay, filtering and interpreting the information she was offering me by passing it through the mind of an objective observer: myself. Who understood nothing, really, of what it was like to be anyone but himself.

Somehow—it was one of those automatic, unconscious adjustments—I altered the focus of my perceptions. All old frames of reference fell away and I let myself lose any sense of the separateness of our identities.

I was her. Fully, unconditionally, inextricably.

And I understood.

Figures flitted about her, shadowy, baffling, maddening. Brothers, sisters, parents, friends: they were all strangers to her. Everyone on Kansas Four was a stranger to her. And always would be.

She hated her body not because it was weak or unsightly but because it was her prison. She was enclosed within it as though within narrow stone walls. It hung about her, a cage of flesh, holding her down, pinning her to this lovely world called Kansas Four where she knew only pain and isolation and estrangement. Her body—her perfectly acceptable, healthy body—had become hateful to her because it was the emblem and symbol of her soul's imprisonment. Wild and incurably restless by temperament, she had failed to find a way to live within the smothering predictability of Kansas Four, a planet where she would never be anything but an internal outlaw. The only way she could leave Kansas Four was to surrender the body that tied her to it; and so she had turned against it with fury and loathing, rejecting it, abandoning it, despising it, detesting it. No one could ever understand that who beheld her from the outside.

But I understood.

I understood much more than that, in that one flashing moment of communion that she and I had. I came to see what she meant when she said that I was her twin, her double, her other self. Of course we were wholly different, I the sober, staid, plodding, diligent man, and she the reckless, volatile, impulsive, tempestuous girl. But beneath all that we were the same:misfits, outsiders, troubled wanderers through worlds we had never made. We had found vastly differing ways to cope with our pain. Yet we were one and the same, two halves of a single entity.

We will remain together always now, I told myself.

And in that moment our communion broke. She broke it—it must have been she, fearful of letting this new intimacy grow too deep—and I found myself apart from her once again, still playing host to her in my brain but separated from her by the boundaries of my own individuality, my own selfhood. I felt her nearby, within me, a warm but discrete presence. Still within me, yes. But separate again.

15.

There was shipwork to do. For days, now, Vox's invasion of me had been a startling distraction. But I dared not let myself forget that we were in the midst of a traversal of heaven. The lives of us all, and of our passengers, depended on the proper execution of our duties: even mine. And worlds awaited the bounty that we bore. My task of the moment was to oversee spinaround acquisition.

I told Vox to leave me temporarily while I went through the routines of acquisition. I would be jacked to other crewmen for a time; they might very well be able to detect her within me; there was no telling what might happen. But she refused. "No," she said. "I won't leave you. I don't want to go out there. But I'll hide, deep down, the way I did when I was upset with you."

"Vox—" I began.

"No. Please. I don't want to talk about it."

There was no time to argue the point. I could feel the depth and intensity of her stubborn determination.

"Hide, then," I said. "If that's what you want to do."

I made my way down out of the Eye to Engine Deck.

The rest of the acquisition team was already assembled in the Great Navigation Hall: Fresco, Raebuck, Roacher. Raebuck's role was to see to it that communications channels were kept open, Fresco's to set up the navigation coordinates, and Roacher, as power engineer, would monitor fluctuations in drain and input-output cycling. My function was to give the cues at each stage of acquisition. In truth I was pretty much redundant, since Raebuck and Fresco and Roacher had been doing this sort of thing a dozen times a voyage for scores of voyages and they had little need of my guidance. The deeper truth was that they were redundant too, for 49 Henry Henry would oversee us all, and the intelligence was quite capable of setting up the entire process without any human help. Nevertheless there were formalities to observe, and not inane ones.

Intelligences are far superior to humans in mental capacity, interfacing capability, and reaction time, but even so they are nothing but servants, and artificial servants at that, lacking in any real awareness of human fragility or human ethical complexity. They must only be used as tools, not decision-makers. A society which delegates responsibilities of life and death to its servants will eventually find the servants' hands at its throat. As for me, novice that I was, my role was valid as well: the focal point of the enterprise, the prime initiator, the conductor and observer of the process. Perhaps anyone could perform those functions, but the fact remained that someone had to, and by tradition that someone was the captain. Call it a ritual, call it a highly stylized dance, if you will. But there is no getting away from the human need for ritual and stylization. Such aspects of a process may not seem essential, but they are valuable and significant, and ultimately they can be seen to be essential as well.

"Shall we begin?" Fresco asked.

We jacked up, Roacher directly into the ship, Raebuck into Roacher, Fresco to me, me into the ship.

"Simulation," I said.

Raebuck keyed in the first code and the vast echoing space that was the Great Navigation Hall came alive with pulsing light: a representation of heaven all about us, the lines of force, the spinaround nodes, the stars, the planets. We moved unhinderedly in free fall, drifting as casually as angels. We could easily have believed we were starwalking.

The simulacrum of the ship was a bright arrow of fierce light just below us and to the left. Ahead, throbbing like a nest of twining angry serpents, was the globe that represented the Lasciate Ogni Speranza spinaround point, tightly-wound dull gray cables shot through with strands of fierce scarlet.

"Enter approach mode," I said. "Activate receptors. Begin threshold equalization. Begin momentum comparison. Prepare for acceleration uptick. Check angular velocity. Begin spin consolidation. Enter displacement select. Extend mast. Prepare for acquisition receptivity."

At each command the proper man touched a control key or pressed a directive panel or simply sent an impulse shooting through the jack hookup by which he was connected, directly or indirectly, to the mind of the ship. Out of courtesy to me, they waited until the commands were given, but the speed with which they obeyed told me that their minds were already in motion even as I spoke.

"It's really exciting, isn't it?" Vox said suddenly.

"For God's sake, Vox! What are you trying to do?"

For all I knew, the others had heard her outburst as clearly as though it had come across a loudspeaker.

"I mean," she went on, "I never imagined it was anything like this. I can feel the whole—"

I shot her a sharp, anguished order to keep quiet. Her surfacing like this, after my warning to her, was a lunatic act. In the silence that followed I felt a kind of inner reverberation, a sulky twanging of displeasure coming from her. But I had no time to worry about Vox's moods now.

Arcing patterns of displacement power went ricocheting through the Great Navigation Hall as our mast came forth—not the underpinning for a set of sails, as it would be on a vessel that plied planetary seas, but rather a giant antenna to link us to the spinaround point ahead—and the ship and the spinaround point reached toward one another like grappling many-armed wrestlers. Hot streaks of crimson and emerald and gold and amethyst speared the air, vaulting and rebounding. The spinaround point, activated now and trembling between energy states, was enfolding us in its million tentacles, capturing us, making ready to whirl on its axis and hurl us swiftly onward toward the next way-station in our journey across heaven.

"Acquisition," Raebuck announced.

"Proceed to capture acceptance," I said.

"Acceptance," said Raebuck.

"Directional mode," I said. "Dimensional grid eleven."

"Dimensional grid eleven," Fresco repeated.

The whole hall seemed on fire now.

"Wonderful," Vox murmured. "So beautiful—"

"Vox!"

"Request spin authorization," said Fresco.

"Spin authorization granted," I said. "Grid eleven."

"Grid eleven," Fresco said again. "Spin achieved."

A tremor went rippling through me—and through Fresco, through Raebuck, through Roacher. It was the ship, in the persona of 49 Henry Henry, completing the acquisition process. We had been captured by Lasciate Ogni Speranza, we had undergone velocity absorption and redirection, we had had new spin imparted to us, and we had been sent soaring off through heaven toward our upcoming port of call. I heard Vox sobbing within me, not a sob of despair but one of ecstasy, of fulfillment.

We all unjacked. Raebuck, that dour man, managed a little smile as he turned to me.

"Nicely done, captain," he said.

"Yes," said Fresco. "Very nice. You're a quick learner."

I saw Roacher studying me with those little shining eyes of his. Go on, you bastard, I thought. You give me a compliment too now, if you know how.

But all he did was stare. I shrugged and turned away.

What Roacher thought or said made little difference to me, I told myself.

As we left the Great Navigation Hall in our separate directions Fresco fell in alongside me. Without a word we trudged together toward the transit trackers that were waiting for us. Just as I was about to board mine he—or was it she?—said softly, "Captain?"

"What is it, Fresco?"

Fresco leaned close. Soft sly eyes, tricksy little smile; and yet I felt some warmth coming from the navigator.

"It's a very dangerous game, captain."

"I don't know what you mean."

"Yes, you do," Fresco said. "No use pretending. We were jacked together in there. I felt things. I know."

There was nothing I could say, so I said nothing.

After a moment Fresco said, "I like you. I won't harm you. But Roacher knows too. I don't know if he knew before, but he certainly knows now. If I were you, I'd find that very troublesome, captain. Just a word to the wise. All right?"

16.

Only a fool would have remained on such a course as I had been following. Vox saw the risks as well as I. There was no hiding anything from anyone any longer; if Roacher knew, then Bulgar knew, and soon it would be all over the ship. No question, either, but that 49 Henry Henry knew. In the intimacies of our navigation-hall contact, Vox must have been as apparent to them as a red scarf around my forehead.

There was no point in taking her to task for revealing her presence within me like that during acquisition. What was done was done. At first it had seemed impossible to

understand why she had done such a thing; but then it became all too easy to comprehend. It was the same sort of
unpredictable, unexamined, impulsive behavior that had led
her to go barging into a suspended passenger's mind and
cause his death. She was simply not one who paused to
think before acting. That kind of behavior has always been
bewildering to me. She was my opposite as well as my double. And yet had I not done a Vox-like thing myself, taking
her into me, when she appealed to me for sanctuary, without
stopping at all to consider the consequences?

"Where can I go?" she asked, desperate. "If I move
around the ship freely again they'll track me and close me
off. And then they'll eradicate me. They'll—"

"Easy," I said. "Don't panic. I'll hide you where they
won't find you."

"Inside some passenger?"

"We can't try that again. There's no way to prepare the
passenger for what's happening to him, and he'll panic. No.
I'll put you in one of the annexes. Or maybe one of the
virtualities."

"The what?"

"The additional cargo area. The subspace extensions
that surround the ship."

She gasped. "Those aren't even real! I was in them, when
I was traveling around the ship. Those are just clusters of
probability waves!"

"You'll be safe there," I said.

"I'm afraid. It's bad enough that I'm not real any more.
But to be stored in a place that isn't real either—"

"You're as real as I am. And the outstructures are just
as real as the rest of the ship. It's a different quality of
reality, that's all. Nothing bad will happen to you out there.
You've told me yourself that you've already been in them,
right? And got out again without any problems. They won't

be able to detect you there, Vox. But I tell you this, that if you stay in me, or anywhere else in the main part of the ship, they'll track you down and find you and eradicate you. And probably eradicate me right along with you."

"Do you mean that?" she said, sounding chastened.

"Come on. There isn't much time."

On the pretext of a routine inventory check—well within my table of responsibilities—I obtained access to one of the virtualities. It was the storehouse where the probability stabilizers were kept. No one was likely to search for her there. The chances of our encountering a zone of probability turbulence between here and Cul-de-Sac were minimal; and in the ordinary course of a voyage nobody cared to enter any of the virtualities.

I had lied to Vox, or at least committed a half-truth, by leading her to believe that all our outstructures are of an equal level of reality. Certainly the annexes are tangible, solid; they differ from the ship proper only in the spin of their dimensional polarity. They are invisible except when activated, and they involve us in no additional expenditure of fuel, but there is no uncertainty about their existence, which is why we entrust valuable cargo to them, and on some occasions even passengers.

The extensions are a level further removed from basic reality. They are skewed not only in dimensional polarity but in temporal contiguity: that is, we carry them with us under time displacement, generally ten to twenty virtual years in the past or future. The risks of this are extremely minor and the payoff in reduction of generating cost is great. Still, we are measurably more cautious about what sort of cargo we keep in them.

As for the virtualities—

Their name itself implies their uncertainty. They are purely probabilistic entities, existing most of the time in the stochastic void that surrounds the ship. In simpler words, whether they are actually there or not at any given time is a matter worth wagering on. We know how to access them at the time of greatest probability, and our techniques are quite reliable, which is why we can use them for overflow ladings when our cargo uptake is unusually heavy. But in general we prefer not to entrust anything very important to them, since a virtuality's range of access times can fluctuate in an extreme way, from a matter of microseconds to a matter of megayears, and that can make quick recall a chancy affair.

Knowing all this, I put Vox in a virtuality anyway.

I had to hide her. And I had to hide her in a place where no one would look. The risk that I'd be unable to call her up again because of virtuality fluctuation was a small one. The risk was much greater that she would be detected, and she and I both punished, if I let her remain in any area of the ship that had a higher order of probability.

"I want you to stay here until the coast is clear," I told her sternly. "No impulsive journeys around the ship, no excursions into adjoining outstructures, no little trips of any kind, regardless of how restless you get. Is that clear? I'll call you up from here as soon as I think it's safe."

"I'll miss you, Adam."

"The same here. But this is how it has to be."

"I know."

"If you're discovered, I'll deny I know anything about you. I mean that, Vox."

"I understand."

"You won't be stuck in here long. I promise you that."

"Will you visit me?"

"That wouldn't be wise," I said.

"But maybe you will anyway."

"Maybe. I don't know." I opened the access channel. The

virtuality gaped before us. "Go on," I said. "In with you. In. Now. Go, Vox. Go."

I could feel her leaving me. It was almost like an amputation. The silence, the emptiness, that descended on me suddenly was ten times as deep as what I had felt when she had merely been hiding within me. She was gone, now. For the first time in days, I was truly alone.

I closed off the virtuality.

When I returned to the Eye, Roacher was waiting for me near the command bridge.

"You have a moment, captain?"

"What is it, Roacher."

"The missing matrix. We have proof it's still on board ship."

"Proof?"

"You know what I mean. You felt it just like I did while we were doing acquisition. It said something. It spoke. It was right in there in the navigation hall with us, captain."

I met his luminescent gaze levelly and said in an even voice, "I was giving my complete attention to what we were doing, Roacher. Spinaround acquisition isn't second nature to me the way it is to you. I had no time to notice any matrixes floating around in there."

"You didn't?"

"No. Does that disappoint you?"

"That might mean that you're the one carrying the matrix," he said.

"How so?"

"If it's in you, down on a subneural level, you might not even be aware of it. But we would be. Raebuck, Fresco, me. We all detected something, captain. If it wasn't in us it would have to be in you. We can't have a matrix riding around inside our captain, you know. No telling how that could distort his judgment. What dangers that might lead us into."

"I'm not carrying any matrixes, Roacher."

"Can we be sure of that?"

"Would you like to have a look?"

"A jackup, you mean? You and me?"

The notion disgusted me. But I had to make the offer.

"A—jackup, yes," I said. "Communion. You and me, Roacher. Right now. Come on, we'll measure the bandwidths and do the matching. Let's get this over with."

He contemplated me a long while, as if calculating the likelihood that I was bluffing. In the end he must have decided that I was too naive to be able to play the game out to so hazardous a turn. He knew that I wouldn't bluff, that I was confident he would find me untenanted or I never would have made the offer.

"No," he said finally. "We don't need to bother with that."

"Are you sure?"

"If you say you're clean—"

"But I might be carrying her and not even know it," I said. "You told me that yourself."

"Forget it. You'd know, if you had her in you."

"You'll never be certain of that unless you look. Let's jackup, Roacher."

He scowled. "Forget it," he said again, and turned away. "You must be clean, if you're this eager for jacking. But I'll tell you this, captain. We're going to find her, wherever she's hiding. And when we do—"

He left the threat unfinished. I stood staring at his retreating form until he was lost to view.

17.

For a few days everything seemed back to normal. We sped onward toward Cul-de-Sac. I went through the round of my regular tasks, however meaningless they seemed to me. Most of them did. I had not yet achieved any sense that the *Sword of Orion* was under my command in anything but the most hypothetical way. Still, I did what I had to do.

No one spoke of the missing matrix within my hearing. On those rare occasions when I encountered some other member of the crew while I moved about the ship, I could tell by the hooded look of his eyes that I was still under suspicion. But they had no proof. The matrix was no longer in any way evident on board. The ship's intelligences were unable to find the slightest trace of its presence.

I was alone, and oh! it was a painful business for me.

I suppose that once you have tasted that kind of round-the-clock communion, that sort of perpetual jacking, you are never the same again. I don't know: there is no real information available on cases of possession by free matrix, only shipboard folklore, scarcely to be taken seriously. All I can judge by is my own misery now that Vox was actually gone. She was only a half-grown girl, a wild coltish thing, unstable, unformed; and yet, and yet, she had lived within me and we had come toward one another to construct the deepest sort of sharing, what was almost a kind of marriage. You could call it that.

After five or six days I knew I had to see her again. Whatever the risks.

I accessed the virtuality and sent a signal into it that I was coming in. There was no reply; and for one terrible moment I feared the worst, that in the mysterious workings of the virtuality she had somehow been engulfed and destroyed. But that was not the case. I stepped through the glowing pink-edged field of light that was the gateway to the virtuality, and instantly I felt her near me, clinging tight, trembling with joy.

She held back, though, from entering me. She wanted me to tell her it was safe. I beckoned her in; and then came that sharp warm moment I remembered so well, as she slipped down into my neural network and we became one.

"I can only stay a little while," I said. "It's still very chancy for me to be with you."

"Oh, Adam, Adam, it's been so awful for me in here—"

"I know. I can imagine."

"Are they still looking for me?"

"I think they're starting to put you out of their minds," I said. And we both laughed at the play on words that that phrase implied.

I didn't dare remain more than a few minutes. I had only wanted to touch souls with her briefly, to reassure myself that she was all right and to ease the pain of separation. But it was irregular for a captain to enter a virtuality at all. To stay in one for any length of time exposed me to real risk of detection.

But my next visit was longer, and the one after that longer still. We were like furtive lovers meeting in a dark forest for hasty delicious trysts. Hidden there in that not-quite-real out-structure of the ship we would join our two selves and whisper together with urgent intensity until I felt it was time for me to leave. She would always try to keep me longer; but her resistance to my departure was never great, nor did she ever suggest accompanying me back into the stable sector of the ship. She had come to understand that the only place we could meet was in the virtuality.

We were nearing the vicinity of Cul-de-Sac now. Soon we would go to worldward and the shoreships would travel out to meet us, so that we could download the cargo that was meant for them. It was time to begin considering the problem of what would happen to Vox when we reached our destination.

That was something I was unwilling to face. However I tried, I could not force myself to confront the difficulties that I knew lay just ahead.

But she could.

"We must be getting close to Cul-de-Sac now," she said.

"We'll be there soon, yes."

"I've been thinking about that. How I'm going to deal with that."

"What do you mean?"

"I'm a lost soul," she said. "Literally. There's no way I can come to life again."

"I don't under—"

"Adam, don't you see?" she cried fiercely. "I can't just float down to Cul-de-Sac and grab myself a body and put myself on the roster of colonists. And you can't possibly smuggle me down there while nobody's looking. The first time anyone ran an inventory check, or did passport control, I'd be dead. No, the only way I can get there is to be neatly packed up again in my original storage circuit. And even if I could figure out how to get back into that, I'd be simply handing myself over for punishment or even eradication. I'm listed as missing on the manifest, right? And I'm wanted for causing the death of that passenger. Now I turn up again, in my storage circuit. You think they'll just download me nicely to Cul-de-Sac and give me the body that's waiting for me there? Not very likely. Not likely that I'll ever get out of that circuit alive, is it, once I go back in? Assuming I could go back in in the first place. I don't know how a storage circuit is operated, do you? And there's nobody you can ask."

"What are you trying to say, Vox?"

"I'm not trying to say anything. I'm saying it. I have to leave the ship on my own and disappear."

"No. You can't do that!"

"Sure I can. It'll be just like starwalking. I can go anywhere I please. Right through the skin of the ship, out into heaven. And keep on going."

"To Cul-de-Sac?"

"You're being stupid," she said. "Not to Cul-de-Sac, no. Not to anywhere. That's all over for me, the idea of getting a new body. I have no legal existence any more. I've messed myself up. All right: I admit it. I'll take what's coming to me. It won't be so bad, Adam. I'll go starwalking. Outward and outward and outward, forever and ever."

"You mustn't," I said. "Stay here with me."

"Where? In this empty storage unit out here?"

"No," I told her. "Within me. The way we are right now. The way we were before."

"How long do you think we could carry that off?" she asked.

I didn't answer.

"Every time you have to jack into the machinery I'll have to hide myself down deep," she said. "And I can't guarantee that I'll go deep enough, or that I'll stay down there long enough. Sooner or later they'll notice me. They'll find me. They'll eradicate me and they'll throw you out of the Service, or maybe they'll eradicate you too. No, Adam. It couldn't possibly work. And I'm not going to destroy you with me. I've done enough harm to you already."

"Vox—"

"No. This is how it has to be."

18.

And this is how it was. We were deep in the Spook Cluster now, and the Vainglory Archipelago burned bright on my realspace screen. Somewhere down there was the planet called Cul-de-Sac. Before we came to worldward of it, Vox would have to slip away into the great night of heaven.

Making a worldward approach is perhaps the most difficult maneuver a starship must achieve; and the captain must go to the edge of his abilities along with everyone else. Novice at my trade though I was, I would be called on to perform complex and challenging processes. If I failed at them, other crewmen might cut in and intervene, or, if necessary, the ship's intelligences might override; but if that came to pass my career would be destroyed, and there was the small but finite possibility, I suppose, that the ship itself could be gravely damaged or even lost.

I was determined, all the same, to give Vox the best send-off I could.

On the morning of our approach I stood for a time on Outerscreen Level, staring down at the world that called itself Cul-de-Sac. It glowed like a red eye in the night. I knew that it was the world Vox had chosen for herself, but all the same it seemed repellent to me, almost evil. I felt that way about all the worlds of the shore people now. The Service had changed me; and I knew that the change was irreversible. Never again would I go down to one of those worlds. The starship was my world now.

I went to the virtuality where Vox was waiting.

"Come," I said, and she entered me.

Together we crossed the ship to the Great Navigation Hall.

The approach team had already gathered: Raebuck,

Fresco, Roacher, again, along with Pedregal, who would su-
pervise the downloading of cargo. The intelligence on duty
was 612 Jason. I greeted them with quick nods and we
jacked ourselves together in approach series.

Almost at once I felt Roacher probing within me,
searching for the fugitive intelligence that he still thought I
might be harboring. Vox shrank back, deep out of sight. I
didn't care. Let him probe, I thought. This will all be over
soon.

"Request approach instructions," Fresco said.

"Simulation," I ordered.

The fiery red eye of Cul-de-Sac sprang into vivid representation before us in the hall. On the other side of us was
the simulacrum of the ship, surrounded by sheets of white
flame that rippled like the blaze of the aurora.

I gave the command and we entered approach mode.

We could not, of course, come closer to planetskin than
a million shiplengths, or Cul-de-Sac's inexorable forces
would rip us apart. But we had to line the ship up with its
extended mast aimed at the planet's equator, and hold ourselves firm in that position while the shoreships of Cul-de-
Sac came swarming up from their red world to receive their
cargo from us.

612 Jason fed me the coordinates and I gave them to
Fresco, while Raebuck kept the channels clear and Roacher
saw to it that we had enough power for what we had to do.
But as I passed the data along to Fresco, it was with every
sign reversed. My purpose was to aim the mast not downward to Cul-de-Sac but outward toward the stars of heaven.

At first none of them noticed. Everything seemed to be
going serenely. Because my reversals were exact, only the
closest examination of the ship's position would indicate
our 180-degree displacement.

Floating in the free fall of the Great Navigation Hall, I

felt almost as though I could detect the movements of the ship. An illusion, I knew. But a powerful one. The vast ten-kilometer-long needle that was the Sword of Orion seemed to hang suspended, motionless, and then to begin slowly, slowly to turn, tipping itself on its axis, reaching for the stars with its mighty mast. Easily, easily, slowly, silently—

What joy that was, feeling the ship in my hand!

The ship was mine. I had mastered it.

"Captain," Fresco said softly.

"Easy on, Fresco. Keep feeding power."

"Captain, the signs don't look right—"

"Easy on. Easy."

"Give me a coordinates check, captain."

"Another minute," I told him.

"But—"

"Easy on, Fresco."

Now I felt restlessness too from Pedregal, and a slow chilly stirring of interrogation from Raebuck; and then Roacher probed me again, perhaps seeking Vox, perhaps simply trying to discover what was going on. They knew something was wrong, but they weren't sure what it was.

We were nearly at full extension, now. Within me there was an electrical trembling: Vox rising through the levels of my mind, nearing the surface, preparing for departure.

"Captain, we're turned the wrong way!" Fresco cried.

"I know," I said. "Easy on. We'll swing around in a moment."

"He's gone crazy!" Pedregal blurted.

I felt Vox slipping free of my mind. But somehow I found myself still aware of her movements, I suppose because I was jacked into 612 Jason and 612 Jason was monitoring everything. Easily, serenely, Vox melted into the skin of the ship.

"Captain!" Fresco yelled, and began to struggle with me for control.

I held the navigator at arm's length and watched in a strange and wonderful calmness as Vox passed through the ship's circuitry all in an instant and emerged at the tip of the mast, facing the stars. And cast herself adrift.

Because I had turned the ship around, she could not be captured and acquired by Cul-de-Sac's powerful navigational grid, but would be free to move outward into heaven. For her it would be a kind of floating out to sea, now. After a time she would be so far out that she could no longer key into the shipboard bioprocessors that sustained the patterns of her consciousness, and, though the web of electrical impulses that was the Vox matrix would travel outward and onward forever, the set of identity responses that was Vox herself would lose focus soon, would begin to waver and blur. In a little while, or perhaps not so little, but inevitably, her sense of herself as an independent entity would be lost. Which is to say, she would die.

I followed her as long as I could. I saw a spark traveling across the great night. And then nothing.

"All right," I said to Fresco. "Now let's turn the ship the right way around and give them their cargo."

19.

That was many years ago. Perhaps no one else remembers those events, which seem so dreamlike now even to me. The *Sword of Orion* has carried me nearly everwhere in the galaxy since then. On some voyages I have been captain; on others, a downloader, a supercargo, a mind-wiper, even sometimes a push-cell. It makes no difference how we serve, in the Service.

I often think of her. There was a time when thinking of her meant coming to terms with feelings of grief and pain and irrecoverable loss, but no longer, not for many years. She must be long dead now, however durable and resilient the spark of her might have been. And yet she still lives. Of that much I am certain. There is a place within me where I can reach her warmth, her strength, her quirky vitality, her impulsive suddenness. I can feel those aspects of her, those gifts of her brief time of sanctuary within me, as a living presence still, and I think I always will, as I make my way from world to tethered world, as I journey onward everlastingly spanning the dark light-years in this great ship of heaven.

An Open Letter to Our Valued Readers

What do Raymond Chandler, Arthur C. Clarke, Isaac Asimov, Irving Wallace, Ben Bova, Stuart Kaminsky and over a dozen other authors have in common? They are all part of an exciting new line of **ibooks** distributed by Simon and Schuster.

 ibooks represent the best of the future and the best of the past...a voyage into the future of books that unites traditional printed books with the excitement of the web.

Please join us in developing the first new publishing imprint of the 21st century.

We're planning terrific offers for ibooks readers...virtual reading groups where you can chat online about ibooks authors...message boards where you can communicate with fellow readers...downloadable free chapters of ibooks for your reading pleasure...free readers services such as a directory of where to find electronic books on the web...special discounts on books and other items of interest to readers...

The evolution of the book is www.ibooksinc.com.